I0773545

The Silversaar Legacy

Book 1

When Things Are Set Right

Jordan St. James

House of Q LLC

Knoxville

Published in the United States by House of Q LLC, Knoxville, TN.

ISBN (Paperback) 979-8-218-08356-4

HouseofQLLC.com

A mother bereft.

A captive released.

An ancient power awakens.

I

Daphne

The fever came without warning during the night. At sunup, the village shaman called upon the elvish gods, but they remained silent. Unresponsive to the available remedies, the child's temperature climbed. Her tears ran dry, and in less than a day, Aeryn's inconsolable baby had become listless.

When Rathma returned to the Haranae household that afternoon, she took one look at the child and pronounced she'd be dead by morning without a miracle.

"Prepare yourselves," the shaman said.

It felt like the ground swung out from beneath Aeryn. She bounced her nine-month-old to hide the shaking in her own limbs. She dabbed Daphne's burning head with a cool cloth. Heat seeped into her fingers.

Aeryn's mind raced in search of an answer. She set her jaw. "No. I don't accept that. I can't. There must be something we can do."

Rathma's face softened. "Aeryn...."

Ignoring the shaman, Aeryn turned to her mother, Verelle. "What about the herb you gave to Samuel? You said it'll cure most illnesses. Would it fix whatever's wrong with Daphne?"

"Blue leatherleaf?" Verelle said. "It should. It's a seven-hour hike to the grove." Verelle turned to her husband. "Bartholomew, if you or I hurry—"

Aeryn's aged father nodded. "I'll get ready."

Aeryn watched him hobble out of the room, followed by Rathma. His war wound had been acting up for weeks. He would never make it back in time.

She hugged her child tighter as necessity settled over her. "Poppa can't go. There's no time," she said. "I'm going. I'll run through the night."

Her mother didn't protest.

"Do you know where it is?" Verelle asked. "It only grows in one place. You can't forage for it elsewhere."

"I know where it is. There's a waterfall and a pool." Aeryn scanned the room for her boots. Daphne whimpered and stuck out her bottom lip.

Aeryn's throat thickened painfully. It tore her apart to leave her baby like this. Daphne needed her mother, and wouldn't understand why Aeryn wasn't there to comfort her. But what choice was there? She'd die without the miracle herb, and Aeryn was the only person equipped to retrieve it.

The sooner she left, the sooner she'd get back with the cure.

Aeryn rested her daughter gently on her bed. She stroked the damp chocolate curls atop her head. No longer strong enough to wriggle or cry, Daphne rocked her head toward Aeryn. She took slow shallow breaths.

Aeryn leaned over her, and croaked a few lines of a lullaby about crickets in the meadow. A tear escaped down her cheek, cutting the song short. She planted a kiss on her baby's burning forehead. "It's okay, little feather. I'll be back soon. I'll make you better."

Verelle laid a hand on Aeryn's shoulder. She took the cloth from her, dipped it into a bowl of cool water, and dabbed the baby's skin.

Aeryn hurried across her room, moved her lute out of the way, and snatched her leather boots from the corner. She slung a satchel over her shoulder. Bartholomew limped into Aeryn's room after showing Rathma to the door. He assessed the situation and understood immediately.

"Aeryn, bring your bow. Just in case," he said.

"Okay." Aeryn laced her boots. Urgency pressed upon her, but her mind sharpened into focus.

Get there, get the plant, and get back.

Or Daphne would die.

Before she left, she turned her attention on the still, pallid form of her child. Pain returned to her throat. She gave her one more kiss on the top of her head.

"Please hang on. Your momma loves you. I'll be back, I promise."

Aeryn bolted from the house and straight to the great forest, Ravenwood, which was Merioake's wild backyard. Her golden brown hair flew out behind her as she shot like an arrow through the trees. She leaped over fallen branches and dodged jagged rocks, sensing their presence before she even saw them. She kicked up the smells of foliage and mushrooms, which entered her nose with each sharp intake of breath. The rattle of arrows in her quiver provided a rhythm to her pace. Insects hummed and forest birds argued, ignorant to Aeryn's race below the canopy.

Late afternoon dipped into dusk and Aeryn's legs and lungs begged for a break. She refused them.

She couldn't afford to stop, but was forced to when she misjudged a leap over a downed tree. She barked her shin and landed facedown in the detritus on the other side.

Aeryn grabbed her leg, wincing. She gasped for air and broke into a coughing fit. She needed water.

She gave herself a minute, forcing her body back under control. Then she pulled herself to her feet and pressed through the pain. She set her focus to the grove, the one place in Errebos the herb grew. There was a pool at the grove. She could drink there.

Darkness spread rapidly through the forest. Aeryn's eyes adjusted to the dimness. The night creatures crept out of hiding to blink from the shadows, howl, or fiddle their calls. The forest was unsafe at night, but a different fear snapped at Aeryn's heels as the image of her sick baby lodged in her mind.

Urging her onward.

At long last, the trees opened upon a grove blanketed with blue flowers and thick green foliage. A small waterfall fed a bubbling pool nearby.

Aeryn waded through the knee-high plants, staggering to the water's edge, and collapsed. She scooped handful after handful of fresh water to her mouth. Panting, she ran a cool, wet hand over her face, then turned her attention to the grove itself.

The moonlight reflected off the indigo petals and bathed the clearing in a bluish glow. This was a sacred, protected place. A remnant of magic in the world, her mother speculated.

"Get the whole plant," Verelle said before she left. "Roots, leaves, flowers. All of it."

Aeryn ripped a plant out of the dirt. She uprooted four more handfuls and shoved them into her satchel. After one final drought from the pool, she rose, and hurried back the way she came.

Gray morning light cracked through the gaps in the foliage as she neared the edge of the wood. The trees thinned and her village materialized before her.

Aeryn leaned into the final push. Arms and legs pumping, her muscles screaming for mercy, she flew along the empty lane and didn't slow until she reached her parents house.

Rathma was leaving.

What was she doing here so early in the morning?

The old woman leaned on her gnarled staff, met Aeryn's eyes, and shook her head.

Dread sunk its teeth into Aeryn's heart, ready to rip it from her body. Without a word to the shaman, she took the stairs two at a time and burst into the house. Elion, Samuel, and Tarra congregated in the living area. Their eyes were raw from crying.

No, no, no.

Aeryn crashed through the house and bounded up the stairs to her bedroom. She rushed in, satchel in hand, and froze.

Daphne laid on the bed, eyes shut. Her chest was still. Beside the baby, Verelle leaned her head in her arms, and wept. She hadn't noticed Aeryn come in.

Bartholomew rose. His eyes were damp. He took a few unsteady steps toward Aeryn. "Aeryn, I'm so sorry."

A cry of anguish caught in Aeryn's throat, and for a moment, she couldn't breathe. The satchel hit the floor. She staggered to her lifeless child and dropped to her knees.

She tenderly scooped Daphne into her arms. A wail escaped from a place deep inside Aeryn. Grief wracked her body. Her cries filled the house as she hugged her child to her breast.

She failed.

Daphne was gone.

2

The Cost of Arrows

Smears of blood coated Aeryn's palms.

She pressed one hand onto the buck's buff shoulder, and gripped the arrow shaft with the other. It had been a clean shot, and given her dwindling supply of arrows, she didn't want to break another one.

But as she pulled, the arrowhead caught on some inner structure of the deer. She felt the telltale snap and a second later held only a shaft. She growled and flung it away from her. It clacked against a nearby tree trunk, then fell to the forest floor.

A familiar grackle alighted on the stag's rump. He rasped and fixed Aeryn with his bright eye.

She swiped a wisp of hair away from her face with the back of her hand. A glance at her quiver showed only three arrows left.

An old discomfort twisted inside her chest.

She really needed to learn how to make those.

"I suppose we're going back, Weaver," she said.

Weaver made a chacking sound in reply.

"No, not to stay. We'll visit the tannery. Sell the hide. Get some arrows." She patted the buck. "The boys'll give me a good price for this fella. Enough to supply for longer than three weeks out here."

Weaver flitted to her shoulder and picked at the fur along

her collar. He wanted the seeds inside her breast pocket.

She gave the bird a nudge with her cheek. "Not now, Greedy. I'm a mess."

Aeryn spent the day skinning the deer, preparing the meat, and trying not to think about her upcoming visit to Merioake.

A month ago, she turned thirty years old. Most elves her age were paired off by now, having spent their twenties learning the family trades, falling in love, and enjoying their youth. Her family expected she'd take up the mantle running the tannery alongside her brothers, but she celebrated the elvish mark of adulthood by declaring her intent to leave town. After several arguments and a week of preparation, she hugged her siblings, kissed her parents goodbye, and left Merioake behind, with the understanding she'd be back.

Back, before Samuel's baby entered the world.

Back, with a decision to participate in the family's trade.

She spent the last month in Ravenwood, away from civilization. She lived off the land, bathed in the streams, and slept under the dense canopy. As an adept hunter, Ravenwood was a source of provision even before leaving home. It was familiar and comfortable. The forest, which spanned most of the South, had long been her sanctuary.

She wasn't looking forward to leaving it, but arrows don't make themselves.

At sunup, she wove sprigs of ivy into her braid and donned a loose-fitting set of homemade clothes, pieced together from the hides of several pikdeer with the short chestnut hair still attached.

Her long wrapped top, adorned with strips of rabbit fur and shells sewn into the hem, left her strong arms bare. She tied a rope belt around her trim waist, giving her the hint of a figure. She slung her possum-fur vest over it all. If ever there was a time to look as though she belonged to the forest, it was today.

Pushing aside her impending dread, she left her camp with the buckskin, and set foot in her hometown just before midday.

Merioake consisted of mostly elves, with a sizable human minority. Situated along the northern edge of Ravenwood in the province of Thoen in the South, trees were many and old, but sparse enough to allow a small village to thrive. Most homes were built low in the trees, whereas shops were erected along a series of well-worn natural roads.

Dozens of familiar faces wove through the village, busy about their work. Folks ran errands and visited with neighbors. Children chased dragonflies. The ancient-looking shaman ambled along in her tasseled robe. A sheepdog barked.

Aeryn drew funny looks from villagers almost immediately. The elves of Thoen kept a neat appearance, favoring comfortable, fitted clothing. The styles were humble yet refined, characterized by trim leather, practical fabrics, and the occasional bright, flowing skirt. Furs were for the Illwalii, or humans who lived in the far North, or even the orcs. Not a respectable Thoenite.

In her hurry down Merchants Row, she rubbed shoulders with a pretty she-elf who caught Aeryn by the arm. Aeryn stopped, finding herself face-to-face with her old friend, Sariel.

"Aeryn?" The young lady's blue eyes lit up, but her smile

took a forced, awkward quality. Sariel's eyes swept over Aeryn, assessing. "I thought you were moving into the woods permanently."

Aeryn forced a smile. "Nice to see you too."

"What am I thinking?" Sariel gave her head a small shake, and swooped in to give Aeryn a stiff hug. "So...are you back?"

"Only resupplying."

Sariel visibly relaxed. "Oh. Hard to tell, you know. Even when you were here, you were barely ever around. Busy with...well, busy."

Aeryn shifted the weight of her pack and Sariel cleared her throat then touched Aeryn's arm in a pat gesture.

"I wish there was more time," she said with ambiguous sincerity. "I feel like I hardly know you these days. We were the closest of friends growing up."

It was true. She and Sariel sang together and were inseparable until adolescence when their interests diverged. Aeryn pursued the bow in her spare time, and kept company with other archers. Sariel threw herself into pursuing the attention of young men.

A thick silence wedged between the two ladies. Sariel turned the delicate gold band on her finger. Aeryn arched an eyebrow as curiosity got the better of her.

"Are you engaged?" Aeryn asked.

"I am." Sariel pressed her lips together in an expression of unmistakable guilt. "To Gideon."

The words hit like a punch to the gut.

"Oh." It was all Aeryn could muster. She adjusted the weight of her pack again and scrambled for a way out of this conversation.

"I understand there's history with you two, but we're all older now," Sariel said, as if that made it better. "We're happy. He's a good man."

Aeryn let out a bark of laughter. "Don't justify yourself to me. You know what he did."

Sariel shrugged, and wouldn't meet her eyes.

Aeryn's stomach tightened. She watched her old friend for the length of a breath as realization slid into place. "You believe him now, don't you?"

"I – I don't know," Sariel said, still avoiding Aeryn's eyes as she wrung her fingers.

Aeryn was finished. Without wasting another moment, she left Sariel standing speechless in the road. She marched to *Haranae Tannery and Leatherworks* and thrust open the door. It jangled violently upon her entry and made a nearby rack of belts wobble.

Aeryn's father and her twin brother Elion stood at the butcher block counter. Each wore a leather apron, each with his shoulder-length hair fastened at the nape of the neck.

Elion recovered from her abrupt entrance first.

"Behold!" He spread his arms. "The gods have blessed us this day. The forest has entered our very establishment."

He rolled his hand in a mock bow.

"We are honored by your presence. How may we serve you, O Spirit of the Forest?"

Aeryn gave her brother a wry look.

He continued. "May we interest you in some leather? We have a special this day on slacks."

"Funny, Elion."

Aeryn swung the door shut and joined them at the counter. The smell of tanned skins mingled with the aroma of fresh cut wood, smoke, and sweaty men at work. Intact skins hung along the back wall, while finished leather goods were tactfully displayed at the front of the shop. She could see into the back room where someone had stretched a hide over a wooden hoop.

"No, Aeryn, you are the funny one," Elion said with a grin. "Your insistence on dressing like one of the Illwalii remains the laughing stock of the people."

"You know I don't care."

"Oh, we know," Elion said.

Aeryn pecked her father on the cheek. He looked a little grayer than when she last saw him.

"Have you decided to leave the Ravenwood early?" Bartholomew asked, brightening. "Ready to don the apron and start tanning?"

He was so proud of the Haranae livelihood. With little variation, the elves trained their children in the family's line of work, and it was a point of honor to continue the family business. As an elvish woman, she had more flexibility to choose whether she wanted to follow her mother's path, herbalism, or her father's. It would even be acceptable to adopt the trade of her husband, if she ever married. Tanning remained the most practical and stable choice, given the demand for leather goods.

That, and her notable lack of prospects.

She didn't have the heart to tell them, since it would be an affront to tradition, but she'd do anything to avoid working in Merioake.

"I wasn't planning on it," Aeryn said. "I have until Samuel's baby arrives before I have to make a decision. Is he around?"

"No, Samuel took the day," Bartholomew said.

"Must be why it's so quiet," Aeryn said. "Where's the fussbudget?"

"Be kind, he's your brother," Bartholomew said. "He's helping Tarra prepare the nursery. Your mother's there, and Tarra's mother. It's become an event."

"Oh. I suppose that's sweet."

"Are you staying for lunch?" Bartholomew asked. "I have something for you back at the house."

"I can't. Long walk back to camp." Aeryn scratched at the back of her head, and her eyes darted to Elion, who understood some of her moods.

"Well, don't leave yet." Bartholomew untied his apron and rested it on the counter. He pulled the door open with a jingle. "I'll be back in ten or so minutes."

"You're in quite the hurry to get back to the woods," Elion said when their father left.

"I have until Samuel and Tarra have the baby."

"You don't have to tell me," he said as he lifted a palm. "So why have you graced us with your presence?"

Aeryn hoisted the buckskin from her pack onto the counter. "I brought a present."

Elion gave a low whistle. "Big feller."

"How much?"

"I thought he was a present," he said in jest. He inspected the skin. "Twelve silvers."

"How about thirteen?"

"How about ten."

"Eleven, and ten pounds of salt." She pointed to a barrel brimming with the whitish, rocky crystals, just inside the back room. Salt kept the skins from rotting, so she didn't have to hurry to Merioake every time she caught a hide worth selling.

Elion thought for a moment, then rapped the counter once with his knuckles. "Deal."

He grabbed a burlap sack, tossed it onto the counter, and went to the back room to count out the money. Aeryn fiddled with a coin pouch from a display box beside her. She recognized the pattern sewn into the front as one of the popular designs she made a while ago.

"Are you planning to tell me who put the thorn in your boot this morning?" Elion said as he plopped the coins on the counter. "And because I fear it bears saying, please don't adorn your boots with actual thorns."

Aeryn turned the coin pouch over in her hands, debating how much to say. "I ran into Sariel."

"Ah." Elion grabbed the burlap sack and stepped just

inside the doorway to the backroom to scoop the salt. "I learned the news last week. She used to be your close friend, too."

"Some friend."

Aeryn tossed the coin pouch back into its shallow wooden box with a flick of her wrist.

"I need arrows," she said as she scraped the coins off the counter and dropped them into her own coin purse. "If Father returns before I do, tell him I'm at the smith's."

Weaver, who refused to come indoors, landed on Aeryn's shoulder the moment she stepped out of the stuffy shop. She wove her way down the lane to the smithy on the corner.

Aeryn liked the blacksmith, a human named Kazmuk. He had bright blue eyes and skin the exact color and texture of tanned leather. Kazmuk stayed out of town gossip. Business was business, and he didn't play favorites. He took pride in his work and was pleased to show it off for those who appreciated it.

The smithy's front door swung wide as she reached for the handle. A handsome, raven-haired elf strolled outside. The color drained from his face when his eyes met Aeryn's. He kept his expression otherwise impassive, which kindled her ire.

Aeryn's stomach tightened. No one made her feel simultaneously enraged and like crawling under a rock like Gideon.

"I know you prefer pretending I don't exist, but you're blocking the door," she said. "Move."

Gideon reddened. He let the door swing shut out of her grasp.

She cut her eyes at him, unable to resist the opportunity to dig. "I heard you and Sariel are engaged."

He lifted his chin. "We are."

"How long do you think that'll last? She'll flirt with anything that moves."

Gideon frowned. "You think I've had a pleasant time these years? Sariel actually gave me a chance."

"How touching."

He pinched the bridge of his nose.

"I won't apologize for desiring a normal life. You could've had one too." Gideon dropped his voice. "If you listened to me then, no one would've even known."

"I would know!" Aeryn took a step at him so that she was only inches from his face. She clenched her hands into fists and she fought to control her voice. "I think about her every day."

For the last six years.

"Would you hush?" Gideon's eyes darted to the startled passersby who slowed and turned their heads. Crimson splotches crawled up his neck.

He was uncomfortable.

Good.

He straightened his blue tunic, and fixed her with a chilly glance.

"Enjoy your time alone in the woods." He stepped around her to saunter on his way. "Try to keep your legs closed."

Aeryn dropped her pack. Lunging at him, she pulled back her fist, but strong hands grabbed her by the arm and yanked her back. The punch never landed.

She spat a curse at Gideon so loud her voice shook. A passing mother gasped, and clapped her hands over her child's ears. She scowled at Aeryn as she hurried her son along.

Gideon whirled around, realizing he narrowly escaped a knock to the back of the head. Aeryn repeated herself. A crowd materialized as more passersby stopped to stare. Gideon took an unsteady step away, thought better of engaging further, and with one last bewildered glare at Aeryn, hurried toward the fletcher's where he worked.

Aeryn struggled against Kazmuk's grasp. "Let go!"

The smith held firm. "Aeryn, ye settle!"

Aeryn's cheeks burned as the villagers murmured about, "that Haranae girl," and shook their heads. She hardened her face against the hot tears which wanted to erupt down her cheeks. She would not let them see her cry.

"Move along, ye gawkin' lot." Kazmuk bellowed at the crowd, shooing them away with his free, meaty arm while still holding firm onto Aeryn. As the villagers dispersed, Kazmuk turned his attention to Aeryn. "I'ma guess ye here fer arrows?"

She nodded and tugged her arm.

"Can't let ye in my smithy all wild," he said. "I'ma let ye go now. Ye gonna run after trouble, or come get what ye came fer?"

Aeryn nodded again and the smith released her. He plucked her bow from the ground and handed it back to her. "C'mon. I got somethin' to show ye."

The acrid smell of the smithy greeted Aeryn as she stepped through the doorway. Kazmuk's apprentice worked the bellows. The clang of metal on metal rang in her ears. With the forge ablaze, it was warmer and stuffy inside.

She followed Kazmuk to a rack of arrows he kept on hand. He slipped on a heavy glove and produced an arrow with an unusual tip.

"Mechanical head. Watch." Kazmuk pressed the barbs which retracted and clicked into place, making the tip narrow, but razor sharp. "When the arrow penetrates the beast, pressure triggers the barbs." He pushed the tip of the arrow to demonstrate. The barbs snapped outward. "Goes deep. Holds in place."

Aeryn examined the arrow, intrigued. "How much?"

"Four silvers."

"For one?"

"Aye."

She handed it back. "What else do you have?"

"Been makin' more bodkins of late." He grabbed a couple arrows with sharp pyramid tips to show her. "The long ones pass through ring mail, these short ones can cut through plate armor."

"Folks around here buy these?"

"Not usually. Most folk like havin' a few, fer emergencies. Marauders and the like," Kazmuk said. "Mostly I keep 'em in stock for when the Imperials come through. Had some a day ago. Bought me clean out."

Aeryn looked closely at the bodkin tip. "I can't imagine shooting people in heavy armor any time soon."

"Ye sure? They said they were trackin' a prisoner who might've gone into the Ravenwood."

"I'll take my chances."

Aeryn perused Kazmuk's stock and left with a sheave's worth of arrows. Twenty broadheads of various sizes, four blunts for hunting birds. As she made her way back to the tannery, some villagers from the crowd earlier pointed, and watched her pass, whispering to their neighbors.

Heat crawled up her neck. She had to get out of here.

She'd make due without the salt. Elion and her father would just have to understand if she left without saying goodbye.

As she turned onto Market Street, she spotted her father marching unevenly up the road. He held a stringed instrument with a curved body in both hands.

"Aeryn, I thought you planned to wait for me at the tannery," he said as he approached.

Guilt pricked her. "Why are you carrying my old lute?"

"Your mother and I cleaned the storage loft last week." Bartholomew held it out to her. "Thought you might want to take it with you."

A pang twisted inside her chest. Six years went by since she played the instrument.

She didn't want to touch it.

She didn't even want to look at it.

"I haven't played in a long time. I probably wouldn't remember how," she said.

"Nonsense. It's all up here." Bartholomew tapped his temple. "The fingers remember. Take it. This too." He pulled a fuzzy brown object from his pocket and passed it to Aeryn.

"A rabbit's foot?" she asked as she turned it over.

"I've spoken with Rathma," he said. "Now, before you dismiss it, hear me. She told me you were in need of some luck."

"That old fraud also told you and mother that you'd have three sons."

Bartholomew thought for a moment. "Maybe she was referring to a son-in-law. In the future."

"Poppa, I hope you didn't pay her too much for this."

"I'd feel better if you carried it. I worry about you, out there by yourself."

Aeryn stifled a sigh at the familiar conversation. "I know Ravenwood. I'm fine."

"Know it or not, it's still dangerous," he said with emphasis. "Bandits. Wolves. What if a dragon reappears?"

"Then I know who to call upon." Aeryn smiled at her father.

"You don't have to go back, Aeryn."

"I do. I left all my belongings there."

"You understand what I mean," Bartholomew said. He looked affectionately at her. "Why wait another two months? Stay. Establish yourself here, even if you prefer the herbalist hut to the tannery. You could settle down, and be happy."

Aeryn balked inwardly. A dragon reappearing in Ravenwood would be more likely. She shifted the weight of her pack. "I should go. Don't want to travel by dark."

Bartholomew sighed. He couldn't argue with that. He held out the lute for her to take. Aeryn took one last glance at the pretty carved wood.

She never wanted to see it again.

Aeryn didn't have it in her to continue the conversation. She simply shook her head and hugged her father goodbye.

"Watch out for panthers," he said. "Don't speak to strange men. In fact, avoid strange men altogether."

Weaver followed Aeryn into the forest, gliding overhead and flitting from branch to branch. Her tension eased the deeper she traveled. Halfway through the afternoon, a brief shower pattered the leaves overhead. Due to the thick overgrowth, Aeryn only experienced a light drizzle. The humid air was thick with the scents of dirt and mushrooms and fresh green growth.

As the sun neared the end of its course across the sky, the woods dimmed, and Aeryn noticed boot prints in the soft earth. Though only ten minutes from her campsite, she decided to follow the tracks to see whether they wound back to the main path.

They didn't.

The prints meandered through the forest, then made straight for her camp, just visible in the distance.

Aeryn crouched in the underbrush and unshouldered her pack, careful to avoid rustling the knotweed. The presence of nearby strangers in the woods always demanded caution.

She signaled to Weaver and pulled a seed from her breast pocket. "Fly ahead. See if there are people."

He plucked the seed from her fingers and took flight.

She waited and listened, but only heard the drip of wet

leaves, the normal creaks and groans of the forest, and the far-off chirrup of birds. She tried not to imagine strange hikers rifling through her belongings, stealing her food, or worse.

After a long minute, Weaver returned.

Men waited outside her camp.

3

Intruders

Aeryn's pulse quickened. Hunters from town rarely came this far.

Kazmuk's mention of Imperials and prisoners came to mind. If the men were the law keepers of Errebos, she needn't worry, but what if these were the escaped prisoners?

She needed more information. It wouldn't be safe to expose herself until then. She tucked her backpack under the knotweed and gripped her bow, just in case.

She offered Weaver another seed. "Show me where."

Weaver glided through the trees without a sound. She crept closer to camp, keeping her eyes on the blackbird's movements. He perched on a branch outside of the clearing. Directly beneath him, three men crouched low in the brush, their backs to her.

Why were they lying in wait?

She took a steadying breath. With a hand on her quiver to keep the arrows from rattling, she inched forward. Every few feet she paused to take cover behind trees and brush. Finally she stopped, hidden by an overgrown fern, twenty feet from them. She strained her eyes and ears for information.

Two unshaven humans and an elf crouched in the undergrowth. Their navy Imperial uniforms were disheveled, and they looked filthy, unlike the disciplined appearance Aeryn expected from Imperials. Even the elf's appearance was unkempt, which further struck Aeryn as odd given her people's priority on cleanliness. The elf balanced a short bow across his lap. The others each grasped a short sword.

The skinnier of the two humans smacked the back of his neck. "Blast these biters! How much longer, you reckon? These woods give me the creeps."

"It's getting late," the elf said. "He's gotta come back sometime."

"The sooner the better." The skinny man smacked another bug on his forearm. "I heard savage wood elves infest these woods. My mate knew a man who was skewered to death by their arrows, then skinned alive, before they ate him."

"You're an idiot, Percy," the elf said.

"This camp seems awfully small. Didn't Stonebreaker have a group?" Percy leaned closer to the other human with greasy hair. "Karl, what if it ain't his camp? Look at those underclothes hangin' over there. Don't those seem a little small?"

"You saying I can't track a man?" the second human said. "He's here."

"Say he is. That don't concern you?" Percy asked. "There's only three of us."

Karl smacked his comrade upside the head. "What are you, a coward? He's a slave. Been on the run for weeks. How do you think he's fared?"

Percy wrinkled his nose at Karl, rubbing his head. "Point taken..."

"Look. We have our orders. We get him alive," Karl said. "Preferably before Jasper's group. I got a wager we'll find him first."

They quieted for a moment.

Aeryn tried to make sense of what she was hearing. Why were Imperials tracking slaves? Slavery was illegal.

"What if it's a woman's camp?" Percy asked, his tone changing, as though the thought intrigued him.

Karl snorted. "Well, we ain't leaving empty handed."

The elf snickered.

Aeryn's muscles tensed with the single minded urge to get away. Imperials or not, these were bad men. She hoped the dripping leaves covered any noise she caused as she made her retreat. As she crept backward, a branch snapped underfoot.

She froze.

"Did you hear that?" The elf craned his neck to squint in her direction. The others fell silent.

Careful not to move a muscle, Aeryn prayed to whatever gods might be listening that the men wouldn't spot her through the foliage.

After a minute which felt like an eternity, Percy relaxed. "Losing your touch, Lucan. Probably only a squirrel."

The elf grunted.

Percy swatted another insect, then stood. "I can't wait no more. I gotta go leak."

"Bring your sword, idiot," Karl said.

Percy snatched it off the ground and crammed it in the scabbard. He fiddled with his belt buckle as he ambled out of the brush straight toward Aeryn.

Panic exploded inside Aeryn. There was no time.

She grabbed an arrow.

The next moment he pushed aside the fern where she hid. He halted, eyes wide with terror. He hollered and fumbled for his sword. "Wood elf!"

Aeryn took a step back, lifted her bow, and fired. At close range, the arrow sunk deep into his chest. With rapid skill from years of practice, she nocked another and sent it at the elf.

Percy staggered. He clutched at the wound and dropped to one knee, while behind him, the second arrow found its target's throat. The elf hit the ground gurgling.

Before she could draw a third, Karl rushed at her, sword flashing. He sliced the exposed skin above Aeryn's elbow.

She cried out, and reeled back to avoid another cut, but caught her heel on an exposed root. She landed hard on her back in the dirt.

Karl swooped upon her like a bird of prey. She scrambled backward, out of his grasp. She tried to get to her feet, but he caught her by the ankle.

Aeryn screamed and yanked. With her free foot, she kicked until her heel connected with his face and he let go. She leapt to her feet and fled into the forest. In her haste, it felt like her arms and legs were going to fly off.

The crunch of boots over undergrowth told her Karl was chasing her, and gaining.

She felt a sudden tug as the man grabbed the back of her

collar. He whirled her around, and struck her in the face. "You ugly elf! You just killed two of my men!"

Splitting pain shot through Aeryn's head. Still holding onto her vest, he thrust her at the nearest tree, pinned her to the trunk by the neck, and squeezed.

Cut off from air, her sense of panic spiked to new heights. Aeryn fought to pry his fingers away. They wouldn't budge. She clawed his hands and arms, then dug her nails into the exposed skin.

Undeterred, he clenched his hands painfully into her neck, harder than before. The man's face was bloodied from where she kicked him. He bared his teeth and Aeryn stared at his twisted features.

Water filled her eyes.

Remembering her hunting knife, she groped at her belt. Her fingertips met the hilt. In an instant, she grasped the handle and thrust the blade into his ribs.

He grunted. His expression slackened and the pressure around her neck lessened immediately. Aeryn broke free of his grasp. He toppled into the fallen leaves with a crunch and breathed his last.

She held her tender neck and coughed violently. Her eyes watered and ears rang. The warm, stinging gash on her arm streamed freely.

A hoarse sob escaped her lips.

It was over.

She was alive.

Her eyes fell to the body at her feet and she felt like she might throw up.

She killed three men in uniform.

She couldn't stay here.

She grasped her bow and spilled arrows with quaking hands. Her legs trembled as she retrieved her backpack and hurried into her camp. She tried to avoid looking at the dead men.

Frantic, she broke camp quicker than ever before. She crammed extra clothes, her sketchbook, hunting trap, and cooking pot into her bag. She released the rope which strung her food bundle from the branches overhead, and shoved it inside with her medicine kit. Last, she fixed her bedroll to the top of her pack.

Weaver descended from the branches and landed on Aeryn's leanto. She reached for him, and he stepped onto her finger. Pulling him close to her chest, she scanned the area and strained her ears. The forest was quiet.

Her eyes landed on the lifeless forms of her attackers.

What if someone came here and saw them? The men mentioned another group. Aeryn didn't trust them to be any less dangerous.

With no time to waste, she slung her pack over her shoulders, and fled.

❏

Aeryn's legs refused to stop, and her heart hammered from the exertion. After an hour of hard-going, travel grew trickier. Dusk fell and the nighttime creatures emerged with their chittering, howling cacophony.

Her muscles begged for a break, but where was she? Blind terror had driven her deeper into Ravenwood, heedless of direction.

Weaver, who mostly rode atop the pack, fluttered to a nearby tree. It was taller than the others. Dropping her bag at the base of the trunk, she hoisted herself into the branches. She climbed as high as safely possible in the low light.

The cool evening air enveloped her as she breached the canopy. The just-setting sun cast red and purple streaks across the twinkling indigo backdrop. The forest spread out before her like a sea of deep, leafy green. In the distance, the dark mountains in Illwali rose against the eastern horizon.

Aeryn settled in the branches and absorbed the view. She knew where she was now.

How could a place so beautiful invite such violence?

Weaver alighted on a branch beside her. As she caught her breath, the weight of what happened hammered her in the chest.

Aeryn remembered the first time she killed an animal. She was twelve, hunting under her father's tutelage. She was surprised to find that she could do it, but it gave her the shakes, and that night in the privacy of her room, she cried. She grew up a little bit that day, part of her callusing over in order to survive in a world which included death.

It was a brutal part of the natural order. *The law of the forest.* Their life, for hers. The elves weren't meant to subsist without meat. Still, she never killed lightly, even after all these years.

She'd never killed a person. She never needed to. Not until now.

In the past, she wondered what she'd do if ever faced with a violent attacker. Could she take a person's life if the choice was either to kill them, or be raped and murdered?

Turns out, she could, and making the choice to lift the bow wasn't that hard.

That scared her.

Killing a soldier of Errebos was a capital offense. She killed three. There were no witnesses to prove she acted in defense. If she went to the authorities about her attackers, they might turn around and arrest her for murder, or interference of official duties at best.

Why were they attempting to recapture escaped slaves anyway? What might they do to keep their activity quiet?

If she went home and told her family, they would believe her. But her parents would lose their minds. This would only prove all their concerns about her choice to leave the village were justified.

Maybe they were right after all.

Elion would keep his head. Weaver tolerated Elion, so maybe she could send him a message. But then what? She was an outlaw now.

Was this more judgment from the gods? They hadn't poured out a full measure yet?

Aeryn's head throbbed. Weaver squawked and ruffled his feathers. He was tired and cranky. Her own fatigue was catching up with her. She'd form a plan in the morning. She was too far from Merioake, and too exhausted to travel further today, though she doubted she'd get much sleep. Ravenwood was dangerous enough at night without the threat of more corrupt Imperials and violent ex-slaves roaming the woods. The only mercy was she didn't know anyone, woodsman or not, willing to travel through Ravenwood by dark, except for an emergency.

Back on the forest floor, she slung her bag over her shoulder. She kept her bow in hand and pressed on for a suitable place to rest before what light remained disappeared completely.

The trickle of running water alerted her to her growing thirst. The desire to drink drove her toward a stream which cut through the terrain nearby. She followed its banks to a clearing where the break in the canopy allowed swaths of dusky moonlight to bathe the area in dim light.

As she stepped out of the cover of the trees, Aeryn's heart skipped. Her breath caught.

A broad, armored human slumped against a fallen tree. His helmet had been dumped at his feet. One arm rested awkwardly across his middle. The other rested on a battle axe at his side. An arrow protruded from his right shoulder. His hair was the color of wet sand and he had a short, scruffy beard.

One of his eyes was swollen shut and he stared hard at her across the clearing. His chest rose and fell with the labored breaths of an injured animal.

Mustering his strength, he tensed, and hoisted his axe for action. "So, are you here to kill me?"

4

Grim Stonebreaker

Aeryn gaped at him. He looked half-dead, so how was he even holding that?

"No!" she cried.

He paused. "Okay."

The man slumped against the log, sinking lower and allowing the axe to thunk into the grass at his side.

Aeryn studied him for a moment, pained at the sight. He was semi-conscious and still breathing heavily. He wasn't dressed like an Imperial, which relieved her, but he was a wreck.

He cracked an eye and watched her inch closer.

"You have an arrow sticking out of you," she said.

"I know," he said, unphased.

She hesitated. "If you let me, I can remove it."

The man regarded her with his one unswollen eye for a beat. "Okay."

He shut his eye, and took a few more heavy breaths, as though summoning his strength. He grunted in discomfort as he shifted his body to offer his shoulder.

Aeryn rested her belongings and inspected the wound. The arrow penetrated the minute gap between his backplate and spaulder. With permission, she removed the shoulder piece, and cut back some of the leather and fabric which was wet and sticky with blood. The arrowhead was completely embedded.

She took a steadying breath. She had a strong stomach, but wasn't used to seeing arrows sticking out of people.

"I'm going to pull it straight out," she said. "It's going to hurt, and I'm sorry."

"I can handle it."

Her eyes darted to the axe at his side. What if he reacted strongly when she yanked it out?

"Mind if I move your axe first?"

"I like my axe."

"Yes, it looks very sharp."

She left the shoulder to grasp the weapon with two hands, then dragged it a few feet away, out of his reach.

"There. Nice and safe." Returning to his shoulder, she took a deep breath. "Try to stay still. Ready?"

His muscles tensed as she wrapped her hands around the arrow shaft. She pulled, firmly and steadily. He barely flinched. With a shucking noise, the arrow came out, followed by a gush of blood.

It was in one piece.

Relief washed over Aeryn and she realized she had been holding her breath. She recognized the arrowhead as the mechanical barbed variety Kazmuk showed her earlier that day.

Was this the prisoner the Imperials mentioned to Kazmuk? What did those men call him? Stonebreaker?

She tossed the arrow to the ground where the man could see it. She pulled her handkerchief from her pocket and applied gentle pressure to slow the bleeding.

"Thank you," the man said, pulling Aeryn out of her own head.

"You're welcome. What's your name?"

"Grim Stonebreaker," he said, his voice groggy.

That answers that.

When she imagined a fugitive on the run for weeks, she expected someone gaunt and ragged, or wild and dangerous. Not a mountain of muscle in plate armor. Questions tangled in her mind, but more pressing was Grim, drifting off right in front of her.

She rapped his metal chestpiece with a finger. "Hey. Wake up. No dying."

His eyes fluttered and he took a sudden breath.

"Stay awake for now," she said. "You can talk to me if it helps."

He bobbed his head. "Okay."

"I'm Aeryn. When was the last time you ate?"

He thought for a minute. "Two days ago."

"I have some food and water I can share." She checked the handkerchief.

As she waited for the bleeding to slow, she tried to recall the contents of her medicine kit. She glanced at the throbbing wound on her own arm. It needed attention too.

"Grim," she said, and he cracked his eye to look at her again. "Can you hold this on your shoulder for me? I need some light before I can clean and stitch this..." Her eyes passed over his bloody armor. "...and whatever else needs it. What else hurts?"

"Everything."

She conceded with a nod.

With effort, the man reached across his body to press the cloth.

Aeryn dumped the contents of her backpack, found her tinderbox and some dry kindling. She took a few minutes to get a small campfire crackling. She knelt by the man with her medicine kit, food, and water.

"Before stitches, chew this. It helps with pain." She passed him a sprig of gingerwort, and offered her waterskin to wash it down.

Water sloshed down his front as he drank. He handed it back and sighed.

"Eat some venison. It's salty, so drink more water. Let me get your gauntlet off before you eat," she said.

He cooperated as she unclasped the gauntlet and pulled it off. A series of unfamiliar symbols were tattooed down each knuckle. Something tickled at the back of her mind, just out of reach. She wanted to ask what the marks meant, but he was drooping again.

She tapped him gingerly. "Hey. Sleep later."

He grunted, his head lolling upright. "Okay," he said with very little energy.

"Eat. It'll help you get better." Aeryn passed him a sizable hunk of venison as she took over at his shoulder wound.

She worked quietly, cleaning and stitching as he ate.

"Did Imperials do this to you?" she asked, as much to get an answer as to keep him from drifting off again.

"Not Imperials," he said. "Cords."

"Who is *Cords?*"

"Slavers. Look for the black cord," he said. "It's how you know."

He coughed and his whole body contracted in discomfort. She waited for him to stop, not wanting to cause any more pain. When she finished on his shoulder, she moved to the gash on the back of his leg.

"You were a slave?" she asked carefully.

"I was."

"Where? For how long?"

Grim thought for a moment. He flinched as she cleaned the wound. "There was a mine in the mountains. I was there since I was eight."

Aeryn's fingers paused over her work, and she cocked her head. "Eight years old?"

"Eight years old."

❏

Grim was bloody and bruised everywhere. Apart from the gash on his shoulder, it was likely the impact from the arrow cracked bone. He sustained a deep gash on his calf, and Aeryn suspected a broken rib. He had numerous older bruises. Scars covered his back, giving the skin a mottled, lacy appearance.

Perhaps it was exhaustion, or the amount of blood he lost, but he was remarkably cooperative as she cleaned, wrapped, treated, and stitched. He relaxed, and mostly kept his eyes shut as she worked and asked questions. She kept him talking, but his answers grew less coherent as the night wore on.

By the time she finished, his filthy armor lay piled beside the log. She salvaged some of his shirt for a sling to keep his shoulder in place. She brewed him an extra strong dose of medicinal tea for pain, and asked him to eat a few more pieces of venison. Half asleep, he grunted consent and complied.

She helped him ease into a suitable position for rest with his back against the log and his toes toward the fire.

"I'm going to be awake for awhile," she said as she spread a blanket over him. "If you awake and need medicine, there's more."

Grim's eyes were already closed. His face relaxed as he mumbled something unintelligible, then slipped into sleep.

At the stream's edge, she let the cool water flow over her blood-stained hands, and tried not to think about what she'd fled from before finding this strange man. She stretched her neck. Her stomach growled and she realized she had skipped supper.

Aeryn stowed her supplies. She grabbed a few more hunks of meat, a handful of nuts, and her second blanket. She plopped on the grassy earth beside Grim. She chewed her meal in silence, staring into the fire.

Her reluctant visit to Merioake that morning felt like ages ago. The world was not the same place anymore. Aeryn wasn't sure what to believe. As far as she knew, slavery didn't exist in the continent. Yet here was Grim. The scars which laced his back made a compelling case.

A cool breeze ruffled the leaves. She shivered and pulled the blanket around her shoulders.

The past few hours had been a needed distraction, but she

had to return to her old camp. Everyone in Merioak knew she was staying in Ravenwood. If anyone trekked that way and saw the dead bodies at a recently abandoned campsite, there'd be trouble.

Grim would need help tomorrow, but she could spare a couple hours away to bury the Imperials and hide any evidence of what she'd done.

5

Doubts

Aeryn woke with a start in the muted light of early morning. She had fallen asleep on the bare ground some time after midnight. Her bones felt stiff, her neck ached where the man choked her, and the wound on her arm throbbed.

She peaked beneath her bandage and grimaced. The stitches she performed on herself in the low light with her non-dominant hand would leave an ugly scar.

A few feet away, Grim slept upright, propped against the log. Beads of sweat coated his forehead. His complexion looked grayer than it should. He breathed heavily and turned his head, frowning in his sleep.

He needed more medicine.

She rechecked the stores of her herbalism kit. The supply of gingerwort concerned her least. The herb grew all over Ravenwood.

She might need some fever sorrel if his temperature remained high. It usually reduced fevers and made the person comfortable, though it wouldn't fix the cause. So hopefully Grim was only hot and sweaty because of the wool blanket, not some brewing infection.

She fed fresh kindling to the dying embers of the campfire, and set the kettle beside the smoldering logs. Weaver landed nearby to investigate as she shredded herbs and tossed them into the cup.

Finding this dull, the blackbird fluttered to Aeryn's shoulder and attempted to preen her hair.

"I know. I'm a mess," Aeryn said. Her life circumstances didn't allow her much room for girliness, but meticulously neat hair was one thing she prided herself on.

There were more important matters to attend to this morning.

Her eyes wandered to Grim.

He was no native to the southern provinces. If she wasn't sure before, she was now. The humans of Thoen tended to stand only slightly taller than the elves, with dusky complexions and light brown to black hair. Even the humans in neighboring Illwali were almost exclusively dark-haired with tan skin and dark, almond shaped eyes. Grim was too tall, too pale, and too blonde to be from around here.

He resembled the brash Northern mercenaries she saw pass through town as a child.

How did a Northerner end up in the southern mountains as a slave?

The kettle sang. When she finished a dose of tea for herself, she got to work on a serving for Grim.

He needed his own cup.

She'd figure that out later. The first priority after Grim was treated and situated, was her old campsite. She needed to bury those bodies, or whatever was left of them.

Grim gasped awake. He cast a bleary-eyed gape at his surroundings. "My gloves. I need them."

Aeryn crouched beside him.

"You mean your gauntlets? They're over there." She burned her fingers on his forehead, and frowned. "How about some medicine and food? Good morning, by the way."

Grim blinked at her, perplexed. "Herm said never take them off."

"I don't recommend putting them back on. They'll probably make you uncomfortable. And sick, if you eat with them. They're filthy."

Grim's jaw chattered. His eyes passed over the camp again, then refocused on Aeryn, full of confusion. "Eat them?"

"Here. Medicine," she said. She put the cup into his free hand. "Do you remember my name?"

He gulped the tea, winced as he swallowed, and shook his head.

"It's okay. I only told you four times yesterday. I'm Aeryn. You're in Ravenwood forest. I found you yesterday," she said. "Sound familiar?"

Grim's breathing relaxed slightly as the medicine seeped into his body. "You removed the arrow."

Aeryn smiled. "Right. Do you need to relieve yourself? I'll help you get to the bushes, but you have to take care of your own business. Don't get any ideas."

Grim nodded.

He grunted as he tried to hoist himself off the ground. Aeryn slung his free arm over her shoulder and helped him up. Standing, he was more than a head taller than her, and heavy. He smelled terrible. His sides and neck were covered with bug bites. She made a mental note to collect some citraneem while she was out. Being an elf, the biters left Aeryn alone, but the humans in her village often used the pleasant smelling herb to repel insects.

As she helped him limp to the bushes outside the clearing, his heat seeped into her, making her sweat. She allowed him some privacy, then supported his weight as he hobbled back to his spot.

Grim eased against the log, shivering and breathing hard. He shut his eyes to rest, but a cough made him shudder. Aeryn's brows pitched in the center as his body contracted in pain.

His condition was a major snag in her plan. She couldn't leave him like this. He was so unfocused and weak, if danger came upon their camp, he was as good as dead. External danger aside, he might die anyway without care in his current state.

The urgency to bury the Imperials tugged on her mind. She needed him stable enough to leave him for the morning.

"You should eat. Food makes things better." She grabbed a handful of nuts and dried fruit and knelt beside him.

Grim crunched on a single nut and then relaxed against the log, still panting. "Are my gloves here?"

"Grim, you don't have gloves. You don't need them. You have a fever and it's going to be a warm day," she said. "You need to rest and eat some food. I'm going to check your bandages, okay?"

Grim took a few heavy breaths and then nodded.

Aeryn peeled back the bandage at his shoulder. Her stomach sank.

The stitches held, but that was the extent of the good news.

The entire area was flaming red, swollen, and hot.

"How bad?" he asked.

She dabbed the cloudy fluid seeping from the wound. "How long was the arrow in your shoulder before I pulled it out?"

He thought for a moment. "They attacked at sunup."

All day.

Aeryn took a deep breath. She only knew one treatment for a wound this severely infected. She felt like she might be sick, in no small part because she knew what that entailed.

"You need leatherleaf."

"Another plant?"

"Yes. It cures infection. All kinds of sickness, actually. Kept my brother from dying after the dunderhead gobbled a bunch of poison berries as a kid." She removed the dirty bandage entirely.

Her thoughts ran, picking up speed.

If someone discovered the bodies, her family, vigilant townsfolk, and the authorities would search the woods. They'd discover her and Grim. They'd figure out she killed the Imperials. She'd be arrested for murder. Since Grim was running from crooked soldiers who wanted to return him to slavery and would probably do anything to keep their activities from exposure, they'd spin it so she'd also be guilty of aiding an abetting a fugitive. She'd be hung, and Grim would be sent back to the mine where they'd make an example of him.

She couldn't afford to leave the evidence of what she'd done to those soldiers. Her old camp was an hour away, like the leatherleaf grove but in the opposite direction. Given Grim's state of health, she didn't have time to go to both places.

She didn't want to go to the grove at all.

Yet he was going to die of infection if he didn't get the herb soon.

Grim interrupted Aeryn's spiraling flow of thought as he suddenly lurched to the side and coughed up his stomach contents. He wiped his mouth with the back of his free hand and eased into a sitting position again. Shivering, he hugged his body and caught his breath.

"Naren?" he said in a groggy voice, his eyes closed.

"Aeryn."

"Aeryn..." He rocked his head in her direction. "My gloves."

His lucid moment had passed.

Urgency pushed against Aeryn. She watched him for a moment, as she settled her mind. "Grim, I'll be back in a little while."

He murmured, "Mhmm," although she doubted he understood.

Aeryn grabbed her bow and slung her quiver and satchel, then disappeared into the treeline.

❖

Six years, and the grove looked exactly the same.

A familiar ache twisted in Aeryn's chest as her last visit replayed in her mind, rushing through her like the torrent of water cascading down the rockface. Battering her. Threatening to drown her.

Not now.

She knelt at the grove's edge and ripped handfuls of the blue leatherleaf from the earth until her satchel bulged. It was too bad the plant grew nowhere else and couldn't be preserved. She didn't want to come back here again.

She paused a moment, and ran her fingers over the soft indigo blooms blanketing the earth beside her. It kicked up a spicy fragrance which tickled the inside of her nose.

The regular haunting accusations thrummed in her mind. *You couldn't save her. You weren't fast enough. She's gone because of you. You failed as a mother.*

She pulled herself away, and hurried back to camp at a full-out run. She couldn't afford to give the pain an opportunity to latch on right now. She didn't have much time before she had another dead person on her hands.

❚

She found Grim as she left him, still alive. White-lipped and sweaty, he stirred as she knelt beside him and uncapped her waterskin.

"You seem surprised to see me," Aeryn said as she helped him take a drink. "Are you going to vomit?"

"No," he said, jaw chattering. He watched her unload heaps of blue leatherleaf from her bag. She washed the dirt from the roots and got to work grinding it into a paste as the kettle warmed beside the fire.

Like gingerwort, the leathery leaves and mild blue flowers for which the plant derived its name could be brewed as a medicinal tea, or ground into a paste for direct application. If anything could ensure a grievous wound would heal without infection, it was blue leatherleaf.

So she was told.

"I have more medicine for pain," she said as she worked. "This blue plant is the one I told you about. You can drink some, and I'll put some on your stitches. It'll kill the infection, which'll make your fever go down too. You'll feel better."

Grim nodded.

"Do you like blueberries?" she said, trying to keep the conversation light. "I passed some bushes closeby."

He shifted his weight. "Never had 'em."

"Oh, you'll like them," she said.

It took a few minutes to grind a thick paste and brew a strong dose of medicinal tea. She poured the hot water over gingerwort with fever sorrel and handed him the cup. He passed it back empty. She wasn't sure if the leatherleaf could be mixed with other herbs, so she made what she imagined was a double dosage of it separately, then rechecked his wounds.

His stitches, which she left clean and treated, looked worse than they did at sunrise. They'd turned greenish-black. She cleaned them again, smeared the poultice over the wounds, and waited for it to take effect.

After years of regarding the plant as a miracle herb, she expected a more miraculous effect. The leatherleaf seemed to operate at the pace of any other medicine.

Feeling a little let down, Aeryn busied herself nearby as

Grim eased into a feverish sleep. *Alright. No instantaneous healing.*

"That doesn't mean the medicine isn't working on him," she said to Weaver as she cleaned up. The pressing need to attend to her old campsite prodded her. "Once it does its work, we can go back to the old camp. This afternoon. Right now, he's too sick to leave. I need you with me to keep a lookout. How long does it take to dig graves for three men, anyway?"

Weaver rasped. He had no idea what she was talking about beyond *you with me* and *lookout.* It didn't matter. She needed to hear a voice outside her own head. As she washed bandages, her mind turned over her dilemma.

Grim awoke abruptly, startling Aeryn. He squinted at the sky. "Did you see it?"

"See what?" she asked. She scanned the gap in the trees.

"The dragon."

Aeryn tested his forehead. He was still feverish and delirious. "No dragon, Grim."

"They said they eat children."

"I'm sure they do," she said. "But I live in this forest. If there was a dragon here, I'd know it by now."

Grim's expression slackened. He rested his head, hugging his body. "Okay."

Aeryn's opportunity to return to her camp slipped away with the hours of daylight. Despite the frequent doses of leatherleaf, Grim's physical and mental condition worsened. The fever climbed and pain from his injuries kept him from sound rest. When he drifted off, it wasn't long before nightmares assailed and he awoke with a start, panicked and confused.

He experienced brief periods of lucidity following a dosage of medicine. Aeryn tried to keep him engaged while he was awake. Keeping his axe nearby provided him some solace, not that he was capable of wielding it, though he thought he was. He wanted to bring it with him when she helped him travel again to the bushes that afternoon.

"No, it can wait for you here." Aeryn grunted as he leaned on her for balance.

"If there's a dragon, I need my axe."

Aeryn had given up trying to convince him there were no dragons in the woods. "I'll make sure none sneak up on you."

This seemed acceptable to him.

They hobbled past the pile of armor. She considered it. Plate armor was expensive.

"Grim?" she said. "Where'd you get your nice armor, if you were a slave?"

He rumbled in his chest and replied with conviction. "I killed a man."

"I see."

Hopefully that was delirium too.

By sundown, Grim had deteriorated so much that he could do little but cooperate with Aeryn's efforts to keep him alive. He was in-and-out of consciousness every hour or two. Aeryn kept vigilant through the night, only resting in short bursts while she sat upright, head propped on her knees.

In the morning Weaver landed on her shoulder to pick at her collar for seeds. She peevishly shooed him away. He fluttered to the ground and glared at her.

"Don't look at me like that."

The rasp of the mortar and pestle shifted into unpleasant grinding as she prepared a fresh batch of blue leatherleaf poultice for Grim's shoulder.

She was exhausted, and doubts snagged her like thorns trapped in her sock. She expected stronger results by now.

The arrow had been lodged in his shoulder for a full day. What if the damage was too much for the herb to overcome?

She wondered if she'd made a grievous mistake going to the grove, instead of her old camp. She might've saved herself by dealing with the bodies of the Imperials. Now it might be too late.

Instead, she was here, helping someone who, despite her efforts, might still die.

She questioned whether it was wrong to leave him, to take care of herself, if he was just going to die anyway.

The thought made her uncomfortable. It felt wrong.

She wrestled with it nonetheless.

She finished grinding the paste and stared at it.

She left her baby for this herb.

It was supposed to cure anything, but what if the promise of blue leatherleaf was only a myth? Or somehow worsened his condition? The idea that Aeryn traveled the grove for a lie, when she should've been at her dying child's side, was too much to bear.

Aeryn ran a hand down her weary face and glanced at

Grim, resting nearby.

The herb gave him some relief when administered, even if temporarily. That was something.

Aeryn's mother wouldn't lead her astray. Verelle knew her medicines.

Aeryn released the breath which lodged painfully in her chest.

Whatever sickness raged inside Grim's body was waging a valiant war to destroy him. He might not prevail, but she would do her best to help him win.

If it's too late, at least he wouldn't die alone.

She tossed a seed to Weaver. He turned his beak up and flew away, but returned for it when he thought she wasn't looking.

That afternoon, when Grim drifted into a fitful sleep, an idea came to Aeryn, and she whistled for Weaver. He landed on her knee, attentive.

"Weaver, you're a clever boy."

The grackle puffed his chest, showing off his gleaming plumage.

"I need you to go back to my old camp. Do you remember where?"

He nipped her on the leg.

"Ouch. Don't get offended, I had to ask," she said. "Go there. Check for men. Dead men. Come back and tell me what you find." She handed him a seed, and he flew into the trees.

Nerves kept Aeryn from taking the opportunity for a nap.

She washed dirty bandages and prepared Grim's next round of medicine. Aeryn's gaze drifted to the markings which covered each of his fingers.

When she first saw the symbols, a hint of familiarity tugged at her memory. The feeling resurfaced now, though she couldn't pin it down.

Weaver returned within an hour. He dropped a circular black cord with a metal clasp in front of her.

"That was fast. Good boy. What of the men?"

Weaver made a series of *cack* and *churr* sounds.

"Wolf food, huh?" she said.

The wild animals got them after all. Aeryn felt relieved, but only slightly. Animals might drag bloody, ravaged uniforms anywhere. If found, it might entice some of the more vigilant townsfolk to seek the dangerous beasts responsible.

There wasn't much to do about that.

Aeryn prodded the black cord. It looked like a bracelet, but was crusted with dried blood. "What's this, a present? Did you find this at camp?"

Weaver chirruped affirmatively. He flitted to her shoulder and pecked at her collar for his reward.

Grim mentioned something about a black cord when they met. He'd been talking about the slavers.

Why were these Imperials involved with slavers?

Grim might know, but asking him now and getting a coherent answer was out of the question.

Over the next few days, Aeryn fell into a routine. She administered medicine, treated wounds, and tried to keep Grim hydrated and comfortable. She rested when she could and didn't leave camp except to check her trap or gather berries from a patch a couple minutes walk from the clearing.

The mercy in this was that constant care for another person helped distract Aeryn's mind from the trauma of being attacked and killing three people. She usually didn't sleep for long enough stretches to relive the ordeal in her dreams.

Usually.

If there was one thing she wanted, it was answers. Too much of what Grim said in his incoherent ramblings didn't mesh with the world as she knew it.

On the third day of fever, Aeryn sat cross-legged near Grim with her lunch. His breathing changed and the trembling stopped. Grim's face relaxed.

Fearing the worst, Aeryn almost dropped her bowl. She checked for breathing and touched his head. It felt cool. She chanced a peak at the arrow wound. It was dry and the skin around it appeared normal.

Aeryn rubbed her exhausted face, so relieved she thought she might cry. The infection was gone. He'd only eased into a peaceful sleep.

6

Gloves

When Grim awoke in the late afternoon, the first thing he noticed was his gnawing hunger, and the second was the elvish woman. She seemed genuinely relieved, happy even, to see him awake. She was eager to get him upright and eating. To this, Grim had no objections. He was ravenous.

The next thing he noticed was his tattoos. He was supposed to keep those covered.

As he adjusted himself with the log at his back, he felt unsure what to do with his hands. The arm with the injured shoulder rested against his bare chest in a sling, with his knuckles hanging out the end, for anyone to see. He moved his free arm over the end of his fingers, and tried to tuck his hand from view, but couldn't figure out how to do it without sending a shock of pain to his broken shoulder.

"Do I have gloves somewhere?" he asked, trying to sound nonchalant.

"Oh, your favorite question," the she-elf said without looking up, as she bent over the simmering cook pot.

She was slender, with strong arms, and silky elbow-length hair which fell over her shoulder as she ladled food into a dish. She wore patchy buckskin trousers which ballooned where she tucked them into her boots, and a loose-fitting shirt made from the same type of fuzzy animal skin.

"Sorry, no gloves. I looked among your things, but I found nothing. Don't worry, I didn't steal any of your coins." As she offered him the bowl, she noticed Grim awkwardly trying to hide his knuckles, and she gave him a funny look. "Why? Do you need them?"

"I just…" Grim shifted. He felt more exposed over his fingers than the fact he had no shirt to cover his scars, in front of a woman no less. "I like to keep my hands covered."

There was a pause.

"Okay…" The she-elf handed him the bowl of food, and retook her place near the fire a few feet away.

Grim's concern about his gloves was momentarily overpowered by the need to eat. The hunger which clung to his ribs made his muscles weak, and it was hard to think about much else. Grim wasn't entirely sure what was in the dish, but it smelled better than anything served at the mines, and it tasted like salvation.

"What is this?" he asked, as he balanced the dish in his lap and spooned another enormous bite into his mouth.

She watched him inhale another mouthful. "Pork, orange potatoes, wild onion…"

"No, no, I've had meat and potatoes. What did you put in this?" Grim asked. "This is better than anything I've ever tasted."

She sat a little straighter, and a small smile crept onto her lips. "Thank you."

He lifted the dish to his mouth to drink the cloudy broth.

"Is there more?" he asked after his third helping.

She was still on her first. "That's all of it."

"Oh." He felt genuinely disappointed. They sat without speaking for a full thirty seconds. With food, strength started to seep into his body and his thoughts regained focus.

Grim was unaccustomed to women. The mines were exclusively male. Mostly filthy, uncouth humans. She was the opposite in every way. Her hair was neat, she sat up straight, and rather than inhaling her food, she took her time, turning her spoon over after every bite to lick the other side. Which was odd. In the mines, you ate fast, or you didn't eat.

Maybe she didn't like it. She was still on her first helping, after all.

"I can finish it, if you don't want the rest," he said helpfully.

"I'm actually enjoying this quite a lot," she said, turning over the spoon and popping it back into her mouth.

"But you're not done."

She attempted to suppress a smirk. "Just because I don't devour my food like some beast, doesn't mean I dislike it."

"Oh."

"I suppose I'm not surprised you have an appetite. You haven't eaten in three days."

Grim's mind worked over his predicament. He knew it'd been a while. "Three days?"

"Yes. You almost died."

He stiffened. Grim furrowed his brow and watched her for a moment. The past few days were fuzzy. He knew he'd been injured, and very sick, and she'd looked after him. A growing sense of unease leaked into his mind.

She'd saved his life? Why? What did she want, and why hadn't she mentioned it yet? Most perplexing of all, she seemed genuine about helping him. Kind, even.

No one was that selfless.

Maybe she was bad at extorting favors.

"So what do you want?" he asked at last.

She stopped with her spoon halfway to her mouth. "What are you talking about?"

His eyes narrowed. "Who are you?"

"You don't remember my name, do you?" she asked. When he remained quiet, she sighed, plunked her spoon back in her bowl, and spoke slowly. "I'm Aeryn. I live here. I found you. You were injured. Does any of this sound familiar?"

It did. He continued to stare at her, trying to figure out the catch.

She took his delay for a lack of understanding, and repeated herself, slower and a little louder. "I'm *Aeryn*..."

"I got that," he said, raising his free hand. "I'm trying to figure out why you helped me."

"So you wouldn't die," she said, emphasizing with both hands. "A primary goal of treating injuries."

He eyed her warily. Was she serious?

"You're welcome," she said, annoyed. "Gods. You save someone's life and you think the first thing they'd say is *thank you*, not..." and she lowered her voice to imitate Grim, "...*what do you want?"*

She rolled her eyes and jabbed her spoon around the cloudy broth in her bowl.

A blackbird Grim noticed hovering around the campsite chittered. Aeryn dipped her head toward the bird in a mock bow. "Thank you, Weaver."

Was that bird...laughing?

Aeryn returned her focus to her food, her annoyance still palpable. Grim watched her for a moment as she took another painfully slow bite. His mind worked over the situation, and he weighed whether he believed her.

She seemed sincere.

He wasn't really sure what to do with that.

He remained quiet for a minute, then said, "Thank you."

Aeryn glanced at him out of the corner of her eye and gave a tiny nod.

By the time she was done, which felt like hours, her mood improved. She stacked her dirty dish on top of his, and pivoted toward him.

"Alright. You asked if I wanted something," she said looking him in the face. "I do."

Grim hesitated. *Here it was.* "What is it?"

"Conversation."

"Conversation?"

"You have been severely lacking in conversation these past few days. I have questions," Aeryn folded her hands in her lap. "Given that I've treated your injuries, your infection, and your lice, I think it's fair if I get some answers."

Grim met her eyes, detecting only honest curiosity. If all she wanted was some answers, that was more than reasonable. After all, she had saved his life, and he felt significantly less itchy.

"I guess I owe you that much," Grim said.

Aeryn flicked the hair away from her shoulder with the back of her hand and adjusted herself to get more comfortable. She dove into the first question. "Were you really a slave?"

He dipped his chin. "I was."

"In Illwali?"

"I don't know what *Illwali* is. I was in a mine somewhere in the mountains."

Aeryn thought for a moment, but accepted the answer. "This group, *Cord*, enslaved you?"

"No, they're called the Loom," he said. "The individual members are called Cords."

"Do they often work with Imperials?"

"Those are soldiers, right?"

She nodded. "For the Empire."

"Not that I'm aware."

Aeryn's brows pressed together in thought for a moment before she continued. "How'd you end up here?"

"The Loom took me from my family when I was eight. I don't remember anything before then," he said. "They put me in the mines, where I worked until recently. I started a revolt, and got out with some others. Cords tracked us into the forest. They attacked, and I was the only one who survived."

Aeryn's expression shifted as she listened. "I'm sorry for what you went through. Your parents must be worried about you."

At the mention of his parents, there was a tightness in his chest. He didn't remember them. He sometimes wondered if they were alive, and at what point they had given up on finding him, if they even bothered to look. He also contended with the possibility they put him there. Hearing what some of the other men had done, or had been done to them, he knew people weren't above wickedness to their own flesh and blood. He remembered the day, after his first beating at the hands of the taskmaster, when he realized no one was coming to save him.

Grim tried to shrug, but winced as a jolt of pain shot down his arm. He forgot about his shoulder. "Was that all?" he asked.

"No." Aeryn tilted her head toward his pile of armor. "Did you really kill someone for that armor?"

"Yes. A slaver."

If that made her uneasy, she took it remarkably well. Aeryn thought for another moment, then dug something out from beneath her backpack and tossed it into the grass between them. "Does this mean anything to you?"

Grim's whole body tensed as his eyes fell on the black bracelet.

"Where'd you find this?" he asked, his tone serious.

"Answer my question first," she shot back.

"The Cords wear them. Higher ranked Cords have it tattooed on their arm. It identifies them," he said. "Where'd you get this?"

Aeryn hesitated. She opened her mouth, but no words came out. Dropping her gaze, she touched her neck. Grim noticed for the first time that the discolored marks which mottled the skin on her neck were bruises. His frown deepened. Had she met the owner of that cord already?

"Aeryn," he said, his tone urgent.

She took a steadying breath. "There were men at my old camp, the day I found you. They were looking for you. The bracelet was theirs. But they were dressed like Imperials, so–"

"What?" Grim went rigid. "What did you tell them?"

"I didn't tell them anything," she said, her voice tightening. "I overheard them and I tried to get away."

"Did they follow you?"

"No."

"Are you sure? If they're in the woods, and they find me, they're going to capture or kill me and drag you off too," he said. "How certain are you?"

"They're dead, Grim."

He studied her for a moment. "All of them? How many?"

"Yes, all of them."

"You killed them?"

Aeryn stiffened. "I defended myself," she said, her wide green eyes suddenly fierce. "I know what they would've done. What they tried to do. What choice did I have? It was me or them."

"But they're dead?" He had to be sure.

She nodded, her fire simmering.

"Good," he said, able to relax again. "How many?"

"Three."

Grim raised his eyebrows. She handled herself against three Cords and came out practically unscathed? That was impressive.

She rubbed her arm and Grim noticed a set of stitches which looked about as fresh as the ones on his leg.

He jerked his chin towards the black corded bracelet in the grass. "Those men were Cords, not Imperials. The ones who attacked me and my men were dressed like soldiers too. Probably to blend in."

Aeryn's eyes searched his face, almost begging. "Are you sure?"

His mind traveled to the familiar slavers who tried to recapture him and got what they deserved. "I'm sure."

Aeryn's shoulders relaxed. She leaned her head back and tears came to her eyes.

Grim watched the display of emotion, utterly perplexed. "Are you in pain?"

She swiped the water from one eye and then the other. She sniffed, regaining her composure.

"No. Relieved," she said. "I thought they were soldiers. I had no way to prove I defended myself. If someone found out, I'd've been hung."

The blackbird chose that moment to leave his perch in a nearby tree and fly to Aeryn's shoulder and preen her hair.

"This is my friend Weaver." The bird climbed onto her finger and she held him for Grim to better see the creature. Weaver puffed his chest to show off his iridescent blue-black feathers. She set him on the log where he pounced upon a beetle. The fire crackled, and she eased her back against the trunk to watch the blackbird with a tired, but easy smile.

Feeling more at ease himself, Grim wanted to keep talking with her. Aeryn seemed capable and decent, and he had questions, too.

"Where are we?" he asked.

She pulled her gaze from Weaver. "We're in the Ravenwood region of the Southern Forest."

He stared at her blankly.

"Hold on," she said. She retrieved a leatherbound book which rested nearby amongst her belongings, then settled cross-legged beside him. She opened to a blank page. Using a charcoal pencil, she began to draw. "You'll have to excuse my depiction of the Empire. I'm better at birds and flowers."

She drew the rough shape of the land, like a fat square with lumpy sides and rounded edges. Grim watched with rapt interest as she divided the continent into eight sections, shaded the bottom third of the map with light, loopy swirls for a forest. She made a series of serrated lines, like arrow points, in each cardinal direction for mountains.

She inched closer so he could see.

"Here's Errebos. There are eight provinces." She touched her pencil to the southwestern one. "We're here in Thoen, in a part of the forest called Ravenwood."

She made a dot for their estimated whereabouts in the sprawling southern wood, and another just above it. "This is my hometown, Merioake. It's about a day's hike north of where we are right now. It's considered a border village, because it sits on the edge of the forest, so there's quite a few humans. In the South as a whole, you'll mostly find elves."

She tapped the four clusters of points she'd made for mountains.

"These are the Four Peaks. Really, they're ranges with a lot of peaks."

Grim stopped her to point to the closest set of mountains in the neighboring province. "I think the mines are here. After I left, I led a group west into the woods."

"That's Illwali," she said with a nod. "It's the most mountainous and wild of the three elvish provinces. I'd guess you're originally from here." She circled the area which encompassed the Northern Mountains. "Noemar."

"Why do you say that?"

"You look like the Northerners I've seen before. Tall and blonde," she said. "I don't know if you've ever seen a Thoenite, but you don't look like them, or the Illwalii."

His eyes worked over the map for a minute, and she handed him the sketchbook for a better look. Had he really been dragged across the continent?

Aeryn nodded to Grim's hands. "What do your tattoos say?"

Grim looked over his knuckles. "I have no idea. I can't read."

"You tattooed your hands, and you don't know what it

says?"

"I didn't put them there."

"Did the Loom do it to you?"

He shook his head. "I had them before I got to the mine. That I do remember."

"You were tattooed before you were eight?" she asked carefully.

"No, I think I was born with them."

Aeryn raised a dubious eyebrow. "Do you know how tattoos work?"

He gave her a wry look.

She gave it right back. "Excuse me, but it's the most unbelievable thing you've told me so far."

"I'm telling you the truth." He handed the sketchbook back to her. "I've always had them."

"Why are you so concerned about keeping them covered?" she said, peering closer at his hand.

Grim followed her gaze to the symbols on his knuckles. "There was a slave in the mines, Herm, who told me to. The Loom didn't interact with us much except to dole out punishment, and Herm's job was to communicate orders. He tried to help us along. When I got there, it was dark. They tossed us into this room, or cave, I'm not really sure. Herm was there to acclimate us. He took one look at my hands, gave me a pair of gloves, and told me never to take them off unless I wanted to lose my fingers. So I never did."

Aeryn gave him a bewildered look. "Why would anyone take your fingers?"

"Herm told me later it was because I look like a Baldomar," he said. "He said they were heroes a long time ago with markings called runes, like these." He turned his hand over.

Startled, Aeryn tilted her head. Her eyes widened, as though something important occurred to her. "What did he call them?"

"Runes."

"No, no, the people."

"Baldomar."

She snapped her fingers. "That's what it is. All this time, your tattoos were itching something in my memory, but I couldn't place it. I've heard of those people. My father fought in the last war. He told me about them."

"Did he know any?"

Aeryn shook her head. "He fought in the South. From what he says, the war here was very different from the war in the North, but everyone heard about the Baldomar back then. They were a mighty clan, but they were wiped out in the years of the war. Many thousands of them died." She gave his knuckles a curious glance as she tilted her head. "I wonder if you're descended from them?"

"You just said they all died."

She waved her hand as though shooing a fly. "History exaggerates all the time. They're probably only mostly dead."

"How long ago was this?" he asked.

"The war ended a hundred years ago."

A hundred years? "How old is your father?"

"Old enough to have fought in the war," she said. "Most elves, if they're healthy and stay out of trouble, can live to be two-hundred."

"How old are you?"

"Thirty," she said. "How old are you? Thirty five? Thirty seven?"

"I'm not completely sure." He thought for a moment. Based on the timing of newer slaves' arriavals, and those who kept track of how long they worked in the mine in comparison to others, he deduced that he'd been there for almost fifteen years. He worked the math in his head. "Twenty-two or twenty-three?"

"Oh. You look older." Her eyes fell to his knuckles once more, then back to meet his eyes. "Well, I don't think you have to worry about anyone chopping off your fingers, now that you're free. If they say something inflammatory, I can't tell. They make you look tough."

He snorted, amused, and she returned the smirk.

"Last question," she said. "Can you keep watch for a little while?" She tried to pin back a yawn. "I need to shut my eyes."

He nodded.

"Thanks." She stood and stretched her back. "Do you need medicine for pain?"

"I can manage."

"Right," she said. "When you decide you don't want to suffer needlessly, there's a cup of medicinal tea prepared by the fire. For pain."

Grim's eyes traveled to the cup, and he considered.

"If a predatory turtle climbs out to warm itself, avoid its mouth."

He looked at her with a hint of concern. "A what?"

"The crooked reeds among the straight," she said, as though the phrase ought to make sense. "They think they're very sneaky, but they're incredibly stupid and bad tempered. They won't differentiate between a worm or your toes, so stay out of lunging distance." Noting the look of concern in his brow, she added, "Don't worry, they're slow on land. If you're really concerned, you can wake me. I'll throw him back in the stream."

Well, if she wasn't worried about it....

Aeryn traveled to her bedroll. "Glad you kicked the infection. Don't kill me in my sleep."

"Ha!" Grim's face cracked into a smile as he threw his head back with a laugh. "I like my sleep too. Who's gonna keep watch if I do that?"

Aeryn raised both eyebrows at his jarring attempt at humor. "So, I'm dead meat as soon as you don't need me to keep watch? Very comforting." She snickered, but the laughter didn't reach her eyes. Then the light moment was over.

Maybe that was the wrong thing for him to say. Too familiar.

Aeryn watched him for a moment, her mind working. "Listen. You need to recover, and it's going to be a while before you're well enough to hike toward civilization. I'm willing to help you here, as long as you follow the ground rules."

"What are those?" he asked, trying not to sound as wary as

he felt. She needn't convince him that he required her help if he wanted to live, and she knew Grim wasn't in the position to negotiate.

She ticked off her fingers. "You keep clean. Do your fair share of work as you're able. Don't be a pervert."

That shouldn't be a problem. Making a mental note not to stare, he dipped his chin. "Okay."

"And so we're clear, if I get the sense you intend to harm me, I will leave you to the forest." She looked him steadily in the eye, and spoke evenly.

He believed her.

"Understood," Grim said.

"Good." Aeryn climbed under her covers. She didn't turn her back to him.

His eyes passed over the campsite, noting his axe within reach, her cooking and medicine supplies neatly arranged nearby, and a few items of clothing hung up to dry. Weaver strutted by his feet, on the hunt for insects, every so often turning his bright eye on Grim as though watching him, or hoping he dropped a crumb. Or both. The fire crackled and joined the trickle of the stream coursing behind them and the crickets eked out their songs. An owl hooted in the distance.

This would be his life until he got better. Here, with Aeryn and the bird.

She was capable, and while he couldn't be entirely certain, he didn't detect ulterior motives for helping him. He liked talking to her, and she made him laugh.

She was also an excellent cook.

"Aeryn?" he asked, before she drifted off. "Can we have more of that pork tomorrow?"

She propped herself on an elbow. "I set up my trap, so let's see if I catch anything. Which reminds me…" She pointed into the woods. "Don't go that way if you have to use the bushes."

He took a breath, feeling more at ease than he ever felt in his life. Once he recovered his strength, he could start planning his vengeance against the Loom. For now, as long as Aeryn was willing, this seemed like a good place to be.

7

Plans

A week after the fever left, Grim pointed Aeryn in the direction of his old campsite, for additional supplies.

She smelled the camp before she saw it. The carnage was terrible, confirming what he told her about his attackers. Unguarded, the wild animals tore the site apart. Flies buzzed over the remains of what the scavengers left behind. Two rats tumbled out of a breastplate, snarling over the rotting bits left inside. Clubs, swords, bows, and personal belongings were scattered everywhere. She found tattered swaths of blue Imperial uniform, but not the body it belonged to.

Aeryn didn't think it would be healthy to spend more than a few minutes picking through the debris. She managed to find some proper clothes and boots for Grim, dishes, a tinder box, and a heavy canvas pack. No gloves. Among the wreckage, she found two sheaves of arrows, including the expensive mechanical variety made by Kazmuk.

All this helped hold them over as Grim recovered. Food in Ravenwood was plentiful. Between her hunting skills and her trap, Aeryn had no trouble catching what they needed in meat. She found time to brain-tan a few skins, leaving the furs on, in hopes of storing up the materials required to make more clothing for herself.

Grim abided by the terms she set. She quickly discovered

he disliked idleness, so at times Aeryn was forced to order him to take it easy, lest he reinjure himself. She never caught him leering at her. The concept of regular washing was probably the biggest adjustment for him.

By now, he was healthy, and Aeryn was running out of time in Ravenwood. Samuel and Tarra's baby was due soon, which meant she was expected back in town to take up her place at the family business. A pang twisted inside Aeryn at the thought of a new baby in the family.

It was easy to avoid thinking about it, until the day the bear wandered into their campsite with the foolish notion that standing on its hind legs to challenge Grim for his supper was a wise idea.

"I can't believe you beat the bear to death with a stick," Aeryn said as she got to work skinning it. "In three blows. Didn't think that was possible."

"I'm used to a pickaxe on stone. A bear's skull is a little more yielding," Grim said from the stump where he sat beside her.

Aeryn grimaced.

"*That is* why they call me Stonebreaker," he said.

She stopped her work to look him in the face, incredulous. "Stonebreaker isn't your real name? Two months, and I'm learning this now?"

"You thought my real name was *Stonebreaker*?" he asked, as though the idea were both ridiculous and amusing.

"Oh right. I guess, because I didn't see you break any stones, I should've known." She threw her filthy hands in the air. "Of course I thought your name was Stonebreaker! Let me guess.

Your birth name isn't really Grim either."

"It's what they called me at the mine." He shrugged. "I told you, I don't remember anything before I was taken, including my real name."

Aeryn blinked slowly once, then returned her attention to skinning the beast. "Will it bother you if I continue to call you Grim?"

"What else would you call me?"

"I don't know. Bearkiller?"

"Bearkiller Stonebreaker? Really?"

Aeryn's mouth twitched into a smile. She liked his humor. "You'd get used to it."

He snorted and shook his head.

Aeryn wrinkled her nose at the pungent aroma of the bear's flesh. "I can tell you right now, this bear's eaten a lot of fish. He's going to taste terrible. Practically inedible."

"Inedible?" Grim asked. "Seems like a waste."

"I know, but do you want to eat fish-flavored bear meat?"

"How bad could it be?"

"I'll save you some, and you can tell me. We'll bury the rest."

Movement at the edge of the campsite caught the corner of her eye as a dinner-plate-sized predatory turtle inched its way around one of the lean-tos, toward the low-burning campfire.

"We have a visitor," she said.

"I got him." Grim hoisted himself from the stump beside Aeryn to deal with the turtle.

The creature hissed, and opened its beak-like maw as Grim planted his feet wide of snapping range. He grasped the edge of the shell with two hands, and carried the ornery beast back to the stream, where he tossed it unceremoniously back into the water. The turtle's belly smacked the surface before it submerged and drifted downstream. There, it wedged itself in the reeds to wait for some unsuspecting victim, foolish enough not to notice the crooked reeds among the straight.

"You're getting good at turtle-tossing," she said as Grim resettled beside her. "I'm going to need you to help me roll this over soon. I'll try to keep it as intact as possible. I don't have the salt to preserve this, so we should figure out what we want to do with it before it rots."

"What are the options?"

"Bearskins make valuable rugs, but we can't split a rug, and tanning it is a lot of work," she said. "It's that, or we sell the skin and split the coin. I know my brothers will give us a good price."

"Your brothers, the tanners?"

Aeryn nodded.

"Fine with me," he said. "How soon before it rots?"

"We should get it there as soon as possible."

"Tomorrow?"

"Yeah." As she worked, she tried to hide the discomfort which bloomed in her chest. She knew this was coming. "Which means this is our last night here."

"Oh. Okay." He grew quiet.

They hadn't discussed future plans, but it was probably

time. In fact, over the last two months, they didn't discuss much. It was one of the things she liked about him. He didn't get too personal. Their arrangement was exactly that. An arrangement.

Still, he was good for company.

Grim did well in the forest, mostly because of her, but life in the woods didn't suit most humans. She wondered whether he'd want to stay in Merioake, or go his separate way. He was sharp and diligent, so finding suitable work in town would be easy, especially considering humans didn't abide by as strict vocational traditions as the elves. He had options, and she could almost picture him working alongside Kazmuk at the smithy.

Her thoughts returned to her family business obligations, and thoughts of family made Aeryn's mind turn to his. She could never quite shake how badly his parents must miss him, if they were alive.

"You're almost completely better," she said as she moved the bear's arm out of the way. "Any idea what you'll do as a free man?"

Grim nodded. His expression darkened and he rotated his shoulder. "As soon as I'm comfortable swinging my axe, I'm going back to the mine."

Aeryn shot him a startled look. He didn't notice.

"I'm going to find the people who enslaved me, and make them pay," he said with an undercurrent of menace.

Disturbed, Aeryn stopped her work again and leaned back on her haunches to meet his eyes. "So, revenge?"

Grim dipped his chin once.

"That's a terrible idea," she said flatly. "You should find your family."

"I can do that afterwards. I'm here now," Grim said. "I'll go, kill any remaining Cords at the mine, and then I'll find my family."

"You're gonna get yourself killed," she said, her concern mounting.

He frowned at her. "They deserve what they have coming. I won't delay justice."

"I know you want their blood. But their death isn't going to give you back those years of your life," she said.

"Of course it won't. Doesn't mean I want them to live," he said, his voice strengthening. "If I don't ensure they get what they deserve, no one will."

"Grim, some injustices can't be corrected. Not by us."

Grim dropped into quiet thought, the frown turning to a scowl. If Aeryn was completely unfamiliar with him, she might be intimidated. But between the quiet and the look in his eye, she could tell that he was considering her words, even if he didn't like them.

For his own good, Aeryn was unwilling to back down on this one.

"Look, you're free now," she said, her voice softening. "You can finally find your people. Aren't you the least bit curious where you came from? Who you might've been?"

Grim took a deep breath in the way he tended to when frustrated. "Listen. I'll help you with this bear and then I'm going to sleep."

Conversation over.

"Fine," she said.

A disquieted mood settled over the camp. They worked without speaking, Grim in deep thought, and Aeryn trying to make sense of the sunken feeling in her middle. He wasn't her friend, so why did she feel disappointed?

The Loom took him from his family. Beat him. Forced him into hard labor. Broke men in front of him. Tried to break him. They deserved worse than anything Grim could do to them, and she was sure he could do a lot of damage.

Of course he wanted them to pay. That was natural.

He also wanted the best chance at surviving the riot and getting out. That's why, based on the little he told her, it took so long watching, waiting, planning. If he simply wanted to cause as much havoc as possible, irrespective of his own survival, he would've struck out at them a long time ago.

Now he was about to throw his life away in a failed attempt at vengeance. If he didn't die, he'd be giving up his chance at freedom.

She wanted no part of it. Maybe this was simply the sort of person he was. Truthfully, she didn't really know him.

They finished the work on the bear without speaking to each other beyond brief, work-related comments. *Move that here. Hand me that rope. Take this.*

After a meager sprinkling of what remained of the salt supply, they wrapped and hung the bearskin, then buried the carcass outside of camp. It took longer than either of them wanted, and it was well past dark when Grim finally skulked toward his lean-to.

"I'll try to keep it down," Aeryn said over her shoulder as she untied her clothesline. She didn't have many belongings here, but if they were to reach Merioake before sundown the next day, she couldn't waste time packing in the morning.

He continued toward his sleeping area without acknowledging. But instead of crawling into his bed, he paused, his back to her. He stood like that for the length of three breaths, long enough for Aeryn to wonder what he was brooding about. Finally, he forced out a breath.

"Fine," he said, turning to square off with her.

She gave him a questioning appraisal. "Fine?"

"To finding my family. Your bright idea." Though he sounded like the very words were costing him dearly, there was a force behind them, and a resolve in his posture which meant the silent war he'd been waging within himself had been decided.

"You're not going back to the mine for revenge-killing?" she asked.

"No," he said definitively, as much to himself as to her. "You're right. Going back is suicide. I'm going to get out of the South. Go to Noemar. Try to find them."

A shard of relief cut through her. A genuine smile spread across her lips. "Good."

He drew his mouth into a line, thought for a moment, then nodded his head, like he was settling the matter within himself again.

"Can I get a real map in Merioake?" he asked.

"Yeah," she said. "I'll take you around town. I'll help you get everything you need before you go."

"Okay."

8

Spite

Aeryn kept two feet in the grass as she eased the plank swing back and forth. She hummed to the chubby cheeked baby girl in her arms. This wasn't how she expected motherhood to be, but a fierce, protective love filled her heart to the brim. Daphne's eyes grew heavy. *Her little feather.* Music floated on the breeze around them, and grew louder.

Or was that real music?

Aeryn opened her eyes from sleep.

A few feet away, Grim shook the dead leaves off his blanket. *Was he singing?* That would be a new development. She righted herself and the remnants of her dream dissolved. "Good morning."

"Morning."

They stopped a few hours outside Merioake the night before. It took longer than expected to properly break camp at sunup, and Grim was no woodsman. His armor was hot and heavy, and their packs were full of all their belongings, plus the bear skin.

She shook out her possum fur vest, which she'd bunched up to use as a pillow, and slipped it over the sleeveless tunic which had been one of her earliest attempts at homemade hide clothing. Weaver swooped to the ground beside her with a *good-morning-I'll-take-a-seed-now* rasp. She fished a seed from her breast pocket and tossed it to him, and he caught it before it hit the ground.

"I think I want a horse," Grim said.

"You can't afford a horse," Aeryn said, still groggy, as she crammed some leftovers into her mouth.

"Eventually, though. I want one."

They ate in companionable silence. Aeryn imagined Grim astride his steed in his shiny armor, with a bowl of blueberries in one arm, and she smiled to herself.

Strangely, a pleasant anticipation crept into her body as she considered the day ahead. Normally, reentering Merioake filled her with dread, but she'd never been away from her family for this long. She looked forward to their faces. They expected an answer about the family trade, and she wasn't looking forward to that conversation. In a few short hours, she'd help Grim collect his supplies, then point him northward. After all the effort of helping him recover, she'd send him off on a satisfying note. It felt good.

They finished a quick breakfast, including the remaining berries he overpicked yesterday, while Weaver foraged for insects at their feet. Grim tossed a berry to Weaver who caught it in midair.

"I think you found the way to Weaver's heart," Aeryn said with a smirk. In Weaver's mind, Grim was *Big Food-Giver.* Sometimes *Grim Food-Giver.*

As Grim refastened the bear hide to his pack, she dusted off her slouchy pikdeer leggings and ran her fingers through her hair like a comb before tying a quick braid over her shoulder. No time for ivy today.

"We'll stop at my house first. I have a real map somewhere,

so you don't have to buy one," she said. "Then we'll go to the tannery, split the money from the bearskin, and I'll take you around to get any other supplies you might need before you set out."

She grinned.

"Sounds good." He gave the ties on his pack one last tug, then slung it over his shoulder along with his axe.

As the trees of Ravenwood thinned into the village, Aeryn's nerves crawled around inside her, clawing at her good mood. They must've been an odd sight, she in her loose-fitting furry clothes, he in his gleaming plate armor with his axe slung over one shoulder. He was enormous compared to the relatively short villagers. His armor alone was probably worth more than the finest dress of the wealthiest elf in town. Aeryn took a certain bitter satisfaction in the eyebrows she raised.

"Why are some of the houses in trees?" Grim asked as he observed a nearby home constructed in the boughs of a sprawling elm.

"Because we're elves," she said as if it were the most obvious thing in the world.

"Oh."

"My house actually belongs to my parents. They built it," Aeryn said, pulling her eyes off the half-constructed new home a pair of former friends were building during their engagement. She marshaled on. "Elves remain part of their parents' household until they marry. At least, it's like that here. I hear traditions are looser in some of the more human-populated areas."

Grim nodded his understanding.

She imagined how the conversation might go when she arrived at the house.

Mother, Father, I met this escaped slave in the woods after I killed three men. I thought they were Imperials, but don't worry, he assured me there weren't really soldiers, and I think he's a reliable source. I don't know his real name, but we've been camping together for two months, and I'm sending him away now.

Somehow the blunt truth didn't present like a viable option.

If she wasn't careful, they might try to physically restrain her from ever entering the forest again. She decided to keep it simple. Her parents didn't need to know everything. She hoped Grim had the sense not to mention either of their violent encounters with the slavers.

She coached him as she led the way along the shady lane to her parents' house.

"When you meet my parents, be sure you use the greeting, *may the trees shade your path,*" she said.

"May the trees shade your path?"

"Yes. You don't have to say it to everyone, but it's the elvish custom, and it's respectful," she said. "If someone says it to you first, you reply, *and may the fruit fall sweetly to your hand.*"

Grim nodded, committing the phrase to memory.

"Don't worry, my family speaks common like I do, so you'll understand them," she said.

"Okay."

As she climbed the stairs to the front door, she heard the

voices of her brothers, and the laugh of her sister-in-law. Aeryn's muscles tightened. What if the baby was here already?

She knocked on the freshly painted mauve door and dropped her voice. "You should take off your helmet. Leave your axe outside. No one will steal it."

He pulled it off, mussed his hair, and rested his weapon against the railing. Aeryn heard feet move from inside the house.

Better not risk it.

"Don't mention that you or I killed anyone," she said in a hurried whisper. She could feel Grim's eyes on her, and a second later, the door flew inward.

Elion's face brightened. "The Spirit of the Forest returns!" He noticed Grim at her side, and tipped his head back to look him in the face. "...With a Northerner? Why, hello."

"Elion, this Grim," she said, only to be interrupted as Tarra's voice carried from inside.

"Aeryn's back?"

Aeryn looked past Elion to see her human sister-in-law hoist herself out of a comfortable armchair, hand on her rounded belly. *No baby yet.* She wore a linen dress with fluttery sleeves and a red sash tied at the ribs, accentuating her rounded middle. She had a mop of honey brown ringlets, a few shades lighter than her skin, and olive green eyes, similar to Aeryn and her brothers. She waddled toward the door, genuinely pleased to see Aeryn.

"Come give me a hug!"

Grinning, Aeryn stepped around her brother, waving for Grim to follow her in, and caught Tarra in a squeeze.

Grim had to duck to avoid thunking his forehead on the lintel. He hung back as the family greeted each other, looking too big for the snug living area, which was already crowded with seating, a tea table, and a reuniting family.

Verelle met them at the door, and her eyes crinkled into a smile. Her straight, graying hair fell below her shoulders, and she had a tan complexion more like Aeryn's. She folded Aeryn into a hug which lasted a little longer than it usually did.

Drawn in by the excitement, Bartholomew entered the room from the kitchen, followed by Samuel. Samuel took his dark hair and paler complexion from their father. He took some pride at being the tallest in the family. They noticed Grim immediately, but addressed Aeryn first.

"Aeryn!" Bartholomew beamed at his daughter, hobbling over while leaning on his cane.

"About time," Samuel said, as he came alongside Tarra, handing her a glass of water. It wasn't mean-spirited, but the hint of expectation in his voice prodded Aeryn, irritating her. He gave his sister a genuine smile, which redeemed him for the moment.

"We were beginning to wonder whether you'd taken root," Bartholomew said. "It's been two months without a word."

Aeryn gave him a peck on the cheek. "I missed you too, Poppa."

"Who do we have here?" Bartholomew asked, turning his attention to Grim.

"May the trees shade your path," Grim said, his eyes darting to Aeryn to make sure he worded it correctly. She gave him a tiny approving nod.

"And may the fruit fall sweetly to your hand," Bartholomew said, appreciating the remark. But his gaze jumped to Aeryn, full of questions, such as, *Who is this enormous bearded man, and why have you brought him to the house? Should I be concerned?*

"This is Grim Stonebreaker," Aeryn said. "We met in Ravenwood."

Verelle smiled warmly up at Grim. "It's a pleasure to meet you, Grim. I'm Verelle, Aeryn's mother." She gestured gracefully. "This is my husband, Bartholomew."

Bartholomew's expression shifted from curiosity to concern in an instant. "In Ravenwood, you say?"

Aeryn could almost hear the follow up question. *Didn't I tell you to avoid strange men?*

She forced a smile.

"When?" he asked.

"Two months ago," Aeryn replied, trying to keep her voice light.

Bartholomew's smile disappeared. "What have you been doing alone in the woods for the last two months?"

Aeryn felt her temperature rise. She was about to slip into elvish and ask *What is that supposed to mean?* But Grim beat her to the reply.

"She's been helping me recover," he said. "She saved my life."

"Saved your life?" Slight panic rippled across

Bartholomew's expression, as though he were unsure whether to be proud of his daughter, or disbelieve what he was hearing. Shocked faces jumped between Grim and Aeryn.

"What happened to you?" Elion asked.

Aeryn's mouth ran dry and she forced herself not to give Grim a warning look, silently willing him not to mention anything particularly violent.

"I was injured," Grim said.

"What were you doing before you were injured?" Bartholomew asked.

"I was a slave in the mountains."

"A slave?" Bartholomew asked, incredulous.

"Since I was eight, up until recently."

"He's heading to Noemar to find his family," Aeryn said, before anyone jumped in with questions which might precipitate a response requiring words like *revolt, attacked in the woods by bad men,* or *only survivor.* "I was planning on taking him around town to make sure he gets the supplies he needs before he sets out."

"Are either of you hungry?" Verelle asked. "Lunch will be ready in a half-hour, if Grim doesn't have to leave right away."

On the other end of the room, the oval wooden table with curved benches designed for two people each, stood bearing plates, cups, a bowl of fruit, a basket of bread, and a vase of cut flowers, ready for a meal.

"Speaking of which, I should check the smoker," Elion said. "Negotiated the joint purchase of sixteen cattle with the Alishers last month, and we're about to partake in the firstfruits of that agreement."

Excusing himself, he passed through the kitchen, and out the back door.

Samuel took a sip of his own glass of water. "He's a little proud of himself for brokering the deal."

An uncomfortable memory prodded Aeryn. One of the butcher's sons, Javaan Alisher, used to be her friend. After she became pregnant, he started coming around more often, offering kindness, which Aeryn found surprising considering he was always better friends with Gideon than her, and she would've expected him to take Gideon's side. She soon discovered that, whatever he believed, he assumed Aeryn got on her back easily. With her already pregnant, the risk of consequences for him were nonexistent. He was the first person she ever slapped in the face.

"What are the terms?" Aeryn asked, trying to nudge aside the memory and take interest in her brother's success.

"We get the hides, and half price on any meat we purchase coming from the cow," Samuel said. "Are you actually taking an interest in the family business?"

Aeryn bristled. She resisted the urge to cut her eyes at him.

"Come and sit down," Verelle said, ushering them into the living area. Grim followed Aeryn, taking the seat on the couch situated perpendicular to her own, turning the three-seater into a two-seater. The furniture groaned under his weight and he craned his neck to take in the cozy surroundings and modest decor.

Verelle offered them each a glass of water and Elion returned, pulling one of the short, curved benches into the living area for additional seating.

"So, the mountains?" Bartholomew asked Grim once everyone was situated. "Illwali is a long way from Noemar."

Grim dipped his chin. He met the elvish faces which watched him with curiosity.

"As a slave?" Bartholomew didn't believe it.

"Poppa, he's telling the truth," Aeryn said, slipping into elvish. Most humans in Merioake spoke the language, but it was considered rude to switch from the common tongue into elvish in the presence of an unfamiliar human. Grim only knew a few words, so the convention applied.

But Aeryn knew where this was headed, and her father was going to create an awkward situation quickly.

"Oh, is that what he told you?" Bartholomew asked, keeping to elvish.

"Yes, it is," Aeryn said. Her frustration spiked at having her judgment questioned.

"Slavery has been illegal for a hundred years, Aeryn."

Aeryn turned her palms up, not wishing to have this discussion now. Or ever.

Verelle's gentle voice cut in. "Barth, these things happened during and after the war. It's not terribly unbelievable."

Aeryn's father sucked his teeth, dissatisfied but momentarily pacified.

Tarra returned the conversation to the common tongue. "We were discussing our little turtle problem before you arrived," she said.

"Oh?" Aeryn asked, grateful for her changing the subject.

"Yes, we have a new resident who's claimed the bank of the creek behind our house. Normally I wouldn't bother. They're easy enough to avoid, but with the baby coming..." Tarra shrugged her shoulders. "Your mother was just saying it reminds her of Fat Loughie."

Aeryn's shoulders relaxed. "Oh, I remember Fat Loughie!" She turned to Grim, to fill him in on the story.

"Fat Loughie was a predatory turtle living in the pond behind the house when Elion and I were children. Little thing. We would toss him into the pond, and he'd crawl back out for more."

"There was something wrong with that animal," Samuel said.

"Don't insult Fat Loughie. You only say that because he bit you. Who gets bitten by a predatory turtle?" Aeryn said, chuckling.

Then she noticed the bandage wrapped around Samuel's palm.

"What happened to your hand?"

"We don't need to talk about it," Samuel said, more stiff than necessary.

Samuel was an indoorsy type. The running joke was that his wife, a pregnant human baker, had better woodsmanship than he did. Aeryn didn't push it, but she caught Elion's eye. Suppressing a smirk, he mouthed the word *turtle.*

"The only thing this one has in common with Fat Loughie is persistence," Samuel said. "With the baby coming, it won't be long before he or she is toddling around. I don't want my child losing a hand."

Tarra rubbed her pregnant belly, and gave Samuel an affectionate twinkle of the eyes. "He's a good Poppa already."

Aeryn tried to ignore the twist in her gut. She wanted to be happy for them. They'd done things right, and were about to welcome their first child into the world. The thought of the new baby in the family made Aeryn itch to get back to the forest. She'd be alone, but life in Merioake was about to get harder to bear, making solitude in the woods preferable.

Verelle took a sip from her teacup. "So, Aeryn...you'll be staying?"

Aeryn felt her muscles tense. This wasn't a question of whether she'd reenter the forest, but whether she'd begin working at the tannery full time.

She scanned the expectant faces around the room, feeling like a wretch. She knew the terms of her stay in Ravenwood. Time was up. But now faced with the prospect of life here, dread gnawed at her insides.

She couldn't do it.

Not yet.

Aeryn chewed on her lip. "I thought I'd wait a little–"

"*What?*"

Startled by the abrupt uptick in volume, Aeryn turned to see Elion, livid. She might expect such a reaction from Samuel, but not him. His face was tight and his eyes flashed as he switched into elvish.

"What do you mean, *wait a little*? What about the family

business?"

Caught off guard by his sudden confrontational tone, she took a moment to harness her thoughts, before continuing the conversation in elvish. "I can't join the tannery yet."

Heavy silence fell over the room until Bartholomew spoke one word. "Explain."

Aeryn shifted in her seat. "I'm not ready."

Samuel's face hardened. He was the picture of responsibility, and out of anyone, showed the least patience for Aeryn's delays to join the business. Biting back his frustration, he shook his head, as though unsurprised.

Elion's brow bent into a deeper frown, and his voice grew uncharacteristically harsh. "Aeryn, stop thinking about yourself, and start thinking about this family. Haven't you brought enough shame on this family with your foolish choices?"

The words stung. For a moment, she stared at him, speechless.

"This is our livelihood," Elion said, his voice strengthening with each word. "Do you have any regard for our family's honor? Any gratitude for what's been poured into you?"

Samuel, who initially seemed equally surprised at Elion's outburst, took the opportunity to enter the conversation. "Consider, Aeryn. Father and I spent seven years training you. Since then you've spent more time running around the forest than actually participating in the family trade."

"Running around the forest?" Aeryn said, recovering a bit. She was used to the diatribe from him, so her retort came more naturally. "Is that what you call meat on the table? Were the skins I brought to the tannery a waste?

"Aeryn, enough," Elion said, shouting. "What you describe is not the same as acting like a functioning member of this family. Yet you defend it!"

Aeryn opened her mouth to argue, but Elion raised a hand, cutting her off.

"No, Aeryn. No," he said, getting worked up and rising to his feet. "I don't want to hear more excuses. You know I've always defended you. I've always understood you need time. You were grieving. I never pressured you."

He took a step toward her, his face bent with repressed anger turned loose.

"We all know participating in this business requires you to stand up straight and look the other villagers in the eye after how they treated you. You've been avoiding it." He patted his palm to his chest. "We have to bear the embarrassment of your delays. Father more than anyone."

Heat rushed to her face, and the urge to justify herself welled within her.

Frustration tangled up in the bend of Elion's mouth, and his shoulders sagged. "If you go back into that forest, you might as well not come back."

"Elion!" Verelle said, visibly distressed at the conflict between her children.

Eyes burning with indignation, he held Aeryn's gaze for the length of a breath, waiting to see whether his words had any impact.

Aeryn fought back hot tears. Feeling more like a wretch than ever, part of her wished she could relent, but it wasn't that simple. She swallowed the lump in her throat, forcing the tears back in, and hardened her expression. He'd never been forced to live down even half of what she experienced on a regular basis. *How dare he?*

Reading the shift in his sister, Elion brushed his hands roughly together and held them in front of himself. He marched halfway to the door, turned to jab a finger in Aeryn's direction, and shouted. "I'm done defending you."

He stormed out the front door, letting the screen clatter behind him.

Samuel gave another shake of the head, and looked meaningfully at Tarra. She'd been quiet, gravely watching the argument in elvish unfold before her. She understood every word. While she was decidedly staying out of it, Samuel had her support.

Grim sat unnaturally still on the couch, leaning on his knees. Alert. Taking it all in, but understanding nothing.

Aeryn met his eyes in apology.

Bartholomew noticed.

"Aeryn, are you pregnant?" he asked, still in elvish.

Her mouth hung ajar. "Poppa! Really?"

At the same time, Verelle cast a weary gaze at her husband. "Barth."

"What am I supposed to think, Verelle? She arrives after months away. Announces she's been living with a strange man in the woods who sold her a tale of woe. Now she wants to avoid the tannery again. I have to ask." Bartholomew refocused on Aeryn. "Answer the question."

"No!" Aeryn said, shouting. "Gods, that's what you think of me? *We all know what great judgment Aeryn uses. Better make sure she's not pregnant again.*"

Verelle reached a pacifying hand toward her. "Aeryn, that's not what we think."

"Since we're on the subject of your judgment," Bartholomew said, ignoring his wife. "I heard what happened on your last visit. Kazmuk had to restrain you from attacking Gideon in the street, correct?"

Aeryn crossed her arms and shrugged. "Not my proudest moment, I'll admit."

"You think?"

"Yes. If I moved quicker, I could've knocked him across his head."

Bartholomew threw his hands in the air. "I knew you staying in Ravenwood was a mistake."

"No, coming back was." The words were meant to sting, and she meant every word.

Bartholomew stood, leaning heavily on his cane. He clamped his mouth shut for several long seconds. Still visibly upset, he calmed himself enough to keep his voice level.

"Your brother is right," he said. "You've had your stint living like an Illwalii. You're lucky this man here didn't murder you. You have no idea how dangerous this world can be. It's time to come home. You have a place here. You don't even know how good you have it."

Aeryn's jaw set. He had no idea to what extent she understood the dangers of this world, but it was the last statement which crawled under her skin and stirred up her ire the most.

She had it good here?

He never lost a child.

He never had to live with being the sort of used goods no one wanted.

Everything here haunted her, and whenever she thought she might experience a good day, all she had to do was step outside and meet the faces of her neighbors, and she was cured of the notion.

Many believed the lies Gideon pedaled to save face. They whispered behind her back, saying the baby's death was judgment from the gods for bearing a child out of wedlock. They even said it to her face, as if she didn't know what she did with Gideon was wrong. It didn't matter how many times her parents reiterated that the gods didn't punish children for the sins of their parents.

She was just supposed to endure this, for the sake of participating in the family trade, like a respectable elf.

You're a childless pariah, Aeryn, and the town thinks you're a whore. But at least you have a place in the family business, and the opportunity to avoid embarrassing us further. It's not like you have other options.

Was that what *having it good* looked like?

In her fury, an idea entered her mind which was equal parts retaliation and self preservation. By all metrics, it was risky, but she had to get out of here, and the perfect excuse to delay her surrender to the family trade was sitting five feet away.

She stuck out her chin. "I can't begin at the tannery yet."

"Good gods. Why not?"

"I'm leaving with Grim to help him find his family." Aeryn popped to her feet and shifted back to the common language. "Come on, Grim."

She marched them out the front door.

9

A Lie

Aeryn paused with Grim on the landing just outside her parent's front door.

"I'm coming with you," she said to him. It wasn't a question.

"Really?" He sounded mildly surprised, though unopposed to the idea.

"Yeah. I want to help you find your family."

It took him only a second to decide what he thought of that. "Okay," he said. He nodded toward the house. "But what was that all about?"

Aeryn hesitated for a breath. She dropped her gaze to adjust her pack. "They're not happy. They don't think it's a good idea for me to go with you."

Which was true enough, but as far as answering the question went, it was a lie. She felt a nudge against her conscience, but admitting that her family was livid over her avoidance of her life and obligations felt even worse.

"They're probably right," he said, as though stating a matter of fact, not trying to talk her out of it. "If I had a daughter, I wouldn't want her going with me either."

She raised an eyebrow and met his face again. "Are you saying you're dangerous?"

"I am dangerous," he said, again as if stating that water was wet. "Didn't you realize that?"

Aeryn's insides shifted uneasily. Maybe this wasn't a good idea. She hesitated again, then resolved herself. "Well, so am I."

She slipped her pack over one shoulder.

"I gotta go back in and get my things. Wait here. Give me the bearskin."

Aeryn pulled the door open, bringing the harried conversation inside to halt. All four remaining family members were standing, dour in appearance. Father was hard. Mother was distressed and upset with him. Avoiding their faces and without slowing, she crossed the room in a few steps and hurled the bearskin at Samuel. He staggered under the weight.

"Here. Consider it a gift for the baby," she said. Without waiting for a response, she took the stairs to the second floor two at a time.

Aeryn's room was as she left it, with a strand of ivy draped around the doorframe. The walls were decorated with pressed flowers mounted on heavy parchment and drawings she was particularly proud of. Her half-spent candles sat atop the chest. The dusty lute leaned against the wall in the empty corner where Daphne's crib once stood. The bag of salt she left behind on her last visit had been tucked just inside the door.

Aeryn yanked open her chest of drawers. She indiscriminately scooped an armful of leggings, tunics, socks, and undergarments into her arms and crammed them into her pack. It occurred to her that Noemar was probably chilly, being in the

North, so she grabbed her nice leather jacket with the furry lining that she used in the mild winters of Thoen. Though half the clothes which lay dormant in her drawers weren't made of fuzzy animal hides, it didn't seem to matter right now.

In one of the drawers, she found the pouch of money she'd been saving. Fingers swimming through it, she counted mostly silvers and coppers, and three gold coins. It wasn't much, but it was better than nothing, and enough to get started. If she were richer, they might be able to afford horses, or pay for transport, but Aeryn came from a working class family, and life in the woods didn't present many opportunities for accumulating wealth. She and Grim would be traveling on foot.

From the shelf above the chest, she snagged the two books she'd used in lessons growing up. One was a book of history, religion, reading, and the practical arts. The other was oriented around plants, animals, and the natural world. She couldn't remember which book had the map of Errebos, so she brought them both.

She bustled around her room, collecting a few odd items, making sure she didn't forget anything. Spare boot laces. Gloves for cold weather. An extra spool of thread and sewing needles. A pencil. The bag of salt. She had few possessions, so it was fast. She left her lute untouched.

She gave herself a moment's pause at the top of the stairs. She could hear footsteps and terse voices on the first floor. Samuel, her father, Tarra.

Was she really going to do this? She'd never left Thoen,

never even left the Ravenwood region. She was going to trek across the country, in hopes of finding a strange man's family, if they weren't dead already.

It was that, or the tannery.

Better to not prolong goodbyes.

Still simmering, she took the stairs as gracefully as the extra weight would allow. She slowed as she reentered the room and met the faces awash with disappointment and disbelief. Bartholomew's expression was still hard. Samuel looked up from the bearhide, bewildered, with Tarra at his side.

"Goodbye," Aeryn said as she moved toward the door.

"Aeryn, wait."

Verelle hurried into the room with a burlap bag. The concern on her brow was unmistakable, like a woman unable to hold back the tide. Her nose was red, her eyes glassy, and she blinked rapidly to keep the liquid at bay as she forced the bag into Aeryn's hands.

"There's some food, and a set of warm clothes, and some other things..." Tears filled her eyes, and she caught Aeryn in a tight hug.

Aeryn's heart twisted as her mother held onto her, and she hugged her back.

"I have to do this," she said in a whisper so only Verelle could hear.

"I know," Verelle said. "But I fear I'll never see you again."

Now Aeryn was fighting to keep it together. "I love you Momma." Then, loud enough for the others to hear, "I'll give you my answer about the tannery when I get back."

The suggestion that Aeryn would return provided Verelle with a measure of comfort. She looked less despairing as she released Aeryn, and swiped the liquid from her eyes. "Are you leaving right away?"

"We have to go to the store. Then, yes."

Verelle barely kept her composure. She smoothed Aeryn's hair, adjusting her braid over her shoulder. "I love you. Be safe. Be smart."

"I will." Aeryn placed her hand on the door, with a last glance at her family. Father's mouth was still bunched in frustration and anger. No goodbye from him, then.

"Did you kill this bear?" Samuel asked, the slimy pelt still in his hands.

"Grim did," Aeryn said. "Three blows to the head with a stick. Never seen anything like it."

She left.

🖊

"I owe you half of what we would've gotten for the bear," Aeryn said as she led the way as briskly to the market district. Normally, she moved at a quicker pace, but her bulging pack, her bow and quiver, and the sack from her mother made her feel more cumbersome than normal. She managed to keep a steady pace, though she knew she'd have to do some rearranging if travel was to be at all comfortable. Grim, meanwhile, being taller, took longer strides, his heavy gear barely slowing him now that they'd exited the denser parts of the forest.

"It's fine," Grim said.

"No. Fair's fair," she said. She dug into her belt pouch with her free hand. She estimated what the skin would've sold for, worked the math in her head, and counted out the coins, dropping them in Grim's palm.

In town, they acquired several pounds of travel-worthy rations, a waterskin and waterproof bedroll for Grim, rope, and some personal items. The outfitter only had two sets of traveling clothes Grim's size. He bought them both.

Unless Grim was a fantastic actor, it became immediately apparent that he had almost no experience exchanging tender with shop owners and merchants. After a quick side discussion about the value of coins, Aeryn led by example for her own purchases, then stood aside to give him the practice.

She ignored the questioning looks of the familiar merchants, and the passersby who gawked openly. No one asked her business, or who Grim was. The questioning leers told Aeryn they had their speculations. None of them good.

At the smithy, Aeryn resupplied her store of arrows and Kazmuk sharpened Grim's axe. If Kazmuk had the inclination she was leaving Thoen, he didn't let on until he gave her a sincere nod and wished her good luck.

She felt emotionally spent after the onslaught from her family, but the business of supplying themselves provided a distraction. She noticed activity in the tannery. Elion was back at work. She kept moving, too upset to attempt a civil goodbye.

He said his piece already.

Some careful rearranging made their loads bearable. As they purchased a couple steaming sausages from the market, Aeryn noticed Gideon and Sariel enter the tavern across the road. For a moment her eyes locked with Sariel. To Aeryn's surprise, she felt pricked with sadness at the sight of her old friend. Gideon placed his hand on Sariel's back and directed her inside. He noticed Aeryn watching them, and in an instant, Aeryn's pang of sadness was outweighed. She used two fingers to flick the tip of her pointed ear at him and turned away.

Grim raised an eyebrow. "What was that?"

"A parting gesture." She paused, rethinking her choice of words. "Actually, don't do that to anyone. You'll make enemies quickly."

Nerves prickled inside Aeryn as they took the main road which led out of town, north towards Proimos. She couldn't describe how she felt.

The thought of leaving Thoen, especially with this stranger, felt scary, but good. It was a worthy partnership benefiting them both.

Her appreciation for this was dampened by the circumstances surrounding the departure.

She'd lied to Grim. Normally, she tried not to lie to anyone. But that was the least of her concern.

She knew leaving would reflect more poorly on her family than any previous attempt to avoid her obligations. But maybe, when they finished nursing their offense or believing she was a selfish wretch, they'd finally realize what staying here cost her.

Maybe by the time she came back, it wouldn't matter anymore. Time and space might help everyone.

"You sure dragons aren't an issue?" Grim asked, pulling Aeryn out of her thoughts.

Aeryn almost laughed. "They haven't been an issue since the war."

"What was the war about?"

Aeryn waved a hand. "Only everything. Fights between people groups. Dragons causing problems." Aeryn shifted the weight of her satchel at her side. "The Imperials stepped in to help, led by Erebin the first, and they united the nations into a single empire, Errebos. Before that, Thoen used to be independent, but far more dangerous. Mostly from the dragons."

"You ever meet one?"

"No. You?"

"I've seen 'em. Never met one."

"Really?"

"Flying high in the mountains," he said. "Cords used to point them out and warn the newcomers what awaited them if they tried to escape."

As they neared the edge of town, Aeryn finally heard her name. Slowing, she looked over her shoulder, and saw her father hurrying after them.

Her countenance hardened.

"Aeryn, wait," Bartholomew said, his limp more pronounced in his haste.

"Father, you can't talk me out of leaving."

He slowed as he reached the pair of them, and Aeryn realized what he held in his hand.

"I want you to take this," Bartholomew said.

He presented her with the finely crafted short sword he carried during the war. With it, he slayed the dragon of Mogmurch, the encounter which ended his time in the elvish military, sending him home to Aeryn's mother with a limp. The sword wasn't a sword to Bartholomew; it represented how the war changed him, and how he'd defined his life. He was immensely proud of what he'd accomplished with it. Apart from the house, it was his most valued material possession.

Aeryn fell quiet and still. "Poppa."

"I won't accept no for an answer. You're my daughter. I want you to be able to protect yourself." He forced it into her hands. "Always carry it."

He looked tired. Older and sad. It made Aeryn want to start crying, despite her resolve.

She gave her father a hug.

"I hope you'll never need to use it," he said, when he released her. His eyes traveled to Grim, then resettled on Aeryn. "Your mother and I love you, Aeryn. We just want you to be wise and safe."

"I love you too."

10

Offers

The first two days of travel were sunny and mild. The forested areas grew thinner, replaced by smaller woods and grassy fields. Aeryn and Grim kept to the main road, passing only a few travelers. They camped off the path beneath the stars.

The third evening, they were chased off a farmer's land. After finding a more suitable location, Aeryn awoke in the middle of the night to a thievish fox with its nose in her pack. They rose to a steady drizzle which leaked from the sky and dampened their belongings. The rain picked up throughout the day. Travel was miserable and by early afternoon, so were Aeryn and Grim.

Aeryn wiped her running nose and pointed to a village sign ahead, which read, *Welcome to Pineham.*

"Let's find an inn," she said. "I don't want to sleep in this."

The rain plinked against Grim's armor. He coughed. "No objections."

Shops and houses lined the muddy streets. Lanterns glowed from within the windows. Most businesses appeared to be open, but there were very few people outdoors. Old men sat in rocking chairs beneath storefront awnings and watched Aeryn and Grim pass. Human children squealed in delight as they launched themselves barefoot into muddy puddles.

In the middle of town, a sign hanging from a tavern and

inn bore the name *The Purple Pint* in lilac and green lettering. Inside, an inviting fire crackled in the hearth on the far end of the tavern. Two older humans sat at the bar in conversation with the barkeep. The dining room boasted eight wooden plank tables of various sizes, but was otherwise sparse of patrons.

The graying man behind the bar stared, as Aeryn and Grim clomped into the establishment, muddy and bedraggled.

"Can I help you?" the man asked.

"Do you have room available for two people?" Aeryn asked as a puddle formed around her feet.

"Yes, Lady, I do. I got rooms with one large bed, or two single cots. Same cost. Five silvers. Eight if you'd like it to include suppers for two people."

A flicker of hesitation nudged Aeryn, reminding her of the impropriety of sharing a room with a man she wasn't married to. Yes, they'd been camping in the forest together, but that felt different. It was, at first, borne of necessity. In Ravenwood, there was space to step away for the privacy to change, bathe, or relieve themselves. They each had their own lean-to for shelter. But she wondered if Grim understood the strangeness of it, or even cared.

This would be his first time staying in civilization as a free man, and for that matter, her first stay at an inn too. At that price, they weren't going to have much money to spare. They'd have to talk about that.

She never once caught him staring, so hopefully he didn't start now.

"The room with two beds." Aeryn strode to the counter

and counted eight silver coins from her belt pouch. Grim joined her at the bar and removed his helmet.

One of the patrons at the counter snickered. "Them Imperial boys ain't gonna be too happy you gave away that room, Odo."

"Then those Imperial boys shoulda got here sooner. I got a business to run," the barkeep shot back. He took the money and smiled cordially at Aeryn. "I'm Odo. Proprietor. You are..?"

"Aeryn. This is Grim."

"Aeryn and Grim, welcome."

Odo disappeared into the backroom and returned a moment later with a brass key on a purple ribbon. He led them to a staircase on the far end of the room opposite the hearth, and up the creaky, wooden steps as he rattled off a few rules.

"No open flames in the room. No weird rituals, magic, or blood sacrifices...."

Aeryn and Grim shared an alarmed look.

"...The tavern can get a little noisy some nights, but I ask you to keep it down upstairs after dark."

A narrow hall ran down the second floor, with two doors on either side and one at the end. Odo unlocked the second door on the right and allowed it to swing open onto a modest room with two single cots and a narrow table between them. Gray light seeped through the threadbare curtain above the beds. A small set of drawers and a wash basin stood on the right side of the room. A changing screen and a chair stood along the left.

"Hooks behind the door to hang your things. Come on

down when you're hungry. Food'll be hot," Odo said as he handed the key to Aeryn. "I forgot to mention that drinks aren't included in the meal. Anything else you need? Towels maybe?"

Aeryn shivered. "Yes, please."

"I'll grab two." He surveyed Grim. "Or...seven. Hold on."

Odo bustled down the hall to a supply closet at the end. Aeryn plodded into the room and dropped her bag on the floor. She wanted to collapse onto the bed, but didn't want to sleep on a wet surface later. Odo returned with a stack of six towels, and shut the door behind him as he left.

Grim surveyed the room as she pulled off her boots and set them near the door. "New experience, huh?" she said.

"Mhmm."

"I've never stayed at an inn, either. This place is quite nice." Aeryn tossed half of the towels onto the cot nearest him. She dug into her pack for an extra set of clothes. The naturally waterproof finish of the leather kept the contents dry.

She stepped behind the changing curtain and peeled off her wet things. She wrung her hair out and towel-dried as much as possible. She slipped a dry tunic over her head, and her second pair of loose-fitting buckskin leggings. Not feeling the same urge to present like she belonged to the woods, and because she was chilly from the rain, she pulled on a pink open-front sweater her mother crocheted for her, back when Verelle still hoped Aeryn might stop wearing furry homemade clothing. She tied a leather belt around her waist, but decided it was probably safe to keep the sword in the room, instead of wearing it to supper. When she stepped out from behind the curtain, Grim was still removing his armor.

"Want a hand?" she asked.

"It'll be faster," he said.

She helped him with the difficult to reach parts. He stepped behind the screen to change, and emerged a minute later in a new charcoal gray shirt and brown slacks. He rubbed a towel on his head.

Aeryn sat on the edge of her cot and gave it a bounce to test the sturdiness. "Think the bed is long enough for you?"

For an answer, he flopped onto his cot and inched upward so his head was at the top, near the wall. There wasn't an inch to spare at his feet. He closed his eyes and sighed. "If I didn't have to dry my armor, I'd go to sleep right now."

Aeryn plucked a spaulder off the floor. "Give me one of those towels, and I'll help you finish so we can eat. I'm so hungry I could eat a mule."

The cot creaked as he hoisted himself upright and got to work on the armor. "Thank you for covering the cost."

"Don't worry about it," she said. "After last night, I realized it may not be safe to camp out all the way to Noemar. We should try to stay at inns when we can."

"I'll pay for the next one." He placed his dry helmet at the foot of his bed. "Remind me what the coins are worth?"

"Ten copper coins to one silver. Ten silvers to one gold. Ten gold to one platinum," she said. "How much do you have?"

Grim checked his belt pouch on the side table. "A gold, six silvers and ten coppers. You?"

"Five silvers, and four coppers."

"That's not enough to get to Noemar, is it?"

"No. We'll need to earn some money along the way."

They finished drying and hung their wet things over every suitable surface. They slipped on their shoes and followed their growling stomachs downstairs. Raised voices in the dining room grew louder as they creaked down the steps.

Four soaking humans and a blonde elf dressed in Imperial uniforms stood at the bar. Like the humans of Pineham, they were taller than the native folk of Merioake with varying complexions, smooth faces, and postures that bore a sense of dignity.

One of the men, who kept his dark brown hair tied at the nape of his neck, argued vehemently with Odo.

"No way," Odo said. "It ain't my fault you brought more men on the job."

The group noticed Aeryn and Grim enter the dining room. Grim stiffened and eyed them with suspicion.

One of the men stuck his narrow chin out at Grim. "What are you looking at?"

The elf smacked his comrade on the shoulder with the back of his hand, then regarded Grim and Aeryn with a courteous nod. "My apologies. It's been a long day."

The man with the dark ponytail surveyed the interruption to his argument, then returned his attention to Odo. "If you want the dragon whiskey delivered tomorrow, the price just went up. Two gold each."

"Bosh," Odo said. "That's more than double what I paid

you last time."

"Circumstances change. Greater need for security."

"Security? You're armed Imperials! Who's goin' to trouble you on the road? That's why I hired you last time!"

Aeryn led the way to the far end of the bar and took a seat with Grim. She lowered her voice. "Relax, Grim. You're acting like a crooked reed among the straight. Those are real Imperials. No black cord."

"Imperials normally haggle with the locals over side jobs?"

"They almost never came to Merioake, so I don't know."

Aeryn eyed the group for a moment as they argued with Odo. The elf noticed, and he gave her a small smile.

She turned back to Grim. "It doesn't sound like official duties to me."

"Where's this place they're talking about? On our way?"

"Woodby? Yeah. Unless we stay here another night for work, we could get there by mid-afternoon tomorrow."

Across the bar the argument rose to full shouting.

"Hey!" Grim called down the counter, so loud it made Aeryn jump. "We'll do it for less."

The shouts died at once.

The Imperials glowered at Grim. The one with the ponytail, with the narrow-chinned man at his shoulder, took a step toward them. "Shut your trap, before I shut it for you."

Grim's stool scraped across the wooden floor as he stood. "I'd love it if you would."

Aeryn's eyes widened and concerns flickered across her

thoughts. Until now she had never seen him handle conflict outside of their own minor squabbles. *What was he doing?*

"I need the whiskey delivered to Woodby tomorrow," Odo said. He didn't seem at all disturbed by the posturing. "You able to do that?"

"We're going that way anyway," Grim said. "Give us the job, and we'll do it for half of what this lot's demanding."

Odo smacked his hands together and glanced at the Imperials. He made a chuffing noise. "Deal."

The ponytailed Imperial stalked toward Grim. "Mind your own business, boy."

Grim drew to his full height, broadening his shoulders, and stepped forward to meet him. "What are you, deaf? It is my business. He just gave me the job. Why don't you mind yours?"

Oh, dirt.

Aeryn braced herself for conflict. The Imperial placed his hand on his sword. The skinny chinned man followed his leader toward Grim, while the others hung back, looking as uncomfortable as Aeryn felt.

The ponytailed man narrowed his eyes. "I'd watch out if I were you. Roads are real dangerous. Be a shame if a stretch got overlooked, and you and that little elf ran into some trouble."

"Alright now, Luther." One of the soldiers with a shaved head touched the ponytailed man on the shoulder. "C'mon. Let's dry off and get a drink. This isn't worth the trouble."

Reluctantly, Luther pulled himself away.

"You better remember who you're talking to and show

some respect," he said, giving Grim a last, appraising look. He bumped Grim's shoulder as he passed.

Grim's fists tightened as Luther stalked to the hearth and sat with his fellow officers. Aeryn tapped him on the arm and gave a firm shake of the head. *Don't follow.*

Grim breathed deeply, then sunk into the stool beside Aeryn.

"Imperials ain't what they used to be," Odo said, dropping his voice.

"I hope we didn't cause you any future trouble with them," Aeryn said.

Odo waved. "Boys'll get over it. There's all kinds of side work floating around the continent. They'll have no shortage of jobs if they want 'em."

"Is that typical?" Aeryn asked. "I didn't think the Imperials wanted soldiers taking side work while enlisted."

"Like I said, they ain't what they used to be. In the days of the war, even fifty years ago, the position came with honor. Young men flocked from all over Errebos to join. But now?" Odo shook his head. "We've had peace so long, they're little more than glorified guards. Low morale, little opportunity for advancement, and not much to do. Many take mercenary work or side jobs to better themselves. Not strictly allowed, but they do it."

He knocked on the bar with a knuckle.

"Though, I hear the orcs are givin' em trouble in Kharsh. So these boys better be grateful they don't have to go face those tusked monsters."

A handful of chatty patrons entered and grabbed a table.

"Ya'll must be starved. I'll grab each of you a plate. And tell you what. You're saving me a lot of money taking the dragon whiskey to Woodby," Odo said. "Pint of the finest mead in Thoen, on the house." He bustled away and greeted another barkeep who emerged from the back room.

Aeryn followed Grim's scowl across the tavern. The Imperials hadn't noticed they were being watched yet.

She nudged Grim with her elbow. "Let it go. You keep staring them down, a fight's going to break out."

"I hate people like that."

"You and I, both. But let's try not to get arrested four days into the journey," she said. "You ever had mead?"

Grim shook his head. "Is that alcohol?"

"There's some in it. It's not strong. It tastes like honey."

Odo emerged from the backroom with a tray. He slid steaming plates of potatoes, soggy greens, and roasted bird slathered in gravy in front of them. He placed a pewter mug brimming with fragrant, frothy drink beside each plate.

"Enjoy," Odo said. "I gotta see to the other customers. Talk to me in the morning. I'll have the cart of dragon whiskey ready to go for you two."

They tucked in. Aeryn devoured half her plate before she remembered to take a sip of the foamy honey-brown liquid in her mug. Grim finished his food long before Aeryn, and chugged his drink in a few gulps, pronouncing it, "good." He scanned the tavern as he tapped his thumb on the bar.

"You should try chewing your food," Aeryn said as she took a bite, turned her spoon over and stuck it back in her mouth to licked the other side clean. "You always finish before me."

"That's because you double-lick your spoon."

"Excuse me?"

Grim demonstrated with his own utensil. He plopped it back onto his dish with a smirk.

He was teasing her.

"Alright, Bearkiller Stonebreaker," she said with a little grin. "If you can sit still long enough for me to finish, we'll play a game when I'm done."

"What kind of game?" he asked, almost suspicious.

She called down the bar for Odo. "Odo! What kind of games do you have?"

"Darts." He waggled a finger toward the dartboard near the stairs. "Peg jump. Pass the pikdeer."

"That one!"

Odo grabbed a small basket from the shelf behind the counter and slid it towards Aeryn. "Don't lose them."

Aeryn removed a rules scorecard and a few curls of scrap parchment. At the bottom of the basket, she found a charcoal stump and two dice-sized sculptures of the miniature deerlike creatures which roamed all over Thoen. They were carved from wood.

She held up the tiny pikdeer between two fingers. Each was marked with a dot on one side.

"Here's how it works. On your turn, you roll them like dice. You score points based on how they land." She pointed at the numbers and amateurish diagrams on the scorecard. Aeryn spent a minute running through the rules, the caveats for building up a score, and the ways you could lose it.

Grim examined the simple game pieces for a moment. "Alright. You go first."

Aeryn took another bite of food, then shook them in her palm and cast them on the bartop. "Five!" She clapped once. "I'm rolling again."

In the gloomy weather, the sun resigned itself early, and the tavern filled with additional staff and patrons willing to brave the rain.

Grim caught on quickly and won the first game of Pass the Pikdeer because Aeryn pushed her luck too far and lost her points. She won the second game.

"Best out of three?" she asked as she took a sip from her mug.

Grim covered a yawn with his fist and shook his head. "I want to get some rest. Are you still working on your drink?"

"I'm almost done. You can head upstairs if you want. You don't have to wait for me." Aeryn passed him the room key. "I'll be up soon."

Grim heaved his bulk from the stool, crossed the tavern and creaked up the stairs.

Odo came by. "Where'd your traveling pal go?"

"He's tired," she said with a smile. "Tell me, what's special about dragon whiskey?"

"Special family recipe. Made right here and shipped

throughout Thoen," he said with pride. "Put Pineham on the map."

The elvish Imperial appeared beside her and leaned on the bar.

"Would you like to try some?" he said, his brown eyes smiling at her.

Aeryn swirled the mead in the bottom third of her mug. "I don't know if I could drink another pint."

"It doesn't come in a pint," Odo said. He set two tiny glasses on the bar, uncorked a bottle, and poured the reddish-amber liquid into them. He pushed them toward Aeryn and the Imperial.

She took a small, wary sip, which tingled her throat on the way down. "Ooh, that's strong."

"You're supposed to drink it all at once," Odo said, a little like he was talking to an idiot.

The Imperial threw his back and Aeryn followed his example, wincing as she swallowed. Warmth spread throughout her chest. Her body relaxed as a sensation of lightness crept down her limbs and over her mind, blunting the sharpness and putting her at ease.

A clatter of dishes from the kitchen pulled Odo away.

The elvish Imperial pointed to the empty stool beside her. "Is your companion still sitting here?"

She shook her head. He was much better looking dry and up close. She subtly looked him over as he eased into the seat. His uniform fit him well.

He noticed her looking and flashed a white grin. "I'm Thomas."

She could feel her face grow warmer by the second. She returned the smile. "Aeryn."

She pulled her hair over her shoulder and sat up a little straighter. In Merioake, she didn't get approached at all. But why not here? He had been trying to catch her eye since she walked in the room.

They enjoyed each other's company at the bar for a while. Thomas was courteous, confident, and he made Aeryn laugh. He was the sort of elf who, under different circumstances, Aeryn would've wanted to see again.

He bought her another thimble of dragon whiskey as someone started to eek out a tune on a fiddle. A few patrons filtered to the open space in the center of the tavern to dance.

She grabbed the basket of Pass the Pikdeer, gave it a wiggle, and arched an eyebrow. "Feel like pressing your luck?"

"Maybe," he said with a grin. He gently took the basket from her hand and set it back on the bar. He nudged her arm with his. "How about a dance?"

He stood and offered his hand.

Aeryn looked at his open palm, then back at his handsome, open face.

She would never see him again.

It was one dance.

She placed her hand in his. They traveled to the open floor, twirling and laughing.

One dance turned into another, and another. She hadn't been held in a long time, and she liked it.

She didn't want to leave, but she'd lost track of how long she had been down here. She told Grim she'd be up soon, and she hoped she didn't disturb his sleep coming in. She was starting to feel tired herself, so she pulled away after the fourth dance.

"Thank you for the company, and the drinks," she said. "But I should go upstairs. I have a job tomorrow."

Thomas stepped to the side of the room with her. "Don't go."

"Thomas…" she said, somewhat flattered he wanted to keep spending time with her.

"I mean on the job. Send your partner instead."

Aeryn wrinkled her brow. "What?"

Thomas moved closer to her. "I have the option to be in Pineham for a few days. Stay with me. We can get to know each other."

She smiled at him, feeling a little disappointed. "I've enjoyed the time with you this evening, but I really can't," she said, hoping she sounded as sincere as she felt. "I promised to help him travel to Noemar."

"What if you sent him ahead of you? Have him wait for you in Woodby, and meet him later." He ran his hand down the length of her arm, and he met her eyes. "Stay."

Aeryn's insides shifted uncomfortably as she started to catch his meaning.

Dropping his voice, he leaned closer to be heard over the music. "I have a room upstairs to myself."

He brushed her hair out of her face, as his eyes traveled to her mouth. He moved in to kiss her.

Aeryn pulled back, flustered. "I have to go."

She didn't bother to say goodbye, but shot up the stairs, catching her toe on a tread halfway up.

Her eyes adjusted to the unlit hallway. With her mind running, and heart beating faster than normal, she paused outside of her and Grim's room. She shut her eyes for a moment, trying to identify exactly what she was feeling, but the dragon whisky made her thoughts feel slippery. It was as if the butterflies which had been happily performing all kinds of pleasant acrobatics for the last hour suddenly grew oily, or wanted to bite her.

She forced out a breath, and jiggled the handle, finding it locked. She rapped on the door. "Grim, it's Aeryn. Let me in."

She suddenly felt very warm. She pulled off her pink sweater, wadding it into a bundle.

She heard the groaning of the cot on the other side of the door as Grim lifted himself from his bed, the creak of floorboards, then the click of the lock. Grim let her into the room, which was darker now with no candle and curtains drawn. Being an elf, her eyesight was stronger in low light than a human's, and she plodded quickly and unhindered past him, crawling into her cot with the sweater. She flopped face first onto her makeshift pillow.

"Enjoy the rest of your drink?" Grim asked as he locked the door, and tripped over his boot on the way back to bed.

She grunted into her sweater.

As Grim got comfortable, she turned her head to look at him, debating whether or not to say anything about what just happened.

She hiccuped.

Aeryn tried to put it out of her mind. It was done. Tomorrow, she and Grim would earn some money together. He did that.

She cast her arm ungracefully outward, across the small gap between their beds, and smacked him lightly on the arm. Moving only her fingertips, she patted him twice, then let her hand slide limply between the beds.

"Thank you for securing the job. You did good," she said.

He wrinkled his brow, looked at his arm where she touched him, then back at her. "What was that for?"

"What was what for? You can't take a compliment?"

"You're drunk, aren't you?"

Aeryn paused. "I tried the dragon whiskey."

The temperature in the room shifted instantly.

"How much did you spend?" he said in an accusatory tone.

"I didn't spend anything," she said defensively. "I was bought a drink."

"A drink?"

"Two drinks."

"By who?"

"The elvish Imperial," she said. "His name is Thomas."

"Did he try to talk you out of the job?" Grim asked. He was leaning on an elbow now, straining his eyes and frowning at her in the dark.

"What?" She wrinkled her nose. "No. I mean, not really.

We didn't talk about it much."

"Not really? What does that mean?"

"Well, he tried to get me to stay with him."

"What do you mean, *stay with him*?"

Aeryn huffed, and propped herself on her elbows. "He wanted you to go on the job, so I could stay with him. In his room. Alone."

Grim stared at her in the dark, perplexed for a moment, until realization dawned.

"Oh," he said as if the idea surprised him.

Aeryn pulled her chin inward. "What do you mean, *oh*? I'm a very attractive elf."

"Wha – no, I mean..." Grim stuttered over his words for a moment.

Aeryn flopped onto her pillow. "Anyway, I told him no," she said with an air. "Because I'm a classy lady."

She hiccuped again.

Grim shook his head and forced out a breath. "I'm going to sleep. You need to sleep too."

"I will go to sleep when I'm good and ready," she said. "Don't boss me."

II

Trouble

Sunshine cracked through the curtains the next morning. With their belongings mostly dry, they dressed, packed, and ate breakfast out of their rations to avoid spending more money. Then they headed downstairs to find Odo.

Though the music and activity lasted until late, the tavern was clean and orderly. Odo emerged from the kitchen wearing an apron. An overweight striped cat trotted after him and hopped onto the bar.

"Sleep well, I hope?" Odo said. "Ya'll hungry? I got porridge and bacon and eggs made to order."

"We're all set," Grim said.

"Suit yourself. C'mon back. Lemme show you what you'll be delivering."

Aeryn gave the cat a scratch behind the ears and followed Odo and Grim through the kitchen to a loading and receiving area in the back. A crate sat in a wooden cart with two large wheels, two legs, and two handles.

Odo tapped the top of the crate. "I've already nailed it shut, and I'd ask you not to crack it open. You can push or pull the cart. Don't drag the legs, and don't let it tip. Finest dragon whiskey in all of Thoen, here. You're bringing it to Jandar Berringer at The Laughing Boar on Straight Street in Woodby. He'll pay you the other half when you get there."

He dug three gold coins out of his apron pocket, thanked them, and they left.

The road cut through the land, over gentle hills, beside open fields and small farms, and the occasional cluster of trees. With little shade, the summer sun beat upon them mercilessly, as though making up for the downpour the day before.

In the sun, the clothes which were damp in the morning dried within twenty minutes, only to dampen again from sweat. Aeryn's loose hide clothing felt heavy and hot. The southern forest was notoriously warm, but the shade made it bearable. She let her vest hang open to give the sleeveless tunic underneath some air, and she tied her hair in a neat swirl to get it off her neck. Grim suffered more than Aeryn in his plate armor. There was enough room in the cart for their bags and weapons, which helped.

They took turns with the cart. Aeryn felt she had better control when she pushed it in front of her like a wheelbarrow, but Grim preferred to hitch it up and pull it behind him. Weaver glided nearby, and eventually settled atop the load for a snooze.

After two hours of travel they approached an outcropping of trees beside a gargantuan boulder.

"You want to stop for a rest?" Aeryn asked, a few paces behind the cart. "Or switch? I can take another turn."

"A little further," Grim said at the head of their procession. They rattled halfway past the rocky outcropping when he stopped abruptly. Weaver squawked and fluttered to Aeryn's shoulder.

Three armed men in plainclothes emerged from behind the boulder. They strolled into the road like they owned it, barring the path ahead. Each wore a cloth mask which covered their faces from the nose down, and each carried a sword.

A swish of feet over grass drew Aeryn's attention behind her. Another armed man with longer hair and a similar mask darted into the road behind Aeryn.

They were hemmed in.

One of the bandits ahead pointed his sword at Grim and Aeryn. "You stumbled down our road. Drop the cart. Empty your pockets."

Another brandished his shortsword. "Don't get any ideas, or we will cut you open like a pig. Throw your weapons on the ground."

Grim released the wagon handles with a clatter. "You want my weapon?"

He grasped his axe with two hands, hauling it from the wagon bed. With no intention of surrendering, he closed the gap between himself and the bandits in a few strides.

The two closest bandits took a nervous step away as he advanced. "Back off, I'm warning you!"

Grim ignored their orders. One of them thrust his sword, and Grim swung.

Weaver shrieked. He swooped behind Aeryn.

The man at the rear rushed at her. With a gasp, she lunged for a weapon in the cart, but he caught her with one arm around the shoulders and yanked her away.

Aeryn screamed. She writhed like an animal caught in a snare. Overhead, Weaver dove at her attacker. The man swiped at the bird with his sword and missed. In the moment of distraction, Aeryn sunk her teeth into his arm and he released her with a yell.

She raced to the cart with the man on her heels. She dove for the first weapon within reach and grasped her bow. Whirling around, she swung it like a club.

The bow smacked her pursuer across the head. He staggered sideways and fell hard into the dirt. Aeryn fumbled for an arrow and pulled a small broadhead from the quiver.

The man at her feet stirred, attempting to right himself.

She nocked, turned her weapon upon him, and fired.

He cried out in agony as the arrow sunk into his shoulder and drove him back onto the ground.

"Don't kill me!" he cried in elvish.

A weight dropped through Aeryn's stomach. She recognized his voice.

On the opposite side of the cart, metal clanged on metal. Aeryn heard the wet crack of bone, followed by a man's scream.

Grim threw his axe to the ground to grasp the last bandit standing by the collar. The man's arm hung with an unnatural crook at his side, his sword in the dirt. The other two bandits lied motionless, bleeding in the road.

Grim pulled back his fist and pummeled the attacker. Even from the opposite side of the cart, Aeryn heard the crunch of mashed cartilage and broken bones. Grim struck again, sending a spray of blood into the air, and the bandit's body went limp.

Grim's face contorted in rage as he continued to hammer the disfigured man with less restraint than a rabid animal tearing its prey to pieces.

"Grim, stop!" Aeryn screamed as he drew back for yet another punch.

He paused and his attention snapped to Aeryn, noting her horrified expression and the fourth attacker at her feet. He dropped the bandit, and ran over.

The man at Aeryn's feet grasped at the arrow, writhing in agony. At Grim's approach, his eyes bulged. He tried to get up and wriggle away.

Grim gave Aeryn a brief appraisal. Seeing she wasn't bleeding, he bent to grab the man by the collar, eliciting another cry of pain. He yanked the mask down, confirming what Aeryn already knew.

"Don't kill me, please!" Thomas cried. "I didn't hurt anyone. I won't say anything."

"Those your pals from the tavern last night?" Grim said, his voice full of menace.

"Yes." Thomas' voice quavered. "I didn't want to come, but Luther's mind was set. I only came to try to hold them back from killing you."

"But you were fine sending Grim into their hands," Aeryn said, her volume rising. "As long as it got me into your bed."

"Aeryn, no, I..."

"You tried to kill my bird." Her limbs trembled with her swelling indignation.

She crouched. Pressing one hand to his chest, she grabbed the arrow shaft roughly with the other, and yanked it out.

He screamed.

"Shut up!" she said. "Grim, move."

Grim released Thomas, and stepped clear as Aeryn rose, bow in hand. She looked down on Thomas with disdain. His shirt was drenched from the shoulder. He breathed heavily, despair and desperation mingled upon his bloodied face.

Aeryn let him squirm under the weight of it for a moment.

She tossed the arrow into the cart, drew her bow across her body, and swung it at him with all her strength.

He fell over unconscious, bleeding profusely from the arrow wound, but alive.

Aeryn felt sick. She didn't want to think about what would've happened if he succeeded in dragging her off. Weaver landed on her shoulder and she pulled him close. She felt like she might cry or throw up if she stood here any longer.

She assessed Grim. "Is that your blood or theirs?"

"Mostly theirs," he said in a hurry. "You're gonna let him live?"

"I can't kill him in cold blood, Grim," she said.

"This is a mistake," he said, his tone firm.

"I'm not an animal!" Her chest heaved. "You're scaring me!"

For a flicker of a moment, Grim looked taken aback, almost like she had slapped him.

Aeryn dropped her eyes to Thomas, bleeding at her feet,

and resisted the urge to kick him. "Help me drag him off the road."

Aeryn pulled the masks off the other three men and recognized them as Luther and two other Imperials from The Purple Pint. Luther was dead. Another was cleaved in the chest. Only one who attacked Grim was alive, but barely.

They heaved the bodies behind the boulder where Aeryn found their rucksacks stuffed with uniforms, and a coil of rope.

Grim took the swords, flung them in the wagon bed and hitched up the handles. "Let's move."

12

Consequences

For the first ten minutes they hurried along without a word. The boulder grew smaller in the distance and eventually disappeared when they crested the next hill.

Aeryn felt like she was struggling to keep afloat in churning waters. The world was a much more treacherous place than she ever imagined, and she lived in a time of supposed peace. The Imperials were supposed to be upholders of law and justice. Yet these ones acted like ruffians.

If these Imperials could act like thugs, what about the men in uniform she killed before meeting Grim?

What if they were Imperials after all?

The concerns of Aeryn's father swirled into her mind. What if Grim lied to her, and he really was a murderer? Truth was, she didn't really know him. Apart from the disturbing savagery with which he fought those men on the road, Grim knew Thomas was an Imperial, and though he posed no immediate threat, Grim still thought they should kill him. He was clearly more dangerous than she realized.

If he lied to her, not only did she nurse a fugitive back to health, but she was also an Imperial-killer. A capital criminal, several times over.

Aeryn's head swam, and her legs began to shake. "I need a

moment."

She staggered to the side of the road, crouched, and put her head in her hands. Closing her eyes, she took some deep breaths. *What have I gotten myself into?*

Grim creaked to a stop, rested the cart with a rattle and rotated his shoulder. "We should put as much distance as possible between ourselves and that rock."

That rock.

Not, *those people.*

Aeryn shot to her feet. "You just killed several men. We almost died. I'm allowed one minute."

"We can't afford that, Aeryn. You left one alive. He'll talk," Grim said. "If, or when, the Imperials come after us, we need as big of a head start as possible."

"Those men in Ravenwood. Were they really Cords? Slavers?" she said. "How did you know? Are you sure?"

Grim wrinkled his brow. "Where is this coming from?"

"Grim, I just knowingly assaulted an Imperial soldier," she said as she marched toward him. "And right before I met you, I killed three men in uniform. I have no way to prove I acted in self-defense. I have no way to prove they weren't Imperials, except your word."

His mouth dipped into a stern frown. "You think I lied to you?"

Aeryn rubbed a hand under her tingling nose. "I don't know what to think. Now I know Imperials can be despicable, and you have no qualms about slaughtering them."

"They tried to kill me, Aeryn, and would've done who knows what to you," he said, his voice rising. He took a few strides toward her. "I don't understand why it surprises you that officials are corrupt."

Aeryn held her ground and lifted her chin to look him in the face.

"Answer my question, Grim," she said, her voice thickening with emotion. She met his eyes, searching out the truth. "Were the men in Ravenwood really Cords?"

"Yes, they were Cords. Slavers and murderers," Grim said, his words clipped. "You think I don't know my enemy? They took fifteen years of my life. The one called Jasper? I was his favorite one to torment. You've seen the scars on my back."

Grim's steely blue eyes blazed like they were on fire.

"I have only ever told you the truth," he said. "You saved my life, and I owe you that much. But if you don't trust me, I don't know what to say to you."

Holding his gaze, the liquid collecting in Aeryn's eyes spilled over, and she swiped it away with her slender, shaky fingers.

She believed him before.

It would have to be enough.

Before she could respond, Grim continued, controlling his tone and dropping to a normal volume.

"Look. I recognize that helping me has been more than you bargained for, but we can't stay here." He took a breath. "Let's just get this cargo to Woodby and sell the swords. We'll split the money, and if you want to take off, fine."

"Why would you think that?" she said, irritated by his assumption. "I just had to know, Grim. Don't be stupid."

She pushed past him and hiked up the cart.

"Your shoulder's bothering you. I can tell."

He watched her, perplexed for a moment, and then joined her along the path.

They continued at a quick but steady pace. They decided against stopping for lunch, and ate as they walked. Aeryn discovered, due to the fox the other night, she was out of food.

Eventually they passed farms, then a spattering of houses before entering the town proper. Woodby was larger and more prosperous than Pineham. In the afternoon sunshine, the town teemed with activity. Townsfolk hung colorful banners overhead which spanned the cobbled street. Merchants parked their carts throughout town, and humans and elves in equal numbers worked together arranging tables, chairs, and games on the lawn outside town hall. Others stacked kindling in the center of the square for what promised to be a sizable bonfire later. The smells of fresh produce, popped corn, and roasted meat traveled on the air.

It took Aeryn a moment, but when she saw the sun symbol printed on the pennant flags, realization struck. "Today's the summer festival."

"What's that?" Grim asked.

"A holiday to celebrate the longest day of the year. I completely forgot."

"What does that mean for us?"

She shrugged as a group of children with streamers darted in front of them. "Usually towns and villages host their own celebrations, which means increased patrols in and around town. But we didn't see many travelers until we got closer, and they were all coming here. I think we have some time before anyone finds...you know, and starts asking questions."

"Let's deliver this whiskey, get what we need, and go," he said. He squinted at the sign posted on the corner. "Is that Straight Street?"

Aeryn read the sign.

"No. Next one over. Wait," Aeryn said, stopping him. "These might raise some questions if we leave them out."

She loaded the swords carefully into her pack, while tying her father's sword to her side.

The Laughing Boar was situated halfway down Straight Street, not far from the village square. Shiny, well crafted tables were spaced throughout the spacious dining room. Plaques decorated the walls. At a table near the window, a slender brunette elf in a blue dress bickered with a gnarled middle-age human. They paused their argument to watch with interest as Grim wheeled the cart inside. Two barkeeps worked behind the counter while they conversed with a well-dressed half-elf Aeryn took to be a city official.

The lady behind the bar stopped stacking mugs. "Delivery?"

Grim rested the cart and approached the bar with Aeryn. "Yes, for Jandar."

She leaned over the bar for a better look at the cart and

gasped. "Is that dragon whiskey? Oy, you're just in time." She bustled to the back room. "Jandar!"

"Those Imperials finally show up with me dragon whiskey?" A heavyset man with a crooked nose and wide face emerged from the back room. He took one look at Grim and Aeryn. "I thought Odo was sendin' Imperials with me whiskey."

"He hired us last minute," Aeryn said.

The man shrugged. "Well, let's see the damage."

Jandar grabbed a crowbar mounted on the wall behind the bar, and pried the crate open.

"Slap me thrice!" he cried as he looked over the contents. He gave Grim a jolly pat. "A lot more than usually shows up. Usually at least one bottle's broken, and at least two bottles missing from me order. I gotsta tell Odo he should use you two again."

He dug in his apron and dropped a few gold coins into Grim's hand.

"Holiday's always a good time, and'll be extra fun with this." Jandar plucked a bottle from the crate and gave it a waggle. He waved them over to the bar. "You gotsta try. Thimble, on the house. And tell you what, if you're stayin', I'll give you a room at half price."

The lady behind the bar slid a few small glasses to Jandar who poured the reddish brown liquid as Grim passed Aeryn her half of the money.

"Oy, Wolfie, Ophelia," Jandar said to the pair by the window. "Dragon whiskey?"

"I must decline," the elf said as she folded her hands

delicately on the table. "It'll be a clear night, and if I wish to commune with the stars, I need a clear mind."

Her companion poured a handful of bone dice onto the table. "The dice say it's going to rain."

The elf rolled her eyes.

"How about you, Wolfie?" Jandar asked.

"Is a frog's butt watertight?" the man cried with a jovial grin, drawing a strange glance from his companion, Aeryn, and Grim. Snickering, he hoisted himself from his chair and pattered to the bar in his sandals. "I'll have Fifi's thimble, since she doesn't want it."

"Sure, but you're payin' for it," Jandar said with a wheezy chuckle. He slid the thimble of liquor to Aeryn and one to Grim. Grim drank his in one gulp, and coughed. Aeryn felt like it'd be rude to decline, so she threw hers back and immediately regretted it. After the screaming earlier, it felt like her throat was on fire.

"Like molten gold of a dragon's hoard, this drink," Jandar said as he corked the bottle. "How about that room? Looks sparse in here now, but they'll fill quick with people stayin' for the holiday."

"We need to be on our way," Grim said.

"Could you point us in the direction of a smith, or general store?" Aeryn asked.

Jandar gestured to the window. "Gotsta general store a few doors down. Smith around the corner on Toble Road. Good luck findin' anyone still open. Most businesses closed early preparin' for the festival."

"Are those the only ones in town?" Aeryn asked.

"The only smithy, yes. There's another store down on Peony," Jandar said. "Possible one of them's still open. Otherwise you'll have to wait 'til tomorrow."

"Alright, let's hurry," Aeryn said. "Thank you, sir." Aeryn shouldered her pack, heavier now with the weight of the swords which stuck out at the top, and led the way out of The Laughing Boar.

The streets swarmed with merry townsfolk and the smell of cooking fires, bread, and fresh produce made Aeryn's stomach groan with hunger. Two men rolled a gigantic wheel of cheese down the street, and led by an enthusiastic young boy who took his job of hollering for people to make way very seriously.

They wove their way through the bustling street to the general store, but found it locked. It was the same at the smiths, and the second store on Peony.

"How badly do you need to resupply your food?" Grim asked. "I've got a day's worth."

"I'm out of everything except nuts," she said. "We could press on to the next city, but we'll be crossing into Proimos. We wouldn't get there until sundown. I remember my father said the bigger cities, especially human ones, tend to be walled and they shut the gates at dusk."

"We'd be locked out?"

"Even if we made it there on time, their celebration'll be even bigger than here. There's no guarantee any business will be open." Aeryn rubbed her head. "I could try to hunt, but we're in unfamiliar territory. I don't know how long it'll take me to catch something."

"Let's see if Jandar's offer still stands. We'll stay the night, resupply in the morning," Grim said.

They made their way back to The Laughing Boar.

"If what you say is true, the festival should give us extra time," Grim said. "Besides, it's not like the Imperials know where we're going after Woodby."

Aeryn's insides went rigid. She recalled her conversation with Thomas the night before. *I promised to go to Noemar with him.*

It seemed benign, even noble, when it came out of her mouth.

Now it made her feel sick.

Grim pulled the heavy door open. He exchanged some words and coins with Jandar, but Aeryn only half-listened. Her mind roiled.

Thomas might keep quiet like he said, but she doubted it. From here, Imperials would track them all the way to Noemar. She and Grim would be arrested. Grim would never make it home, or find his family. Their journey would be over before it even started.

What was she thinking? They'd never take Grim alive.

If she and Grim didn't perish when the Imperial caught up with them, they'd spend the rest of their lives on the run. Her parents would hear that she was wanted for assaulting an officer five days after leaving home. Her wanted poster would be displayed in town, right beside Grim's. She could never show her face in Merioake again, even if she wanted to.

How could she let this happen? She couldn't blame the dragon whiskey. This was her fault. Now she and Grim were not safe.

He needed to know.

✦

"Jandar said this is the last room to fit two," Grim said as Aeryn followed him inside the second-floor room. The lodgings were nicer than in Pineham, with painted walls, a hay mattress instead of a cot, and a side table with a glass lantern and a wash basin. But there was only one bed.

Grim locked the door. He swung his bag to the floor, resting his axe against the wall, and started to unfasten his armor. "I can sleep on the floor, I don't care. I gotta get this armor off."

Aeryn let her own pack drop off her shoulders. She sank stiffly into a wooden chair near the wash table. She placed both hands on her knees and took a deep breath to avoid throwing up.

"What's wrong with you?" Grim asked as he added his breastplate in the growing pile of armor. His shirt was soaked through with sweat. Aeryn could smell him across the room.

She summoned her courage and got to the point. "They know we're going to Noemar after Woodby."

Grim stared at her a moment. "How?"

"Thomas. The elvish Imperial. I told him."

Grim's eyes looked like they were on fire again. "You told him where we're going?"

"I thought we were just talking–"

"Is that what you thought?" His voice strained as he took a

step toward her.

She stood, her own voice rising with her. "How was I supposed to know he was planning to rob us? I thought we were just having a pleasant conversation and a dance."

"A dance? I thought you said he talked to you."

"He did – and he asked me to dance," Aeryn said, realizing this bothered him even more.

"And you said yes." Grim shook his head. "Is this going to be a problem?"

"What is that supposed to mean? I just told you, they know where we're going."

"No, I mean, is this normal for you?" he said.

She pulled her chin back. "Excuse me?"

"I didn't think you were the sort to lose all common sense the moment some elf shows interest."

His words hit like a strike.

The accusation was the same sentiment which dogged her mind and kept her from holding her head high in Merioake.

A fire ignited with a wrenching sensation in Aeryn's core. Drawing back her fist, she flew across the room and punched him in the chest.

"What do you take me for? A weak willed whore?" she cried.

She hammered her fists into his chest, again and again, as she continued to shout.

"I've made the mistake of getting close to someone, and I know what happens! He'll take your heart – and shred it – along with your dignity. He'll turn your friends against you – turn the town against you. Now I'm a pariah. No, I'm not going to let that happen again!"

With each blow, the pent-up viscera from years of rejection exploded from her.

He just stood there and took it.

She wasn't sure when the water started to stream down her cheeks, but finally she stopped yelling, her arms resting against his chest, fists tight. She hung her head and a small sob escaped her lips.

"It was just a dance," she said, quieter, her voice hoarse. Her shoulders shook as she started to cry. "It was just a dance."

Head down, she unclenched her fists as hot tears flowed to the tip of her nose.

Grim placed one hand, and then the other tentatively on her shoulders. She lifted her chin to meet his face.

The hardness in his expression was gone. His eyes were damp. Though she didn't see it happen, she noticed the salty streak left on his dirty face from an escaped droplet which rolled a short distance before it soaked into his beard.

She threw her body into his chest and locked her arms around him, eyes shut tight as she finished her cry. He gently returned the hug.

"You couldn't've known about the elf," he said after a minute, his voice a low rumble.

She sniffed, and drew a shaky, cleansing breath. "I'm sorry I hit you."

He was quiet for a moment. "I forgive you."

13

Fortune

Downstairs, Aeryn ordered suppers while Grim changed clothes and washed up. She felt lighter in the chest after reconciling with Grim, but the arguments, violence, labor, and associated stress of the day left her body and mind exhausted.

There was a possibility she couldn't return home.

She tried to remind herself she wanted to get away from Merioake anyway, which was why she'd volunteered to help this strange Northerner hike to the opposite end of the continent. But she had imagined she'd return, either ready to face her future in the tannery, or with a good reason not to. The thought of never seeing her family again unsettled her.

She tried to push the matter from her mind. She'd figure it out later.

For now, the thing to do was to follow through with Grim, and avoid arrest. If their partnership wasn't sealed when leaving Merioake, it certainly was now.

While she waited for their food, she watched the busy town through the large, single-pane windows with her back to the bar. She kept alert for any passing soldiers. She saw none. A few more patrons conversed in the tavern, but it seemed the whole town was outside in the streets.

Still seated near the window, the she-elf and her

companion spoke in furtive tones over a plate of cheese and fruit. The elf noticed Aeryn and waved her over. She was much older than Aeryn, but younger than Aeryn's parents. Up close, Aeryn noticed the man's face was disfigured with scars. Three of the fingers on one hand were missing their tips up to the knuckle. He reeked of liquor.

"There is a blackbird outside looking for you," the she-elf said with a light accent Aeryn didn't recognize from a lifetime in Thoen, or even her few brushes with the Illwalii.

Sure enough, Weaver marched back and forth in front of the window, occasionally fluttering out of the way of a passerby who stepped too close.

Aeryn tapped the glass. Weaver fixed her with his bright eye. Satisfied, he launched himself into the air and perched in a nearby lilac bush.

"Do you speak with animals?" Aeryn asked her.

"I do. I learned from my late husband. He was a falconer," she said, her eyes smiling. She pulled out a chair for Aeryn, inviting her to sit. "The bird seems very fond of you."

"Yes, and food." Aeryn smiled as she slid into the chair. "My mother taught me how a few years ago. We nursed the little guy back to health after he flew into the side of my house. His name is Weaver."

"My name is Ophelia, and this is my friend, Wolfe," she said, gesturing to the human across the table.

Wolfe crinkled his eyes and waved a leathery hand.

"I hope the evening festivities don't disturb Weaver too much. The stars tell me there'll be fireworks competing with their glory this evening." Ophelia gazed wistfully toward the heavens through the window.

"Fireworks?" Aeryn asked, intrigued. "What are they like?"

"Colorful and dead loud!" Wolfe said, smacking the table in his excitement.

Ophelia gasped and pointed out the window. "We're in luck! The early stars have shown themselves."

Though there was still plenty of daylight, three twinkles dotted the sky near the faint shape of the moon.

Wolfe groaned in a loaded-sort-of-way. "It's a bad omen."

"It is not," Ophelia said. "See? The position of *Adelaide* and *Elysande,* with their proximity to the lunar placement, in this moon phase... and *Jax* joining the heavenly dance..."

"Doom," Wolfe said with a lofty shake of his head. "All I'm hearing is doom."

Ophelia rolled her eyes and returned her attention to the heavens.

Wolfe leaned forward in his chair. "She's always looking at the stars. Thinks they tell her things."

"I can hear you," Ophelia said, her voice indignant as she pulled her focus from the sky again. "I'm sitting right here. For your information, they do."

Wolfe waved a hand. "Hooey."

Grim emerged downstairs and scanned the room for Aeryn. She waved to him and introduced Ophelia and Wolfe. "They were telling me about the celebration in town tonight."

"Also, the stars," Ophelia said with an energetic smile and a bob of the head.

"Yes, and the stars," Aeryn said. Grim nodded slowly and Aeryn pulled out a chair. "Supper's coming."

"Will you two join the festival this evening?" Ophelia asked. "Aeryn, and Grim, was it?"

Aeryn's insides shifted. She didn't recall introducing herself by name. Ophelia must've overheard their names when Grim secured the room from Jandar, or even from Weaver. If Imperials really were coming after them in the near future, it was probably unwise to tell others too much information about themselves or their plans.

"We haven't discussed it," Aeryn said.

"It's the most important holiday of the season, and ya'd stay in?" Wolfe said. "Who stays in on a day like today?"

"It's been a long day," Grim said.

"Ophelia, I'm curious," Aeryn asked, wishing to change the subject. "What sorts of things do the stars tell you?"

Ophelia brightened at the question and she checked the sky again. "They say, *trust your companions.*"

"Hold on, where's my lucky one?" Wolfe said, as the barkeep brought plates heaping with soft bread, cold chicken smeared with herbs, and summer vegetables for Aeryn and Grim, with a pint of mead each. Wolfe scanned the table and lifted his plate of cheese. "Oh, right!"

He dropped the plate with a clatter, drawing a sharp look from the barkeep, then popped a tooth out of the back of his mouth with a faint shucking noise. He flicked a piece of food out of the grooves, then showed it to Aeryn and Grim. There were black squiggles carved into its sides.

"My lucky die," he said.

Aeryn and Grim stopped chewing to stare.

Wolfe cast the tooth along with the rest of his bone dice on the table. "They say, *be careful who ya trust.*"

Ophelia folded her arms. "Put that back. You're making them uncomfortable."

Aeryn shifted in her seat. The tattoos on Grim's knuckles caught her eye. They looked similar in style to the marks on Wolfe's lucky tooth.

Ophelia noticed too.

"Grim, what an unusual set of tattoos," she said. "Do they hold any meaning to you?"

Grim glanced absently at his hand and shook his head.

Aeryn arched an eyebrow. "Wolfe, do you read runes?"

"Yes, Lady Aeryn, I most certainly do." Wolfe straightened his vest importantly.

"No, he does not," Ophelia said, flatly. "Almost no one does."

"I should be more specific." Wolfe gestured with both hands to his bone dice. "I can read these runes. Sort of. But if ya're wondering what those tattoos say, I'm afraid I can't help ya there."

Wolfe jammed his lucky tooth into his back gums. He leaned forward, and lowered his voice, his jovial nature now sober.

"But I'd keep those covered if it were me."

Grim stopped chewing for the second time. "Why?"

Wolfe kept his voice low and gave him a knowing look. "Just do yourself a favor and get some gloves. I haven't seen a Baldomar in years, but I know one when I see one."

Grim straightened in his chair, and exchanged a look with Aeryn. Herm's warning about gloves came into her mind, and no doubt, his.

Wolfe's chairlegs scraped the wooden floor as he pushed back from the table and rose unsteadily. "Now if ya excuse me, Jandar has several bottles of dragon whiskey, and one of them is calling my name. Lady Aeryn, Master Grim. Don't miss them fireworks."

He winked and forced a smile, then pattered to the bar like he was a much older man than he looked.

Ophelia sighed almost imperceptibly as she watched her friend purchase more alcohol. She smoothed away her concern and refocused on Grim and Aeryn. "We're setting up a fortune-teller's booth this evening. I hope to see you around." She rose and smiled sincerely. "Good luck."

She met Wolfe at the door and they left together.

Aeryn dropped her voice as she took another bite of chicken. "What do you think?"

"If it's safe enough to stay here tonight, we might as well go out. Staying in'll probably just draw attention," he said. "I'm interested in these fireworks."

"Oh. Me too." Aeryn poked him in the knuckle. "I meant, about Wolfe's comment about the gloves and the Baldomar. Sounded like Herm."

"Yeah..." Grim thought for a moment. "Nothing I can do about it now, though."

He chugged his pint of mead and waited for Aeryn to finish her meal, watching the town through the window like a sentry.

❐

Before they went out, Grim shaved his face with the razor he purchased before leaving Thoen. Aeryn found the ordeal fascinating. She stood beside him near the washtable and small hanging mirror to watch. He made a slow stroke, rinsing the blade every few inches, as it cleaned his cheek inch by inch, like a sheep on shearing day.

After a minute, he paused with the razor poised beside his bristly cheek, and gave her a sidelong glance. "Is there something else you can do?"

"Am I making you uncomfortable?" she asked.

"Yes."

"Sorry." She backed off and sat cross-legged on the bed. "I didn't realize shaving a beard took so long. Elvish men don't grow as much facial hair. It takes my father less than a minute to clean his chin."

"Well, I haven't done this before. It's not like the Loom handed out razors," Grim said. "I'd rather not flay my skin off."

When he was done, he asked Aeryn to check for missed spots. She had never seen him without a beard. He had a scar on his chin, but he looked younger and fresher, and different than he had that morning, which was the idea.

"Does it feel cooler?" she asked, scanning his face and neck.

"Much." He rinsed the razor and dried it. He ran a hand through his hair, making it stick up on end, then smoothed it back down.

Outside, the air was still thick and warm, and the town square and the adjacent village green thrummed with activity. Lively music carried from a podium near the town hall. Several vendors gave away samples of their goods in celebration of the holiday. Aeryn and Grim tried a new species of caramel-colored popped corn with an herbish flavor and a soft cheese which tasted like flowers. They spotted the fortune-teller's booth but avoided it when they noticed Wolfe and Ophelia bickering in front of a customer.

"The dice don't lie," Wolfe said, trying to tempt Ophelia's customer to come to him instead. "Last week, they predicted a mad escape. Next day, Benny Nessik's pig got loose in the town square and it took an hour to wrangle it."

"Your dice also predicted I'd be run over by a manure cart," Ophelia said.

"Heh, heh. Yeah, they did…"

Aeryn gave a Grim a look as they steered themselves away. "Pretty sure fortune-telling is all bunk anyway."

The festival was a distraction from her worries, but couldn't blot them out completely.

As the sun set, the atmosphere of anticipation over the town rose, reaching its peak as the first rocket of light shot into the sky. The buzzing crowd, which had gathered on the green, fell quiet. The rocket seemed to die out before it exploded in a dazzling spray of red and yellow against the blackening sky, accompanied by a deafening pop.

Aeryn and Grim flinched at the first boom. But after the initial shock, they stood side by side, holding their ears and grinning at the sky like kids. And for a little bit, Aeryn completely forgot about the turmoil earlier that day.

Weaver spent the evening huddled under Aeryn's hair. He was cranky and flustered and nipped her more than once, but eventually settled. The moment the fireworks finished, he fluttered off to find a place to roost in peace for the night.

The crowds dispersed with cheering. Aeryn and Grim made their way back to The Laughing Boar exhausted. Aeryn collapsed on the hay mattress, and Grim unfurled his bedroll. He winced as he stretched his neck and shoulder.

Aeryn's conscience pricked her. Sighing, she slapped the bed. She heaved herself off the mattress, then walked to his bedroll, and lied on it.

"Take the bed," she said. "Your shoulder."

He watched her for a moment. "Seriously? You're just going to lay on my mat?"

"Don't argue with me." She gave him a ginger pat on the leg and rolled over. "Toss me a blanket, will you?"

Aeryn woke in the morning, sprawled on the floor, to the sound of clanking armor. She rubbed the sleep from her eyes and propped herself on one elbow. Grim strapped a greave to his shin.

"Wait." She hoisted herself up, groggy. "Don't put that

on."

Grim paused. "Why not?"

She stretched her back. "You should ditch the heavy armor and keep one of the swords."

He looked at her like she'd grown another eyeball. "Absolutely not. We were attacked on the road yesterday."

"Then wear the chest piece, store the rest, and carry a sword at your side like a normal person," she said. "If you haven't noticed, most people don't walk around in full plate, lugging a two-handed axe. You look like you're being escorted to war by an unarmored woman and a bird."

Grim scanned his pile of armor. "I like carrying my axe."

"If the Imperials come after us, we don't want to stand out. I probably wouldn't have thought about it if you hadn't shaved. It was a good idea to change your appearance." Aeryn yawned. "Gods, you snore like a bear. I'm shocked I'm even alive after two months of this."

Grim considered, conceded with a sigh, then unstrapped the shin piece.

They spent some time reorganizing their packs to accommodate Grim's pieces of armor, and took an inventory of their supplies. Grim slung one of the short swords at his side but strapped his axe to his back for quick access if needed.

Aeryn opened the book to the page with the map and laid it on the bed. It wasn't very detailed, but it featured all the major landmarks, cities, some larger towns, and a few major roads. She placed a finger on the dot labeled Woodby in northeast Thoen. She traced the short line which connected Woodby to Fieldgate, across the border between Thoen and Proimos, the Imperial Province.

Fieldgate was a major trading post situated in southeast Proimos near the convergence of several provinces. Thoen sat to its south, Illwali to its southeast corner, and Wholls, the heartlands, to the east. Major routes led to and from the city, including roads which cut westward directly to the capital city Nyassa, and to all of the neighboring provinces, including Noemar directly north and Kharsh in the northwest.

"We can reach Fieldgate by midday," Aeryn said. "From there, we can take any number of routes out of the city." Aeryn pointed to some of their options. "We can go straight to Noemar through Proimos. It's the fastest and most direct route. But the Imperials may expect it, and it takes us past Kharsh. I don't know about the situation with the orcs who live there. I've never met one, but I hear they're aggressive."

She pointed to another road out of Fieldgate.

"Noemar spans most of the continent like a hat. We can still get there if we bear northeast out of the city. We'll cross the heartlands. Mostly human farmers. It'll take longer, and we'll arrive further east, but with potentially fewer hazards," she said. "I'm told the heartlands are fruitful with crops and roaming game, so finding food may be less challenging this way."

"Heartlands," he said decisively. "It doesn't matter if we take a longer route, as long as we get there."

They finished packing. Aeryn gently tore the map from the book. She kept it, her hunting knife, and a handful of medicinal herbs and bandages in a side pocket. She secured her father's sword at her side, and kept her bow strung and quiver strapped to the side of her pack for easy access, in case they passed a roaming herd of pikdeer.

Downstairs, they devoured a hearty breakfast, returned their key to Jandar, and stepped into the fresh morning air. They splashed through a few puddles that formed along the cobbled lane from an overnight shower and visited the blacksmith first. There, they sold the remaining three swords for a decent price. Afterward they made their way back to the general store on Straight Street to restock their rations.

Aeryn stood by, allowing Grim the practice of exchanging coins with the clerk, when Ophelia and Wolfe entered the store.

"Greetings!" Ophelia said, brimming with energy.

Wolfe cringed at the sound of her voice.

"I had a feeling our paths would cross again," she said. "The stars, you know."

Wolfe grunted. "I'm sure it had nothing to do with the bird hanging around outside. I gotta find this blasted hazelroot."

"How did Weaver fare with the noise last night?" Ophelia asked, ignoring Wolfe as he blundered around the store in search of the herb known to help with the after effects of heavy drinking. To Aeryn, a general store seemed like an odd place to find it, but she hadn't seen an herbalist in town.

"Fussy, but he settled," Aeryn said with a polite smile. "Is Wolfe alright? I have gingerwort. It'll help with a headache, at least." She dug into her side pocket for the pain reliever.

"That's very kind," Ophelia said, interrupted by Wolfe, who knocked over a display rack near the storefront window, turning every head in the store.

Outside, a group of six Imperials marched along Straight Street toward The Laughing Boar.

A weight dropped through Aeryn's stomach. She shot a look at Grim. He noticed them too. He finished his transaction with the clerk, and they crammed their supplies into their bags.

"We have to go. Now." Grim strode to the window and checked the lane, before stepping outside. "Aeryn, come on."

Grim nodded goodbye to Wolfe and pulled the door open.

"Goodbye," Aeryn said, as she pressed a sprig of gingerwort into Ophelia's hand. She hurried out the door and followed Grim in the opposite direction of The Laughing Boar.

Neither spoke. They wove their way through Woodby, never traveling the same road for long. They checked over their shoulders frequently, trying not to appear as nervous as they felt while they hurried past townsfolk. The markets, town buildings, and workplaces at the center of town shifted into residential neighborhoods. They avoided the main road until they neared the edge of town.

As they left Woodby, the road out of Thoen spanned before them. Aeryn checked over her shoulder for Imperials and her predicament settled upon her.

She was a fugitive.

14

Lowhoods

Aeryn tried to keep her mind on staying ahead of the authorities.

"Should we get off the road?" Grim asked.

"I don't know my way around these parts," she said. "If we trek to Fieldgate off the path, it'll take us longer. If we stay on the road, we can stay ahead of the Imperials. I don't think they've made it this far."

After an hour, they crested a hill and gazed upon Proimos for the first time.

A mammoth city spread before them in the distance. The road led to Fieldgate through a spattering of farms and up to the south gate. The city was so massive, she couldn't see any other roads leading from it, even from their vantage point.

Aeryn, who had never left Thoen before, had expected to feel something profound upon leaving her home province for the first time. But the sense of significance was dampened by the urgent drive to get out of the area lest she be thrown into jail and executed.

"How populated with soldiers do you think it is?" Grim said as they marched.

"It's a major trading city in the Imperial province. So, a few," Aeryn said. "I'm hoping we can disappear in the crowd, then find the road heading east out of there."

They passed more travelers as they neared the city. Most were on foot, but some creaked past in wagons pulled by teams of oxen. The road was too sparse to hide in a crowd yet.

Closer to the city, a few clusters of Imperials were on patrol. Aeryn held her breath, but the soldiers only barked at them and the other passersby to make way.

Another half a dozen soldiers stood guard on either side of the gate. They watched intently as she and Grim drew near. One of the Imperials gave them an appraising once-over and murmured something to his partner.

Aeryn could feel her pulse in her ears. She swallowed hard and avoided eye contact. Grim's tension seeped from him, but she didn't dare chance a nervous glance in his direction. She hoped he had the sense not to glower.

They approached as casually as possible and crossed halfway through the gate when one of the guards bellowed at them.

"Hey, where do you think you're going? Stop right there." The Imperial, a broad man with close-cropped brown hair and a gap between his two front teeth, strutted toward them. He held a sword loosely in his hand. "I've given you a lawful order. Now, halt."

Eyes wide and heart racing, Aeryn slowed to a stop, Grim beside her.

"Is there a problem, sir?" she asked, as benignly as she could muster.

"Yeah, there's a problem." He planted himself a few feet away and gestured between Aeryn and Grim with his sword. "You're coming through my gate without paying the gate tax."

The tension in her chest relaxed. Of course there would be a gate tax. This was the Imperial province. *They would tax the air you breathe, if they could,* Samuel would murmur when the tax collectors came to town. The Imperials started charging as soon as a person reached adulthood. The humans sometimes resented that the elves, who aged differently, had ten or more years than the humans did before they began paying. Rather than issue a flat age for all citizens, the Empire was willing to accept the temporary delay of ten to fifteen years to keep the peace with the elves. With double the lifespan of a healthy human, they could squeeze a hundred more years of taxes out of them, so it was worth it.

Aeryn reached for her belt pouch. "How much is it?"

"Four gold apiece."

Thinking she misheard, she cocked her head. "Four gold? You mean copper?"

"Four. Gold. Each."

He waited.

Aeryn shared a concerned look with Grim, then said to the officer, "We don't have that kind of money."

A guard nearby shifted his weight and spoke to the one addressing Aeryn. "Nathan, give it up. Let 'em pass."

Let them pass? Did they frequently waive gate taxes, or was there none at all?

The broad Imperial, Nathan, ignored his comrade. He cut his eyes at Grim. "How about that chest piece? Or the axe sticking out of your bag?"

Grim stiffened. "Come and take it. See what happens."

Heat rushed over Aeryn's body. That was the wrong thing to say. Instantly the guards within earshot tensed and reached for their swords.

"Better watch your mouth," Nathan said. "You passed through our gate. Either pay the tax, or there's a nice jail cell waiting for you."

"We'll just leave," Aeryn said, hands raised in a pacifying gesture. They could take the long way around the city. She took a tentative step backward.

"Too late," Nathan said. "You pay, or you sit in a cell until you can pay."

Aeryn's mind raced. This wasn't right. This wasn't legal. But what could they do? They had to get out of here. This Imperial was apparently as rogue as the ones they encountered on the road the day before, and they weren't going to be able to fight their way out of this one if it came to it.

"Tell you what, I'll make you a deal," Nathan said after a moment. "You do me a favor, save me some time, and I'll waive the gate tax."

"What favor?" she asked, wary.

"Relax. I need a delivery made across town. Do it, and you can even keep what they pay you when you arrive."

"And if we don't?" Grim asked.

"Then we arrest you for trying to enter the city illegally. Trust me, girlie, I wouldn't want to double up with some of those prisoners. Been a long time since many of them have seen a woman," Nathan said. He gave Aeryn a lingering appraisal which made her skin crawl. "Make your decision before we make it for you."

"Fine," Aeryn said. "What do you need delivered?"

"Smart girl." Nathan patted his comrade, the guard who suggested Aeryn and Grim be allowed to pass. "Get the crate."

The other man scoffed. "Your dealings, Nathan, not mine."

Nathan scowled at the man, then marched into the gatehouse himself. He emerged a moment later, heaving a wooden crate by its handles on either side. He dropped it at Aeryn's feet.

"This goes to Milo at Lowhoods on Slinger Alley," he said. "Use the back entrance."

"Which way?" Aeryn asked.

"What, you want directions too? Figure it out. I have a gate to guard." Nathan pointed his sword at them and raised his eyebrows. "If you even think about not delivering that crate, I warn you, I will make sure Milo knows who to look for. You'll be lucky if the Imperials get to you before he does."

Aeryn cast a grave look at Grim. She grasped one handle of the crate and he took the other. They hoisted it off the ground and carried it, as quickly as possible, into the city.

The paved streets boiled with more people than Aeryn had ever seen in one place in her life. Due to its proximity to three other regions, the people displayed a variety of physical characteristics, but beige to bronze skin with dark hair and brown eyes seemed to be the dominant feature of the Proimos natives, almost all of which were human.

When they were out of earshot of the guards, Grim spoke over his shoulder to Aeryn. "I don't like this."

"What choice did we have? We don't pay, they lock us up," Aeryn said. "How long do you think it'd take for them to figure out they have two fugitives in custody?"

Grim frowned at a street sign. He bellowed at a merchant on the corner to point them toward Slinger Alley. The merchant gave them an odd look from behind his cart loaded with knick knacks and colored candles, but directed them deeper into the city, bearing east.

"I'm more concerned about why he's willing to forgo payment," Aeryn said. "Especially when he was so keen on extorting us."

"Worth it to him," Grim said. "We'll probably get paid less than he would, which helps this Milo. Now Milo owes Nathan a favor."

"I guess that makes sense."

They lugged the crate through crowded streets which grew dirtier by the block. Trash lined the road. Half the street lamps had broken glass. Run-down, partially boarded buildings stood too close together. The air reeked of onions and putrid water. The people they passed weren't much better. Most appeared dirty, and all looked poor. Several eyed Aeryn and Grim with seemingly nefarious interest.

They cut through a section of streets less populated with loitering and traffic. As they turned a corner, a man's desperate cries made them draw to a sudden stop.

Three men in Imperial garb hauled a manacled prisoner down an alley, barking orders. "Shut up! Stop struggling and march."

The shackled man noticed Aeryn and Grim turn onto the street. In a renewed frenzy, he yelled all the louder.

"Help me! They aren't really Imperials!" His wild, terrified eyes fixed on Grim and Aeryn and his pleas grew frantic. "They're not Imperials!"

Grim hesitated for only a moment. He released his end of the crate, which thunked onto the ground. He let the pack fall from his shoulders, and reached for his axe. "Aeryn, you with me?"

Aeryn's heart seized. The men in Ravenwood and the officers on the road to Woodby gave her no choice but to fight back.

This was different.

But who yells that the men in uniform were imposters, unless they really were? How could she remain idle while these supposed guards dragged this man away?

This could've been her. It could've been Grim.

For an answer, she dropped her end of the crate and reached for her bow.

One of the guards turned to see who the prisoner was screaming for, just as Aeryn and Grim armed themselves. He hollered at them. "Stay where you are!"

Aeryn nocked and aimed her bow at the guard. Maybe the threat of an arrow in the chest would be persuasive enough for the imposters to stand down.

"Let him go, now," she said in her most commanding voice.

"They killed for those uniforms!" The prisoner struggled

against the grip of the other two guards. He continued to scream for help as they dragged him between the buildings. "They aren't who they say they are!"

Grim marched toward the guard at the mouth of the alley, axe cocked for action. "She gave you an order."

The guard took a nervous step away from Grim and reached for his sword. "Get back!"

The man slashed.

Grim blocked with the handle of his axe and parried, turning the weapon upon his attacker. Barely slowing down, Grim dislodged his axe from the man's body as the guard hit the ground in a pool of his own blood. Aeryn flinched, her throat closing up. She pulled her eyes off the slain man as Grim pursued the others down the alley. Thinking fast, she rushed after him.

In the alley, the yells and the chaos of full-out combat assaulted her ears. Battle fury, the likes of which she'd only glimpsed yesterday, exploded from Grim as he engaged the next nearest man. The third guard noticed Aeryn, but thrust the prisoner aside and rushed at Grim, considering him the biggest threat.

Aeryn released her arrow. With rapid reflexes, she drew another and sent it cutting through the air. Both sunk into the man who surged to stab Grim while he was engaged. The man fell before he got close enough to prick him. The guard entangled with Grim lasted only a few moments longer before he met his fate.

Grim yanked his axe free. His chest heaved as he surveyed for the next threat, eyes wild with battle-focus. It had only lasted a few moments, but it was over.

Aeryn lowered her bow as Grim marched a few steps in her direction at the mouth of the alley. She felt cold, almost numb, like she was standing outside herself, unable to see anything but the violence they just wrought. Grim grabbed the first fallen guard and dragged him by the shirt out of the open.

She noticed a gash on his arm, which brought her back to herself. "Grim, you're bleeding."

He regarded the wound. "Later. Prisoner first."

Aeryn poked a head out of the alleyway to appraise the road. The street was still empty, but it wouldn't be for long. Aeryn noticed a threadbare curtain shift in one of the many windows of a nearby three-story slum along this stretch. A hundred pairs of eyes could've seen them behind those windows. Aeryn slunk back into the shadows.

What have I done? The thought entered her mind for the second time in two days. Afraid at what was becoming of her, Aeryn's head sloshed. She reached a hand to steady herself against the brick wall.

She had just killed someone. Not in self-defense. Not by accident. Intentionally, because a stranger claimed they were imposters, like the Cords in Ravenwood. Her eyes went unfocused for a moment, then landed on the hand of one of the fallen guards.

A twisted rope, dyed black, with a metal clasp encircled his wrist.

Despite the carnage in the alley, and the horror of what had just happened, a sense of relief plunged through her, seeping into her bones. The sudden confirmation made her feel weak.

Cords were real. Granted, this meant the Loom had a presence in Fieldgate. But it also meant Grim told her the truth. He really had been taken, enslaved as a child by a criminal organization with a wider reach than Aeryn imagined possible. She hadn't killed Imperials in Ravenwood after all, but despicable slavers.

Together, she and Grim stopped them from hurting someone else. That made it more bearable.

As Grim checked over the prisoner, Aeryn crouched beside the fallen man.

"Grim." She held up the man's wrist. "They're in Fieldgate."

His eyes landed on the black cord and his face hardened. "See if you can find keys."

The prisoner, a gaunt middle-aged man in rags with stringy dark hair and a scraggly beard, broke into a cry of relief.

"Oh, thank you! You saved me. You believed me," the man said as Aeryn searched. "They were going to take me to...to..."

"Are you hurt?" Grim asked the man.

"I'll be alright." The prisoner's voice quavered.

Aeryn found a set of keys dangling from the belt of the second body she checked. She unhooked the keyring with shaky fingers and fumbled through the keys for one that looked like it fit the manacles. She crouched beside the prisoner. "Let me see your hands."

The man presented his wrists. The first two keys Aeryn tried didn't fit, but the third clicked in the lock and the manacles popped open.

He rubbed his wrists, and looked at Aeryn and then Grim with strange, amber-colored eyes. "Thank you. You saved my life."

Grim gave the man a hand up. "Be careful."

"Of course," the man said with a vigorous nod. "Of course. I will not forget this when things are set right. Thank you."

He fled.

"Grim, are you alright?" Aeryn asked.

"The Loom is in the city," Grim said, his face taught with concern. "We have to get out of here."

"Would they recognize you if they spotted you?"

"It depends how far word of the revolt traveled. They might have a description." He looked at his knuckles. "Maybe I should get some gloves."

"Grim, did you know these were Cords when you attacked?" she asked.

He thought for a moment, and looked Aeryn in the eye. "I believed the man."

She nodded. "Me too."

He jerked his chin toward the carnage at their feet. "Let's search the bodies. See if we can find anything valuable."

Aeryn bent beside the man pierced by her arrows. They may've been slavers, but looting the bodies of the dead still made her feel like a reprobate. She scraped a gold coin, four silvers, and six coppers from his belt pouch. Grim checked the other bodies, and pointed out the black cord around each of their wrists.

"Wait," Aeryn said before they stepped into the street again. "Your arm."

She retrieved a bandage from her side pocket and wrapped it around the cut. Blood soaked through immediately.

"It can wait," Grim said. "Let's get rid of this crate, get paid, and get out." He shouldered his pack. They lifted the cargo and hurried on their way before anyone came down the lane.

They made two more turns, each down increasingly seedy roads. Broken bottles, dirty rags, and food scraps littered the road. Apart from dilapidated tenement houses, they passed an alchemist's shop with windows so dirty it was impossible to see inside, three different pubs with an assortment of unfriendly-looking patrons loitering outside, and a brothel a few doors down from Lowhoods. Unkempt ladies in low-cut, off-the-shoulder dresses with snarled hair eyeballed Grim. One made some remarks about taking good care of him. He kept his gaze fixed forward and ignored them.

Lowhoods was a gambling house, and surprisingly busy for so early in the morning. They heaved the crate down a narrow gap between the buildings to the back alley. There was one door.

Aeryn freed a hand from their load and banged it with her fist. A small window in the door slid open. A pointed, dirty face scowled at them.

"Who're ya? Whadda ya want?" the man in the window said. Rancid breath rolled out of the window and hit Aeryn in the face.

Aeryn cringed. "Delivery for Milo. From Nathan."

The dirty-faced man regarded Aeryn, Grim, and the crate. He slid the window shut with a clatter. A moment later, the door swung inward.

The man wore a black leather vest with no shirt underneath. He looked like he hadn't bathed in a month. He held the door with one hand and gestured to a dark stairway to his left. "Right down there."

Grim led the way down, and paused at the door at the bottom of the stairs. The dirty man in the vest trotted after them, then maneuvered himself to the front of the procession. He pushed the door open into a room lit with several hanging lanterns.

"Milo, delivery."

Four men conferred around a rough-hewn wooden table littered with parchment. One of them, a bald man with a scarred lip waved them in with a flick of the hand. He appeared to be in charge.

"From Nathan, I presume?" he said.

"That's what they says," the dirty man said. He entered the room behind Aeryn and Grim, shut the door, and locked it.

"Set it on the table." Milo collected the parchments to make room for the crate.

The whole room was piled shoulder-high with crates and barrels of various sizes. When Milo snapped his fingers at one of the other men at the table, the man retrieved a crowbar from atop a stack nearby.

"I suppose Nathan mentioned I'd pay you?" Milo said as Aeryn and Grim heaved the crate onto the table.

"Yes," Aeryn said.

The associate placed the crowbar in Milo's hand. Aeryn's eyes fell to the black band tattooed around Milo's wrist, then the cord dangling from every other wrist in the room.

Aeryn's mouth dried and she took a step backward toward Grim, bumping into him. He noticed it too. Grim's hand moved to his sword hilt and they inched toward the door as Milo pried the crate open with a crack.

Milo dropped the iron bar heavily onto the table beside the crate, then dug inside. He lifted a navy Imperial uniform, shook it out and set it on the table beside the crowbar.

Then another, and another.

"Looks like they're all here," Milo said after rooting to the bottom of the box. He fixed Aeryn and Grim with a cold stare. "Your payment."

Milo waved his hand at his associates.

"Kill them."

15

The Silver Shadow

Aeryn didn't have time to grab her bow. The men rushed upon them, swords drawn. She pulled her father's shortsword and swung wildly, deflecting a swipe from the nearest attacker with dumb luck.

She screamed, and Grim surged into action with a roar, to take on his own assailant.

Driven back, she slashed wide and clipped the man in the arm. He yelled and redoubled his attack.

She was no good with a sword. She needed her bow.

She dodged a stab and brought her blade down upon his shoulder, into his neck. Horrorstruck, she pulled her blade free with a wet scrape against bone, and he collapsed. His cohort nearly lost his footing as he stumbled over him. From a few feet away, Grim took the opportunity to run him through.

On the other side of the table, Milo's eyes darted around the room, and Aeryn became suddenly aware that he was the only Cord still standing. Grim had dispatched his attackers more quickly than she had the one. Milo drew a longsword, and stepped around the table to swing at Aeryn, who was closest. She flew out of the way and screamed again.

A chair flew across the room, breaking against Milo's body. Milo shielded himself as Grim rushed at him. One swipe and his bald head rolled across the ground, while his body fell at Grim's feet. Blood splattered Aeryn's clothes and arms, and pooled on the cellar floor.

Before Aeryn had time to react, Grim grabbed her by the elbow. "C'mon!"

The door was open. He took the stairs two at a time. Aeryn flew after him like a shot into the back alley.

Side by side, they dashed along the narrow path behind Lowhoods and cut between a pair of buildings, their packs clunking violently as they ran.

Shouts emitted from behind, igniting the fire in Aeryn's legs. The commotion had drawn the attention of those in the upper level of the gambling house. The smack of many feet behind them grew louder.

Aeryn chanced a backward glance. Four men with drawn swords flew around the corner in pursuit.

"They're behind us!" she cried. She led the way down another alley, and then another, Grim at her heels.

The yells and pounding of feet drew nearer. She pumped her arms and legs, pushing herself to go faster. In this dense, unfamiliar city, she had no idea where she was going. As they raced down another lane, she scanned for any way of escape, any place to turn, or hide.

"Aeryn!"

Grim took a sharp right and she ran after him. He made a quick left into an alcove where he stopped, dropped his pack, and unhooked his axe.

"We're going to have to fight," he said. "Get ready."

Aeryn dropped her bag beside his and readied her bow. She aimed for the corner, and took a steadying breath, prepared to skewer the first Cord who took the turn.

The gallop of feet crescendoed. The first man flew around the corner and Aeryn sent an arrow into his chest. He hit the ground, and the man directly after stumbled over him. He tumbled onto the cobbled street with a crack.

The other two Cord's darted around the corner, avoiding the collision.

Axe in hand, Grim tensed, ready to charge, when a mechanical shuttering sound drew their attention. One of the Cords staggered and fell, pierced in the heart by a crossbow bolt.

A few paces up the lane, Wolfe lowered his crossbow to reload the second bolt he held in his teeth. His scarred face was serious with deadly focus.

Grim burst forth and cut down the last Cord still upright. At this, the one who tripped over his comrade scrambled to his feet and attempted to flee. He made it only a few feet before Grim stopped him for good.

Ophelia emerged, and trotted over to Aeryn. "Are either of you injured?"

"What are you doing here?" Aeryn said, looking from Ophelia to Wolfe. "I mean, I'm grateful, but how did...?"

"No time. Talk later," Wolfe said. "Grab your bags and follow me."

Wolfe led the way up the narrow street, away from the pile

of dead criminals. Aeryn and Grim didn't argue. They shouldered their belongings and followed at a trot. Ophelia took the rear.

A few blocks away, Wolfe steered them behind a shuttered, two-story house with a flat roof. He unlocked the heavy back door and waved them inside, holding the door for light while Ophelia lit a lamp.

"What is this place?" Aeryn asked.

"Safe lodging," Wolfe said.

While he secured the many locks, Ophelia ushered Aeryn and Grim through the neat kitchen into the next room. Between the kitchen and living area, a ladder led to the second floor. Bare walls enclosed a small living space with a woven blue rug, a simple couch, low table, and two chairs. A hallway to the left led to a closet, and Aeryn presumed based on the layout, a front door.

Weaver's high-pitched creaky calls carried through the one shuttered window.

"You'll be safe here in case your pursuers come around," Ophelia said. "Thankfully, we can hear the Imperials coming four blocks away, bossing everyone out of their paths. There's a trap door under the mat where you can hide, if need be."

"How did you know the Imperials are looking for us?" Aeryn asked, half-expecting Ophelia to reference the stars in her answer.

But the airy-fairy act had been dropped for a businesslike, no nonsense demeanor.

"You just slaughtered several men. Cords or not, it's the Imperial's duty to look into these things," Ophelia said. "Besides, we spoke with the group you two skirted in Woodby."

Aeryn and Grim exchanged a tense glance.

"Relax," Wolfe said as he sank into a wooden chair opposite the couch. "We told 'em ya're heavily bearded. Why don't ya sit down?"

Grim scratched the stubble on his cheek. He remained standing. "You two know about the Loom?"

Wolfe scoffed.

"'Course we do." He turned his face to give them a better view of the scar which ran from the corner of his mouth nearly to his ear. "They gave me this. Took these too."

He held his right hand to show the missing ends of his fingers. Leaning against the back of his chair he unhooked a hip flask. An unfocused, disquieted look entered his eye.

"Took a lot more than that." He took a swig. The jovial man they'd met in The Laughing Boar was gone for the moment. "I see ya didn't take my advice about the gloves, ya stubborn Northerner. Here."

He reached into his back pocket and retrieved a pair of olive colored gloves with open fingertips. He tossed them onto the table.

"Did you two follow us here?" Aeryn asked.

"Yes and no," Ophelia said as she took the chair beside Wolfe. "We hoped to find you, but didn't know exactly where to look. We...had a little help."

Wolfe snickered and patted his belly. "Go on, admit it, Fifi. The bone dice don't lie."

"*Bone dice* told you where to find us?" Aeryn asked. "You mean, the lucky tooth?"

"Apparently," Ophelia said with a hint of annoyance.

"Why?" Grim asked. "What do you want?"

Ophelia folded her hands primly atop her lap. She gestured for the pair to sit, and waited to speak until they had settled on the wicker couch.

"We work with a covert organization called Silver Shadow." She hooked a thumb around a delicate silver chain around her neck and showed them the round pendant. Etched on the silver disk was a wing of some kind, with four stars along its edge. Wolfe pulled a similar pendant out of his shirt collar. "I don't suppose you've heard of us?"

Grim slowly shook his head.

"No matter. The Shadow was formed by an order of monks in Noemar during the war with the goal of undermining the Loom," Ophelia said as she tucked the pendant back into her blouse. "I'm not sure what you're doing so far south, but we can connect you with the Silver Shadow spies who specialize in helping you reach the Enclave. They're called the Chain."

"What's the Enclave?" Grim said.

"Where the remaining Baldomar live, of course."

"Remaining Baldomar?" Grim glanced at Aeryn.

"Yes. The Shadow helped those who survived the hand-hunt disappear," she said. "The Enclave was established as a place where your people can live in safety."

"The hand hunt?" Aeryn said, recalling Grim's story about

Herm and the warning to keep his fingers covered, lest he lose them. From the look on Grim's face, he was remembering the same thing.

"The Loom's effort to eradicate your people, Grim."

Grim leaned forward in his seat and he pointed to the marks on his knuckles. "You're saying I'm a Baldomar...?"

Wolfe took another sip from his flask. "Yup."

"...and the Loom is connected to killing off my people...?"

Wolfe dipped his chin in the affirmative. "Responsible for it."

Grim's face darkened momentarily, but he continued. "There are others like me, with runes on their knuckles, somewhere in hiding?"

"I'm truly surprised this is news to you, Grim," Ophelia said. "Didn't your parents have runes?"

"I don't remember my parents," Grim said. "The Loom took me from my family and sent me to work in the mines in Illwali when I was eight years old. I was there for fifteen years. I don't remember anything before then."

Silence fell over the room.

"Ya're lucky the Loom didn't realize what ya are," Wolfe said. "Or they'd've lopped your hands off."

"But why?" he asked.

"Because there's dragon magic in them runes."

The lines across Grim's forehead appeared. "What?"

Ophelia cleared her throat. "How much do you know about the war, or the Baldomar's part in it?"

Grim rubbed his brow as he recalled.

"Aeryn told me it was a hundred years ago. Conflict between groups and with dragons. The Imperials united the people and fought back the dragons to near-extinction. I know that the Baldomar were a warrior clan, but I thought they were all dead." He caught Aeryn's eye. "Or, mostly dead."

"So...ya two don't know much," Wolfe said.

"Excuse you," Aeryn said. "My father fought in the war."

"So did I," Wolfe said, unoffended.

Aeryn squinted at him. "That's not possible."

"Why not?"

"You're human. It ended a hundred years ago," she said. "You look like you might be forty or fifty."

Wolfe slapped his knee and chuckled. "Hear that, Fifi? I look young." He reached into his mouth and plucked out his lucky tooth. He rolled it onto the table. "That's why. A blessing. Or a curse, depending how ya look at things."

"Do you at least know about the kings and queens of the peaks?" Ophelia asked.

Aeryn shook her head. "Who are they?"

"They are, or were, the ruling dragons. Very old, very powerful. Very different from the feral beasts of elvish scarytales," she said. "The King of the West was a glorious purple dragon named Malachai."

Wolfe scoffed and took another swig from his flask.

Ophelia shot him a look. "It's not blasphemous to call him what he was. He was the embodiment of discipline and order. Bold and charismatic by all accounts. He attracted zealous admirers who worshiped him. They called themselves The Loyal Ones Of Malachai, or the Loom."

Satisfied that she had everyone's full attention, Ophelia straightened her posture and assumed the manner of speech Aeryn had heard a hundred times. For the elves, storytelling, especially true stories, was an important part of their culture, and Ophelia assumed the posture and tone of a story-teller now.

"Malachai came to crave the worship of humans in particular," she said. "He was especially harsh toward those in nearby lands who would not bow the knee. He used cruelty and cunning to exploit the infighting amongst the peoples in order to consolidate power. Dragons under his dominion, along with his cult, sowed chaos throughout the land. Finally, Silversaar, the King of the North, and the embodiment of wisdom, made a controversial decision."

Ophelia's eyes brightened as she said his name, and she leaned forward.

"Silversaar had befriended a particular clan of humans, the Baldomar. They were fearless and determined to stand against Malachai. Silversaar used his magic to impart a gift. The unique set of symbols on your hands, Grim, are the remnants of that gift. There is magic in the runes. Silversaar caused the people to learn them. The war shifted.

"However, this enraged Malachai. He saw this as a betrayal, an affront to order. Before this, only dragons could use magic. He decided to make Silversaar pay."

Ophelia's expression grew somber.

"He directed his cult to target the Baldomar without

mercy. Rune Reapers collected their knuckles like trophies. Malachai even killed Silversaar's mate. He positioned himself for victory.

"Silversaar was grief-stricken. Seeing no other way to end the war, he used the last of his magic to bind Malachai in the humble form of a man. Silversaar disappeared, taking the knowledge of the runes with him.

"The Loom, for a time, continued Malachai's mission. They sought knowledge of the runes themselves, believing magic would restore their lord. They believed they'd find this knowledge hidden in the belly of a mountain, where most powerful dragons like to hide their treasure. They never did. Over time, with the object of their worship gone, the Loom shifted its interests to other criminal endeavors. Smuggling, assassinations, slavery...they didn't discriminate. I'm afraid the world has been a very dangerous place for Baldomar, even after Malachai's fall. Those who survived went into hiding."

Grim listened intently. His expression was grave. From the set of his jaw and the bend in his brown, Aeryn knew he was turning everything over in his mind.

Ophelia's voice softened. "We are on your side. Wolfe and I can help you reach your people, if you'll let us."

Grim remained quiet for a long moment, then met Aeryn's eyes. There were things he wanted to discuss.

"Can you give us a few minutes?" he said to Ophelia.

"Of course." Ophelia stood and offered them a sincere smile before she followed Wolfe into the kitchen. "You needn't make a decision right now. If you'd like to sleep on it, you'll be safe here."

Grim waited for Ophelia and Wolfe to exit the room, then turned his attention to Aeryn. "Do you trust those two?"

"I think if they meant us harm, we'd be dead," she said. "Or in an Imperial jail cell right now."

Grim mulled this over for a moment and dipped his head in agreement. "Do you believe their story?"

"I think I do."

"You know, that Imperial at the gate sent us to Cords, knowing it'd mean our deaths," Grim said.

"I know," she said, feeling cold in her belly. *How closely intertwined were the Imperials and the Loom anyway?* "You think he recognized you?"

"I don't know. Maybe." Serious and contemplative, Grim stared at his hands, folded in front of him. "I have a clan."

Aeryn tucked one foot under the other leg and shifted to look at him directly. "Grim, if your family is still alive, they're probably at the Enclave."

Grim continued to stare at his hands, but his eyes grew unfocused and his frown deepened. "The Loom needs to be stopped."

Aeryn watched him with a nudge of concern. She didn't want to think about the Loom, the faces of the slain Cords, or the trauma and violence they'd wrought upon her life. But that was his every waking moment, for years. His thirst for justice was understandable, but a renewed interest in vengeance wouldn't end well for either of them, especially considering the breadth and capabilities of the Loom.

Grim was smart.

He had to know that.

"Grim, think about your family," she said, counting on his better judgment.

He pulled his gaze off his knuckles, conflict knotted in his brow when he met her face.

Of course he knew.

It pained him.

The sight made a surge of feelings well within her. She wanted to reach out and catch him in a hug, and beg him not to choose the path of destruction.

Instead, she stayed where she was and swallowed the tightness in her throat. "We'll find them. I promise."

"Excuse me, Aeryn?" Ophelia poked her head into the room. "If I went to the roof to speak with Weaver, do you think he'd settle down, or consent to come indoors? I'm concerned his persistent squawking will draw attention."

Sure enough, Weaver's racket had continued. He was flustered and worried.

"You can try," Aeryn said. "If he doesn't settle, I'll talk to him. He won't come indoors, though, so don't waste your time."

Ophelia took the ladder to the second floor where she could access the flat roof. Wolfe shuffled into the room bearing a tray with a kettle and cups. He set the platter noisily on the table and handed Grim and Aeryn each a mug.

"Tea. 'Cause ya've been in an ordeal."

He produced his hip flask and poured a dollop of its smelly

liquid into his own steaming mug.

"I like my tea a little stronger," he said, settling in his own chair with a snicker.

Aeryn sniffed her cup, detecting only mint. The flavor was unusual, but soothing. She eased against the back of the couch, and her eyes fell to the splatter of blood on her pikdeer leggings. A strangled, sunken feeling pulled at her insides. She couldn't look away. The moments she made her lethal decisions replayed in her thoughts. She saw their faces in her mind, and watched their deaths. She heard their yells, smelled their sweat and the coppery scent of spilled blood. She felt the press of the bowstring against her calloused fingertips...

"Lady Aeryn."

Wolfe's heartland drawl interrupted her thoughts, drawing her back into the room. Her eyes fluttered, and she gave him her attention.

"Watching someone die in front of ya, knowing ya had a part in it, is a heavy thing," he said. "There'd be something wrong with ya if ya didn't feel that."

Aeryn's throat tightened painfully. She bobbed her head. The coldness in her limbs was a contrast to the sinking feeling in her middle. She pulled the mug of tea closer to herself, inhaling the steam.

Wolfe leaned forward. "Those were not innocent men. This is the Loom. It's always your life or theirs. If they didn't kill ya, they woulda dragged ya off, sold ya to the highest bidder, or stuck ya in one of their brothels, and not before each of 'em got a piece of ya first. Ya two did what ya had to."

The frankness with which Wolfe spoke wasn't meant to excuse or mitigate what happened. He simply stated it as fact, gleaned from the experience as a seasoned veteran who'd seen what would've happened, and somehow still has a soul.

A soul medicated by strong drink, but a soul nonetheless.

Aeryn looked to Grim, who was watching her.

His face was awash in a mixture of emotions, but one of them was agreement. Wolfe's words resonated with him. She couldn't pin down what weighed heaviest on his mind, but he was handling their ordeal better than she was in this moment. Maybe he was just accustomed to the heinousness of the Loom, or maybe he'd cope in his dreams. The nightmares which shook him from sleep had lessened over their stay in Ravenwood, but perhaps they were going to start again. Maybe they would for her too.

Grim was a harder person than her, but he had a soul too. As he looked at Aeryn, she more fully realized the level of trust he not only placed in her, but which she was placing in him. She had an ally to count on in this dangerous world, and she took a measure of comfort in that. Knowing she was that ally for someone else strengthened her.

"Wolfe, where is the Enclave?" Grim asked.

"In Noemar," Wolfe said.

"What's it like?" Aeryn asked.

"Noemar? Cold."

"No, the Enclave."

Wolfe took a long drink from his mug. "Also cold."

Aeryn settled deeper into the couch and took another sip, and another, then drained the cup. She sighed as its refreshing warmth spread through her body. Her thoughts grew fuzzy and eyelids drooped.

The last thing she heard before she passed out was Grim's empty cup clunk against the floor.

16

The Rune Reaper

"Where is he?"

The Rune Reeper's belt jangled with each heavy step. As he strode across the parlor of the gambling house, severed fingers swayed from the black cord around his neck.

Three men, low-level scum, trembled in silence as they avoided looking directly at him. Ulfur could smell the terror seeping from their pores.

"You were supposed to have had him by now," he said. "You said you tracked him here. So where is he?"

"He–he got away, Sir," said one of the men with a metal stud in his nose. "We found the guards slaughtered."

"He got away," Ulfur said.

The Cords fell quiet.

Ulfur paced silently, seething, then grabbed the nearest Cord, a skinny man with a vest and no shirt who smelled particularly foul. Shirtless yelped as Ulfur wrapped him in a headlock, and with one swift motion, snapped his neck.

"Imagine my displeasure," Ulfur said, his voice conversational as he allowed the lifeless body to collapse on the floor. "I received word to hurry to Fieldgate. When I arrived, I learned he'd gotten away. Again. In addition, *half of the Fieldgate cell is dead.*"

Unleashing a roar, Ulfur overturned a nearby table. The

remaining two Cords quailed as Ulfur broke off a table leg and stalked toward them.

"I want an explanation," he said, his voice elevated and menacing. "Did his powers come back?"

"We—we think he had help," Nose Stud said.

"Enlighten me."

The door swung wide and one of Ulfur's men dragged a prostitute inside by the hair. He pushed her forward. The woman cursed at him, standing straighter and smoothing her shabby dress. Her eyes were bloodshot, and she had bruises over her arms.

"This whore says she saw something," the hunter said.

Ulfur lowered the table leg and let it clatter to the floor. He looked the woman up and down. Her gaze darted from Ulfur's one milky eye to his grotesque necklace. She blanched, and hugged her arms to herself. She took the tiniest step away.

"I mighta saw somethin'..." she said, looking anywhere but at him.

Ulfur's mouth curled into a faint smile. He slowly crossed the room. When he reached out his hand, she recoiled, but he caught her. He pressed only his fingertips against her scalp.

Cold seeped from his touch. She screamed for a brief moment, then her breath caught. Her face contorted.

He stroked the fingers around his neck, each marked with a symbol he found unique and useful. His hand brushed the symbol allowing him to worm through her memory. He felt its power leak into his own hand, crawl up his arm, through his mind, and down the other arm, into the hand grasping the woman by the forehead.

Through the prostitute's eyes, he watched a gruesome scene unfold, when something gave him pause.

A little she-elf?

That was unexpected.

What was she, some zealot, or do-gooder?

He wormed deeper into the woman's mind.

The she-elf slipped into the shadowy alley, and the whore stepped away from the window where she'd been watching.

Ulfur pried his hand off the woman's face, leaving blackened prints where his fingertips touched her head. She dropped to her knees, and dissolved in tears.

Ulfur gasped for air and his eyelids drooped. He swayed, then caught himself, grabbing onto the necklace. His muscles felt heavy and depleted. Using the runes this way drained him of energy. It always did. But this was an extraordinary circumstance.

"Ready my carriage," he said to the hunter, his voice gravelly. "Find out what you can about the wood elf. Alert our men at the gates. She doesn't leave this city. She'll lead us to him."

He lumbered stiffly toward the door following his hunter toward the waiting carriage.

"Where...where are you going?" Nose Stud asked.

"To summon our forces across Noemar," Ulfur said. "He's loose."

17

Noemar

Aeryn's eyes fluttered open. Her body jostled in rhythm with the clatter of wheels on a bumpy road and the jingle of horse tackle. Her head throbbed. *Where am I?*

With a hand to her temple, she eased herself upright. Grim lay beside her in the back of a covered wagon. He was unconscious, and his skin had a grayish cast.

She strained her eyes.

Was he breathing?

Without warning, a wave of nausea rolled over her. She threw herself toward the flap at the rear of the wagon, leaned her upper body out, and retched. The bitterness of bile and sour taste of stomach acid mingled in her mouth.

The wagon lurched to a stop.

Her empty stomach contorted again. She gagged and hacked. A slender woman in a blue skirt emerged in Aeryn's peripheral.

"I'm sorry, dear. I know it's unpleasant," said a familiar female voice. The person held Aeryn's hair back as she finished another round of vomit.

"Ophelia?" Aeryn blinked as the brunette elf came into focus. She wiped her mouth with the back of her hand, and remembered Grim's motionless body. "Oh gods!"

Aeryn clambored to his side, and pressed her ear to his chest. His heartbeat was near imperceptible. She grabbed him by his shirt and shook.

"Grim, wake up!" She shook him again, more desperate than before, as her voice thickened. "*Get up!*"

"Aeryn, he's fine," Ophelia said. "I wouldn't shake him. It's a nasty shock waking from Trystal's Tease."

Aeryn turned on her. "What is that?"

"It's the substance discovered by the alchemist Trystal Tevane, which put you to sleep for the last four days."

"Four days? When did…" Aeryn's head swirled back in time for the last thing she remembered.

The tea.

Grim drew a sudden breath. He reached for his head, then promptly turned over to vomit. Wolfe peered inside from his perch at the driver's seat. He grimaced and rummaged for a bucket for Grim.

Aeryn's voice rose, hoarse. "You drugged us?"

"To be precise, it's a type of poison," Ophelia said as she climbed into the wagon from the rear. "But no need for alarm. I'm a poisoner, and very well-practiced. You two will be fine."

"Poison?" Aeryn said, starting to feel panicked. "Who are you people?"

Grim retched again.

Their belongings, including their weapons, lay piled along the side of the wagon bed. Aeryn lunged for her hunting knife. She brandished it at Wolfe at the head of the wagon, then Ophelia at the rear.

Quick as a wasp, Ophelia grasped Aeryn by the wrist, precisely triggering the muscles in Aeryn's hand to seize.

Aeryn released the blade involuntarily. She swore and rubbed her wrist.

"You will not pull a knife on me in my wagon. Thank you," Ophelia said. "Sit."

Even as Ophelia spoke, Aeryn's ears buzzed and her vision grew spotty. Her head had the sloshing feeling it always got after spinning on the rope swing at her parents house. Her shaky legs buckled beneath her.

"It was the only way to get you out of the city," Ophelia said. "Imperials were checking every person and cart to come in and out of Fieldgate. The poison placed you into a deep sleep, mimicking death. Wolfe and I posed as grieving family members who needed to bury our relatives outside the city."

Grim sat upright, resting his forearms on his bent knees while panting.

Aeryn took a few more deep breaths through her nose as her vision cleared. Grim's color returned, but he kept his eyes shut, looking just as miserable as Aeryn felt a few moments earlier.

As soon as Ophelia came into focus again, she fixed her with a dark look. "You drugged and transported us without our permission. Do you realize how violating that is?"

"I understand you're upset. But the longer we delayed, the riskier things grew for everyone," Ophelia said. "Your lives are not the only ones at stake."

Aeryn's hard stare eased a smidgeon. She hadn't considered the possible danger Ophelia and Wolfe accepted by helping them, if that's really what they were doing.

They had confronted several Cords in Fieldgate to save them, and ushered them towards refuge. They risked arrest by smuggling them out of the Imperial's hands.

But poisoning?

"If you're struggling to trust us, then look." Ophelia pointed. "Your weapons, your money, all your belongings are there. If we meant you harm, why would we let you keep any of that?"

"Ya'll need food in your bellies." Wolfe stepped into the wagon bed, knelt beside Aeryn, and produced a hard biscuit from his pocket.

She scoffed. "If you think I'm taking food from you..."

Wolfe gave her a tired look. He broke off the corner, popped it in his mouth, and held the rest out. "Look, not poison."

Aeryn watched him swallow before she took the biscuit, broke it, and passed half to Grim. Even with the lingering bitterness in her mouth, chewing the biscuit felt like salvation. Energy seeped into her body like rain to thirsty roots. It wasn't nearly enough to fill her, but her growling stomach settled. Her simmering ire cooled.

Grim finished eating, rubbed his temple, and winced. "Where are we?"

"About a half day from Fogness March in Noemar," Wolfe said.

Aeryn started. "We're in Noemar?"

"Yep. Gone almost nonstop. Pippa and Hugh need rest,

but they don't sleep like people do." Wolfe jerked his thumb toward the front of the wagon. "Them's the horses."

The chill in the air made more sense now. A brisk wind passed through the gap in the canvas of the covered wagon, and made Aeryn rub the goosebumps on her bare arms.

"My apologies, Lady Aeryn. I know it's a long way from Thoen," Wolfe said. "We can see about getting ya back home once things settle down, but it wasn't safe to stay."

Aeryn shook her head vigorously and regretted it. "No. I promised I'd help Grim find his family. We were planning to come here together before everything…"

"…Went to pot?"

"Yeah."

"Well, that works."

A sudden thought made her gasp. "Where's Weaver? Did you leave him in Fieldgate?"

"He's followed the whole time." Ophelia said, her eyes smiling. "Usually perched atop the wagon, but he's taken a liking to Hugh."

"Is our food and water still here?" Grim asked.

Ophelia handed them their waterskins, then produced two small loaves of bread from a basket beside her, along with a pouch of nuts. "You'll find your food in your bag where you left it. Here. Start mild, and don't eat too much, too quickly, or you'll make yourself sick again. Grim, you had an open gash on your arm. I stitched it when we left Fieldgate, but you'll want to remove those in a week."

"Ya'll have any questions, or can we get rollin' again?"

Wolfe said.

Aeryn and Grim shook their heads. Wolfe wiped the mess off the floor, took Grim's bucket, then climbed onto the driver's bench with Ophelia. With a jolly word and a flick of the reins, the wagon creaked into motion. Aeryn and Grim sat quietly together nibbling the bread as the wagon bounced along. The wagon bed was crowded with blankets, food, tools, and backpacks.

Weaver alighted on the tail of the wagon in the gap between the canvas flaps. He rasped a greeting to Aeryn. Relieved at the sight of him, she dug a seed from her breast pocket and tossed it to him. He snagged it before it hit the ground, then fluttered back to his perch atop the cover.

Aeryn took a deep breath as she chewed. She and Grim were alive. Weaver was here. They were in the North. And despite the manner in which Ophelia and Wolfe got them there, they seemed sincere.

Aeryn nudged Grim. "You alright?"

He snorted. "Hungry. Feel like I got kicked in the head."

They rested and ate as their grogginess wore off. Aeryn's head still ached, and her body felt stiff, but she felt stronger after eating.

After an hour, Wolfe pulled off the road. He peered inside the wagon and grinned. "Breaktime. Why don't ya come outside and see the North."

The cool air enveloped them as they stepped out the back together. It felt crisp and smelled faintly of pine, different from the humidity and grassy, deciduous smells of Thoen. The road cut through a dark green landscape dotted with evergreens and low shrubs. Thin clouds drifted across the gray-blue sky. Snowcapped mountains rose against the skyline in the distance like the points of a crown.

Grim breathed deeply and his face relaxed into the smile of a man who had finally returned home after a long time away. It made Aeryn beam.

Wolfe unlatched the horses, a black mare and a chestnut stallion. Aeryn watched the horses with interest. The animals weren't native to the Southern Forest, but could be found in border villages in the possession of the wealthy. They were beautiful creatures, with powerful, muscular bodies and gentle eyes. She longed to touch their velvety smooth necks.

Instead, Aeryn fished her jacket from the bottom of her backpack, and she and Grim each took the opportunity to change out of their blood stained clothes. Her possum vest survived, but the rest was by now, beyond repair, and she never wanted to see those splatters again. She buried the hide clothing in an abandoned gopher burrow beneath a shrub.

They rested for an hour, then piled into the wagon and continued their journey.

"Got an old friend in the Chain who lives outside of Fogness," Wolfe said. "First stop on the way to the Enclave."

"You're not taking us there directly?" Aeryn asked, trying to remember the conversation back in Fieldgate. Had she missed something?

"Not our post."

"Oh." Aeryn was surprised at the tug of disappointment in her chest. She was just getting used to Wolfe and Ophelia. "What is your post?"

"We're assigned to investigate potential Loom activity around Thoen's border," Ophelia said. "We do a considerable amount of work in Fieldgate."

"...Poisoning?"

"Well, yes. But only bad people."

"And unsuspecting guests in your home?" Grim added.

"There's that too."

"It's too risky for all Shadows to know the Enclave's location," Wolfe said. "That information is reserved for a trusted few, called the Keepers. If ya two're sticking together, then we get ya both to the Chain, and the Chain'll get ya to the Keepers in Goldbur Gren, and they'll bring ya safely to the Enclave."

Grim looked at Aeryn as though to ask, *Are we really doing this?* She gave a small smile and a nod. He dipped his chin in return. "Alright," he said to Wolfe and Ophelia. "Chain it is."

A thought occurred to Aerny. "Wolfe, if you found us with your dice, couldn't they help you find the Enclave?"

He shook his head. "Big difference between finding a small, warded territory hidden somewhere in Noemar, and figuring out which street to turn down when I already know two folk are nearby."

"What do you mean, *warded?*" Grim asked.

"Protected by magic. Runes put in place back when the first generation knew how to use them." Wolfe chuckled and elbowed Ophelia in the ribs. "Like how she asked about my bone dice and not your stars?"

Ophelia rolled her eyes.

They followed a dirt road for twenty minutes beyond a sprawl of modest cabins. Wolfe eased the wagon to a stop in front of a fatigued farmhouse. The windows were shuttered. Smoke puffed from the chimney. A weathered barn with a side yard and a chicken coop stood at the rear of the property. The animals had retreated for the evening.

"Stay in the wagon," Ophelia said. "We'll be right back."

She and Wolfe hopped off the bench. Pulling their collars higher around their necks, they swished through the yard as the chilly breeze ruffled the high grass. Aeryn peered through the tent flap to watch, and made room for Grim to join her.

Wolfe and Ophelia waited at the front door for a full minute before an older human, as weathered as his house, opened the door looking perplexed.

His raised voice carried across the yard. "No."

Wolfe argued, but was too garbled to understand.

"I'm out, that's why," the weathered old man said. "I'm out. You of all folk ought to respect that."

Wolfe argued some more, but Ophelia interrupted. Voices dropped to a normal volume. They spoke for a few moments. When they parted ways, no one looked happy. The old man shut the door hard, and Ophelia and Wolfe marched back to the wagon. They climbed in without a word and drove around the back of the property.

"Aeryn, light the lamp," Ophelia said as they stopped outside the barn. Wolfe hopped down to open the latch and he held the door for Ophelia to drive the wagon inside. Weaver swooped in and perched in the rafters alongside some pigeons.

The barn was dark, with only the glow of the lamp for light. It smelled like hay and livestock. The wind buffeted the rickety walls, forcing its way in through cracks. Though chilly, it provided better shelter against the wind than the wagon cover alone.

Ophelia threw the canvas flaps open, allowing herself the space to sit primly on the wagon's edge. "Change of plans. Our host is unable to help."

Wolfe scoffed. "Unable."

Ophelia drew her mouth into a terse line. "He's permitted us to stay for the night. We leave at sunup for Fogness March. We'll resupply and acquire some proper clothing for the North. Wolfe and I will make contact with a Shadow stationed there who can give us a better idea of how to move you two in the right direction."

Wolfe dug through his belongings and retrieved a bottle of alcohol. He yanked the cork with his teeth and spit it out. He took a swig, then attended to the horses.

Aeryn and Grim unearthed some food from their bags. After a brief supper, they huddled inside the wagon, wrapped in heavy blankets. Ophelia asked Aeryn and Grim how they met, and they shared the bare bones of the story.

"What made you decide to leave Thoen?" Ophelia asked Aeryn.

Aeryn pushed the uncomfortable thoughts of her family's tannery from her mind. Grim held her gaze for a moment, and she offered him a small smile. "I wanted to help Grim find his family."

It wasn't *untrue*, as far as general statements went, but it wasn't the reason she left, and her conscience pricked her for lying again.

She'd committed to it.

There wasn't any going back now.

Wolfe said the wagon was too stuffy and stiff for his old bones, and after drinking half his bottle of liquor, he passed out in a pile of hay. Ophelia spent some time gazing at the night sky through a gap in the shutters, before she curled up in her own pile, loaded with blankets.

Aeryn and Grim each took a side of the wagon bed, with plenty of space between them. The canvas cover trapped some heat, but not much.

It felt like sleeping outside in the winter in Thoen, only colder. The elves' bodies adapted to their natural environments, but one day in Noemar wasn't enough time to adjust after decades of living in a warm climate. She shivered under her covers until she couldn't take it anymore.

"Grim?" The brief whisper hid the shaky quality to her voice.

"Hm?" He grunted, lifting his head to squint at her in the dark.

"Can we sleep back to back? I'm sorry, but I'm freezing,"

she said, her words punctuated by the chatter of her jaw.

"Yeah, it's fine." he said, sounding relieved and not bothering to hide the quaver in his own husky whisper.

"Thank you."

He shifted to the center of the wagon and adjusted himself, turning over, while Aeryn scooted closer, her back to his.

"Oh gods. That's right, you don't have a jacket."

She pressed her back harder against his. With some rearranging of the blankets and the trapped body heat, their shivering lessened within a few minutes. She tried to fall asleep, but despite her fatigue, she now felt very awake.

She could feel him breathing, and knew he wasn't sleeping either. She wondered if he felt awkward sleeping so close. She did, but she tried not to overthink it. They were desperate for warmth, and it was the practical thing to do considering their circumstances. At least by now she trusted him to keep his hands to himself.

She nudged him in the back of the ribs with her elbow. "I'm glad we made it to Noemar."

"Me too," he said. He quieted for a moment. "Thank you."

Aeryn smiled to herself as a warm, pleased feeling spread in her mind. She drifted into a heavy sleep.

Ophelia shook them at sunup. Hungry and cold, they hitched up the horses, and left the barn behind.

"It's important to maintain discretion as you travel, whether with us or the Chain," Ophelia said. "Grim, unless you're in private, keep your gloves on. Aeryn, your manner of dress assimilates well, but I'm afraid there are frightfully few elves in Noemar. You cannot hide what you are, but if you keep your hood up, you might avoid attracting too much attention."

It took an hour to reach Fogness March. The small city was muddy, crowded, and fenced by a wooden stockade. Most townsfolk were tall, broad humans, half of whom were flaxen-haired. A quarter looked like they'd come from Proimos. The appearance of the remaining quarter fell somewhere in between. Aeryn noted a few elves, all of whom stood taller and thicker than Thoenites, with pale skin and dark hair. Ophelia blended in, but Aeryn, being short, tan, and with lighter brown hair stood out as a foreigner. It was like stepping into Merioake, but in reverse.

Their wagon trundled through uneven roads to the market and parked outside of an outfitters.

"Ya'll need proper attire," Wolfe said. "Ya think it's cold now, wait til summer comes to an end. Get some warmer clothes. Ya'll probably want some warmer boots too."

Unlike the outfitter in Thoen, Grim found warm clothing, boots, and a heavy jacket his size with ease. Aeryn found canvas trousers, good against the wind, and a pair of wooly leggings to layer underneath. According to the clerk, the fur-lined boots she chose were designed for older children, but they fit. She also bought a warmer shirt and a wool sweater in yellow, her favorite color, along with gloves and a slouchy hat to cover her ears. It felt odd to dress in anything besides the homemade furry hide clothing she'd grown accustomed to over the last six years. While her remaining pair of pikdeer leggings and possum-fur vest would serve well here, her sleeveless or loose-fitting shirts were now too airy to wear alone.

It was a good thing they raided the belt pouches of the slain Cords in the alley. Ophelia and Wolfe offered to pay, explaining the Shadow allots funds for such needs, but both Grim and Aeryn felt uncomfortable taking the money.

They piled into the wagon, arms loaded with supplies, and Wolfe flicked the reins. He drove along several streets, casually glancing around. After the fourth muddy lane, Ophelia murmured, "You don't remember where it is, do you?"

"It's been over ten years since I've been in Fogness." Wolfe pulled his dice out of his pocket and rolled them on the bench in the empty space between them. He bunched his wiry eyebrows and rolled again.

They turned down another lane and Wolfe smacked his leg.

"Look at that. A confectioner. How about candy?" He glanced over his shoulder and winked.

Ahead, a sign with curly white letters read *Mintbark Confectioners* and dangled from a small building with large front windows.

"By candy," Aeryn asked, "do you mean…"

Ophelia held a finger to her lips for quiet, and nodded once. "But also, candy."

Wolfe directed the horses to stop alongside the building.

"Ya two, stay with the wagon," he said to Aeryn and Grim. He sniffed the air like a hound and they all caught the scent of sausages emanating from the meatseller's cart across the street. "On second thought, rations didn't cut it for me this morning. Now don't be too proud..." He dug in his coin pouch and handed Grim a silver and a few coppers. "Grab sausages for us all while Ophelia and I have a little conversation with the confectioner."

Wolfe and Ophelia entered the shop and exchanged words with a burly, ginger headed man behind the counter. From across the street, Aeryn and Grim had a clear view of them through the storefront window.

As they stood in line at the meat cart, Aeryn scanned the wrists of several passersby. She didn't see any black cords, and relaxed a little. The line moved.

"What's candy?" Grim asked.

"A treat made with sugar or honey. I've only had it once," she said. "At my brother's wedding. His in-laws insisted on importing some for guests."

They stepped forward in line.

"What's it like?" Grim asked.

"An elvish wedding, or candy?"

"...Candy."

"Sweeter than you might expect."

The array of meats made Aeryn's stomach groan, vocalizing so loudly Grim cast her an amused glace. After purchasing the steaming food, they waited for a gap in traffic to cross the road.

Halfway across and without warning, Grim yelled as if in pain. He plowed into Aeryn, knocking the food out of her hands. He stumbled to one knee, and dropped the remaining meat in the muddy street.

"What's wrong with you?" Aeryn staggered, but kept her

balance.

Face strained, he held his gloved hands in front of him. "*My hands are on fire.*"

His hands looked fine.

An oncoming carriage maintained its speed, rattling toward them. In a hurry, she wrapped her arm around his shoulder. "Let me help you."

He tried to stand, but staggered again. "Augh!" He gritted his teeth. His body tightened involuntarily. "Aeryn, they're burning!"

The carriage halted abruptly only a few feet away. The horse champed its bit and snorted hot breath at them while the cabby waved his arm, frustrated. "Get out of the road!"

"What's going on?" A gravelly male voice came from within the carriage. The window slid open and a man with combed salt-and-pepper hair and one eye the color of milk craned his neck to assess the delay.

"Some idiot's falling all over the road," the cabby said. He waved his arm, this time with a rude gesture. "Move it!"

Grim noticed the man in the carriage as he attempted to steady himself. The man with the cloudy eye watched him with curiosity, and his hand shifted to grab at something around his neck.

Grim shuddered again, wincing. "Gah!"

Aeryn slung his arm over her shoulder, wrapped her arm around his ribs, and heaved. "Lean on me. We gotta get out of the street."

She strained under his weight. Grim dragged his feet as

Aeryn led him unsteadily toward their ride.

Traffic resumed the moment there was an inch of clearance and sprayed the backs of the legs with mud.

Ophelia and Wolfe emerged from the shop, looking concerned, and helped Grim climb into the back of the wagon. They threw the flaps shut, enclosing all four of them in the back.

Grim ripped the gloves off. The runes on his knuckles glowed reddish orange, like hot metal in a forge.

Aeryn's eyes widened. She couldn't keep the alarm out of her voice. "Grim, why are you glowing?"

"You think I know?" he said. "They've never done this before. Wolfe, is this normal?"

"It ain't ever happened with my lucky tooth," Wolfe said. "Never seen such a thing."

"Does it still hurt?" Aeryn asked.

"They're hot, but not like they were a moment ago."

As they watched without speaking, the runes faded from glowing orange, to cooler brown, and finally resumed their normal inky black. The change took less than a minute.

Aeryn gently touched a finger to one of the tattoos. "It's cool."

"They feel normal again." Grim worked his hands, and brought his knuckles closer to examine. He sighed and pulled the gloves back on. He nodded to Wolfe. "What'd you learn in there?"

"The next closest link along the Chain is stationed near Bywinter," Wolfe said.

"How far?"

"Not far as the crow flies. But roads in the North ain't like the roads we traveled further south. All windy, through forests, meandering around mountains. It'll take us two days." Wolfe tutted. "No sausages, I see. Well. This always makes me feel better."

He passed them each a wrapped candy shaped like a maple leaf.

"Melts in your mouth. One more stop for horse feed, and we'll head out."

18

Hunting

The road to Bywinter wound northeast through a pine forest. They passed a few travelers along the path, but were mostly accompanied by the sounds of birds. The day was clear and brisk, like autumn in Merioake, but the temperature plummeted overnight. They pulled over and found a clearing away from the road to camp, keeping watch in shifts.

On the morning of the second day of travel, food supplies started to dwindle. Aeryn's check of her belt pouch confirmed they were almost out of money. After she helped clean up from breakfast, she strung her bow and slung her quiver over her head. "I'm going hunting."

Wolfe stopped filling the horses' nose bags. "Are ya, now?"

"We're low on funds and low on food. If I can catch something, it'll save us some coin and maybe I can sell the hide."

"Assuming nothin' catches ya first." He finished with the nose bags and plodded across the clearing to Aeryn. "How familiar are ya with northern beasts?"

"How different could they be from those in the south?" she said. She tightened the strap of the quiver to keep it from sliding.

Wolfe planted his hands on his hips, and assumed a conversational tone. "Imagine much of the same critters. But bigger. And meaner. If by chance ya ran into a griffon, or a dragon, it'd prolly be the end of ya."

Aeryn stifled a sigh. He sounded like her father with his endless warnings about dangerous beasts she never met. "I appreciate the concern, but I'm still going. We need food."

"Then go with someone."

"I hunt alone."

"It's not safe."

"Wolfe, I don't require supervision," she said, her voice tight with irritation. "I'm not a child."

"Then don't act like one. Use your noggin, Lady Aeryn. We're in unfamiliar territory. Ya could run into trouble."

Aeryn blew out a sigh. "Why don't you consult your dice about it?"

Wolfe flared his nostrils as he dug them from his pocket. Not bothering to look at them and never breaking eye contact, he dropped them on the grass. "Oh look. They says I'm right."

Grim grabbed his axe. "I'll come. Wolfe is right. If you catch something big, you'll need help carrying it."

Aeryn pressed her mouth shut. He just had to preface it with *Wolfe is right,* but he had a point. The only problem was, if Grim came, the chances of catching anything, even something as simple-minded as a pikdeer, diminished.

Maybe she could teach him how to tread carefully through the wood. At least he wasn't wearing full plate anymore.

"Fine. Let's go." She ended the possibility of further discussion on the matter, and led the way into the treeline.

The noises of their camp faded.

It felt good to be surrounded by the trees again, with the smells and the texture of the undergrowth. Grim, who never joined Aeryn on a hunt before, relaxed as they hiked deeper into the forest.

He relaxed too much.

His woodsmanship left her wondering if every edible creature in the vicinity knew they were there. She provided a few gentle suggestions, and while his technique improved, he was still a large human in need of practice. After a quarter hour of crunching over pine needles, Aeryn paused, considering how to put the matter delicately. He'd get there eventually, she was sure of it.

But they needed to eat today.

"I'll have a better chance of catching something if I go ahead a little ways." She held up a hand to stave off protest. "I'll stay within sight. Try to step lighter and avoid swishing the fallen leaves."

Grim saw the sense in this and fell behind. She readied her bow and practically melted into the forest. She crept ahead without a sound, aware of every noise, every smell, every flicker of movement.

Stealthy. Deliberate. Patient.

Weaver hovered nearby, sometimes foraging, other times soaring ahead.

A swish of movement in the distance caught her eye. She changed course and crept after it, though she couldn't decipher what it was.

She followed the shiver of oversized ferns and the faint rustling, moving deeper into the wood. She strained her eyes and ears and thought she glimpsed something large and ruddy brown, but then it was gone again.

The forest was still. No birds sang. No squirrels rummaged in the undergrowth.

She started to suspect the presence of a large predator lurking nearby. Keeping her wits about her, she picked her way onward. The hair on the back of her neck began to prickle.

It was too quiet. Something wasn't right.

The heavy breath of a beast rolled toward her from behind a downed tree. Aeryn knew better than to make any sudden movements. The air bottled in her lungs. She turned slowly toward the source of the hot, musky breath.

Her throat tightened.

The scaly, winged body of a mahogany dragon crouched behind the log. It was as large as a horse with teeth like knives and powerful legs like tree trunks. Its leathery wings were clasped tight to its sides for maneuverability. It watched her with hungry, yellow eyes. The moment she met its gaze, it worked its shoulders for a mere second, then pounced.

Weaver screamed.

Aeryn threw herself out of the way. The dragon landed where she had been a moment before and dug his talons into the dirt instead of her flesh. The beast snarled in frustration at missing his catch. Aeryn clambored to her feet before he reeled on her, and she turned her bow upon him.

The arrow flew wide as the dragon flicked his tail and whipped her. She cried out as the sharp end cut her cheek, narrowly missing her eye.

The beast lunged, snapping his jaws on air as she darted out of the way again. Aeryn also knew better than to turn her back to a predator, or invite it to give chase. She scrambled to put some distance between them while she fumbled for another arrow.

Seeing she wasn't running, the dragon prowled closer, assessing her every move. A wet growl rattled in his belly.

Aeryn fired just as he dove at her. He roared as the arrow pierced his flank.

But this time, he caught her. The impact knocked the wind from her lungs. He held her firm, pinning her to the ground with muscular, taloned paws.

The dragon bared his teeth inches from her face, and his nostrils flared with a great sniff. Eyes bulging, she stared back at him, unable to scream. He was incredibly strong and heavy, and Aeryn felt sure she'd burst under his weight if he didn't decapitate her first.

Then the dragon paused and cocked his head as something like confusion passed over his expression.

Grim crashed into the clearing, axe raised for action. Startled, the dragon released Aeryn. Grim rushed upon him with a yell. He swung his weapon and clipped the dragon on the jaw. The beast reeled back.

Grim advanced on the dragon, roaring. Swipe after swipe, he drove him back. The dragon bellowed and beat his wings. He whipped his tail and swiped at Grim, but Grim fought this dragon with the fury of a god, and for Aeryn, that meant salvation.

Everything hurt, but she managed to stand, grasp her bow, and nock an arrow.

Visibly seething, the dragon roared and launched himself

into the air out of Grim's reach. He reared his neck, parted his jaws, and sent a scorching blast at Grim.

But not before Aeryn took her shot.

The arrow struck the dragon in the side. The blast split the air with a crack and soared wide, missing Grim, but leaving a charred and smoldering hole in the trunk of a nearby tree.

It smelled like lightning.

The dragon's expression shifted. Beast though he was, he was starting to think better of continuing this fight.

With a hasty beat of his wings he pulled back.

Aeryn sensed a retreat coming. But if anything her father told her about dragons was true, that wasn't an option. They were persistent, patient opportunists. Letting him go now only meant he'd attack them on his own terms before they cleared the area.

Rapidly, she pulled another arrow and fired, this time piercing the dragon in the eye. It screamed and pitched right, clipping his wings on the tree branches. It crashed to the ground.

Grim rushed at him, and brought the axe down upon the neck before the beast could rise again.

The dragon's body sagged and its tongue lolled out of his mouth.

He was dead.

Cool relief washed over Aeryn. She came to Grim's side as he dislodged his axe. He noticed the cut on her face, and his eyes swept the length of her.

"Are you hurt?" he asked

Her bones ached, but nothing felt broken. She wiped the

trickle of blood from her cheek. "I'm fine. You?"

He pulled his stitches, and sustained a few cuts which tore through his new coat, but he was otherwise unscathed.

They beheld the lifeless beast at their feet.

"Alright. I'm glad you came with me," Aeryn said. "Thank you."

He nodded to the smoldering tree. The hole left by the dragon's blast was as big as a human head. "I should thank you too, then."

"My father called it *liquid lightning*," Aeryn said. "He said the blast is so hot and powerful, it can hollow out a mountain. Normally, they breathe fire, so you must've made him really angry."

Grim appraised the dragon. "Do you think we can eat it?"

Aeryn made a doubtful hum. "Seems kind of wrong. Eating something that can hold an intelligent conversation with you."

Grim wrinkled his brow. "Did it talk to you?"

"Well, no. Maybe this is a feral one, not a greater one like the ones Ophelia told us about."

"You talk to all kinds of animals. We still eat them."

"Sure, but that's different," she said. "Predators taste bad. Remember the bear?"

He grimaced. He usually ate anything without complaint, but the tough, fishy-flavored meat almost made him lose his stomach contents.

She pulled out her knife and pointed it at the beast for emphasis. "There's good money on a dragon hide. The leather on the wings doesn't need to be tanned and can be sold for armor, and the scales are rare and valuable."

Removing the dragon's hide was much different than skinning a pikdeer. The scales were thick, hard, and tightly packed. Aeryn's hunting knife was not suited for dragons. She removed five palm-sized scales from the side before the knife broke.

Frustrated, she flung the handle into the forest with a growl. "I should've done the wings first."

"Let's go back," Grim said. "We have enough food to last another day. We can sell the scales in Bywinter."

Aeryn wiped her hands clean and looked over the beast, feeling a pull of sadness. She, along with her people, maintained an aversion to hunting for the sake of trophies. Hunting was for food and survival. *Take what you need to live.* Sometimes that meant taking the creature's life to preserve one's own. Still, she hated killing an animal if unable to make full use of it. It felt like a waste.

"It's a shame he had to die," she said. "He's magnificent. Vicious. But magnificent."

Grim snorted. "Make sure you tell that to Wolfe."

She groaned and tipped her head back. "Time to eat my words."

"They probably taste better than dragon meat."

They rolled into the large northern city of Bywinter after dark. The gatekeeper permitted them entry only after a terse exchange and a bribe. He pointed them in the direction of a stable and lodgings, and after securing the horses and wagon, they had precious few silvers between them.

"Wolfe and I can call on a favor for additional funds when we make contact with the Shadow stationed here. We'll reach out in the morning," Ophelia said. "City this size, the Shadow likely has safe lodgings where we can stay while we wait for the Chain. In the meantime, let's grab a warm meal and secure a room."

She led the group across the cobbled street toward a tavern and inn with warm yellow light glowing from the windows.

Most businesses had closed for the day.

"Looks like you'll have to wait until tomorrow to sell the scales." Ophelia craned her neck skyward and smiled dreamily. "My! Those stars are lovely tonight."

At Tallonroses Tavern and Inn, they devoured a modest supper. Ophelia left the table to speak with the barmaid about securing a room, but returned a few minutes later, irked.

"More than we can afford tonight," she said.

Aeryn's heart sank. It was warm and cozy here.

"Is there any work we could do to lower the cost?" Grim said.

"I asked," Ophelia said. "The woman just laughed."

Wolfe cast his bone dice on the table. "She doesn't like ya."

"I care very little," Ophelia said, her tone curt. "I simply forgot how rude Northerners can be."

Wolfe stuffed the bone dice back in his coat pocket. "So where're we staying tonight?"

"When I told her what we could afford, she recommended a back alley, or an inn called The Bloated Heffer, down the street,"

Ophelia said. "She suggested there's not much difference."

"Sounds classy." Wolfe drained the last of his beer.

Ophelia sucked in her cheeks. "I'm willing to take a look, but I may simply track down our contact tonight, to see about the safe lodgings."

Wolfe covered a belch with his fist. "Fifi, it's late. We don't know how long that'll take. We've seen our share of less-than-desirable holes to sleep. How bad could it be?"

They finished their meal and tromped up the road against the brittle wind. Even in the dark, there was a stunning lack of greenery in the dense urban scape. Lanterns hung from iron poles along the stone-laid street, lighting their path. Few people lingered outside until they neared The Bloated Heffer, where boisterous men who reeked of ale loitered outside a pub with a knot of course ladies across the road.

The three-story inn stood in disrepair. One of the street lamps outside was broken. Its shattered glass littered the road, along with what Aeryn hoped was horse manure. Inside, an overweight woman with curly hair, red lips, and a generous amount of cleavage picked her fingernails behind a counter. She appraised the group as they entered.

"What do you want?"

"A room," Ophelia said, her voice clipped. "A large one if you have it."

"We don't."

Ophelia pursed her lips. "Then two rooms, please."

"Paying by the hour, or for the night?"

"Seeing as how we intend to *sleep*, the night."

The woman snorted. "Bless your hearts. Three silvers for a room. Four silvers if you want the bed off the floor."

Aeryn and Grim produced the equivalent of two silvers, and Ophelia and Wolfe came up with the rest. The woman stuck the coins down the front of her dress, then passed them two rusty keys. She waggled a finger toward the staircase on the right. "Rooms eight and nine. Third floor."

"Would it have been cheaper to pay by the hour?" Grim asked as they climbed the groaning staircase. "It's late. If we leave first thing in the morning, we'll only be here a few hours."

"Grim, people only pay by the hour if they've hired a prostitute," Wolfe said.

Grim was quiet for a beat. "Oh."

On the third floor landing, Aeryn lit a lamp. She jammed the key in the lock, and it snapped.

Eyes wide, she tested the handle and found the key didn't matter anyway. The rickety door swung inward.

The tiny room featured a thin, stained hay mattress in the middle of a creaky, unfinished wooden floor. The mattress took up most of the room. From the doorway, the bed looked and smelled like it had been used recently. There was an empty bottle of liquor in the corner, and discolored smudges on the unpainted walls. Most alarming was the hole in the ceiling. A beady-eyed rat the size of a small dog couched in the gap and leered at them with nefarious interest as they appraised their accommodations from the doorway.

Wolfe's voice carried from their room just down the hall.

"Oh look, Fifi. There's a window. The roaches can keep ya company while ya stargaze."

Aeryn curled her lip at the rat. She stomped toward him and clapped her hands. Unphased, he eyed her with contempt, then scurried out of sight into the recesses of the attic.

"Did you see that rat narrow his eyes at me?" Aeryn asked Grim, feeling a sudden chill.

He gave her a funny look. "No."

"Do you think it's too late to get our money back?" she asked.

"You saw where that woman put it. It's one night, and it beats an alley." Grim pointed at the mattress. "But there's no way I'm sleeping on that thing."

They heaved the mattress upright, letting it sag against the far wall, and set up their bedrolls in the opposite corner.

Ophelia rapped her knuckles on the door a few moments later. She winced at the ceiling hole.

"First thing tomorrow, we'll attempt to connect with the Shadow," she said. "He'll know how to call upon the Chain. While we wait, we'll likely have to stay in Bywinter another night. Somewhere else."

The scurry of rat feet overhead drew everyone's attention. As one, they tracked the scritching noise across the ceiling.

"I'm sorry we can't afford more comfortable accommodations tonight," Ophelia said, sincerely apologetic.

"This is fine," Grim said. "Thank you for your help."

"Yes, thank you," Aeryn said, reminding herself this was

better than freezing in the wagon.

Ophelia forced a weary smile.

"I imagine you two must be exhausted after fighting a dragon this morning. Try to rest." She paused before she pulled the door shut behind her. "Keep the door locked."

After some finagling, Aeryn discovered that the door was unable to lock from the inside, so they carefully positioned the axe, jamming it under the handle, then piled their backpacks in front of the door for good measure.

Exhaustion settled heavily upon them as they climbed into their bedrolls and turned out the lamp. It was warm enough that they needn't invade each other's space.

Aeryn strained her eyes at the ceiling hole until her lids grew too heavy to stay open. Though the walls were thin, and indistinct conversational muffles carried from outside or the lower levels, the adjacent rooms were mercifully quiet.

As she started to doze, squeaks and skitters in the wall by her head woke her with a gasp.

Grim jerked awake. He propped himself on one elbow. "What's wrong?"

"It's in the walls!" she hissed. Her heart hammered.

Grim listened as the wall-inhabiting creature gnawed on framing for a moment, only to be joined by a second chewer. The squeaks and squeals took a vicious turn as one vermin battled another. A rodent shrieked. A tiny thud. Then the sound of one creature dragging the body of the other up the wall and into the ceiling.

"He's a monster," Aeryn said.

"Who?"

"The rat. It's him. You saw how he looked at me?" Aeryn said in a whisper. "Like he wanted to chew my ears off while I slept."

Grim sighed and collapsed back onto his bedroll. "You speak with animals. Tell him to leave you alone."

"There's no reasoning with a rat."

"Goodnight, Aeryn."

Aeryn stared at the ceiling overhead. The gnawing continued for a few minutes before the critter decided to scurry back and forth repeatedly, as if rearranging rat furniture in its ceiling lair.

Grim sighed. "Lying here listening to rat feet in the walls is the start of madness."

"You should get your axe," she said. Only half-kidding.

Grim chuckled, and Aeryn laughed too.

19

The Man with the Cloudy Eye

Ophelia knocked gently at sunup. "Wolfe and I are going to step out. It'd be advisable for you to hunker here while we're gone."

"Oh, no," Aeryn said. She stuffed her blanket into her backpack. "It's time to say goodbye to The Bloated Heffer forever."

"The situation with our contact here is sensitive. You can't come with us to drop the message."

"Then we won't. We have to sell the scales."

Wolfe entered the room behind Ophelia. "They're not prisoners, Fifi. We gotta head toward the market district anyway."

They collected their belongings, turned in the key stump to the empty desk downstairs, and stepped into the streets of Bywinter. The day was overcast and brisk. Wolfe squinted in the light and groaned. Aeryn passed him a sprig of gingerwort.

The further they traveled from The Bloated Heffer, Aeryn noticed an increase of maintained buildings and intact street lamps. The road was clear of glass, food scraps, and soiled garments.

There was no grass. It was like the entire city had been laid with the same gray stone.

"Where does one sell dragon scales?" Aeryn asked as they strolled into the market district.

"First of all, stop shouting," Wolfe said.

"No one is shouting, Wolfe," Ophelia said flatly. "A collector or jeweler is a good place to start."

A shop called Poggin's Antiques and Rare Items caught Aeryn's eye. She pointed. "There?"

"Looks promising," Ophelia said brightly. "Our business is nearby. When you're done..." She scanned their surroundings until her eyes landed on an eatery on the corner called Applegriffon's. "Meet there."

⏻

"Grim, I've never had this much money before," Aeryn said as they left Poggin's. "We're rich."

The shopowner, thrilled about the scales, offered three platinum pieces. As intrigued as Aeryn was to hold a platinum coin, she asked for smaller denominations so she and Grim could split it evenly, and to minimize difficulty making change.

"We gotta resupply, but we should try to save as much as we can," he said. "I want to find some work before we leave. We'll need the money eventually. I don't want to be dependent on anyone if I can help it."

"I completely agree, but I'm going to buy a better hunting knife," she said. "You should too."

"I'm going to get breakfast before anything else," Grim replied.

Applegriffon's was cleaner and better furnished than the tavern the previous night. A tall young lady with a fresh face and a fiery red braid introduced herself as Jemma and took their order.

While they waited for their food, Aeryn scanned the dining

room for a job board, but didn't see one.

Jemma returned bearing a tray with two mugs of hot spiced milk and two plates piled with eggs, slabs of ham, and fresh bread. She cast an interested glance at Grim as she placed the food on the table, but he didn't notice.

"Jemma?" Aeryn asked, which pulled her attention away from Grim. "Do you know anyone seeking to hire immediate help around town?"

Jemma considered for a moment. "Our usual busser got kicked by a horse last week, so we could use a set of hands clearing dishes. Mayor's day-of-birth celebration tonight. Expecting a crowd. Also, I know my pop's always looking for labor down at the lumber yard."

"Thank you," Aeryn said. "We'll get back to you before we leave." She wanted to make sure they'd be available before giving Jemma a definite answer. Things with the Chain might move faster than expected.

"Sure thing." Jemma flashed a smile and left them to their meal.

It wasn't until Aeryn and Grim finished their breakfast that Ophelia and Wolfe arrived, which meant more waiting around as they ordered food and ate their own breakfasts. Ophelia was pleased to announce they had a place to stay, and Grim explained the jobs Jemma mentioned and their intention to earn a little money while they had the opportunity.

Ophelia dropped her voice. "I can't stop you. Though I'm concerned about the Loom. I'm certain they're here. But almost everyone in the North wears long sleeves, so they're difficult to identify visually."

"Is it too dangerous to work?" Grim asked.

"Not necessarily," Ophelia said. "But if you insist, Wolfe and I will be nearby to keep an eye on things. If the link in the Chain arrives and needs you to go, be prepared to leave immediately."

Wolfe shrugged. "I'll come with ya to the lumber yard. Put these old bones to work."

"We need an alibi. I want you to draw as little interest as possible," Ophelia continued. "If anyone asks, we're on a religious pilgrimage. That alone should be enough to deter most people from further questioning."

When they finished the meal, Aeryn told Jemma she'd be glad for the bussing job, and Grim asked for directions to the lumber yard. Jemma instructed Aeryn to return about lunchtime and expect to work well into the evening.

The Shadow-run safe lodging was a tiny, albeit sturdy, two-room home in one of the busy, working class residential wards, not far from the market. There was one window, shuddered and positioned high on the wall to deter robbers, and a heavy door with an assortment of locks. The main room was a dusty open space featuring a fireplace, a bare wooden floor, a small countertop with a few dishes, and a rack stocked with folded blankets. Six cots were folded and leaned against the wall, out of the way, near a yoke with two buckets for water, and a broom. The second room was more of a closet, containing a washtub and a chamber pot. That was all the privacy they'd get.

They spent a few minutes in the dim house, lit only by the cracks of daylight slipping through the shuddered window, to set up cots, and settle in.

Ophelia announced she'd take care of water, firewood, and food that afternoon. Aeryn offered to join her before she had to work. Since Grim and Wolfe needed to leave for the lumber yard sooner, Grim gave her some of his coins to pay for his share in supplies.

After a trip to one of the city wells for water, the ladies wandered into town to restock Aeryn's arrows and resupply what they could, given the time.

"How does a person get involved with Silver Shadow?" Aeryn asked as they moved on to the next store for dry goods. She tucked the hunting knives she'd just purchased for her and Grim into her satchel. "I've never even heard of the Silver Shadow until a few days ago."

"With certain exceptions, spies are trained from a young age," Ophelia said. She added, "Though, old enough to make the choice themselves."

"What about you?"

"I was recruited after my husband died."

"Your husband, the falconer?"

"Yes. We left the South together for him to work for one of the noble houses in Proimos. We were only married a short time before he passed. It was long ago," she said, her tone light. "I was an alchemist in Nyassa at the time when some Shadow spies reached out, hoping I'd be willing to utilize my skills against the Loom.

Making the leap to poisoning wasn't difficult."

"Is that how you met Wolfe?"

"That came later. He's been my mentor for some time."

After stowing their purchases back at the residence, Ophelia walked Aeryn to work with instructions.

"I'll be nearby finishing some errands, and I'll stop in for supper," she said. "At the end of the night, wait for Wolfe or I to escort you. Do not leave alone."

Aeryn arrived at Applegriffon's just before midday, ready to work. Jemma handed her a rectangular wooden bucket with a handle. "For dirty dishes. C'mon. I'll show you what to do and introduce you to the rest of the staff."

Aeryn decided she liked Jemma. She was friendly, energetic, and helpful. Clearing tables wasn't complicated, but it kept Aeryn moving constantly. After the midday rush, Jemma invited Aeryn to sit for a break. She handed her a plate with meat and vegetables stuffed into a crusty roll and winked.

"One of the upsides. Free food," she said. "Hope it's okay I left the garnish off. I noticed both you and your blonde companion ate it at breakfast."

Aeryn's cheeks warmed. She hadn't noticed. She never had meals which came with decorations before.

Jemma started, as though catching a slip of the tongue. "Oh, I'm sorry. I assumed you two were friends. You're not...together, are you?"

"We're friends," Aeryn said as they grabbed a table near the back of the restaurant. The word felt odd in her mouth. *Friend* felt like a stretch. Trusted partner, ally, excuse for leaving Merioake, sure. She liked his company, but did he count as a friend when in so many ways they were still strangers to each other?

Jemma looked relieved, and pleased. "So I figured correctly. I didn't think elves and humans paired up often. Then again, we don't have many elves around here."

"They don't. My elder brother married a human, so it's not unheard of. Cultural and lifespan differences are enough to deter most. Though, when you love someone...." Aeryn shrugged and bit into her roll. It was delicious.

Jemma's eyes twinkled in a smile. "That sounds romantic."

"It sounds depressing," Aeryn said with a snort of laughter. "Imagine knowing you're going to outlive your spouse and children by a hundred years."

They made small talk while they ate. Aeryn was forced to use the alibi Ophelia invented. Unfortunately, Jemma found this very interesting.

Jemma leaned forward, her elbow on the table, and rested her chin in his hand. "Which gods do you pray to?"

Aeryn wished they discussed this in greater detail. She was only familiar with the popular gods in Merioake, and she didn't think much of them. "Oh, you know. The good ones."

Jemma cocked her head and gave a thoughtful nod. "I find you can tell a lot about a person by the gods they serve."

"...Sure."

"How about your blonde friend from this morning?"

Jemma asked. "Is he devout?"

"Oh, yes. Single-minded in his focus," Aeryn said, hoping it was enough to extinguish the hopeful glint in Jemma's eye. "He's all religion, no...anything else."

"Really?" Jemma sat up a little straighter. "Tell me more."

Aeryn cleared her throat and said the first thing which came to mind. "He's taken a vow of celibacy."

"Pity. Is he firm in his conviction?"

"Extremely. He's considering becoming a eunuch." Aeryn made a chopping motion with her hand.

Jemma took a bite of her meal and thought for a moment. "You know, that doesn't have to be a problem."

Aeryn raised both eyebrows. She chugged her water and popped to her feet. "Back to work for me."

Business picked up as afternoon stretched into evening. Applegriffon's catered to upper class guests who dressed nicely and smelled cleaner than most of the humans she'd come into contact with so far. Affluent bureaucrats, city officials, and wealthy merchants congregated in one half of the establishment to celebrate with the mayor. Aeryn recognized and greeted Poggin in the crowd. The mayor, a finely dressed, middle aged woman with a sharp eye and sharper tongue, grew louder as the evening progressed, but with her exorbitant spending, the wait staff barely complained.

Ophelia, Wolfe, and Grim stopped in for a late supper. Jemma happily waited on them. As eager as Aeryn was to ask about work in the lumberyard, her own work kept her from conversing for long.

When Jemma brought them a round of mead, she leaned closer to speak to Grim over the din. "Your friend told me you're planning to do the deed."

"What deed?" Grim shot a puzzled look at Aeryn, who stood behind Jemma, clearing a nearby table.

Aeryn bobbed her head eagerly and mouthed the words *play along*.

Oblivious, Jemma pointed to his lap. "You know. Becoming a eunuch."

"A *eunuch*?"

Jemma rested a hand on Grim's shoulder and looked him in the eye. "I respect and admire your devotion."

Grim shifted uncomfortably in his seat. "Thank you?"

Jemma batted her eyes at him then left to attend to her other customers.

"What did you tell her?" Grim asked as soon as Jemma was out of earshot.

"She kept asking questions," Aeryn said as her shoulders climbed toward her ears. "I thought that if I told her you were unavailable then she'd lose interest. So I told her you're celibate and considering...something more permanent. It didn't work."

Wolfe stifled a laugh. "Clearly."

At this point, Aeryn was biting back a laugh.

Grim ran a hand over his crimson face. "You could've said so many other things."

Jemma reappeared at the tableside with a bright smile. "How's everyone's food? Is there anything else I can get you all?"

"We're all set, dear. Thank you," Ophelia said politely.

"Back so soon with the attentive service! Industrious young lady, this one." Wolfe dipped his chin and lifted his pint to Jemma. "Ya keep comin' around, our fella Grim might have to reconsider his oath."

Grim choked on his beverage.

Jemma flushed. Suddenly bashful, she gave a small giggle and her eyes jumped to Grim, who was still coughing.

"I'll get you a glass of water," Jemma said, and she darted away.

"Wolfe, that was uncomfortable for everyone," Ophelia said. "Don't toy with that poor girl."

Wolfe snickered and nudged Grim with his elbow. "Pretty soon we'll have to call ya Grim Heart-breaker."

Grim recovered from his coughing fit. "I will tear that tooth out of your mouth."

Not to be outdone, Wolfe reached into his mouth, plucked out the tooth, and rolled it on the tabletop. "Look! They says ya're gonna have triplets. So much for being a eunuch. And before ya ask, yes, I'll be their godfather."

The evening stayed steadily busy with the mayor's guests leaving, and new ones arriving, on top of what Jemma said was regular business. At one point, as Aeryn emerged from the kitchen, she nearly ran into one of the patrons in the hallway.

She apologized as she tried to step around him.

He didn't move.

The man stood a head taller than her, and was twice as wide. He wore a black leather jacket, buttoned to his chin. There was a bulge in the garment over his heart. A smell of decay hung around him.

Her gaze climbed to his familiar face. She recognized the man with the cloudy eye from the carriage which almost ran them over in Fogness March.

His mouth curled in the corner. "I smell dragon magic."

Aeryn felt her mouth grow dry. "Pardon?"

"Let me see you."

The man searched Aeryn with his eyes, down to the caddy she carried in front of her, and back to her face. Taken aback and feeling violated, Aeryn hugged the caddy tighter to her body.

"You look familiar," he said. He took a step closer, and reached to touch the end of her hair.

Aeryn drew back, and avoided being brushed by his hand. Instead he sniffed the air over her head and Aeryn took another uneasy step away.

"My friend informed me that he purchased a number of dragon scales from a little wood elf today," he said, unphased by her obvious discomfort. "A rare treasure, dragon scales. Imagine his delight when he was able to point her out at supper."

His voice was deep. Both oily and gravelly. It made Aeryn's skin crawl.

"I find dragons have a particular...magical aroma," the man said. "They're inherently magical beasts. I don't know many people equipped to face one alone, and live." He caressed the lump in his jacket over his heart. "Not without power."

Aeryn wanted nothing more than to get away from the man, but she didn't want to turn her back to him either. She inched toward the kitchen, which she thought of as a sort of refuge. Customers weren't allowed back there.

The man continued to watch her with his dead eye. "The man who–"

"Coming through!" Jemma said. She exited the kitchen behind Aeryn and ushered the man to the side.

"Let me help you," Aeryn said. Seizing the opportunity to get away, she scooted around the cloudy-eyed man, staying on Jemma's heels, and followed her into the dining room.

Jemma gave her a curious look. "You alright?"

"The man back there," Aeryn said. "He wouldn't let me pass."

Jemma cast her gaze in his direction. "Him? He's friends with the mayor. In good with the city guard. I don't know what he does."

"He tried to smell my hair."

Jemma wrinkled her nose. "That's not normal."

"What's his name?"

Jemma bunched her mouth to the side as she thought. "Uller? Or Richard? I don't know. But if he or anyone else gets fresh with you, let me know. Usually our customers behave themselves, but every so often, someone has too much to drink and gets handsy. Boss has no patience for it. We'll throw him out."

Aeryn thanked her. She kept alert, and to her relief, the

cloudy-eyed man didn't bother her the rest of the evening. Or even look in her direction. He left a half hour later.

Eventually the mayor's gathering died down. Patrons stumbled from the premises. Aeryn collected the last of the dirty dishes and wiped tables. Tips were divvied, and Aeryn pocketed twenty-two silvers.

"Job well done," Jemma said with a wink. "If you want to come back tomorrow, same time, you should."

A balding middle aged man with bushy eyebrows tapped on the window from outside. Jemma waved.

"It's my pops. I gotta go," she said. "Aeryn, do you want to walk with us? It's not a bad part of town, but in an area with a bunch of full-blooded Northerners who've been drinking, it's safer not to walk home alone in the dark."

"My friend will be here soon," Aeryn said. Through the window, she checked the street for Ophelia.

"Oh. Sorry I'll miss him," Jemma said, misunderstanding. The girl's cheeks turned pink. "Well, goodnight."

Aeryn waited a few more minutes inside Applegriffon's with the other servers for Ophelia to arrive. Grim accompanied her. Aeryn asked how Grim's day at the lumberyard went, and when she shared how much coinage she made, he whistled.

"You earned four times what I made," he said.

"She invited me back tomorrow," Aeryn said. "Ophelia, any word about the Chain?"

"They should be here soon. Plan on another day or two in Bywinter." Ophelia gazed skyword as they strolled in the glow of street lanterns.

Ophelia had kept busy that afternoon, and it showed. She'd swept and dusted. She'd filled any vessel which needed water and arranged food stores neatly on the rack. There was water ready in the kettle for the morning, oats soaking in the cookpot on the counter. Using a combination of their own belongings and the blankets which had been provided, she'd turned each of the bare cots into a comfortable-looking bed. A single daisy sat in a glass on the counter. It made Aeryn smile. It was such a motherly thing to do, and it deepened her appreciation for Ophelia.

The fire in the hearth burned low, casting a jumpy orange glow over the room. Wolfe was already asleep, snoring quietly. One of his arms dangled over the edge of his cot, touching an empty glass bottle which, Aeryn presumed based on the smell, once held some kind of alcoholic beverage before he consumed it all.

"I'm going to get ready for bed," Ophelia said. "Would anyone like to use the water closet first?"

Grim announced he was fine, but Aeryn, who'd been holding it in all afternoon, jumped at the opportunity. She fished a clean set of clothes out of her bag and stepped into the other room to relieve herself and change. She pulled on her new, clean shirt, which was a pretty mossy green, and her comfortable pikdeer leggings. Emerging, she folded her dirty clothes and rested them at the foot of her cot.

Grim set another log on the fire, and Ophelia stepped into the closet to wash up before bed. Wolfe shifted, breaking wind, and the empty bottle slipped from his fingers.

"Our boss wouldn't let Wolfe drink on the job, so he made up for it this evening. He passed out two hours ago." Grim eased himself onto his bed and stretched his neck with a grunt. He pulled off his gloves and set them on top of his pack beside his bed.

"I don't know how he's even alive," Aeryn said. She climbed into her bed. "He drinks enough to kill a mule."

"I think it's his tooth," Grim said. "You know he's a hundred and fifty two years old?"

"That's older than my parents."

"He told me the rune on his tooth was a blessing from one of the Baldomar after the war. Barely aged a day since," he said. "Says the drink doesn't hit him like it used to."

"Some people call that tolerance."

Grim shrugged. "I believe him."

Aeryn pointed at his knuckles. "I wonder what those runes mean. Have they bothered you since Fogness?"

Grim turned his hand over. "Bothered? No. But after we slayed the dragon, they felt odd."

Aeryn propped herself on her elbow. "How so?"

"Warm. While you were working on the scales, I checked them, and they were fading. Like the other day after we climbed back into the wagon."

"Why didn't you say anything?"

"Would you want to point out whenever tattoos you were born with started glowing on their own?" he asked. "It didn't hurt and didn't affect my ability to function."

"What do you think it means?" Aeryn asked.

Grim shrugged and looked at his hand for a long moment. "I've always known they mean something. Can't say I'm any more interested in knowing than I ever have been. I just hope they don't get us killed."

20

What Happened to Weaver

The next few days passed without a word from the Chain. Aeryn and Grim used the time to work.

The Imperials maintained a presence in Bywinter in equal measure to City Guard. Going to and from work, Aeryn saw more City Guard than Imperials, which surprised her because Applegriffon's was in a nice part of town. She expected them to go where the crime was.

They made her less nervous than the Imperials did. When a few Imperials stopped into Applegriffon's for a meal, they took no notice of her. But she suspected that if her and Grim's wanted posters made it to Bywinter before they left, they might be in trouble.

By the morning of the fourth day in the city, Wolfe and Ophelia were uneasy.

"The stars indicate a problem," Ophelia said over breakfast.

"The stars, or the fact he hasn't shown yet?" Wolfe said. He poured a dollop from his hip flask into his morning tea.

Ophelia ignored his early-morning grouchiness. "I know a hermit who can send an animal messenger to find our link in the Chain."

Wolfe stopped with his beverage halfway to his mouth. "Ya

want to call on Sprucepit Mange?"

"*Magne* is reliable. He's been friendly to our cause for years."

"Who is this hermit?" Aeryn asked as she spooned a small bite of oatmeal into her mouth.

"Nutter who lives in Sprucepit," Wolfe said.

"Where's that?" Grim asked.

"Dense part of the woods, north of the city," Wolfe said. "Last time I saw him, he sent his griffon after me."

"He did no such thing," Ophelia said with a little sniff. "You offended her with your jibber-jabber."

"He laughed!" Wolfe said.

Ophelia waved her hand dismissively. "It was humorous. I'm setting out after breakfast. I should be back by tonight. Aeryn, I'll plan on escorting you after your shift, as usual."

"What if the link in the Chain shows before you're back?" Aeryn said.

A sad smile spread across Ophelia's face. "If he needs you to leave right away, then may the stars bear good tidings over you. It's been a pleasure." She reached out, and squeezed their hands. "Whatever happens, I believe we'll see each other again." She crinkled her eyes. "The stars, you know."

Since Aeryn would be the last to leave for the day, she was given charge over the key, with the understanding that whoever finished their business first would come by Applegriffon's and retrieve it from her.

"I'm sure Jemma will be quite happy to see you," Aeryn

said with a smirk. Wolfe snickered, and Grim ran a hand over his face.

The men left for the lumberyard after breakfast. In the absence of company, Aeryn tidied the house, flopped onto her bed, and got right back up again.

"Now I can't sit still. He's influencing me, Weaver," she said as the bird landed on her shoulder the moment she stepped outside. She was wearing her yellow sweater with the possum vest over it. She gave him a seed and nudged him with her cheek. "Next thing you know, I'll be inhaling my food and snoring like a bear."

At Applegriffon's, she waved hello to Jemma. "I know it's not midday, but can I start working now?"

"Sure thing. Mind taking the rubbish out back?"

Aeryn found a small barrel full of trash in the kitchen. She carried it through the back door into the alley, where there was a rubbish cart to dump it. She picked through the food scraps, a butterknife with no handle, and the shards of a broken plate, for something to interest Weaver, and settled on a partially eaten piece of fruit. Behind her, Weaver watched expectantly from his perch on the eaves above the back door.

He rasped, drawing Aeryn's attention.

The man with the cloudy eye from the other night stood in the doorway. He fixed his good eye on Aeryn and his mouth curled into a grin. "I've been looking for you."

A wave of cold rolled over her body. She emptied the trash quickly, careful not to turn her back on the man. "I have to get back to work."

"I verified your story about the dragon. Went to see it myself," he said. He took a heavy step toward her. His belt jingled with his gait. "See, I'm a hunter too."

Aeryn didn't like the hungry look in his eye. She gripped the rubbish barrel tightly, prepared to throw it and make her escape if needed.

"That's very interesting, but like I said, I have to get back to work now." She kept her tone direct, making it clear she didn't wish to continue the conversation.

Two men in black leather of the City Guard appeared behind him. They were equally broad with stern faces and cold eyes. Aeryn recognized them as some of the local guards who had been patrolling the area nearby. They rested their hands on their sword hilts as they positioned themselves about eight feet away from her on either side.

Blocking her escape along both sides of the alley.

One of the guard's sleeves was rolled to the elbow. A black cord dangled from his wrist.

Aeryn tried not to look as afraid as she felt. Her back bumped the rubbish cart as she attempted to keep space between herself and the men.

"I noticed signs of heavy weaponry used against the beast. Too heavy for a little thing like you," the man with the cloudy eye said. "Upon further inquiry, I learned you sold the dragon scales with a blonde Northerner. I knew there had to be someone else. Not who I expected, but someone with something I want."

The stench of decay closed in as he took a step closer. His

jacket hung open in the front and Aeryn's eyes landed on the tattooed human fingers which swayed from a black cord around his neck.

Aeryn blanched, her body seized with sudden panic.

"We can talk about what you did in Fieldgate another time. Where is the Baldomar?" the Rune Reaper asked. His fingers brushed the grotesque necklace. "Don't bother lying. I can tell."

Weaver danced along the eaves and rasped again. Anxious.

Mouth dry, Aeryn fought to keep a steady voice. She lifted her chin in defiance. "I know what you are."

"Then you know your fate if you try to protect him," the Rune Reaper said. "Tell me, how do you think it feels to have the meat peeled from your bones?"

The men closed in on either side of Aeryn like wolves cornering a pikdeer who would soon be torn to pieces.

Aeryn prepared to thrust the barrel at the man on her right and make a run for it.

Sensing her in trouble, Weaver swooped from his perch.

The Rune Reaper's arm moved as quickly as a striking serpent. Without looking or even turning his head, he snatched the bird out of the air with one hand. Weaver squawked once before the man tightened his grasp.

The crunch of bones made Aeryn's breath catch. A scream died on her lips.

The Rune Reaper tossed the crumpled heap of black feathers to the ground. "I, too, am a hunter."

Aeryn swooped to scoop Weaver's body into her shaking

hands. His ribs had caved in, and his neck was broken. He was dead.

Hot tears rushed to her eyes. Her temples pulsed.

For years, he'd been her only friend. Then Grim happened.

This *monster* wanted Grim's fingers dangling from that awful necklace. He would torment and kill anyone who stood in his way.

It's always your life, or theirs.

Aeryn set her jaw and hardened her will into stone. She knew what she had to do.

She grasped the hunting knife tucked into her boot, and lunged.

The Rune Reaper caught her wrist like an iron vice. She struggled and yelled, but he held firm. Unearthly cold seeped from his fingertips.

He pulled her closer until her face was inches away from the severed fingers. The stench of death engulfed her. He sniffed her hair and his throat hummed with pleasure. "His scent lingers on you."

Aeryn struggled and spat a curse at him. "Let go of me!"

He tutted. "Such a foul tongue for such a pretty face. It'd be a shame if you lost it."

Using his free hand, he pried the knife from her grasp. He twirled it in his fingers with the ease of an expert knivesman.

"Tell me where to find the Baldomar," the Rune Reaper said, his tone conversational. "Or you can lead me to him. I don't mind the hunt."

Aeryn spat in his face.

The Rune Reaper thrust her away, betraying the first sign of anger. He wiped the spit off his jaw with the back of his hand.

"Have it your way." He shifted the dagger in his hand, poised to throw it. "Now run."

Aeryn dodged the man on her right and tore out of the alley as fast as her legs would carry her. She sprinted toward the main road and barrelled into traffic. Still clutching Weaver, she looked over her shoulder. The two men from City Guard, both Cords, moved swiftly and determinedly in her direction.

She needed to get to the lumberyard, but she couldn't lead them straight to Grim. That was exactly what they wanted. Wolfe and Ophelia would know what to do. But Wolfe was with Grim, and Ophelia wasn't in the city.

She had to lose these men.

Aeryn plunged into the dense crowd gathered around a street musician. She exited the throng and skirted a horse drawn carriage. Swiftly rounding the nearest corner, she plowed into a man's chest. She reeled back, gaping at a tall Imperial sergeant with pocked skin, and her eyes darted to his curly haired associate, same rank.

"Watch it!" The pocked Imperial said. He snagged her by the arm before she could bolt. "What're you holding?"

She pulled and checked frantically behind her. The heads of her Cord pursuers bobbed through the crowd in her direction. "You have to let me go!"

"I don't have to do anything, thief," the man said. "What do you have?"

Aeryn clutched Weaver tighter to her chest, but he wrenched her hand open. He grimaced, making a disgusted noise, and threw the bird on the ground.

"No!" Aeryn cried. She reached for Weaver, but the man yanked her back.

"Who do you think you're trying to get away from?"

The Cords exited the throng and quickened their pace in her direction.

Aeryn tried to pry the Imperial's fingers from her arm. Tears came to her eyes. "Them! Please! Let me go!"

The Imperial grasping Aeryn squinted down the street. "That's City Guard."

"Give her to me," said the sergeant with the curly hair. "Go see what's the trouble."

The tall Imperial thrust Aeryn toward his comrade and strode down the street, stopping the Cords about fifty feet away.

Aeryn tried in vain to wriggle free from the second man's grasp. She ignored his orders to stop struggling and stomped on his foot. She could barely hear him or anything else over the ringing in her ears. She had to get away. She couldn't let these men get to her, or find Grim. She had to warn him. If she was arrested, it would all be over.

In desperation, Aeryn clawed like a wild animal. When dropping her weight didn't work, she bit the sergeant on the hand.

He yelled and forced her against the nearest building. Face first.

From the distance, the pock-faced Imperial speaking with

Cords hollered at his partner. His voice was thick with fatigue and derision. "*Do you need help?* She's half your size. Get her under control."

"She bit me!" Aeryn's captor forced her hands behind her back. "I'm taking her to lock-up. *Stop–struggling!*"

He clapped a manacle around one wrist before she sent her elbow into his mouth.

"Alright, that's enough."

The Imperial whirled her around and pulled back his fist. She felt a crack of pain in her head, and the next moment, her world went black.

21

Iviss

Aeryn came-to in a damp, windowless room, lit only by the glow of a wall-mounted torch. She had been propped against a dank stone wall, cuffed, and gagged. Her head throbbed where the curly-headed Imperial struck her.

He squatted a few feet away, watching her attentively. "Good. You're awake."

He had the physical appearance of someone who might be from anywhere. He was pale, like the majority of the Northerners she'd seen, but with dark-hair like the inhabitants of Proimos. He had a wiry build of compact muscle. His eyes had a faint shape reminiscent of the Illwalii. Perhaps this was what people from Gallendahli looked like. She'd never met any before.

She swung her foot to kick him.

He braced himself and forced her leg back to the stone floor. "Enough. I don't want to sit on you, but I will."

Aeryn spat a muffled curse at him. Her frantic thoughts jumped around as she tried to orient herself. Where was she? How long had she been unconscious? What if the Rune Reaper had gotten to Grim?

She had to get out of here.

She tried to struggle to her feet, but the man forced her to sit. "Would you be still for one moment? Look."

He yanked a silver pendant out of his uniform collar, and held it for her to see. It had the image of a wing with four stars, identical to those of Ophelia and Wolfe.

"Good," he said. "You recognize it." He tucked the necklace back into his shirt. "Now. Can I remove the gag, or will you begin screaming again?"

Aeryn glowered at him and nodded.

He took it for *yes, you can remove it,* not *yes, I'm gonna pitch a fit,* and untied it. "I'm sorry about that."

Aeryn worked her jaw. "Where am I?"

"In the catacombs beneath Bywinter."

"Who'd you kill for the pendant?"

"It's mine," he said, with strained patience. "I'm an Imperial, but I'm a Silver Shadow first."

"Sure you are."

"I know you're from Thoen. I know you're traveling with a Baldomar. I know you're wanted by the Imperials for crimes I won't mention. And I know you need to get to the Enclave," he said. "I connected with Ophelia the day after you and your companion arrived."

"...You're the Bywinter contact?" Aeryn said, deciding whether or not to believe him. "Aren't you supposed to connect us to the Chain? If so, why am I shackled in a cellar beneath the city?"

"The link in the Chain isn't coming."

"Why not?"

"He's dead. And you're down here because you managed

to run afoul of the Rune Reaper and his hunters." He unclipped a set of keys from his belt. "We need to locate your companion and get out of the city before they reach him. If I unlock you, are you going to try to fight me again?"

Aeryn's mind raced. *Dead? Was that true? What if he wasn't a spy with the Silver Shadow? What if this was a trap?*

She needed to get out of this cuffs.

"No," she said as convincingly as possible.

He arched an eyebrow. "You know, I'm trained to detect deceit."

Aeryn clamped her mouth shut. Hands still cuffed behind her back, she struggled to her feet.

"Look, I can't have you run off. If you go up there alone, they'll find you, and torture you until you give up your friends," he said. "They're not normal Cords. *He's the Rune Reaper–*"

"I know what a Rune Reaper is!"

"Then you know he won't stop until your companion's fingers dangle from his neck. We don't have time to argue," he said, his voice elevated. "Either I have your word that you won't flee, or I leave you here while I go look for the Baldomar, and we can pray the hunters didn't find him while you wasted time being difficult."

Aeryn narrowed her eyes. Whatever he was, she decided she hated him.

"Wasting time?" she said. "This, from the man who knocked me unconscious in the street. How long have I been out anyway?"

"It's only been a few minutes," he said. "Make a decision."

She stuck out her chin. "How do I know you didn't kill someone for that pendant?"

The man rubbed his brow. "I suppose you don't."

"Let me see your wrists."

Exasperated, he held up both hands, pulled up his sleeves to reveal bare wrists. "Satisfied?"

"No. Are you going to unlock me?"

"Are you going to cooperate?"

"What choice do I have? But if I get the inkling you're not who you say, you're dead."

"Very intimidating. Turn around and give me your wrists." He unlocked her. "I'm Iviss, by the way," he said as he returned the manacles and keys to his belt. He offered a small but disarming smile which made her want to like him, and therefore irritated her all the more.

She rubbed her wrists. "Lumberyard. North edge of the city."

Iviss grabbed the torch off the wall. "Follow me."

They took the stone corridors at a jog, down endless turns, past the scuttle of vermin and the trickle of a subterranean stream.

Aeryn briefly considered making a grab for the sword at his side. But Iviss was bigger, stronger, and probably armed with more than the sword alone. Furthermore, she didn't know where she was. She needed him to lead her out of the catacombs to Grim. If he wasn't really a Shadow spy, then she and Grim could take him, and his fate would be his own fault.

With each breath, her mind turned over her situation like

the many sides of Wolfe's dice. Was this really her life now? Thinking three steps ahead to avoid death?

It didn't matter. Grim was in danger.

Weaver was dead.

She had to trust a supposed spy.

Cords knew they were in the city and a Rune Reaper promised to hunt them down.

She quickened her pace and barked at Iviss to move it.

After fifteen minutes, he slowed to a stop in front of an old, stone door. He heaved it open, and they beheld a cellar full of casks and barrels with a set of stairs along one side. On the cellar-side, the door had no visible handle and blended in perfectly to the stone walls.

"Stay quiet," he said in a low voice. He hurried past stores of alcohol and crept up the stairs. Aeryn shadowed him without a sound. At the top, he listened at the door before cracking it open into the back hall of a brewery. Voices emitted from a room nearby. He held his finger to his mouth for quiet and pointed at the back door at the end of the hall.

They crept out of the building and made their way around toward the front. Across the bustling street stood Wamblee Lumber and General Supply. A wide, fenced yard sprawled at the rear of the building.

Aeryn prepared to dart across the lane, but Iviss held her back.

"You see that peddler on the corner?" he said. "Cord. Wait for my signal, and walk calmly across the street. If you run, you'll draw attention. Stand on my right, so he can't see you as well."

They waited for an adequate surge of traffic, then stepped out from the shadows beside the brewery and into the crowd. They wove through people and horses, made it across, and slipped into the building without the peddler noticing.

The supplier's building was warm and smelled like fresh cut wood. A couple customers milled around. One leaned on the counter in conversation with a bushy-eyebrowed man Aeryn recognized as Jemma's father.

"Morning, Sergeant. Lady," he said. Aeryn couldn't tell whether Jemma's father recognized her from their brief passing the other day. "How can I help you this morning?"

Grim's hearty laugh carried through the screen door toward the back of the building. It sent a jolt through Aeryn. Leaving Iviss with Jemma's father, she bolted for the door without a word, nearly breaking it off its hinges as she flew into the lumberyard.

Two burly men lingered by a nearby stack of logs. They stopped their conversation to stare at her. "Lassie, you ain't supposed to be back here."

Grim and Wolfe emerged from another row of lumber, chuckling over something Wolfe said. The grin fell from Grim's face when he saw Aeryn run at him, disheveled, with her tear-stained, swollen face.

"Aeryn, what happened?"

"We need to go now," she said.

Iviss stepped through the back door. He exchanged a word

with the two men who had been lingering, and the laborers went inside. Iviss marched across the yard to meet them.

Grim moved Aeryn aside. He tightened his gloved hands into fists, but Wolfe strode into the space between them.

"Iviss, what's going on?" Wolfe asked.

So they knew each other after all.

Iviss caught the uncertainty in Grim's expression, and flashed his silver pendant. "Rune Reaper and hunters on their way. Time to go."

"Good gods. Which one?"

"Ulfur."

They marched toward the building, but Iviss stopped them before they reentered. He peered through the screen door, then turned around and ushered them away. "They're here."

They ran through the lumberyard to the bolted gate at the side. It was locked, so they climbed the fence and ran along the edge of the property toward the street which ran behind it.

They found a horse tethered outside a thatcher's building.

"Get on," Iviss said.

Grim climbed into the saddle, and pulled Aeryn up behind him. As Iviss worked to untether the horse from its hitching post, a middle aged man stormed from the thatchers, hollering. "Whatdoyou think yer doing?"

Iviss pulled his sword halfway from its sheath and barked at the man in a very convincing way. "Official business. You'll be compensated for your trouble. Now go back inside!"

The man's eyes fell to the sword. With a sour look, he

slunk away into the safety of the building.

"This road'll take ya north out of the city. Head toward the forest, bearing northeast after the first three miles," Wolfe said, taking the house key from Aeryn. "Ya should fall in with Ophelia. Stay off the main path. I'll get your things and meet up with ya soon."

"The hunters think I have Aeryn in lock-up," Iviss said. "I can give them the runaround for a little longer. Buy you some time."

Wolfe pointed at the reins. He gave Grim a few hurried instructions. He slapped the horse on its flanks, and they galloped out of the city as fast as they dared.

22

The Hermitage

They didn't speak until they reached the woods.

"Can you signal Weaver to scout ahead for Ophelia?" Grim asked.

Aeryn scrunched her face to pinch back the tears as she recalled his crumpled body cast into the street like a piece of rubbish. He was still there, maybe shoveled into the ditch, maybe trodden underfoot, or shredded to pieces by a stray dog. Her oldest friend, snatched from life in an instant.

She forced the words out. "He's dead."

Grim listened as she explained everything from the Rune Reaper behind Applegriffon's, to her confrontation with the Imperials, to waking in the catacombs with Iviss there. She also told him about her uncomfortable interaction with the Rune Reaper a few days earlier, and how she recognized him from Fogness. "I just thought he was some perverted official."

Grim grunted as a thought occurred to him.

"What?" Aeryn asked, still clinging to his back.

"Remember how I told you my runes glowed when we were working on the dragon?"

"I remember."

"I mentioned it to Wolfe. He thought it might have

something to do with them responding to the dragon. But if the Rune Reaper is in Bywinter, he either left Fogness March before us, or just after. I don't remember passing a carriage like his along the road," Grim said. "What if he passed along the road when we were hunting?"

Aeryn thought about this, putting together what he suggested. "You think they flared up because the Rune Reaper was close."

"I think it's possible," Grim said after a moment.

Aeryn felt unsure whether this was good, or unsettling. Better to know there's a wolf nearby than be caught unawares.

Riding horseback was bumpier than Aeryn expected. They rode off path for what seemed like three miles, then traveled northeast for a half hour. The forest grew thicker the deeper they went. Despite the dense foliage, a drizzle worked its way through the branches to make them damp and cold. Their horse, a sturdy black gelding with a white stripe, grew fussier by the minute. Eventually, he refused to step over a fallen branch no thicker than Aeryn's arm.

"Come on," Grim said. He gave the horse a jab with his heels, but the steed only shuffled his feet and shook his mane in protest.

"Let me try to talk to him." Aeryn slipped off the horse and stepped lightly to his head. She had never spoken with anything bigger than a pikdeer, but the principle was the same.

Meeting his gentle black eye, she stroked his velvet nose and hushed him. The horse's ears swiveled forward as she whispered nice things. Her consciousness touched his, and instantly, instead of reading the emotions he exuded, she understood his horsey murmurs and whinnies.

"He's nervous and hungry," she said to Grim.

"He has to deal with it. We need to keep going."

Aeryn frowned at Grim, then returned her attention to the horse. She stroked his soft neck. She told him to be brave and press on, and they would rest soon enough. The horse wasn't happy, but afterwards he grew more cooperative.

They rode for an hour with no sign of Ophelia. Wet to the skin and chattering with cold, Aeryn told Grim to stop the horse.

"I think we might be lost. We should've overtaken her by now." She hopped down. "I'm going to climb and get a lay of the land. Then we can decide what to do."

Aeryn hoisted herself into the branches of a nearby oak with low boughs, which was much easier to climb than the prickly evergreens which made up most of the forest. She breached the canopy and scanned the landscape. Bywinter was a tiny mound atop a distant hill. Based on their current location, they had kept the course fairly well.

"We're on path," Aeryn said when she climbed down. "We ought to reach her soon."

"If we don't, we need to find shelter. We have no food, weapons, or fire," Grim said. "I don't like being unarmed."

"I can't imagine many creatures will be out hunting in this weather."

Grim snorted. "At least if we get attacked by a predator, there's a one-in-three chance it eats the horse and not us."

Grim urged the steed onward and Aeryn kept every sense on high alert. Finally, after another twenty minutes, a figure in a blue cloak came into view ahead.

Ophelia.

They overtook her, and the color drained from Ophelia's face as they explained how they were forced to flee Bywinter. She regained her composure quickly, assuming the no-nonsense demeanor Aeryn was growing accustomed to.

"To the hermitage," Ophelia said. "We'll wait for Wolfe there."

They continued for another few miles until they neared a clearing situated beside a cave. The area featured all kinds of tools, a yurt, and a pagoda to shield a small cooking fire from the rain.

"Let me go first," Ophelia said. As she entered the clearing, a large beast prowled out of the shadowy cave. It had a feathered blue-gray head and wings like a bird of prey, and the tawny body of a large wildcat. Aeryn had never seen a griffon, but she'd heard stories about the proud, intelligent predators.

The griffon rasped a warning, but with a word from Ophelia, it relaxed its ruffled plumage and allowed her to approach.

A male elf in gray robes emerged from the yurt. His expression was just as frazzled as his head of wild white hair. He and Ophelia spoke for a few moments. She pointed into the treeline, and he followed with his eyes, noticing Aeryn and Grim, waiting at a distance.

Ophelia waved them on.

The horse, who'd never seen a griffon either, didn't care for the menacing beast who watched them with rapt interest. The griffon lashed its flanks with its tufted tail and clacked its beak. In response, the horse whinnied and shuffled against Grim's attempts to keep him from charging in the opposite direction.

The hermit regarded them with an awkward nod, but wouldn't quite meet their eyes.

"Lady Ophelia tells me you seek refuge." The hermit spoke in a soft voice and with a slight stutter. "I understand you are headed to the Enclave. You may rest here before continuing on your journey."

"Thank you," Grim said as they dismounted, and Aeryn echoed her thanks.

"I hope you don't mind sharing the space with Willa." The hermit gestured toward the cave. He gave the griffon a gentle pat on the head, which she responded to by closing her eyes slightly, only for them to pop back open the moment he took his hand away. "Yes. Willa shall watch over the guests well, won't you, Willa? Ever-vigilant, my Willa…"

The hermit then took control of the horse, giving the animal his undivided attention. "There, there. Out performing important work in this weather? Shall we make you comfortable, Sten? That is your name, yes?"

Aeryn tried to catch his eye, in order to give the traditional elvish greeting out of respect for the older elf, but Magne wasn't keen on eye contact. So she just said it anyway before he walked away from them with Sten. "May the trees shade your path."

Magne looked her in the face, astonished, as though

noticing for the first time she was an elf.

"Oh, yes, the greeting. It's been a long time. What was it?" He dropped his eyes, which grew unfocused again as he fiddled with the reigns. "And the hand falls sweetly to the fruit. No, no. That's backwards. My, my..." Flustered, he shuffled away, leading the horse, continuing to murmur his stream of thought. "...fruit to the hand. Fruit falls sweetly to the hand. Yes, that's it..."

Ophelia brought them into the cave. Inside it was dry. Hay and feathers covered the floor.

"Is there any work we can do to help?" Grim asked, even as his jaw chattered with the cold.

Ophelia shook her head. "Magne means well, but people make him flustered, and Wolfe is on his way, which'll test him more than you realize. Stay here."

Ophelia touched the swollen gash on Aeryn's face. "I'll see if Magne has any herbs to help with swelling."

Aeryn slid to the hay covered floor beside Grim. She stared into the pattering rain outside until the griffon settled by the cave mouth like a sentry. Under different circumstances she would try to befriend it, or speak to it. But the only creature she wanted to talk to lay crumpled in the dirty streets of Bywinter.

She hadn't even wanted Weaver at first. Caring for him was her mother's idea. But as they bonded, the bird gave Aeryn a reason to get out of bed after Daphne died.

The back of her throat tightened and water came to her eyes. She didn't want to relive that time of her life. But the memories were haunting her here. Now. Demanding her attention and eeking out the corners of her eyes.

Grim noticed.

She felt severed from her old life to a greater degree than any of her previous attempts to avoid the tannery had ever accomplished. Things were different now.

"Weaver was my only friend before you." The word didn't feel so foreign in her mouth anymore. Aeryn sniffed hard and swiped the tears from her eyes. "I was worried they'd get to you too."

Aeryn leaned her head on his shoulder. She felt his eyes on the top of her head. He let her stay that way, reminding her she wasn't here alone.

A short while later, Magne and Ophelia came with bowls of porridge. Though bland, it filled their stomachs and warmed them. Magne, though keen to provide for their needs, spoke his every thought in a quiet, ceaseless stream, mostly to himself. He made little eye-contact, and scuttled back to his yurt at the first opportunity.

Ophelia stayed with Aeryn and Grim in the cave. Aeryn watched her communicate with the griffon and listened to the pitter of the rain until she drifted off.

The jingle of horse tackle and male voices outside woke her some time later. The rain had stopped. Ophelia's voice carried indistinctly from the clearing. Aeryn listened as Iviss explained his handler's instructions to help ensure the safe escape of the Baldomar.

"He thinks we should trek through Sprucepit to Wolfwind. Says it'll be faster," Iviss said.

Ophelia sighed. "Assuming we don't meet any more

dragons."

"Any *more* dragons?"

Ophelia briefly explained Aeryn and Grim's run-in while hunting on the road to Bywinter.

Aeryn nudged Grim with her elbow. He cracked an eye. "They're here."

Aeryn's vertebrae popped as they stretched and emerged from the cave to help unload their packs. Wolfe and Iviss were both dressed for the weather. Iviss had ditched his Imperial garb for a brown hooded cloak and the heavy canvas trousers which Aeryn noticed on most working-class folk. He had rubbed some dirt on his cheeks, mouth and chin to give himself the appearance of a beard shadow. His lip was busted and swollen where Aeryn had elbowed him.

Aeryn and Grim brought their belongings to the cave and checked to make sure everything was there. It was. She immediately secured her sword to her belt.

Iviss tapped Aeryn on the arm and opened his hand. Two black feathers rested in his palm. "I got him out of the street."

Aeryn swallowed the lump in her throat. "Thank you."

She plucked them gently from his hand. She winced at the bite marks she left on his skin.

"I'm sorry about that." She pointed to the purple mark, and then nodded at his busted lip. "And that."

He touched the wound on his mouth. "Likewise. Though, word to the wise, it's generally not a good idea to fight an officer."

Aeryn bristled. "Word to the naive, they're often corrupt."

"Thank you for the validation. I feared I'd been infiltrating their organization for the last eight years for nothing," he said. "Not that it matters anymore. Thank you for that, too."

"Excuse me?"

"Had you cooperated, I could've marched you around the corner and let you go without destroying my cover." Iviss took a step closer as Ophelia came over to listen. "But you left me no choice but to arrest you. And because you and the Baldomar are a package deal, and Imperials don't steal horses and lose their prisoners, my cover is finished."

"Iviss, be fair," Ophelia said.

He ignored the warning tone and continued. "So thank you for forcing me to abandon my home and my position in Bywinter."

Aeryn narrowed her eyes.

"I suppose I should've known you were a *helpful* Imperial. Never mind that I was being chased by Cord hunters. Or that the last Imperial we encountered sent us directly to the Loom, and the ones before him tried to kill us on the road." Aeryn took a step toward him, lifting her chin. "What did you expect?"

"I suppose you believe your situation is unique?"

Frustration rose inside Aeryn. In the absence of a well-considered retort, she flicked her ear at him.

Ophelia gasped. "Aeryn!"

"Very ladylike," Iviss said.

"Oh, you're the image of chivalry," Aeryn said, her voice sharp. "How often do you punch women in the street?"

Iviss shook his head and stalked across the clearing to help Wolfe with the horses.

"What's with the ear-flicking?" Grim asked.

"It's a rude gesture for elves," Aeryn said. "Like spitting a curse without words."

"I gathered. I meant, why flick your ear at Iviss?"

Aeryn turned her palms up. "...Were you listening?"

"Don't you think there's enough ways for people to mistreat each other?" he said. "He just saved your life. You're acting like a fool."

Taken aback, Aeryn's frown deepened as she stared back at Grim.

"Grim is right," Ophelia said. "Aeryn, you should apologize."

Aeryn recovered. "Why?" she said, outraged.

"He may have been out of line, but so were you," Ophelia said. "This has been a difficult day for everyone. Keep in mind, his work is extremely dangerous. He just walked away from years of sacrifice, at great personal risk, to help you escape. He's only human. No offense intended, Grim."

"None taken."

Aeryn started at the two of them. She couldn't help feeling a little cornered, even if she knew there was truth to what they said. They watched her with sincerity, waiting for her response.

Willa came up behind Grim and nudged him in the elbow. He glanced at the griffon and patted her head. Willa closed her eyes serenely under the weight of his hand, purring.

Something inside Aeryn relented. She felt the swell of frustration ebb. It had been a terrible day, but Grim was her friend, she was too relieved they were alive and out of danger to stay angry. She took a breath.

"I'm sorry," she said, meeting their eyes.

"Alright, but I'm not really the one you should be saying that to," Grim said.

Aeryn's jaw tightened, and she fought to keep the flash of anger from rising again at the thought of Iviss. Part of her wanted to justify herself. *Fine, maybe I shouldn't have flicked my ear at him, but...*

She crammed her hands in her pockets, and her fingers brushed against Weavers feathers. The stream of defenses running through her mind ground to a halt.

Aeryn was surprised at the sudden tightness in her throat.

She had agonized over the image of her bird in the street, and now she had something to remember him by. Though part of her was annoyed they'd come from Iviss, she wouldn't trade them.

Ophelia tilted her head with meaning toward the opposite side of the clearing, where Iviss was rubbing down the horses.

Aeryn clenched her jaw. Before she could change her mind, she marched toward him, stopping along the horse's flank. She waited for him to look up, or otherwise acknowledge her presence.

He ignored her.

"Can I talk to you, or are you too busy?" she asked, her tone tighter than it probably ought to be for an apology.

He stood up straight, hand on the horse's neck, and looked

her in the face. "Just talk? Sure you didn't forget to jab me in the eye?"

Aeryn stifled a growl. "You aren't making this easy. I came to apologize to you."

They stared at each other darkly for a long moment. At last, Iviss sighed. He broke eye contact, and some of the bitterness in his expression ebbed. He rubbed his hand through his curly hair, making it puff.

"Apology accepted," he said. "I'm sorry, too. It wasn't fair to blame you…" He frowned at something over Aeryn's shoulder. "What's wrong with your companion?"

Across the hermitage, Grim held his hands curled in front of him. They were glowing.

23

The Navigator

"Grim, what's wrong with you?" Aeryn asked as she rushed to his side with Iviss. His conjecture about his runes and proximity to the Rune Reaper came to her mind immediately, which felt like a cold tugging behind her ribs.

With his expression strained, Grim cocked his head as if listening for something near-inaudible. The glow of his knuckles shone through the weave of his gloves. Ophelia hollered for Wolfe, a note of worry in her voice. Willa clacked her beak and danced around him, flustered.

Unfocused, Grim staggered away from the group toward the treeline.

"Hey! Where are you going?" Aeryn said.

Grim shook his head, disoriented. He changed course for the cave. "We can't stay."

Aeryn followed him inside the cave, with the others just behind her.

"Why?" she asked, fearing she already knew.

He brought his fists in front of him. "I don't know. They're urging me to move. I can't explain it." He tossed Aeryn her backpack. "Get your things."

"Your runes are urging you?" Iviss asked slowly. He glanced

warily between Grim and Wolfe. "Is this normal? I thought Baldomar didn't know how to use their runes anymore."

"They don't. But when ya're talking about Baldomar and their runes, there's a wide range of normal. I've seen runes do some funny things," Wolfe said. "That's dragon magic for ya. Sometimes it flares up inexplicably. Usually with good reason."

"Has this happened at all since Fogness?" Ophelia said. "Are you in pain?"

"Not in pain." Grim winced as the runes thrummed brighter through the knit of his gloves. He pulled his attention away from his hands, grabbed the last of his belongings, and marched out of the cave.

"What happened in Fogness March?" Iviss asked.

"We were close to the Rune Reaper," Aeryn said.

"What?" Wolfe asked, alarmed.

"Remember the carriage which almost ran us over in the street? When his runes acted up the first time? That was the Rune Reaper," Aeryn said as she collected the rest of her stuff. "What if he's nearby now?"

A brief silence settled over the cave. Then, as if on cue, Wolfe and Ophelia snatched their belongings off the ground. Iviss followed their lead. Aeryn exited the cave in time to see Grim enter the forest on foot.

"Grim, wait!"

She overtook him and dragged him back to the clearing, where the others emerged, and immediately readied the horses.

Aeryn, Wolfe, and Iviss quickly saddled and tacked their

steeds while Grim paced the treeline like a man consumed. He held his first curled in front of him, with a look of deep concentration, breathing heavily.

"Grim, which way, if any, are your runes prodding ya to go?" Wolfe said.

Still pacing, Grim pointed East.

Wolfe fished his bone dice from his pocket. He dislodged the lucky one from his gums, squatted, and rolled them on the packed earth.

"If we want to get him to the Chain in Wolfwind, we need to bear north," Iviss said.

"Iviss, latch your trap for a moment," Wolfe said. He rolled his dice again. Satisfied, he jammed the lucky tooth back in his mouth, and dropped the rest in his pocket. "Forget the Chain. We're taking him directly to the Keepers."

"Wolfe, I respect your seniority, but we have a protocol designed to keep the Baldomar alive," Iviss said, following him to the next horse. "We can't abandon it without good reason."

"We have a good reason," Wolfe said. "Aeryn, hand me that strap."

"Glowing tattoos?" Iviss said. "I've never heard of such a thing."

"The dice agree," Wolfe said. "I trust the runes. They're indicating the right direction anyway."

Iviss followed Wolfe to the other side of the horse.

"It's not our post," he said. "The procedure is to transfer him to the Chain, not bypass it. We don't know how to reach the

Keepers."

"I do."

"I thought only the Chain knew," Aeryn said as she secured her bag to the steed they stole from Bywinter, Sten.

"I used to be on the Chain," Wolfe said, as he tightened a strap on Hugh.

"My orders are to see these two safely to Wolfwind," Iviss said. "You're asking me to disobey my superior and abandon protocol to trek to the other side of Noemar."

Wolfe rested his hand on his hip flask, and squared off with Iviss. "Iviss, those two are going eastward whether we escort them safely or not. Ophelia and I are gonna help them find their way. No more arguing. Ya coming, or not?"

Iviss looked over the group and worked his jaw. "I guess duty demands that I am."

He heaved his bag onto Pippa's flank and secured it.

Ophelia exchanged a hurried word with the perplexed hermit. She climbed up behind Wolfe, and Grim pulled Aeryn up behind him. Without wasting another moment, he drove his heels into the horse's side and they galloped into the forest.

Grim urged the horse to speed up. Aeryn clung to him, fearing one wrong move would pitch them to their deaths. She was not an experienced rider, and neither was he. Mercifully, Sten did not care for a forced gallop through the woods, and the others quickly caught up.

They continued at a trot, which was about as fast as Grim could make Sten go, until the forest dimmed and Wolfe called for a stop.

"It's too dangerous to go all night," he said. "We're as likely to step off a ravine as stumble into the lair of some nasty beast. Let's find a place to hunker."

They found a hollow where the soil eroded beneath the shallow roots of a gnarled tree. A blanket of graybeard moss hung over the entrance to the burrow, providing some shelter. It was snug with five people, but dry, private, and warm.

As they tethered the horses to a nearby tree, Iviss nudged Aeryn and pointed at Grim. A little ways off, he paced, staring east into the treeline, occasionally glancing at his tattoos.

"Is this typical behavior for him?" Iviss asked.

She watched Grim march three paces, turn, then march three more. Turn. "This is new."

"Is he gonna take off in the night?"

"He's not stupid," she said.

"Can you persuade him to settle, then? I don't want to have to tie him to a tree."

Aeryn shot Iviss a look. "He's not a prisoner, Iviss."

"I'm aware," he said in a measured voice. "I also cannot permit him to be a danger to himself. Wolfe may be fine with skirting procedure, but I'm not. The safety of you two is the priority. I will be forced to intervene unless Grim stops acting like a madman. So can you calm him down?"

Aeryn wasn't sure what Iviss meant by *forced to intervene,* but she assumed it involved attempting to restrain Grim. Not that Iviss stood a chance at doing so. Though irritated, Aeryn detected a sincerity similar to when Iviss presented her with Weaver's feathers. She had to admit, Grim seemed unstable at the moment.

"I'll talk to him," she said.

"Thank you."

Aeryn stepped away from the others to approach Grim. "What's going through your head?"

"If we're not moving, I can't think about anything else," he said. He stopped short and held up his hands, which were glowing faintly through his gloves. "I can't explain it. But I need to follow where they're leading me."

"I believe you," Aeryn said. "Where do you think that is?"

Grim shook his head. "No idea."

Aeryn checked over her shoulder and noticed Iviss watching them. She dropped her voice. "Do you have control over yourself? At the hermitage, it was as if the urge to move took you over."

He resumed pacing. "I have control."

Aeryn watched him for a moment. "...You sure?"

Grim ignored the remark. He breathed heavily, eyes fixed on the glowing runes which had recaptured his attention.

Finally, Aeryn smacked him lightly on the arm. "Alright, Bearkiller. Stop pacing. You're making Iviss nervous that you'll wander off. He floated the idea of tying you to a tree."

Grim actually laughed, which lightened some of Aeryn's tension.

"Yes, clearly the day has taken a toll on his sanity," she said. "But I see his point. You gotta settle."

He drew to a stop, though it seemed to take every ounce of self-control he possessed.

"Are you hungry?" she asked. "Wolfe says no fire. But I have dried fruit."

Grim forced out a breath, nodded, and followed Aeryn back to the others.

24

Practice

Aeryn set up her hunting trap, but caught nothing overnight. She fell asleep with someone's elbow in her spine after waiting to hear Grim's light snoring fill the burrow. Her damp vest had taken on the aroma of a wet dog. It was a cramped and smelly evening.

Wolfe roused the group early for a quick breakfast.

"Grim, how them runes feeling?" Wolfe said. "Still a'glowing?"

Grim peeled back his gloves. Though illuminated, his knuckles were dimmer than the day before. "They still want me to go east."

"Strongly?"

"Strongly."

The look on Iviss' face reminded Aeryn of Samuel in that moment. He held his tongue, and Aeryn thought better of him for it. She understood his hesitation to an extent. The idea of someone's tattoos communicating anything sounded strange. But Iviss hadn't seen what she had before this, and she believed Grim wholeheartedly. If he said they were supposed to go east, then eastward they would go. Aeryn might not be able to confirm why, but she felt like their lives depended on it.

"Grim, it may be too soon to tell, but I think there's a

possibility your runes are leading you to your people," Ophelia said. "The stars were very non-specific. But they indicate we're on the correct course, whatever that is."

At this, Aeryn felt wide awake. Once again, the reality of the task for which they set out settled over her. It was a long way to the other end of Noemar, but with a destination in mind, they might actually find Grim's family within weeks or months.

Wolfe held up a gnarled hand, indicating Ophelia should slow down. "Grim, do your runes seem to indicate a *destination*?"

Grim shook his head, still distracted by his glowing knuckles. "Just east."

"Alright. We'll keep in mind the possibility these runes are warnin' ya away from Ulfur. Eastward is the direction of the Keepers, so if we're headed that way anyway, we might as well plan on getting ya to them."

"Ulfur is the Rune Reaper's name?" Grim asked, his eyes hard as they flicked briefly to Wolfe before resettling on his knuckles.

"Yup. This one, anyhow."

"There's others?" he asked.

Wolfe dropped his eyes and took a pull from his hip flask. "I've been in the South a few years. Haven't really kept abreast of how many of 'em are still roaming the North. Last time I was here, there were three."

"He's the last one," Iviss said.

Wolfe looked up, momentarily sober. Aeryn noticed something like shame emanating from the seasoned spy as he met Iviss' face. Or was that fear?

"Granted, he has hunters who work beneath him," Iviss said. "But as far as our information indicates, he's the last Rune Reaper."

Three quiet seconds passed. The spies' expressions were indecipherable, but Aeryn had the sensation of being outside an issue more relevant to the Silver Shadow.

Wolfe took another sip from his flask. "Lady Aeryn, ya got that map?"

"Look. I appreciate the willingness to help us," Grim said, speaking for the both of them as Aeryn unearthed the map. "But so we're clear. I don't know that this has anything to do with staying away from Ulfur. It feels different. I don't know where these are leading me, but if it's not the Keepers, then I'm not going to the Keepers. I'm following the runes."

"And I'm going with Grim," Aeryn said, passing the map to Wolfe. She gave Grim a tiny nod to let him know she was with him.

The three Shadows were quiet for another three seconds. Not for the first time, Aeryn got the feeling that they were used to being in command of the situation. Iviss and Ophelia especially.

"I completely agree," Wolfe said heartily, settling the matter. He shook out the map. "Let's take a looky here..."

As they crowded closer to see, Wolfe's alcoholic stink bit the inside of Aeryn's nose.

"We're about here," he said, pointing to an area of forest outside of Bywinter on the western side of Noemar. He traced his finger across the province directly east. About halfway across the province, he tapped a dot labeled Goldbur Gren. "The Keepers are here."

"Does that mean the Enclave is somewhere around there?" Aeryn asked. She noticed the majority of the major cities in Noemar were located close to the province's southern border, which mostly drew up to the heartlands. Aeryn only noted three settlements in the far North, and she felt relieved. Her map depicted those areas as covered in ice. Noemar near the border, like where they were now, was cold enough.

"Yup. So let's not dilly-dally." Wolfe clapped Grim on the back, the noise pulling Aeryn out of her thoughts. "Lead on, Master Grim."

Throughout the day, Grim led them relentlessly east through dense forest. His mind settled. The driving urge focused and steadied, and he was able to function normally by lunchtime while still maintaining sensitivity to navigate as the runes led. Wolfe, Ophelia, and Iviss checked frequently to see whether Grim had any inclination of their destination. He didn't.

Iviss' demeanor was much more even than the day before. He didn't argue or grate on Aeryn's nerves. Much. She started to think that perhaps Ophelia was right, and he was a professional who had been pushed to his limit with the stresses of the day before. He asked a lot of questions, and like Ophelia, was curious why she left Thoen with Grim.

"I'm going to help him find his family," she said.

"What about your family? What do they do?"

Aeryn bristled. She wondered how much he knew about the importance of younger elves following in the family trade, or the peculiarity for Aeryn to be here with Grim. Ophelia certainly would, but beyond some initial questions, she'd accepted Aeryn's explanations for leaving, and hadn't brought it up since. For all Ophelia knew, Aeryn didn't have a family.

Aeryn didn't trust Iviss not to push, though. The last thing she wanted, apart from another confrontation with the Rune Reaper, was to explain to Grim how, while she cared about his future, she'd also used him as an excuse to avoid the tannery. At least, she had initially.

"Tanners," she said, and then she changed the subject.

It was difficult to tell whether Iviss was attempting to be friendly, or gather information. He was a spy, after all. But Aeryn liked his whistling. It added levity to the trek through the forest. No one else was bothered by it except for Wolfe, whose temperament grew increasingly sour as the day stretched. He told Iviss to hush up so aggressively that Aeryn felt sorry for him.

When they stopped for a break, Wolfe stalked off to use the bushes and roll his dice in peace.

"What's Wolfe's problem today?" Aeryn asked Ophelia, keeping her voice low.

Ophelia pursed her mouth and thought for a moment.

"A combination of things. It's been a long time since he's escorted a Baldomar. The Chain is...difficult work," she said, choosing her words with care. "Also his liquor is running low. Quite a time for it..."

She smoothed her skirt. "Anyway, expect the mood to worsen. Don't take it personally. I assure you, he's as committed as ever."

The afternoon continued quietly. By evening, Wolfe was almost out of alcohol. He grew so irritable with Ophelia that she threatened to dump the rest of his supply if he didn't correct his attitude. He begrudgingly settled around the campfire with the group, until he gave himself a splinter throwing a log on the fire. After that, he gave up and marched away to bed. Ophelia wandered just beyond the edge of their campsite to stargaze alone.

Iviss tucked the rest of his rations in his bag and pointed to the sword at Aeryn's side. "Mind if I see?"

She pulled it out of the scabbard. He took it in both hands and turned it over. "Fine sword. Elvish made?"

"Yes. It was my father's during the war."

"It's been excellently maintained." He handed it back to her.

A little pang pulled at her, but Aeryn smiled at the thought of her father, and how proud he was of his service.

"If you ever wish to practice during our down time, I'd be happy to spar." Iviss nodded at Grim. "Let's see your sword."

Grim handed it over. Iviss' eyebrow cocked almost imperceptibly.

"Standard issue Imperial short sword, I see." He returned it to Grim. "I'm not going to ask where you got this."

"I'll take you up on the offer to practice," Grim said.

Iviss' face relaxed into a genuine smile which made him

look like he was a normal person. "Excellent. Are you familiar with longswords?"

"No. I like my axe."

"A longsword is easier to maneuver than an axe," Iviss said. "It'll give you more space between you and an enemy than a short sword. You can practice with mine."

Aeryn left them in conversation about the benefits and drawbacks of various weapons to find Ophelia. She sat on a boulder just outside their bivouac and gazed somberly at the heavens. Aeryn hopped onto the boulder beside her. "What do they say tonight?"

"More of the same."

"Which is?"

"Trust your companions." Ophelia knit her brows and frowned at the sky. "Ominous tidings though."

"Anything more specific?"

Ophelia shook her head. "Rarely. There are countless stars, and I only ever glimpse part of the picture." She pulled her gaze away from the sky. "How are you coping with the loss of Weaver?"

Aeryn thought for a moment as the sadness pulled at her. Her mouth flickered into a smile. "He was a good friend."

Ophelia patted her on the arm in a comforting, motherly way. "He was."

Aeryn pulled the feathers Iviss gave her from her pocket. She ran her finger over the smooth blue-black feather. "Would you help me tie these in my hair?"

"Of course."

They returned to the campfire, where Grim and Iviss were

on their feet practicing maneuvers. Ophelia regarded them, seeming pleased. "I'm going to rest. Iviss, wake me for the second watch."

"I will. We'll keep it down," he said.

Aeryn sank cross-legged beside the fire and warmed her hands. But Iviss, who was energized by the practice-session, beckoned her. "How about some practice with that fine elvish sword?"

Aeryn hesitated. As much as she wanted to improve her skill with the sword, accepting help from Iviss had been a struggle from the moment she met him. Though he grated on her less today, they had butted heads enough to make humility difficult, and she didn't want to display her lack of skill. Grim had an excuse for being unfamiliar with the sword, but her father was a veteran.

She rose, trying to recall some of the basics her father showed her years ago. She joined the men in an open space on the opposite side of the campfire. Iviss noticed the feathers in her hair and his eyes crinkled into a smile. Then he launched into instruction.

He was a patient teacher. He didn't assume prior knowledge and didn't patronize her, which helped her relax and actually learn a few things.

Iviss was handy with a weapon, wiry and fast, and she realized that if he had wanted to really hurt her in Bywinter, he could've before she even knew what was happening.

"We should practice again tomorrow," Iviss said. "I want to teach you two some knife skills, too."

"Knife skills?" Aeryn said.

"Yes. The Loom maintains a heavy presence all across

Noemar. I want you two to be prepared," he said. "Do you have a dagger?"

"I have a hunting knife," Grim said.

"Me too," Aeryn said, but then remembered the one she'd recently purchased was lying in the alley behind Applegriffon's. "Actually not anymore."

"You both need a dagger. I'll give you one of mine. I brought a dozen."

Aeryn raised her eyebrows. "A dozen?"

"You can't afford to be short on daggers."

"Is that something you learned as an Imperial?" Aeryn asked, shifting her weight to one leg.

"No. Silver Shadow."

Aeryn thought for a moment. "How'd you become a spy within the Imperials?"

"It was my assignment. Join, work my way up..." he said. He released a slow breath like reluctantly laying down his cares. "Seems the one god had different plans."

Aeryn felt a real twinge of guilt at what she might've unknowingly cost him. "How did you become a spy in the first place?"

Iviss forced a smile. "A story for another time."

Grim massaged the fatigue in the corner of his eyes. "I'm going to bed. Aeryn, you staying up?"

She hesitated a moment. "I'll be there in a minute."

Grim thanked Iviss then sauntered to the bedrolls near Ophelia and Wolfe.

Aeryn regarded Iviss. She hated him yesterday, but today, he wasn't so bad. Ophelia and Wolfe trusted him. He seemed eager to make sure they stayed safe, and Grim was comfortable enough to ask him for lessons.

"Not tired?" Iviss said.

"Exhausted," she said. The words churned in her chest, until she forced them out. "Thank you for helping us get out of the city yesterday. Really."

Iviss dipped his head once. "My duty."

"You said the spy on the Chain was dead. What happened?"

Iviss considered for a moment. "His body was found that morning. He'd been dead a few days. Loom handiwork, no doubt. I was just coming from the scene when you ran into me and the other officer."

"Was the person on the Chain close to you?"

"Personally, no. But Silver Shadows are family to one another, even if we don't work closely."

Aeryn paused, weighing how to best phrase what she wanted to say next. "I don't like how things in Bywinter went."

Iviss watched her, uncertain whether she was about to rehash their conflict yesterday, but careful not to betray what he thought. "Understandable."

"Will you teach me how to fight? Not just knife skills and swords."

"You want to be able to handle yourself if you're unarmed."

"Yes. I've had one too many close calls lately, and I'm not interested in waiting for my luck to run out."

Iviss dipped his chin. "Certainly."

25

The Hermit

Ulfur planted a boot on the beast's feathered neck. He pulled the necrotic spear out of the griffon's chest. The sharp, narrow tip glistened, black with blood.

A few feet away, the white-haired elf was in hysterics. His cheeks were wet, and he was colorless with horror. Two of Ulfur's hunters flanked the hermit, holding him on his knees.

He was pitiful. Weak.

Primed for pulling information.

The Rune Reaper jingled with each step, drawing the hermit's attention away from the dying beast. The elf's jaw trembled, eyes wide like a terrified rabbit.

"Let's not waste time, old man. I followed their tracks. I know they were here, and I know you don't have many years left. You can make this quick." Ulfur jangled with each slow, heavy step. "Or don't. Lose one body part at a time until you tell me what I want to know. It matters little to me."

The hermit quailed, but then clamped his jaw to keep it steady.

Ulfur jerked his chin to the hunter on the right. He grabbed the hermit's mop of hair and pulled his head back. Ulfur stalked nearer. He caressed the severed fingers dangling over his heart and hummed as their power seeped into him. He didn't have to know the meaning of every rune, nor the power unlocked by combining them.

This Baldomar, the one traveling with the wood elf, smelled of a different kind of magic. Perhaps this one was the key to unlocking the full potential of Silversaar's gift.

He'd find him. It was a matter of time.

Ulfur withdrew his crooked knife from his belt. He dragged the tip of it along the elf's jaw. Not enough pressure to make him bleed, but enough to make him lose his mind.

Extracting the information worked better when they were afraid.

With one hand, he grabbed the elf by the side of his head, his fingers pressing against his skull. The magic penetrated his mind like skewers, worming through his misty thoughts.

The elf cried in agony. The skin where Ulfur's fingers touched grew blue with cold, then blackened in necrosis.

Ulfur searched the hermit's mind. Tunneling through thoughts of the griffon, a fondness for an elvish woman wearing blue. The Baldomar. Here, not two days ago. The she-elf from the city had reached him, and they escaped to the hermitage together.

Ulfur pried for more.

There were others.

Two more human men. He recognized the old one. He knew that scar across his cheek. Ulfur gave it to him, and the man had repaid him with his dead eye. *So he was still alive after all this time.*

Reaching further into the hermit's mind, Ulfur came upon

snippets of overheard conversation. The Chain. Wolfwind.

Ulfur released the elf. He felt weak as he staggered back a step.

The elf gasped for air. He was weeping. His whole body shook.

"Such loneliness in your mind, Magne," Ulfur said through ragged breaths. He tutted. "I told you I'd get what I came for."

He left the broken elf in the custody of his hunters to move throughout the camp. There was nothing of value in the yurt. The Baldomar's scent lingered in the cave. He grasped some of the hay from the packed earth and sniffed deeply.

He stuck the hay in his jacket pocket and searched the perimeter of the hermitage. Horses departed at a heavy gallop. They were a little off-course from Wolfwind. He followed the tracks for a few minutes to give his muscles a chance to stop shaking.

This was not the way to Wolfwind.

"What are you not telling me, Magne?" Ulfur said, losing his patience as he stormed back into the clearing. He marched toward the hermit. The elf recoiled at his approach, but Ulfur caught him by the forehead. The elf cried out as Ulfur reached into his mind once more.

A hurried exit. The runes.

The runes were flaring with magic, leading the Baldomar. But where?

Ulfur pressed further, but that was all the hermit knew. An apologetic farewell from the she-elf in blue. A hurried exit. An empty camp.

Ulfur withdrew his hand. The broken elf's head lolled, blackened and bloody from Ulfur's fingertips. He drew a haggard breath.

"We have what we came for," Ulfur said to the hunter on the right. Drawing the knife from his belt, he took a step toward the hermit and drove it home.

The elf wheezed his last breath. Ulfur dropped the body in the dirt. "Find me a swift creature. Alive."

26

Music

Wolfe clanged around their bivouac. He was in a foul mood. Near the campfire, Grim ate breakfast with his eyes on the eastern treeline. Aeryn blinked the sleep from her eyes and lifted herself from her bedroll. Ophelia stirred beside her. A little further away Iviss was stretching.

Aeryn plopped next to Grim. She scooped a spoonful of steaming oatmeal into her dish. "He run out of liquor yet?"

"Early this morning," Grim said.

"You been up a while?"

"Someone had to make breakfast."

Aeryn double licked her spoon, savoring the oatmeal with nuts and berries stirred in. He had added some of the spices she purchased in Bywinter. It warmed her from the inside. She tipped her head back and sighed. "You should make breakfast every day."

Grim gave her a sidelong glance, but his mouth twitched into a smile.

Iviss sauntered over and helped himself to a serving. Ophelia joined them a few moments later.

"Wolfe, have you eaten?" she asked, her voice carrying across camp to where he was sniff-testing his socks.

Wolfe winced and held a palm to his forehead. "Ya think I'm some airy-fairy pronk? Don't mother-hen me, woman!"

Ophelia pursed her lips and cut her eyes at her partner.

"Grim, do your runes still indicate we should go east?" Iviss asked.

Grim dipped his chin.

"Then eastward we continue," Ophelia said, returning to her breakfast.

They were still a few days out from civilization and they rode hard throughout the day. That evening, Wolfe's moodiness gave way as he dissolved into shakes and fever.

"Go to bed," Aeryn told him after a scant supper of rations. She handed him a sprig of gingerwort to help with his headache. Wolfe chewed and swallowed it without water. He shuffled across the camp for bed. He'd been a thorn in the boot all day. While his withdrawal symptoms were the result of his own choices, seeing him so obviously ill prompted a smidgeon of pity in Aeryn.

"I'll take his watch," Grim said.

"I'll hunt first thing tomorrow. We need some fresh food. It'll help." She nudged Grim with her elbow. "You coming?"

"Sure."

The mood lightened after Wolfe went to sleep. Ophelia gazed happily at the stars while Iviss ran through some drills with Grim and Aeryn. Iviss presented them each with a dagger in a black leather case. The blade was short enough to be easily concealed. Its edge was razor sharp.

"Someone skilled isn't going to let you see the knife until it's too late. Avoid situations where someone can get close enough to stab you," Iviss said. "The best way to defend yourself is to keep aware and keep your distance."

"What's the maneuver for disarming someone if they get close enough?" Aeryn asked.

"I don't want you to worry about disarming them. It's too quick and chaotic of a weapon, and it would take a lot of practice to master it," he said. "If you're that close to the attacker, you're going to get cut. At that point, your job is to end it. I'll show you some maneuvers."

They ran through some practice scenarios until they felt comfortable. A brisk wind seeped through the trees to make them shiver, so Ophelia made tea, and Iviss called for a break.

"How about a story?" Ophelia said.

"Do you know any good ones?" Aeryn took the cup of tea in her hands as sat cross legged near the fire.

"I know the best one, and it's true."

Grim and Iviss settled down, and when Ophelia had her own cup of tea, she sat up straight and cleared her throat.

"In the beginning, there were dragons. Some believe they created the world, others say it was the gods, but most agree the dragons helped fill it with beauty. This is why Wholls is called The Heartlands. It is there life began," Ophelia said. "The dragons loved variety. They looked with affection on the people, giving traits they valued, which characterize the different people groups today.

"To the orcs, who were hewn from the rock, they bestowed a fierce independence, sharp intellect, and natural craftsmanship. They became expert builders and tacticians.

"To the elves, who were formed from the trees, they gave longer lifespans, a zest for life, and the ability to acclimate to various natural environments. Aeryn, your keen eyesight and resistance to biting insects attest to this.

"To humans, who were molded from the earth, they gave tenacity, ingenuity, and adaptability. This is why you see humans creating and thriving in every province.

"The first generation of dragons saw themselves as benevolent governors. They were mostly content to let the people govern themselves. They alone had the ability to use magic. They could weave spells, which were temporary, or imbue it into creation. This was permanent. Some of these places still exist in the world today, but many were destroyed.

"Infighting led to people spreading out, and the dividing of nations, and the dragons decided never to bestow magic beyond what remains into creation. Hence why giving the runes to a clan of humans was so controversial."

They warmed up listening to the story of how Takara the dragoness once brought a tree to life, which wrought chaos until the dragoness put a stop to it. Whatever measure Takara used to stop the sentient tree, it altered the landscape ever after. All elves knew this story as the reason why their forest was special, full of trees which grew larger and stronger than anywhere else. The event was the reason they could build homes in the trees without harming the tree. Aeryn had been told this wasn't the case elsewhere in the world. It was also the seed which sparked a longstanding mistrust between the elves and the dragons. She'd never heard the story told with any measure of generosity towards Takara, beyond crediting her with correcting her mistake. Ophelia had a higher view of dragons than most elves.

Wolfe reappeared, his blanket wrapped around his shoulders. He hunkered near the fire, looking haggard.

"Can't sleep?" Grim asked.

Wolfe hiccuped and shook his head.

"Maybe Aeryn can sing you a lullaby," Grim said.

She gave him a questioning eye, surprised he'd volunteer her for such a thing.

"The one with the night birds and crickets in the meadow," Grim continued. "You know the one."

He hummed a line.

Aeryn stopped with her cup inches from her mouth and stared at him. Each note cut to her core like a knife. Instantly she was transported to the last time she sang the lullaby for her baby.

"I haven't heard that one," Ophelia said, brightening. "Did you or someone you know create it?"

"Stop it!" Aeryn said, bringing an abrupt end to the tune. "How do you know that song? Where did you hear it?"

Grim frowned. "From you. You sing it in your sleep sometimes."

"I sing it in my sleep?" Heat rushed to Aeryn's cheeks and her mouth dried up. It felt like a pit dropped through her stomach.

"Not all at once, and not every night," he said.

Aeryn's face contorted and she glowered at Grim. To learn that she sang in her sleep in front of everyone was humiliating enough.

Of all the songs in the world, it had to be one she made for her daughter.

"Don't ever sing that song again," Aeryn said, spitting out the words. She turned on Wolfe, her tone savage. "I'm not singing you a lullaby."

Thick silence fell over the camp.

Aeryn scowled into her tea and burned her tongue trying to drink it too fast. Her mind was back six years ago, struggling to push out the memory of the last time she held her child alive and sang that song.

For weeks after Daphne died, she barely ate and couldn't get out of bed, let alone make it through any song. Instead of solace and joy, music brought pain. Every sweet note, an accusation. It broke her down and reminded her that things would never be right again.

"Aeryn?"

Her focus snapped to the present. The others watched her, waiting for a response.

Iviss cleared his throat. The way he said her name told her it wasn't the first time he'd said it. "Are you up for sword practice before you turn in?"

"Oh." Aeryn chugged the last of her tea and popped to her feet. "Yeah. Fine."

Practice was awful. Grim's mention of the lullaby tunneled into her head and heart and threw her off. She confused her maneuvers. Grim outperformed her. She crawled into bed without saying a word to anyone.

Like Wolfe, she spent a restless night, worried that the music would attempt its escape the moment she closed her eyes. How was it that the mere mention of that song threatened to unhinge her?

Painful memories were such opportunists. One moment, everything felt comfortable, and the next moment was a deluge of cold water which drenched her to the bones.

Aeryn woke early the next morning, and shook Grim awake. Grim got ready quietly, grabbing his axe, careful not to disturb Iviss or Wolfe.

Ophelia stoked the campfire and warmed her hands. "Try to be back in an hour or two. I know it's not long, but we should try to leave by midmorning."

They trekked into the woods without speaking.

Aeryn's remedy to clear her mind wasn't working. She failed to notice a wild turkey who scratched in the dirt until Grim pointed it out from forty feet behind her. By then it was too late.

Aeryn tracked the bird. Just as he came into view, a flicker of movement in the distance caught her attention. A wild pig nosed in the brush.

Turkey, or pig?

She took aim and sent an arrow at the pig.

She missed.

Spooked, the boar squealed and dashed into the wood. The turkey scuttled away in the opposite direction.

Aeryn sprinted after the boar like a dart. She grabbed

another arrow as she ran, but tripped over an exposed root and landed prone in the forest detritus. Her arrows spilled from the quiver. The boar disappeared.

Fuming and red with embarrassment, she gathered her arrows and jammed them into her quiver. Grim caught up with her, but she shook her head when he offered a hand to pull her to her feet. She rotated her wrist, which landed awkwardly beneath her when she fell. She winced at the pine needles which embedded in her skin.

"What's going on with you?" Grim asked, his tone direct.

"I fell." She glowered at her palm and plucked out another pine needle.

"You know what I'm talking about, Aeryn. Last night, you were ready to stab someone in the eye when I brought up the lullaby for Wolfe. You've been off since," he said. "It's affected your practice, you woke me up constantly with your rolling around, and now hunting."

Aeryn bunched her face into a deep frown.

"What, you disagree?"

She dropped her eyes and prodded the root with her toe. Her heart rolled around her ribcage, searching for the words that needed escape, but not wanting to expose herself.

"It's the song," she said at last. "It brings up memories."

Grim watched her for a moment. "Did you write it?"

"I did. I haven't sang in a very long time." She scoffed. "Unless you count singing in my sleep. Why didn't you tell me I did that? It's strange."

"I thought you knew."

"How would I know? I lived alone before you came along. Who would've told me? Weaver?"

"Maybe he liked it."

Aeryn snorted.

Grim thought for a moment. "Do you like it?"

"The song?"

"No, singing in general."

Aeryn thought for a moment. Sadness tugged at her heart. She nodded. "I used to have a lute. It's a stringed instrument. A gift from my parents when I turned fifteen." A twitch worked its way to the corner of her mouth. "My friend Sariel and I started a two-person band. We looked for opportunities to sing in the village. She loved impressing those Imperials when they came through town."

Grim arched an eyebrow. "Is it the uniforms?"

She snorted. "For Sariel, the fact that they were young men was intriguing enough. I just wanted to make pretty music."

Grim watched her like he was seeing a new side of her. "You should sing us some of your other songs."

Aeryn took a deep breath and bit her lip as she considered.

"I don't know the first thing about music, but the lullaby is good," he said. "I won't bring it up again if you don't want me to."

Aeryn thought for a moment. Maybe one day. Like Ophelia, who could talk about her late husband while remaining composed.

"Maybe," she said. "We've been gone awhile. Let's head back."

They walked beside each other for a few minutes in companionable silence, when Aeryn stopped him, and pointed.

A hundred feet away, a dozen pikdeer nibbled on the undergrowth. Though still smaller than a normal deer, they were bigger than the variety in Thoen, and their horns had a curve.

Aeryn readied an arrow, creeping as close as she dared without spooking the herd. She took aim and took the shot. She struck the nearest, pinning it to the ground and killing it instantly. The rest of the herd scattered, flashing their white tails as they fled.

Aeryn retrieved her catch. The arrow was intact. She lifted the beast by its horns. "Can you hold it by its back legs for a few minutes while I dress it, or should we get some rope and go after another one?"

"We don't have time to hang it up and look for more. Let's dress it." Grim hoisted the beast off the ground, holding it away from his body. He scanned the woods while Aeryn got to work bleeding the beast and removing its entrails.

"Wolfe was right about the creatures here being bigger and badder. There's good meat on this," Aeryn said as she removed the last of the inedible organs in its belly. "I'm surprised the griffon liked you so much."

"Thanks a lot."

Aeryn rolled her eyes. "You know what I mean. I've always heard they were vicious. I'm a little jealous."

"I think it was the runes, not me. Ophelia said they're fond of magic, remember?" Grim said.

Aeryn's eyes lit up. "Maybe griffons live at the Enclave too.

All those rune-bearers in one place..." Aeryn cut a length of rope and tied the pikdeer closed. "All set."

She met Grim's eyes, feeling a friendly affection for the blonde Northerner. "I hope your family is there, if that's where we're going. They're going to be so happy to see you."

"What if they're not there?"

"Then we keep looking. I told you I'd help you find them. I meant it."

A scurry through the underbrush made them jump. A rabbit shot forth, as if chased by a predator, and collapsed at their feet, panting. Aeryn drew another arrow, prepared for whatever predator might burst through the undergrowth in pursuit, but the forest was still and silent.

The rabbit's rapid breaths made it look like it was shaking. Its fur was damp and ragged, and its feet bloody. The rabbit adjusted its head to observe the two people looming overhead. It had one healthy eye, and one the color of milk.

"Grim, look at his feet. They're raw." Moved with pity, Aeryn crouched. "It's like he pushed himself to exhaustion."

"Look at his eyes. He's not healthy."

Aeryn gently shushed the rabbit. She extended her fingers to stroke his side. She looked the creature in the eye, attempting to connect with it and offer a modicum of comfort before he succumbed. As soon as her mind touched his, she screamed. She pulled her hand away, as if she had burned it, and fumbled for her dagger.

Before she could use it, the beast convulsed. It squealed

with unmistakable agony. Then it was still. Any remaining life in his little body was gone.

Breathing heavily and feeling suddenly shaky, Aeryn stepped away from the creature, pushing Grim to back up. "You were right. We have to go. Those eyes. Those were Ulfur's eyes."

"What are you talking about?" Grim said.

Aeryn shook her head to clear it. "Something was wrong. When I tried to talk to it, it wasn't just the rabbit's consciousness. There was a second presence. It pulled away when I made contact."

"The rabbit was possessed?"

A chill rolled over Aeryn's body and she nodded. "I think he was controlling the rabbit, seeing what it saw, and forcing it to catch up with us."

"We need to get back now."

27

Ten

They ran the rest of the way, the sounds of harried activity from camp carrying into the forest. Ophelia and Iviss were throwing packs onto the backs of the horses. Wolfe leaned against a tree, bent double and sweaty. He blinked at Aeryn and Grim, rubbed his eyes, and blinked again. He called over his shoulder. "They're back."

Ophelia jogged over, placing a hand on her chest. "We were about ready to come find you. I never should've let you go. Saddle up. We packed your things." She offered Wolfe her arm and led him to the horses.

"What's going on here?" Grim asked, following. He gave Wolfe a leg up onto the horse behind Ophelia, then mounted Sten, pulling Aeryn up behind him.

"The dice say we gotta move." Wolfe wiped his clammy forehead. "Some'n coming."

"Ulfur?" Aeryn asked.

"Likely." Wolfe closed his eyes, panting.

"We think he's tracking us with animals," Aeryn said. She explained about the rabbit, their expressions grew more disturbed.

"Keep your bow out," Iviss said, climbing onto Pippa.

They flicked their reins, and urged the horses into the wood at a gallop.

They followed the leading of Grim's runes, riding hard for

a few hours when the trees started to thin. Encountering a shallow stream, they refilled their water skins, then marched the horses through the water for a mile, exiting along the gravel on the other side to minimize tracks. The landscape opened into rockier terrain. Mountains cut the horizon like teeth.

They entered the mountains by midday, stopping only a few minutes at a time before remounting to press on. By afternoon, the pikdeer remained uncooked. Wolfe leaned against Ophelia's back, eyes cracked, muttering and trembling. Ophelia called for a stop.

Aeryn tried to get a fire going to cook the meat before it spoiled. Just as the flame caught, Wolfe cast his die. "Put it out. Back on the horses."

"We've gone hard all day," Aeryn said. It sounded whiney and argumentative, but what she meant was , *Ulfur can't be that close, can he?*

Wolfe's fingers trembled as he rolled again. "We ride through the night. Put that elvish eyesight to good use, Lady Aeryn."

He hobbled toward his mount.

Aeryn had better vision in low light than Grim, so she took over driving the horse, with Grim providing directional shifts as needed. Iviss followed close behind, with Ophelia and Wolfe at the rear. With thinner trees in the mountain pass, the moonlight provided enough light to avoid a grievous accident. But without the forest to buffer the wind, the air felt bitter. By the time the sky lightened to gray, Aeryn's fingers ached from the cold. Everyone looked worn and felt stiff, but they had made it to the other side of the mountain. A town was nestled in the valley below.

Midmorn, they found a cave on the mountainside large enough to fit everyone and the horses. Wolfe staggered to a corner of the cave and curled up on the floor. He didn't bother to unfurl his bedroll. As an afterthought, he pulled his dice out, and still horizontal, cast them on the cave floor. He squinted at them, then laid his head. "Safe for now."

As the men unsaddled the horses, Ophelia set up an area for sleep. Aeryn checked the pikdeer only to be greeted by its rank odor. She shut the cavity, suppressing a gag.

"How desperate are we for food?" she asked the group.

"We have enough rations for a day or two," Grim said. "Maybe longer. Wolfe isn't eating much right now." He nodded at the carcass. "Why? No good?"

In response, Aeryn opened up the cavity and let the stench waft toward him.

He grimaced. "You're not considering cooking that, are you?"

Aeryn shut the cavity. "It'd probably be safe as long as it's thoroughly cooked, though it'd taste terrible."

Grim waved a hand in front of his face. "We're not that desperate," he said. "Bury that outside."

Aeryn heaved it off the cave floor. "I hate waste."

As Aeryn packed the last of the dirt and rocks on the carcass, the tumble of loose stones drew her attention up the mountainside. Eight wooly goats were making their way down the rocky crags, oblivious to her presence. Aeryn dashed into the cave for her bow.

"What's wrong?" Grim asked, tense.

"Goats!" she said with a big grin. She dashed outside and caught one before it could get away.

It was the first fresh meat they'd had in days and it cheered everyone. Wolfe even ate a little before lying back down.

"Ophelia?" Aeryn asked as delicately as possible. "Is he going to be alright?"

The worry lines which had etched into Ophelia's face over the past few days deepened. She kept her voice down. "He has over ten years of alcohol leaving his body. When I worked as an alchemist in Nyassa, on occasion we sold potions to help people handle it. Sometimes they still died."

"He could die?" Aeryn said. She'd heard of people dying from too much drink, but never from quitting.

"He'd be doing considerably worse if not for his lucky tooth," she said. She pressed her lips together and took a moment to gain composure. "We'll see."

Iviss prodded the fire with a stick. "Let's discuss a plan. With Ulfur behind us, we need to keep moving. We'll take the day to rest. The horses need it too. Tomorrow morning, we should go into town. I can attempt to make contact, see if we can acquire some aid. We will not be staying at the inn."

"Why not?" Aeryn asked.

"If you're following someone across the province, who might've stopped in a small town, where's the first place you'd look?"

Aeryn conceded with a nod.

"Any locals we encounter will recognize we're passing travelers. Be as unmemorable as possible. So, Grim, keep your gloves on. Aeryn, with your appearance and your accent, you can't pass as anything but an elf from Thoen, possibly the only one in Noemar. Keep your hood up, or your hair down to cover your ears, and try not to talk to anyone," he said. "We'll pray Wolfe doesn't mutter anything too awkward."

"What if someone asks our business?" Aeryn said.

"Respond with something boring which provides no information," he said. "Or tell them to mind their own business. Remember, we're in the North. Northerners are about as hospitable as the mountains after several feet of snowfall."

Aeryn smirked at Grim. "Jemma was hospitable."

"Jemma was nuts," Grim said.

"Who's Jemma?" Iviss asked.

"A server at Applegriffons. I worked with her while we waited in Bywinter," Aeryn said. "Grim worked with her father at the lumberyard."

Iviss' mind worked to place her. "I'm not sure I know her."

Ophelia spoke up. "Civilian."

"Did you get personal with her?" he asked Grim.

"Personal?" Grim asked.

"He was with one of us the entire time in Bywinter," Ophelia said. "They stuck to their alibi. She doesn't know anything."

Iviss thought for a moment. "The hunters found the lumberyard without tracking Aeryn and me through the catacombs.

Which means Jemma gave Ulfur information. Let's just hope he didn't hurt her for it."

❖

Aeryn stepped outside early the next morning, and froze. The sun was rising behind the eastern mountains and streaked the sky with pink and gold. Two eagles shrieked high over the valley below. The birds circled each other, then crashed together, talons locked, and plummeted. They fell a hundred feet, broke apart, and climbed into the sky to repeat their dance.

It was too good to keep to herself. Aeryn peeked into the cave and hissed at Iviss. "You have to see this."

Iviss, who was on watch and the only other person awake, joined her at the mouth of the cave. Beaming, she pointed at the eagles who were once again in mid-plummet.

"I've never seen eagles," she said.

"They don't have them in Thoen?"

"Not where I lived," she said. "I wish Grim could see this."

"See what?" Grim emerged behind them, scratching his beard and yawning. Aeryn pointed, studying his face as his eyes tracked the winged spectacle over the valley.

His beard was significantly thicker than Iviss', which seemed odd. It depended on the culture, but humans came of age anywhere between sixteen and nineteen. Even if Iviss came of age on the younger end of that range, he claimed he had been a spy in Bywinter for eight years, which would make him older than Grim. Her observation of human men was that they grew hairier with age, yet Iviss only had a few soft whiskers over his lip and chin.

"Iviss, how old are you?" she asked.

"I'm twenty-eight."

"You look younger."

"That's because I'm a eunuch."

Aeryn blinked and exchanged a look with Grim. "You're kidding."

"No. Most Silver Shadows are. You didn't know?"

"No," Aeryn said. "...Is it a requirement?"

"With a few exceptions, yes," he said. "It makes us better spies. We can do our job without the distractions and desires most other men and women face. And because we undergo the procedure before puberty, it allows more versatility when we need to disguise ourselves."

Before...? "How old were you?"

"I was given to the Silver Shadow when I was ten, but I didn't complete my oath until fourteen."

"Ten?" Aeryn's eyebrows jumped up her forehead. "Ophelia said they groomed their spies from a young age, but ten?"

"Ten is typical."

Grim folded his arms across his chest, a shadow passing over him. "Your faction takes kids, castrates them, and turns them into spies?" he said.

Iviss took a breath. "Children are not taken. Parents give them to the organization. Silver Shadow trains them. Provides them skills and values to prepare them for spywork. After the training, if they choose to enter the service, they take an oath and undergo sterilization. Male and female."

"Do parents know that they're giving their children up to be eunuchs and spies?" Aeryn asked.

"They do."

Aeryn struggled to believe what she was hearing. "And they simply make this choice for their children?"

"Parents make all kinds of life-altering decisions for their children," Iviss said. "At the end of training, no one is forced to take the oath or undergo the procedure."

"How many walk away?" Aeryn said, her voice tightening. "They've been left by their parents and raised to do one thing."

Iviss tucked his hands into pockets and considered Aeryn's words, deciding how to best respond.

"Does it disturb you at all?" she said. "Consider what you're fighting against. The Loom kidnaps and enslaves children, and your organization uses children for their own ends."

Iviss took a breath.

"It may not have been my choice to go to the Silver Shadow as a ten-year-old. My mother made the best decision she could. My father was gone, and she had six other mouths to feed," he said. "With the Shadow, she knew I'd be cared for and eventually make a difference in the world. You know what? She was right. Would you care to know my first major mission in Bywinter?"

"What was it?"

"I broke up a Loom-run brothel. I helped young ladies who had been kidnapped by Cords return to their families so they could try to put their lives back together."

Aeryn looked to Grim. His expression was grave.

"I know I'll never have a family in the traditional sense, but I don't need to. My life is not diminished," Iviss said. "You ask if I think it's moral what the Shadow did to me? It doesn't matter. I'm here now, and I've given myself to this work. If I could go back and make a different choice, I wouldn't. I don't know a single Shadow who would."

Grim thought for a moment, and scratched his beard again. Aeryn watched as his course of thought shifted. He still disapproved of the Shadow's methods for acquiring spies, he seemed to accept that they were at least accomplishing some good against a common enemy.

"Okay." He sauntered away to use the bushes.

Aeryn felt unsettled. She rubbed her arms for warmth.

"You're uncomfortable," Iviss observed.

"I'm not uncomfortable."

"You're a terrible liar, too."

She gave him a sidelong glare. He flashed a grin.

They finished the leftover goat for breakfast. Wolfe, though sweaty and bleary-eyed, was able to remain upright. They packed up and descended the mountain, arriving in town a little before midday.

Harskin was larger than Merioake, but smaller than Bywinter, and full of tall fair-haired humans. They received a few curious looks from passersby as they refilled their waterskins and watered the horses at the well. Ophelia stayed outside atop the horse with Wolfe, who leaned against her, half-asleep. They purchased assorted rations at a general store, and eventually came upon a bakery bearing the name *Helen's Fresh Bread.*

Iviss stepped inside for a few moments. When he returned, the shop owner locked the door and drew the curtains. Iviss grabbed Pippa's bridle. "Follow me."

He led them around the back of the building to a yard walled in by tall hedges and a gate. There was a private well, a stable with cows, a couple goats, and chickens. They led the horses into the barn.

"Just grab your belongings," Iviss said. "Helen said she'll take care of the horses."

Grim gave Wolfe a shoulder to lean on as they hobbled out of the stable. At the back door of the building, a brusque woman in a flour-dusted apron waved them inside. Her flaxen hair was swept into a bun and she appeared to be middle-aged.

"Poor Wolfie," the woman said in a thick, northern accent. "He better not hack his sickness all over my breads."

"It's withdrawal," Ophelia said.

"Oh. Well, hurry inside." The woman ushered them in and locked the door. "I'm Helen." She flashed her silver pendant for Aeryn and Grim to see. "This way."

The mouthwatering smells of fresh bread were overpowering. They wove through the kitchen with sacks of wheat and barley on one side, long wooden countertop dusted with flour, a hearth, and an oven like the one Samuel's in-laws used at their bakery. A hallway ran between the kitchen and the storefront, featuring a pantry, a supply closet, and a narrow staircase leading to a second floor.

Halfway down the hall, they stopped in front of a closet with a rack of rolling pins, jams, loaf pans, and dough-cutting tools. The contents of the rack rattled as Helen rollen it out of the way. She pushed a brick on the wall at the back of the closet. There was a scraping noise as the brick gave way under the pressure of her fingers, and a hidden door swung inward. She grabbed an oil lamp from off the rack, lit it, and led the way down a flight of stairs.

"You'll be safe here for the night. I'm the only one in town who knows about the door," Helen said. The dry cellar boasted two two-tiered bunks, a tiny table and chairs, and a chamber pot in the corner. No privacy. Wolfe hobbled to the nearest bunk and flopped onto the lower bed, moaning.

Helen shook her head. "Withdrawal, eh?"

"He requires medicine," Ophelia said.

"I have to reopen and I can't have you accessing the secret door during normal business hours," Helen said, as if that should be obvious. "Tell me what you need, and I'll bring it by suppertime."

Ophelia acquired a scrap of parchment and scrawled a list of ingredients. "If they don't have the potion made already, I can make it, but it'll be costly. Here." She pulled a thin gold band from her pocket and dropped it into Helen's palm. "This should cover it."

Helen slipped the ring and parchment into her apron pocket.

"You know Wolfe?" Aeryn asked Helen.

"Wolfie is a legend. It's good to see him back on the Chain," Helen said. She turned to the group. "You'll have to keep it down. Storefront is directly overhead. There's some extra candles over there. I'll bring you something tasty around suppertime, and we can see about some hot baths."

Since practicing knife skills and swordplay was out of the question, Iviss produced a deck of cards from his pack to kill the time. The game was called Dragon's Bounty, and it was a mixture of luck and strategy. Grim caught on quickly, but Aeryn struggled. She did just well enough to keep her from giving up on the game altogether. Being a new player, she couldn't be certain, but she suspected Iviss started cheating after they got a handle on the rules, and she took some pleasure in Grim outperforming him.

That evening Helen came downstairs and brought several crusty loaves of bread, bowls of creamy chicken and tomato soup, and the potion ingredients for Ophelia. Within ten minutes, Ophelia prepared it and administered it to Wolfe. He relaxed into a peaceful sleep for the first time in days.

"What's the word around here?" Iviss asked as he cleaned his bowl with a piece of bread.

"We had a large contingent of Imperials pass through recently. Managed to acquire a few recruits," Helen said. "Looks like war with Kharsh is inevitable."

"Why?" Aeryn asked.

"Kharsh was the last province to join the Empire of Errebos. It wasn't a popular decision. The warlords were desperate to defend their people against the dragons and the Loom," Iviss said. "Errebos upheld their end of their agreement, but to a limited extent. The tensions have only continued to mount, leading to open fighting, and attacks on both sides of the border."

"We have old allies there. It'd be a shame to lose any," Helen said.

"What's the presence of the Loom here?" Iviss said.

"Same as anywhere else in the North. Spies everywhere," she said. "But, I have cheering news. Seems a little while back, one of their mines down south received a major set-back. *Massive riot.* They've been unable to continue operations."

Grim and Aeryn stopped chewing to exchange a look.

"How'd you hear about it?" Grim asked.

"Our people along the Wholls-Illwali border. Word travels," Helen said. "You know about it?"

"I started it."

Helen and Iviss, who had not yet heard about that detail, beheld Grim with something like awe.

"You started the revolt?" she asked, astonished.

Grim dipped his head, his expression grave.

She smacked the table. "Good gods. Who would've thunk I'd have a hero stayin' in my cellar?"

"I'm not a hero," Grim said. "Everyone else died. Which means I'm the only one who can get justice for what happened to us."

Quiet fell over the room, and Grim finished his meal and set his empty bowl on the table.

"Well I hope I'm not sheltering you so you can run to your death," Helen said. She took Grim's bowl. "I'll get a bath started upstairs. Ladies first."

◩

Since arriving in Noemar, Aeryn hadn't felt anything so refreshing and comforting as that bath. After everyone was clean, they huddled around the hearth in the bakery's kitchen, feeling fresh and smelling much better. Fatigue seeped into their bones and they shuffled back to the cellar once dry.

Wolfe, who could not be disturbed, smelled so bad, no one wanted to double up with him. Iviss took the bunk above him. On the other side of the room, Grim collapsed into the bottom bunk. Aeryn and Ophelia were small enough to share the top.

Aeryn pulled her covers over her shoulders and buried her face into her blanket and drifted off.

But not for long.

"Aeryn. Ophelia. Get up." Grim shook Aeryn out of a sound sleep. Iviss and Wolfe were on their feet, harnessing their packs.

"We have to go now," Grim said. "He's coming."

28

The Bakery

Ulfur wiggled the doorknob of the bakery. Locked. He stroked the fingers dangling from the cord around his neck. A tingling sensation seeped into his own fingers as he touched the rune capable of helping him get around this problem.

Hand on the lock, he heard the characteristic *click*, and opened the door with ease.

His belt jingled quietly as he stepped a heavy boot into the empty bakery, lit only by the glow of the streetlamp outside.

He sniffed the air. It was challenging to detect over the yeasty aroma of rising bread, but the Baldomar's scent lingered here. It grew stronger as he entered the kitchen.

The thrill of the hunt energized him. It had been at least three years since his last Baldomar. There was something distinct about this one which drove Ulfur into single-minded pursuit. Runes Ulfur had not yet collected.

He never expected the news which drew him to Fieldgate would lead to this. It was, he decided, a worthwhile detour from his primary quarry.

At times, years passed without so much as a whisper as to the quarry's whereabouts. There was no telling what magic lied dormant within him, nor the extent of his wrath should he resume his full power. But the object of his pursuit had eluded his grasp for nearly a hundred years, slippery wyrm that he was. A little more time made no difference.

Ulfur heard a mechanical click behind him. He threw his shoulders sideways eight inches, avoiding the crossbow bolt which buried itself in the wall beside his head. He turned around and found the woman, crouched on the stairs, holding a crossbow. Her face was ashen in the moonlight streaming through the window at her back. Their eyes met and she swore.

Ulfur's mouth curled in the corner. "Let's see what you know."

29

A New Plan

Grim watched Aeryn dash forward, dagger in hand. She thrust and Iviss caught her wrist. With her free hand, she grabbed his, and swiveled her knifehand out of his grasp. With blinking speed, she slashed the sheathed weapon across his forearm, then drove it toward his neck. She stopped the weapon an inch from his neck.

She was getting pretty good, Grim thought.

Iviss smacked the dagger out of the way. "Again. Don't forget to slash the neck."

He tapped the side of his neck with two fingers, indicating the blood vessel he wanted her to target.

They ran through the exercise a few more times, building onto the skills Iviss taught them since fleeing Bywinter. In addition to knives and swordplay, Iviss had begun working with Aeryn on unarmed fighting. She was learning all kinds of creative ways to dislocate elbows, break fingers, and maximize pain given her small size.

Grim respected her initiative.

He stood by, watching and waiting for his turn, with Wolfe at his side. The potion Ophelia administered in Harskin had cured Wolfe of his withdrawal symptoms, and he made a full recovery. Just in time, too. As soon as he woke up, he'd rolled the dice and announced they needed to leave immediately.

It had been a week since fleeing the bakery in the middle of the night. They spent three relentless days pushing east before they exited the mountains into shrubby wilderness. According to Wolfe's recollection, they were nearing a mid-sized city called Ingomar. They had come far, but still had two-thirds of Noemar to cross before they reached the eastern end.

"We should consider disguises for heading into the city tomorrow," Iviss said after evening practice. "Ulfur and his hunters are looking for a party of five. Three human men, two elvish women. We propose we enter in two groups, and alter our appearance so he doesn't find anyone matching our description."

"Iviss, on the Chain, we keep together as much as possible," Wolfe said. He warmed his gnarled fingers on the mug of tea, which he no longer spiked with liquor. "Plus, ya're misunderstanding something about Ulfur. He doesn't track like a normal man."

"What do you mean?" Grim asked, even as his thoughts jumped to their disturbing encounter with the possessed rabbit.

Wolfe turned to Aeryn. "When ya saw him, did you notice what he wore around his neck?"

A sickened look passed over Aeryn's face. "Fingers."

Wolfe frowned deeply and dipped his head once. "Fingers. Not just hunting trophies, though they are that too. He wants the runes for their power."

"You said most people don't know how to use them," Grim said.

"True. Folk don't know all of them. Certainly not how to

use the allur."

Grim felt a fidgeting in the back of his mind, like he should know that word. But it remained so far out of reach so as to make him second-guess that he ought to know it at all.

"What's the allur?" he asked.

"That was the gift from Silversaar. See how ya got three runes on each finger? Silversaar helped your people know their symbols, and how to combine them in order to more powerfully use the magic. That's the allur," Wolfe said. "When he disappeared, the knowledge of how to do that disappeared with him."

"Think of it like knowing a few letters of the alphabet," Ophelia said. "You may be able to name the letter and make its sound, but to form a word, you need to understand more than just a letter. You need to understand how they fit together."

It wasn't an analogy Grim could fully appreciate, given his illiteracy, but he understood the jist of it.

"Ulfur has collected the runes for decades, and he knows several symbols, though not how to combine them, thank the gods," Wolfe said. "It's what's made him so effective. He's not only had time to hone traditional tracking skills, but he can use the runes he's collected to enhance his senses, to pull information out of people's minds…"

"…Possess animals…" Grim said.

Aeryn curled her lip. "He kept trying to touch my hair and sniff me. He said…" She glanced uncomfortably at Grim. "He said he could smell you."

"He probably could," Wolfe said.

Grim felt his internal temperature rise, especially at the mention of Ulfur's behavior towards Aeryn. She hadn't mentioned that detail before.

"How long has he done this?" Grim asked Wolfe.

"He's been active since the war."

"Where does he fall within the Loom's ranks?" Grim asked.

Iviss spoke up. "The heads of the Loom are called the circle. It's unclear how many there are. He's one of them. Now, his lust for hunting Baldomar distracts from the Loom's interest in money and influence, but no one who opposes him lives very long. Which makes him quite influential in the Loom's structure."

"All this to say, a disguise might not throw him off our trail," Wolfe said.

"It's still a worthwhile idea," Ophelia said. "It may give civilians we encounter deniability. If he doesn't sense they know something, he's less likely to hurt them."

Grim stared into the fire for a few minutes. He clenched his jaw and cracked his knuckles. He knew Aeryn's idea to find his family was a good one...better than returning to the mines for revenge.

Still, all this time, his hatred for the Loom simmered within him, glowing like a hot coal. The Rune Reaper was like fuel on the fire. This man was a monster, and deserved to die a monster's death.

If Ulfur was on their trail, that meant the opportunity to confront him and settle the score was within Grim's reach.

Beside him, Aeryn nudged his leg with her own, pulling him from his thoughts. She looked up at him with her pretty green eyes.

"I know what you're thinking," she said. "We need to get to the Enclave. If you confront him, he'll kill you on sight."

He stared back at her, hard. Of course she knew what he was thinking.

If he could trust anyone to tell him the truth, or talk him out of a bad idea, it was her. But she was wrong on this one.

Did she still not understand? Was being chased across Noemar by this sadistic murderer not enough? This needed to end.

"No, I'm going to destroy him."

"Grim..."

"He's going to find us. It's a matter of time," Grim said, getting worked up. "Let's set a trap and kill him."

"But you heard what Wolfe said about him using and collecting runes," she said. "He wants yours."

"There's five of us." Grim smacked the back of his hand into the other. "He's a mortal man. This is a perfect opportunity to end this."

"Grim," Wolfe said, cutting off further argument. "We can't risk Ulfur acquiring your knuckles. What's happening in your runes has never happened before. We should trust the runes and stay ahead of him."

"If they're leading us to the Enclave, he's going to follow us all the way there," Grim said, considering how that might put innocent people there at risk. "We should confront him now."

"No," Wolfe said. "But I think ya're onto something. Our best chance of beating him is with other members of the Enclave who can use their runes against him too." He tilted his head in a conceding gesture. "The bit they know, that is."

Grim considered. "Will they be willing to fight?"

Wolfe snorted. "Ya better believe it."

Grim thought for a moment. He'd spent a good portion of his life waiting. Waiting for someone to save him. Waiting for the opportunity to save himself. Waiting to recover. Waiting to reach the Enclave. Waiting to see where the runes led.

If his people were willing to help him get revenge, he could wait a little longer.

"Alright." He threw back his mug, wiped his mouth, and sauntered to the sleeping area.

He called over his shoulder, making sure he caught Aeryn's eye. "Wake me for third. I'm making breakfast."

30

Sleep

"What are ya doin' still looking like a bear? Shave your face and don your armor," Wolfe said. Despite the sobriety, he was still not a morning person.

"You sure Ulfur'll be able to follow us if we're disguised?" Grim asked.

"Oh yeah. He's followed us through wilderness, mountains, in and out of Harskin though we didn't talk to no one," Wolfe said. "We don't want to be identified by any Cords who may be in town. Fifi and the young'un are right. It's mainly to protect civilians."

"Where is Iviss anyway?" Aeryn asked, glancing around for *the young'un*. She combed a coffee-colored liquid through her hair, turning it from honey-brown to ebony, more like the elves they'd seen in the North. "This dye he gave me better come out."

"Within a few washes," Ophelia said as she tied her chin-length hair at the nape of her neck. She had swapped some of her clothes for Iviss' and dabbed some dark makeup above her lip and on her chin, giving her the appearance of a male elf having recently shaved his goatee. A little bit of ash in her hair added about forty years.

The day before, Iviss rode ahead to scout out the city of Ingomar, contact the Shadow stationed there, and acquire access to a safe residence. He returned around suppertime with a key, reporting that the house was ready for them for the next day. He provided no comment about the state of law and disorder, except that the City Guard seemed particularly inept.

"Welcome to the North," he added, wryly.

Aeryn was looking forward to sleeping somewhere with a roof and four walls.

When Iviss emerged from the treeline, Aeryn almost didn't recognize him. He wore one of Ophelia's blue dresses, a blonde wig, and enough makeup for him to pass as an incredibly ugly woman. Grim was unpacking his armor with his back turned. He hadn't noticed Iviss' disguise.

Iviss caught Aeryn's eye. He flashed a grin and held a finger to his lips for quiet. Approaching Grim from behind, he rested a hand on his shoulder, and said in a feminine voice, "Hey."

Grim turned to see who it was, and yelled in surprise, jumping to his feet. Aeryn laughed as Iviss lifted his wig.

"Here's the plan. We enter the city in two groups," Iviss said. "A human-elf pair is uncommon enough to potentially draw attention. Wolfe and I will pose as a couple, with Grim as our hired guard. Aeryn and Ophelia are father and daughter. We stay within line of sight at all times. There's an ally at the stable, two blocks from the house who will help keep an eye on things. No taverns."

It was early afternoon by the time they clopped into the city. Ingomar boasted high sandstone walls and wide cobbled streets, with dirt paths winding off towards residential neighborhoods and less crowded avenues. Houses with thatched roofs stood close together. Aeryn noted a tanners, a smith, several pubs, a jeweler, and houses of worship.

A street artist attempted to garner some business, hollering at Wolfe and Iviss as they passed, and offered to sketch their portraits for a small price. When the artist got a better look at the pair, he made a face and added as a caveat, "I warn you, I'm only as good as my subjects."

The city was crowded with all kinds of people and sellers. There were fishmongers, parchment and ink vendors, someone peddling hand-carved owl figurines claiming they brought luck, a chandler who swore his candles kept away spirits, an apple cart, and at least three different potato farmers. City guards milled about, wearing burgundy uniforms, carrying spears or pikes. A fiddler played on a street corner.

The people's hygiene levels varied, but on the whole Aeryn found the humans tended to tolerate dirtiness more than elves back home, or even the few elves they passed in the city. Her style of dress, however, assimilated to the Northern's clothing so well, she received several praising remarks about her furry vest.

Stabling the horses, Aeryn's eyes passed over the three workers, wondering which of them was the Shadow ally. There was a plain woman of about thirty-five, her teenage son, and an older gentleman who might've been her father. They behaved as though strangers to Aeryn and the rest, though she supposed this was a part of the act.

Iviss subtly led the group on foot, with the three men at the lead, and Ophelia and Aeryn following a distance behind. The safehouse, which was only two blocks from the stables, was a decent-sized cottage, not far from a city well. The main room featured a kitchen area with a woodburning stove on one side, a fireplace along the other, and wooden table with benches in the center. A skinny hallway led from the wide room, with a washroom at the end, and two bedrooms, one on each side of the hall. The windows had glass. Dust particles danced in the beams of light peeking through the curtains.

"For the sake of propriety," Iviss said in his feminine voice. He cleared his throat, seeming to realize it was safe to speak normally again, and continued. "...And no married couples among us, ladies in one room, men in the other." Iviss said as he peered into the bedroom on the right. There were three cots set up in each room, taking up most of the floor space.

"Is it safe to assume ya'll be joining Grim and I, or have ya gotten too much into character?" Wolfe said with a chuckle.

"Wolfe and I will step out for supplies if you'd like to get situated," Ophelia said. "More arrows, Aeryn?"

"Yes, ten broadheads." She dug into her belt pouch for the money.

Ophelia shooed her hand away.

"Don't be ridiculous. Your arrows have benefited us all, and the Shadow's provided us funds for necessities," she said. "So save your money for any extras you might want or need."

"*I need* to liberate myself from this dress," Iviss said, as he scratched under the ribs, shifting the false bosom off-center. He fixed Aeryn and Grim with a look which was difficult to take seriously considering his disguise. "Then I'm challenging both of you to a game of Dragon's Bounty before supper. Prepare yourselves."

The game had been their go-to activity when it was too late to practice. The deck was showing signs of wear. Aeryn had begun to notice that Iviss' eyebrow twitched almost imperceptibly when she suspected him of deceit. It still didn't improve her game.

After Aeryn lost three hands in a row, Ophelia and Wolfe returned with a sack of dry goods, a basket of fruit, several bars of soap, and a sheaf of arrows. They also brought supper, which was several meat pies enough to satisfy everyone's appetites. The food was slightly cold, but it tasted delicious. It was a relief to spend the night somewhere warm and dry with a meal she didn't have to catch or cook.

The evening was immensely comfortable, and a decent distraction from the reasons why they wouldn't be able to stay here more than one night. Full and warm, Aeryn crawled under her covers, using her bundled sweater as a pillow.

She should have been able to get to sleep easily. Across the room, Ophelia fell into a sound sleep within minutes. But Aeryn's mind refused to settle. She tossed and turned.

They were being hunted by a sadistic madman who wanted to cut off Grim's fingers. They also had a plan to finish Ulfur for good. Battle was imminent, and the promise of violence made her stomach feel tight.

What if they didn't make it to the Enclave? How would they be received if they did?

If all went well, and Grim found his family there, what was

Aeryn going to do?

Her argument with her family, especially Elion, returned to her mind in the dark. His biting accusations. The precision of it all.

Still, she missed her brother. She missed them all.

A heaviness settled over her heart. What might her family think if she never returned? Perhaps they didn't want to think about her at this point. She'd brought enough turmoil upon them. Samuel and Tarra's new baby was probably a good distraction.

Aeryn squeezed her eyes tighter, trying to push the thoughts from her mind. She needed to stop thinking about babies, Merioake, the family business, and the sad, worried look on her parents' faces as she said goodbye. It was likely she couldn't go home, even if she wanted to.

Admittedly, when she left, part of Aeryn hoped she would find a good reason not to come back. Now she had one. If her wanted poster made it home, she would be arrested immediately upon her return. More shame on the family.

She considered what it might be like, trying to establish a stable life wherever this village was located. She could start tanning there. She knew how. But would they accept her, being an elf from the South and not a human rune-bearer like the rest of them? Would she even be permitted to stay?

Aeryn opened her eyes to stare at the ceiling. As for what happened after finding Grim's people...she couldn't figure that out right now. The first thing was to make it to the Enclave alive.

She heard the creak of feet in the house, which was odd because she hadn't heard the men's door open. Her heartbeat quickened. Now wide awake and hyper focused, she noted Ophelia's resting form and debated whether to rouse her.

The footsteps creaked in the main living area. It might just be one of the men.

Or not.

Could Ulfur open locks?

Aeryn shifted her covers and rose from her cot as stealthily as possible. She plucked her dagger from where she stored it inside her boots. Keeping her ears pricked for activity, she crept toward the door on woolen sock feet.

The footsteps shifted around a little more, then stilled. If she stepped into the hall, unless the person was on the far left or right, or had his back turned, she'd be seen the moment she opened the door.

There was no way to be sneaky about this. The best she could hope for was to catch whoever it was by surprise. She took two quick breaths, then pulled the door open. Dagger drawn and eyes wild, she flew into the living area like a dart.

She drew to a sudden stop as her eyes landed on Iviss at the table.

"You must really have to go," he said over his cup of tea, with a teasing look. He seemed completely unphased by her sudden appearance, as if elvish women burst into the room brandishing weapons all the time. "You made a wrong turn. Washroom's the other way."

A mixture of relief and embarrassment rolled over Aeryn. She lowered her weapon and slid the blade back into the sheath.

Feeling suddenly warm, she tucked a strand of hair behind her ears. "Oh. Um, thanks."

"Tea?" he asked before she could slink away. He tipped his head towards the kettle beside him at the table. "Water's hot."

Aeryn considered. It was better than lying in her cot, worrying.

"Okay," she said. She grabbed her cup from the end of the table, and slipped into the bench across from him.

"What are you doing awake? It's after midnight," he said.

"I could ask you the same," she said, bringing the cup to her lips. She paused before drinking, and gave it a sniff. It smelled normal, but she gave him a wary glance. "Did you put something in this?"

"I did."

Aeryn felt her ribs tighten and she frowned at him. "What?"

"Tea leaves." He refilled his own cup and took a sip of the same green-brown liquid he'd just poured into Aeryn's. He smiled. "To answer your question, I couldn't sleep either. Grim has a bit of a snoring problem. So I thought I'd make the most of the time, get up, say my prayers."

Aeryn relaxed a little and took a sip. "Sorry to interrupt you."

Iviss shook his head. "No need to apologize. I'm glad for the company."

Aeryn returned the small smile and took another sip.

"Troubles keeping you awake?" he asked.

Aeryn hesitated, which was answer enough.

"It's seeing me in a dress today, isn't it?" he said, filling the silence and keeping a straight face. Aeryn snorted at the joke, which encouraged him to keep going. "It gives me nightmares too. Not my favorite disguise, but duty has its demands."

"You have a favorite disguise?" Aeryn asked, amused.

"Of course."

"I have to hear this."

"I once disguised myself as a circus performer. It was one of my earlier assignments," he said.

"What's a circus?"

His eyes widened, and he blew out a slow breath. "Mayhem. Animal tamers, bearded ladies, freakishly tall men, acrobats, stunts involving fire. It was a smuggling front. I was there to gather information."

"Oh." Aeryn drank more of her tea. It was still unsettling to think of him as a ten-year-old, learning the ins and outs of spywork.

"So what's on your mind?" he asked, coming back to the question. "Is there something you need to get off your chest?"

"Off my chest?" Aeryn wrinkled her brow. "Like a confession?"

Iviss paused. "Maybe that's not the right way to put it. I mean, we're enduring a stressful set of circumstances. If you need to talk about what's bothering you, so you can get to sleep, I'm a very good listener."

Aeryn hesitated, unsure how to respond. He was so duty-oriented, and tended to vacillate between insufferable know-it-all and easy to get along with, it made it difficult to think of him as someone to confide in. Knowing he was a spy, adept at playing a role, made this more complicated. But there was no eyebrow twitch, and something about his demeanor made Aeryn believe he was sincere.

Truthfully, she had a mountain of worries on her mind. Maybe he was right. Perhaps talking a little would help, though she felt unsure how many of her questions about the Enclave he'd know the answer to.

"I'm not quite sure where to start," she said.

"Well, we got the image of me in a dress out of the way," he said with a grin. "How about the reason why you're really here?"

Aeryn frowned.

"What do you mean? I'm helping my friend escape death and find his family," she said, sitting up a little taller.

"I'm not convinced," he said. "No offense, but you don't strike me as that generous of a person."

Aeryn felt herself grow warm. "Excuse me?"

"Your reason makes sense if you and Grim were as close as Wolfe and Ophelia assumed you were when they met you. But you're not romantically involved, and as far as friendship goes, you're some of the least familiar friends I've ever seen," he said. "Yet you were willing to leave your family, home, and livelihood behind to travel across Errebos with someone who's a relative stranger to you? I can't figure out why."

"He's not a stranger," she said, her words more clipped

than she intended. *He wasn't anymore.*

Iviss held up a pacifying hand and arched an eyebrow. "Alright. I'll grant that."

"Generous of you."

"But you didn't leave home out of the kindness of your heart. That's certain."

Aeryn opened her mouth, then shut it again. Iviss took another sip of his tea. It irritated Aeryn how relaxed he seemed. Her frown deepened, but before she responded, he spoke again.

"I have my guesses, but I can't make sense of why you're here."

Aeryn felt a spike of worry and anger rise inside her. She doubted Iviss' guess was any good, but some defensive and overly-curious part of Aeryn goaded her on. "Oh yeah? What guesses are those?"

He thought for a minute, choosing his words carefully. "I'd say you lost something or someone you cared for deeply. It's painful. You desire space from your home so much you were willing to walk away from your livelihood, if it even still exists."

Aeryn could feel the color drain from her face. *How did he...?*

"I'd guess it was one of your parents, considering your father was advanced enough in years to fight in the last war," Iviss continued. "Also given your reaction to the lullaby. You don't really like talking about Merioake. When I suggested getting something off your chest, you jumped to *confession*, which leads me to believe you might feel guilty in some way. You are, at the very least, hiding something."

Aeryn's teeth hurt from clenching her jaw. Her cheeks burned.

He quietly waited for her to respond.

She opened her mouth to argue with him, but no words came. She was aware that each second of delay was probably confirmation in his mind.

Sure, he was wrong about her parents, but uncomfortably accurate about the rest. It was like he had deliberately paid attention to subtle clues which, put together, told him way more about her than she ever intended to show. It flustered her, and in a way, made her feel accused and exposed.

"Well, you're wrong. My parents are alive," she finally said, keeping her voice down, but her tone curt.

He took another sip of tea. "Is that the only thing I'm wrong about?"

Aeryn couldn't hold his gaze. She threw back the rest of her drink and stood. "I'm going to bed."

He reached across the table, grabbed her hand to stop her from leaving.

"Aeryn, I'm not trying to upset you," he said. "I'm not suggesting you're in the wrong for needing a fresh start. I understand how important that can be, trust me."

She pulled her hand free, affronted, and scowled at the man.

Iviss continued, before she stormed away. "I'm saying this as a friend. I'm not sure Grim has figured it out. My impression is he seems to believe your motives for coming on this journey were completely selfless. Ask yourself why."

Aeryn tried to control her breathing as her heart churned inside her chest. She knew the answer. *Because you used and misled him.*

"For the sake of your friendship," he said, "I recommend you tell him eventually. He cares about you."

A fresh wave of guilt roiled inside her. "We're done speaking about this, Iviss."

"Okay," he said, accepting the answer, sitting back in his seat. She left him without a backward glance, slipped into her bed, and crawled into her blankets, feeling like a wretch.

She clamped her eyes shut and she tried to push the thoughts from her mind. His assessment chiseled too close for comfort. She felt like she'd been presented with something ugly she didn't want to look at. She thought about how Grim might take it if he learned she'd used finding his family as an excuse to avoid working alongside her own.

No, she told herself. She cared about his life, and that was true in Ravenwood when she suggested he seek his family instead of revenge. It was true before then. Even if she used Grim's situation to escape her own, it didn't matter anymore. She was here now. He didn't have to know.

She could not escape the nagging feeling that Iviss might be right. Elion's words returned to haunt her, robbing her from sound sleep. *You might as well not come back.*

31

Poison

In the morning, it was like the conversation with Iviss never happened. He was his normal bossy-friendly self, which was fine with Aeryn. She was ready to put the exchange behind her forever.

"Before we leave, I want to stop at the alchemist," Ophelia said as she packed up her belongings. She'd already donned her disguise from the day before. "They were closed when we tried yesterday, and the stars indicate I need to be prepared."

"Prepared for what?" Aeryn asked. "Or did they not specify?"

"Oh, I know what I need to prepare," she said. "Poison."

"Oh." It was still unsettling to think of Ophelia, who in a lot of ways reminded Aeryn of her own mother, as a master poisoner.

Aeryn finished tying Weaver's feathers in her hair, and they met the men in the hall.

The roads were less congested than the afternoon before. Aeryn walked beside Ophelia, while Grim, Wolfe, and Iviss followed a few paces behind. The street boasted rows of shops. Peddlers with their carts were stationed along the road.

Ophelia halted outside of the alchemist's shop, which looked no bigger than a closet.

"It'll be easier if I step inside alone," she said to the group as they drew up behind her. "If you want to shop around for anything you might need or want, stay together and don't go too far."

Ophelia slipped into the alchemy shop with a jingle of the door.

Remembering some of Iviss' tips for keeping alert while in a city space, Aeryn strolled down the street with the men. She perused the shop windows of a bookbinder, a cobbler, and a purveyor of finely crafted wool dresses.

Aeryn slowed as a peddler with a cart full of shiny jewelry caught her eye. Tiered racks displayed metallic rings set with colorful stones, strings of clear glass beads, silver hoop earrings, and a variety of necklaces with pendants ranging from flashy to understated. Aeryn never wore jewelry. It was impractical with hunting, and before slaying the dragon, she was too poor to afford it. When she was younger, she used to wonder what kind of jewelry she might be given when someone asked her to marry him. She'd let go of the idea a long time ago.

But the jewelry was pretty. Weaver would've loved it.

The peddler, a thin older man with a greasy horseshoe of gray hair, noticed Aeryn slow to gaze at his wares.

"Young lady," he said, waving her over. "You like what you see? Come!"

Aeryn stepped closer, her eyes passed over the array of bracelets while the peddler jabbered away.

"All hand-crafted, reputably sourced. I have a range of

products. Surely something to suit your fancy. Like this here." He held up a flashy bangle with citrine charms. "No? A pretty young elf like yourself doesn't strike me like the gaudy type. You prefer something natural looking." He snagged a necklace with a brown leather strap and single jade bead shaped like a leaf. "Yes?"

"I'm not looking to buy," Aeryn said, as Grim came up alongside her, as much to signal to him that she wasn't about to piddle away their funds.

"If you want to try anything on, I'd be happy to oblige," the peddler said. He crinkled his nose and winked at her.

She cast a sly look at Grim.

"What's your favorite color?" she asked, trying to sound natural but avoid Iviss overhearing her. He was loitering with Wolfe a few feet away, and if he heard, he made no indication. If Grim was her friend, she ought to know this.

Grim thought for a moment. "Purple. Or gray. Both are good."

She noticed a spherical glass pendant with a metal clasp resembling a dragon's claw. The tiny glass sphere swirled gray. She squinted at it, and poked it gently with a finger. A whirl of yellow appeared inside the tiny orb.

She pulled back. "Ooh, what just happened?"

The peddler's eyes lit up. "Oh, that's a dragon magic pendant. It can read your mood like a dragon and respond with a change of color."

"It's magic?"

He leaned toward her, like he was letting her in on a secret.

He waved her in, and wouldn't speak until she reluctantly moved half an inch closer.

"It's just what it's called. Really changes color based on your feelings, though." The peddler lifted the pendant, still attached to the rack. The gray sphere swirled pink. "See, it's pink because I'm happy to be talking to a pretty lady such as yourself right now."

Aeryn forced a polite smile at the awkward compliment. She peered at the pendant in the man's palm. She had no desire to waste her money on a novelty item which displayed her feelings to everyone, but it fascinated her nonetheless.

"What do the different colors mean?"

"I only know the one for amorous." He winked at Aeryn again.

She stiffened and took a step away from the man. As she did so, she noticed a delicate silver chain with a familiar pendant hanging from the display. Stopping, she reached for it. It was exactly like the ones Wolfe, Ophelia, and Iviss wore. Grim saw it too.

"Where'd you get this?" she asked, unable to hide the note of accusation in her voice.

The peddler's demeanor changed instantly. He looked the group over, his face turning to stone. His hand traveled slowly toward his hip as he kept his eyes fixed on them.

Before she could react, the peddler whipped a knife from his belt. Aeryn felt herself yanked back by Grim. Wolfe, who had thrust himself between Aeryn and the peddler, took a slash to the hand.

Iviss swooped in. His knife flashed. The peddler grunted.

In the next moment, Iviss lowered the man to the ground. Dead.

"Get his feet," he said, his voice strained under the effort to roll the man beneath his own cart.

Wolfe tucked the man's feet and dropped the curtain, hiding the body. His cut bled profusely. He winced, working his fingers as necrotic black lines crawled rapidly up his hand. He clapped his uninjured palm over the gash to slow the bleeding.

"Time to go," Iviss said.

Keeping alert, they hurried toward the alchemist's shop for Ophelia. Wolfe lagged, sweaty and green. When they paused outside the shop, Aeryn dug into her pack for a bandage for Wolfe, trying to control the shaky feeling in her own hands. Iviss stepped inside, and a few seconds later emerged with Ophelia.

She looked them over. "Loom?"

Wolfe nodded. He gasped for air. "He had...one of our...pendants."

Ophelia grabbed his hand and the color drained from her face. "I'll go back in and get an antidote."

A shriek split the air from up the street. A hysterical woman pointed to the lifeless hand which rolled out from beneath the peddler's cart. Someone else shouted for City Guard.

"No time," Wolfe said, wheezing.

"This will kill you, Wolfe," Ophelia said with emphasis.

He staggered away from her, dragging his feet. "Get...the horses..."

They moved as briskly as possible, but the ten minute walk felt like an hour. Black veins crawled from Wolfe's wound, along his arm and spread up his neck like spider webs.

They rounded a corner and at last, the stables came into view.

With a ragged gasp, Wolfe clutched his heart. He stumbled and collapsed face-first into the middle of the road.

A passing cart narrowly avoided him, and a bystander shrieked. Instantly, a crowd materialized.

"Wolfe!" Aeryn swooped to his side to help him up, while Grim went to the other. Ophelia crouched beside Aeryn to check him for signs of life.

She brought a hand to her mouth. Her face bunched in barely-restrained grief.

"What's going 'ere? Make way." A guard in a burgundy and leather uniform pushed his way through the crowd. He carried a spear.

The guard scrunched his dirty face at Wolfe's sprawled body, displaying his snaggletooth. He regarded Grim, then Aeryn and Ophelia, distraught at Wolfe's side.

"Well, 'e's dead. Get 'im up. Take 'im to the morgue," he said.

Aeryn gaped at the man. "What?"

"You 'eard me," he said. "You lot were with 'im. Can't leave dead bodies laying in the street, or you get a fine. Take 'im to the morgue. Get on."

Another guard with carrot-orange hair shooed gawkers out of the way. He looked dispassionately on the scene. "Oh, not another one."

The first guard scoffed. "You tellin' me? Last week some bloke got run over by a cart. It was a mess. Took a week for the rains to wash it away. Stunk to 'igh 'eaven." He gestured with the butt end of the spear. "Not 'aving that again. Come on, I said get 'im up."

"You heard him." the second guard said. "Off to the morgue with him."

"Wait!" A third guard, this one short and round, pushed through the crowd. "Look at him. He's not healthy. It's the sickness."

The other two guards stiffened and the press of onlookers took a collective step back.

"Oh, not the sickness..."

"Yeah, you see those." The third guard waggled a fat finger, indicating the necrotic black lines webbing up Wolfe's arm and neck. Then he noticed the bloody wound and gasped. "Oh! He's a bleeder. We gotta keep this from spreading and deal with it right-proper. Where's a torch?"

"Here!" A helpful onlooker produced a flaming torch, seemingly from nowhere.

The chubby guard thanked him hastily, then turned to Wolfe without wasting a moment.

"Alright, everyone, get back," he said as he extended the torch toward Wolfe's pant leg, attempting to keep as much space between himself and the dead man as possible.

"No!" Ophelia yelped, throwing herself on top of Wolfe.

The Guards hesitated, and the torch bearer pulled back a smidgeon.

Ophelia continued, trying to maintain her composure. She cleared her throat, remembering her cover. "No, I'm a physician. You have to dispose of the body properly. If you burn him, the ash will get into the air, the disease will spread."

The crowd held its breath while the guards looked at Ophelia for a long moment, like she'd grown a third eye.

"Disease doesn't spread by air," the ginger guard said. "What kind of sorcery is that?"

"No cremating in the street," Iviss cried.

Still disguised as Wolfe's wife, he fanned his face, producing false tears, and he continued his emotional tirade loud enough to put the guards on edge. Aeryn half-listened as Iviss rattled on about the fire risk and penalties of starting a fire in a city space, citing laws she was almost certain he invented on the spot, all while playing the part of an emotionally volatile and extremely knowledgeable widow who would certainly have them charged for crimes if they even tried to ignite the dead man in the road.

By the end of it, the bewildered guards were convinced. The round one with the torch cast around for the bystander who handed it to him.

"You!" he said, as he spotted the man in the crowd. "Get rid of this! What are you doing carrying an open flame in the street? You could start a fire."

"You still can't leave a dead body in the street," the first guard said. "Unless you want a fine, get 'im out of 'ere and be on your way."

There was nothing to do but heave Wolfe's body off the

cobbled road. Grim took one arm and slung it across his shoulder while Iviss took the other. Wolfe sagged in between them, his head lolled forward.

"Where's the morgue?" Ophelia asked, barely keeping her voice steady.

The first guard sighed as though answering was a major inconvenience. He pointed at the nearest intersection. "Go right, then left. Then another left. Straight for a while, and then another right, over a footbridge, and then left."

Ophelia and Aeryn led the way, while Grim and Iviss carried Wolfe along. Ophelia looked over her shoulder at the slumped form of her mentor and dearest friend. He hung like a rag doll between Grim and Iviss.

Aeryn felt numb. It could've been her. Wolfe saved her life, and now he was gone. She put an arm around Ophelia.

"You know..." Grim said. "This isn't much different than when he was alive."

Aeryn's mouth fell open and she gave him a reproachful glare over her shoulder.

Wolfe grunted. "Very funny."

"Agh!" Startled, the men dropped Wolfe. He landed with a grunt in the street, then rolled to his back groaning. Ophelia flew to him and took his face in her hands. She pulled back an eyelid, and checked him over feverishly.

"How...? You're...you're alive." She looked as though she might burst into tears with relief.

Wolfe's head lolled with a dopey grin. "Lucky tooth."

Ophelia choked on a laugh as she blinked back tears. "What's lucky is there's no more alcohol in your system. I don't think your body could handle that much poison, lucky tooth or not."

32

Closer

As it turned out, the incident with the poison dagger wasn't Wolfe's first brush with death, or even his second. Though it took a physical toll on him, by the end of the day, he was joking that he was like a bad fungus the Cords just couldn't get rid of.

In the following weeks, Grim's runes led them perpetually east with little variation. They traveled through small towns, a few cities, hilly countryside, over moors, and through evergreen forest. The group fell into a routine. After the incident in Ingomar, they doubled practice sessions with Iviss. Both Aeryn and Grim were growing adept at handling Sten.

Aeryn hunted more frequently, acquiring food and skins which could be traded when passing through civilization. As a rule, Grim went with her. Enough overlap existed between the flora of Noemar and Thoen that they were often able to forage for edibles, even when hunting proved unfruitful. She showed him which plants were safe for consumption, or good for medicine. She warned him about which berries would kill a man, which nuts would make him violently ill, and which mushrooms would make it look like the world itself was melting. He paid close attention, absorbing as much as possible, and with practice, his woodsmanship markedly improved. The time in the forest was a quiet and temporary reprieve from the rigors of travel, the sore backsides, and the concerns about the Rune Reaper which pressed continually on their minds. Sharing that time in the woods became something they both look forward to.

Some nights, Wolfe roused them to leave right away, but they managed to strike the tense balance of keeping Ulfur on their trail while not letting him get too close. The most alarming of these times came one night outside of Ingomar. Aeryn woke during the third watch to a hot breath on her face. A slavering fox with a milky eye crouched over her head. Watching her sleep.

She shrieked, waking the rest of the camp. She grabbed her bow and swung it like a club, then turned an arrow on the beast and put the creature out of its misery.

As summer neared the end of its course, the chill in the air extended into daytime hours. The few deciduous trees turned golden and scarlet, and they neared the eastern reaches of Noemar.

As they approached the small city of Droghead, and after consulting the dice, they secured a room large enough for the five of them at a dusky tavern and inn. When they came downstairs for a hot supper, a band had started playing.

Iviss spoke with the barkeep while the others grabbed a table in the corner where they could get a good view of the tavern and its occupants.

"I ordered four beers and a water," he said as he slid into the curved bench next to Wolfe.

The tavern was at half-capacity. Aeryn assessed the exits and potential hazards, as was her habit these days. She scanned wrists for a black cord, but saw none.

When the barkeep came bearing drinks on a tray, Aeryn's

body went rigid. His straight jet hair was tied back, and apart from neat whiskers on his chin and the fact he was a human, he bore a strange resemblance to Gideon. Same build in the shoulders. Same gray eyes. Same squared jaw with the same cocky mouth. He slid the pewter mugs onto the table, and when he caught Aeryn staring at him like a startled pikdeer, his brow ticked upward. "You alright there?"

She blinked, dropping her eyes, and pulled her beer to herself, sloshing a little over the brim. She felt her cheeks grow warm. "Fine. Thanks."

He forced an awkward smile, and returned to the bar.

It wasn't the first time Aeryn had been forced to look twice when passing a raven-haired elf who looked too familiar. She took a few gulps of her beer and wrinkled her nose at the flavor, but drank a third of it anyway. "Have you noticed more elves lately?"

"We're close to Gallendahli," Iviss said. "They conduct a considerable amount of trade down the coast with the elves of Dulamein in the Southeast, if I remember correctly. Makes sense."

Grim set his empty mug on the table. "Beer's good."

The song changed to a lively one that made it easy to push thoughts of despicable elves back home out of her mind. Some patrons whooped, or clapped along with the beat, and a few grabbed a partner for dancing. Aeryn's body itched to move. She elbowed Grim. "Hey, Bearkiller. Dance with me."

He cast her a sidelong glance. "Absolutely not."

Aeryn rolled her eyes. "We've all assessed the room. It's not too crowded. No apparent threats. Move your muscles."

"No."

"What are you going to do if a pretty lady at the Enclave bats her eyes at you, and says…" Aeryn raised her pitch while she fluttered her eyelashes. "…*Dance with me, Grim!*"

Wolfe chortled. "He'd prolly ask if she's got something stuck in her eye."

"That would never happen," Grim said flatly.

"Some day, Grim," Aeryn said, "you might be surprised."

"Are you drunk already?" he joked, taking her mug of beer. "Give me that. You don't even like beer."

Aeryn closed her eyes in a dignified manner, not bothering to fight him for it. "No, I am not."

"I'll go," Wolfe said. He hoisted himself off the bench and offered an arm. "How 'bout I show ya a country dance from the heartlands?"

Aeryn took his arm and they skipped onto the dancefloor. Their meal hadn't come by the time the song ended, so she asked Wolfe for one more. The oncoming fight with Ulfur loomed, and after weeks of thinking about little else, numerous close calls, and relentless travel and training, Aeryn was determined to enjoy this little bit of frivolity.

"So ya and Grim sticking together after all this?" Wolfe said. It was more of a statement than a question.

The image of her family at the tannery wiggled in the back of her mind.

"Well, I promised him I'd help him find his parents," she said. "I can't believe I've never asked this, but I don't suppose your dice would be useful in determining whether they're alive?"

They side-skipped to one end of the dancefloor.

"Nah. They're more oriented around immediate issues," Wolfe said. "We tested it already."

"When?"

"Grim asked me in Bywinter." Wolfe twirled Aeryn, clasped her hand and led her frolicking to the other end of the dance floor.

"Are you and Ophelia going back to Fieldgate after all this?" Aeryn asked.

"We'll need to go to Shadow Keep first. Iviss too," Wolfe said. "Being on a team has been good for him. Ya can only be alone so long."

The music came to an end and the tavern clapped for the band. Aeryn followed Wolfe's gaze to the table where Ophelia smiled warmly at them. At her side, Iviss and Grim laughed over something Grim had just mentioned.

Grim noticed her watching the table and smiled at her. There was an intensity, but also a softness which he didn't reserve for anyone else. It was a nice smile, but it made her feel a little wobbly on the inside and made her wonder what exactly he was thinking.

She returned the smile and gave a little wave.

"It's been good for all of us," Wolfe said. He patted her on the shoulder. "Thank ya for the dance, Lady Aeryn. Let's go eat. Have as much dessert as ya want. Life is short!"

Aeryn snickered and dropped her voice. "Says the man who is over a hundred years old."

33

A Welcome of Sorts

Aeryn gripped the bow across her lap. She strained her eyes into the murky treeline, but saw very little. All they had for light was Grim's exposed runes which glowed brightly against the unnatural dark of the forest. She didn't like these woods at all.

Creatures chittered from the shadows and pinpricks of light appeared in the trees where sets of beady eyes watched them pass. A guttural rattle in the darkness, reminiscent of the dragon outside Fogness, made Aeryn reach for an arrow. Dread, the likes of which she'd never felt, smothered her like the dragon's claws pinning her to the earth. She forced her eyes to stay open, but she inched a little closer to Grim. Through all this, he sat tall in the saddle. Though she could feel the tension in his muscles and stiffness of posture, she didn't detect the least bit of terror. It gave her strength.

After leaving Droghead, Grim's runes led them sharply northeast, the first deviation from the straight line they'd traveled since leaving the hermitage. A check of the map indicated they were drawing near to the last mountain range on this end of Noemar. Beyond them lay Gallendahli, which meant they were close to the Enclave.

The trees widened into a small clearing, and the unnatural darkness diminished as the gray autumn light filtered through the pine needle canopy. A few herbs grew among the shrubs at the base of the trees.

"I recognize those," Aeryn said. "Stop for a moment." Grim pulled Sten to a halt. Aeryn slid off the back of it. "I just want to collect a few of these. I'm low on almost everything."

"What are they?" Ophelia asked.

"This one is bindweed. It stops bleeding," Aeryn said as she tore up a handful of the fibrous beige leaf. "Over there is fever sorrel. It lowers a fever."

"What about the one you gave me?" Grim asked.

"Blue leatherleaf will lower fever, but that's because it cures just about anything," Aeryn said. "But it won't grow anywhere else, and the leaves don't keep for long. My mother has tried. She says the grove is magic."

Aeryn packed the bindweed in her satchel and trotted across the clearing to uproot the fever sorrel.

The horses' ears swiveled, and they grew suddenly tense and fidgety. Beyond the dark treeline, a branch snapped.

Aeryn stopped breathing. She shushed the others, and reached for her bow.

Six fierce-looking humans in hide armor burst into the open. Two of the six dropped from the tree branches, while the others emerged from the shadows and behind a gargantuan log. Tall, sturdy, and mostly blonde, they surrounded the group. The ambushers poised their weapons and bellowed for them to surrender.

Grim jumped off Sten. He drew his sword, banged it against his breastplate and hollered back. It was like watching male bears square off and compare their teeth before they used them. In an instant, Iviss was on his feet, at Grim's side, sword in hand.

Aeryn nocked an arrow and turned her attention to the nearest attacker.

Were those tattoos on his knuckles?

Her eyes darted to the next person, and the next. They all had markings on their knuckles, like Grim.

The ambushers closed in around them, shouting orders.

"Drop your weapons!"

"Down on the ground!"

"Wait!" Aeryn cried, catching Grim by the arm before he charged at the nearest person. "Grim! Runes!"

Iviss noticed too. In response, he yanked his Silver Shadow pendant out of his collar. "Don't shoot!"

Ophelia and Wolfe did the same, calling the Baldomar ambushers to hold their fire.

Grim and the other Baldomar hesitated. A sense of confusion rippled through their ranks. A scrawny teenager with a messy knot of sandy hair, gray-blue eyes, and heavy black eye makeup pointed with her hand-axe "Rakel, look at his knuckles!"

"I have eyes, Wynne." A tawny-haired woman with a block face lowered her heavy longbow, but she kept the arrow nocked. The woman strutted forward a few steps. Her steel eyes passed over the group, settling on Grim. His runes still glowed brightly.

"I can see what you are." She turned her attention on Iviss, Wolfe, and Ophelia. "But you're not from the Chain. So how'd you find us?"

"I led them," Grim said.

She wrinkled her brow. "You?"

"Looks like your ears work too."

If she was offended, she didn't show it. The woman, Rakel, kept her face hard, but it was evident that this was all new to her. "How?"

For an answer, Grim held up his clenched fist, flashing his tattoos.

Rakel narrowed her eyes. "Your runes? You expect me to believe that?"

"Rakel," said a ginger haired man with a bear claw necklace. "It's not that far-fetched."

Rakel, who seemed to be the one in charge, ignored him. "Put your sword away and let me see your marks."

"You lower your weapon," Grim said. "Tell your people to do the same."

Rakel wrinkled her nose, then addressed the scouts under her command. "Dally down."

The scouts cautiously obeyed. Once everyone had lowered or put away their weapons, Rakel marched closer and motioned with a quick flick of her fingers for Grim to show his hand. "Let's see 'em."

"Why?"

"To see if I know them." She looked over his knuckles and compared them to her own. "I have this one." She pointed to one of his, then tapped one of the three symbols on her pinkie. The man with the bear claw necklace and the woman on Rakel's right closed in to compare their runes to Grim's.

Aeryn shared a questioning look with Grim, but he seemed as unsure about this behavior as she was.

"Sometimes symbols repeat in families," Rakel said, catching the puzzled expression. "What's your name, Baldomar?"

"Grim."

"Grim what?"

"Stonebreaker."

"Don't know any Stonebreakers."

"I'm not surprised."

Wynne elbowed her way closer. "Why are they glowing?"

"They've been glowing since we left Bywinter," Grim said.

"Bywinter?" Wynne asked. "Where's that? Is that where you're from?"

"No. It's where the Rune Reeper started tracking us."

The mood shifted from curiosity about the newcomer to alarm in an instant. Rakel's eyes bulged with new fury. "Tracking? As in, you led him here?"

"He's not far behind," Grim said. "I assume the Enclave isn't far from here, and that's where you're from. The village needs to prepare for a confrontation. We plan to put an end to him, with as many as are willing."

"I can run back and tell the elders we're coming," Wynne said.

"Quiet, runt." Rakel took a step toward Grim. "The Enclave is supposed to be a place of safety, and you led the Rune Reeper right to us?"

"Rakel," Wolfe said from atop his horse. "It couldn't be avoided."

"No." Rakel gave a rapid shake of her head. "If you come in, he's gonna follow you and it puts us in danger. Go back, and face him out there. If you live, then you can come in."

"I don't think that's your call to make," Grim said.

Rakel's frown deepened at the challenge, but based on the glances from the other scouts, Grim guessed right.

"The elders are not going to be happy with this," Rakel said.

"Won't they want an opportunity to defeat Ulfur?" Aeryn asked.

"No one asked you, wood elf." Rakel turned a scornful eye on Aeryn. She looked her up and down. "I didn't see your pendant. What are you? The help?"

Grim stepped forward to meet Rakel, nose to nose, his expression deadly serious. "She's with me."

Rakel kept her own expression hard, but discomfort flickered across her face, and they all saw it. "Oh, I see. She's with you."

"Yes, you can see. You can hear. Now, how about you think and take us to the elders," Grim said.

Wynne snickered. "He's funny."

Rakel shot her a dark look, and Wynne covered her mouth to hide her smirk. Rakel glowered at him, sticking out her chin. "I don't take orders from you."

"If you don't want to help us kill Ulfur," Grim said, "then

get out of the way."

Rakel took a few steps backward, but kept her eyes locked on the group.

"Get on your horses and follow closely," she said at last. She barked orders for two other scouts to run ahead and inform the elders they were coming, then led the way into the woods.

They followed through thicker forest for nearly a half hour. The path narrowed, forcing them to travel single-file. Aeryn and Grim ducked beneath low branches.

When they stepped out of the wood, Aeryn drank in the gray sky. A village was nestled in the valley before them, hemmed in by mountains to the north and east, and the forest to the south and west. A stream cut through the landscape, passing through the spattering of homesteads. Smoke rose from chimneys. From their vantage point, Aeryn noticed the movement of people.

A lot of people.

Evidently the scouts delivered their message and much of the village had come to receive the newcomers.

Outside the village proper, five older Baldomar stood at the head of the crowd beside the two rangers Rakel sent ahead. There was a tall white-haired man with a neatly trimmed beard, a shorter broad man with a horseshoe of graying auburn hair, a middle-aged woman with a red cloak, an enormous man with partially shaved coiffe of white-blonde hair and facial tattoos, and an ancient-looking lady with impeccable posture and bottlecap spectacles on a beaded chain which made her eyes appear larger than normal.

The elders watched them approach, with Rakel at the head. Behind them, several curious villagers, all with runes on their knuckles, elbowed each other for a glimpse of the newcomers. Even traveling across Noemar, Aeryn had never seen such a concentration of folks who looked like Grim.

The old woman squinted at the oncoming horses. In a disarmingly bold voice, she hollered. "Well, I'll be smickered! Wolfie, is that you?"

Wolfe dipped his head to the old woman. "Jisselle."

The man with the white beard cleared his throat. His piercing green eyes rested momentarily on each person, but settled firmly on Grim.

"Welcome to the Enclave. I'm Harvald Bloch. This is Jisselle Joly, and Tegan Oshea," he said, gesturing to the ladies on his right. "Elric Thar," the stout man with horseshoe hair dipped his chin, "and Nialls Baruch." Nialls crossed his arms over his chest, keeping otherwise still and impassive.

"What's your name, son?" Harvald said.

"Grim Stonebreaker. This is Aeryn Haranae," Grim said. "Also Wolfe, Ophelia, and Iviss, from the Silver Shadow."

"Our scouts informed us you've arrived in an...unorthodox manner, bearing potentially grave news," Harvald said. "Let us move indoors and we shall discuss matters."

Harvald offered his arm to Jisselle, and the crowd parted to let them pass. They led the way back into the tiny town.

Dirt roads wound through the humble village full of huts with thatched roofs, garden plots, stables, and yards for livestock.

Some huts were as small as Magne the hermit's yurt, but others were much larger, like cabins, and the varied shades of wood indicated later additions to increase living space. The smell of cold dirt and cooking fires mingled with the perpetual scent of pine in the air. The people were dressed for chilly weather in long pants, long skirts, and rugged furs, so Aeryn's wardrobe assimilated well. Those who had not been in the crowd earlier stopped their work and conversations with neighbors to watch the procession. A watermill creaked in the distance.

Wynne, who trotted along near the end of the group, quickened her pace. She jogged by Iviss, Wolfe and Ophelia, to come alongside Aeryn and Grim's horse.

"Hello," she said, looking brightly up at them. "I'm Wynne Thar."

Ahead, Elric peered over his shoulder, his brow wrinkled in a question. Wynne grinned and waggled her fingers at him.

"That's my Pop. Also, don't worry about Rakel. She's surly with everyone," she said, then lowered her voice. "Is the Rune Reaper really headed here?"

"Yes," Grim said.

Wynne's eyes widened for a moment. Then her face knit in determination. She cracked her knuckles. "Alright then."

Grim gave her an appraising look.

"How old are you?" Aeryn asked.

"Fifteen," she said. She turned her attention back to Grim. "Grim, can I see your runes? I didn't get a good look back there."

Wynne craned her neck for a look at Grim's knuckles on

the reins.

"Wynne, run ahead and tell your mother we're coming," Elric said. He had dropped his pace to walk alongside his daughter. "Make sure Jai is accounted for."

"Yes, Pop," Wynne said, then waved to Grim and Aeryn. "See you in a bit."

She took off like an arrow up the lane.

"I have room in my barn for your horses, if you'd like to stable them there," Elric said.

"Thank you," Aeryn said.

They traversed the village, which was even smaller than Merioake, arriving at Elric's house within a few minutes. The large hut bore evidence of several additions made over the years. A split rail fence encircled a grassy field with a barn at the rear of the property, along with several different sheds for tools or smoking meat.

A gentle-faced woman with a petite nose and long brown hair waited at the door with her children. She greeted Jisselle and Harvald, who led the group, and stepped aside to allow the elders to enter her home.

Grim and Aeryn dismounted. Wolfe, Ophelia, and Iviss did the same, as Elric's family approached. A little boy dashed from the house, darting between the elders trying to enter the dwelling. He raced to catch up with his family.

"This is my wife, Susi," Elric said, placing his hand on her back. He nodded to a stocky young man who looked like a younger version of himself with hair. "My son, Omri. You've met Wynne already. And my youngest, Jairus."

The boy who was hiding behind his mother blinked up at them. Aeryn smiled at him, and he turned his face into his mother's skirt.

"Collect your belongings, and Omri'll see to the horses," Elric said. "Omri, Jai stays with you. Do not let him out of your sight."

"Yes, Pop."

"What about me?" Wynne asked.

"You were part of the scouts who found them. Get inside."

Wynne's eyes brightened. "I get to be a part of the meeting?"

"Unless you'd like me to find you something else to do."

Wynne suppressed a squeal, and hurried inside along with the others.

Elric and Susi directed them to drop their bags by the door. They followed them into a wide, but crowded, room where the meeting was to be held. It was warm, and well lit with a crackling hearth and lanterns arranged on a long wooden table in the center of the room. Several benches lined the table, and there was a matching pair of rocking chairs in the corner. The elders sat along one side of the table, and Elric and Susi joined them. The scouts were seated along the wall.

"Sit," Harvald said, gesturing to the empty bench opposite the elders. Grim sat in the center seat with Aeryn at his right, and Wolfe at his left. Ophelia took the end beside Wolfe, and Iviss slid onto the bench next to Aeryn.

"We always thank the gods on the occasions when one of our own comes home," Harvald said. "However…the circumstances of your arrival, and the tidings you bring, bid that we not belabor matters. Grim, from your own lips, please tell us what you shared with the scouts."

Grim folded his hands atop the table, leaning forward a little. His face was set in determination, ready to address his people, and rally them to the cause. He looked the man in the eye and spoke in a clear, steady voice.

"When we arrived, I explained that we were unable to connect with the Chain."

He opened his mouth to continue, but Harvald held up a hand to stop him. "Why?"

"They were dead or unwilling," Grim said, refusing to betray the irritation of being immediately interrupted. "My runes began glowing outside of Bywinter, leading us here."

"What do you mean by leading?" Tegan asked, interrupting him again.

"They urged me to move in a particular direction," Grim said. "Ulfur has followed us across Noemar. He is coming."

"Are you sure it's Ulfur?" Tegan asked, her eyes scanning the length of the table, inviting the others to comment or confirm.

"Yes," Aeryn said. "Iviss and Wolfe helped us escape him and his hunters in Bywinter. He has hounded us since, sometimes even possessing animals and running them to death to trail us."

A disturbed look passed over several faces, and the room grew uncomfortably quiet for a moment.

"Is he traveling alone?" Elric asked.

"We don't know," Grim said. "We think it's unlikely."

"How far behind, you reckon?"

"Less than a day," Grim said. "We have the greatest chance of defeating him for good if we confront him together."

"The runes have never done this before," Harvald said.

"Harvald, do you deny the possibility? Everyone's runes are unique. Eventually someone would be born with a combination to do something odd, like lead them across Noemar to us," Tegan said. "It's a lucky thing he got here before Ulfur got ahold of him. Could you imagine Ulfur with the power to come straight to us without warning?"

"He has found us," Harvald said, his voice tightening. "This young man has led him right to us."

"He's given us warning, and he's right," Tegan said, matching his fire with her own. Aeryn decided she liked her. "We can put an end to him forever. Together."

"Here, here!" Elric banged a fist on the table. "We need to prepare ourselves. See about the safe removal of the women, children, sick, and elderly." Aeryn decided she liked him too.

"We still have the problem of three non-Keepers knowing our location," Harvald said.

"Not the most pressing concern," Elric said.

"They shouldn't even be here. Especially Wolfe," Harvald said.

"Harvald, this man has led dozens of our people to safety," Jisselle said, turning a stern eye on him. "Including your mother.

Including my family."

"Our people's blood dirties his hands," Harvald said. "As if one dead family of Baldomar isn't enough. He's a part of the team which has led the Rune Reaper here. It figures he'd be a part of this evil coming upon us."

"Wolfe never betrayed your people," Ophelia said, her voice strong with emotion. "You have to know that."

"Ophelia, stop." Wolfe placed his gnarled hand on Ophelia's arm. Chest heaving, Ophelia met his weary face. "He can be angry. He's right. It was my call to take Ramsey instead of Delan as my second, and a family died because of it."

Ophelia blinked back the liquid pooling on the brim of her eyes. "It's not your fault."

Wolfe lowered his voice. "This isn't the time."

Jisselle pursed her lips and furrowed her brow at Harvald. She shook her head.

"You should be ashamed, Harvald. It was the other spy who cracked. Not. Wolfe." The old woman let her terse words hang in the air for a moment. "Cracked, I remind you, under torture from the abomination-of-a-man headed here." She turned to the elder with the face tattoos. "Nialls, you've been quiet. Thoughts?"

Nialls, who'd been listening impassively with his arms across his chest, took a deep breath. When he spoke, it was with an accent so thick, Aeryn struggled to understand him.

"I do not know these people. The runes leading here," he said with a shrug. "I accept. I believe Grim and Little Elf. If it is Ulfur, I want chance to finish him. We must prepare for fight.

Protect our own. Put runes into use."

Quiet fell over the room.

"Is it settled then?" Tegan said, peering down the bench at the elders' faces.

Jisselle dipped her chin, and Harvald conceded with a nod.

"Very well," Tegan said.

"The elders will make the announcement for the people to prepare themselves at once," Harvald said. "Rakel, double your patrols. We need to know the moment an intruder breaches the warded wood."

"At once, sir." Rakel stood with her rangers and made her way to the door.

"Wynne, you stay," Elric said, stopping his daughter.

Her face fell, but she respected her father enough not to protest in front of everyone.

"You're needed here," he said. "Susi will coordinate for mothers, children, the sick and the elderly. Regroup here with all willing to fight within an hour."

Benches scraped across the floor as everyone remaining in the house stood. The elders hurried out the door. Susi crossed the room to Aeryn, Grim, and the others.

"There's a hut designated for the Keepers when they come. There's another set aside for new Baldomar until they can get on their feet here. Wynne will take you," she said. "Drop off your belongings, and hurry back here."

They followed Wynne through the village to a neighboring

pair of huts, each surrounded by a grassy plot of land. Ophelia, Wolfe, and Iviss dropped their things at the Keeper's Lodge, while Wynne held the door for Grim and Aeryn and stepped out of the way.

"I'll wait out here," she said.

The hut was a single room with two trundle beds. There was a table and chairs near an empty hearth. An unlit lantern and a large woven basket, brimming with blankets, sat atop the table. A set of wooden blocks for children was arranged into a small tower beside the stack of firewood.

Aeryn dropped her pack and weapons onto one of the beds, and Grim on the other.

"Aeryn, this isn't the place," Grim said, keeping his voice low enough not to carry out the open door.

"What are you talking about?" she said.

"Where the runes are leading..." he said, showing her his runes. "This isn't the destination."

Aeryn stared at his still faintly-glowing knuckles for a moment, then met his eyes. "Where, then?"

He led her to the doorway and pointed to a particular mountain east of the village.

"There."

34

Motives

The group returned to Elric's house, where Elric was arguing with Wynne. His elevated voice carried as Omri opened the front door and waved them inside.

"I'm capable," Wynne said, pleading. "Other ladies will be involved. Tegan, Rakel."

"They are grown women who may do as they please," Elric said. "You are my fifteen-year-old daughter. You will help your mother with the women and children."

Wynne assessed Aeryn, Grim, and the others as they entered the wide room, her nostrils flared. "What about Aeryn? She can't be much older than me."

The family's eyes turned on Aeryn, awaiting a response.

"I'm staying with Grim," Aeryn said.

"No more arguing," Susi said, forcing a bowl of fragrant stew into her daughter's hands. "Take a roll, and eat. You lot, come and get some food. You can't plan for battle on an empty stomach."

She waved the newcomers on as she dipped her ladle into the simmering cast iron pot on the hearth. When everyone had a steaming bowl of beef stew and a crusty roll, Elric offered a prayer of thanks to the gods, adding a petition for favor over their enemy. Then they tucked in.

Aeryn found herself squished in between Grim and Wynne

on the bench. Wynne kept peeking past Aeryn for a glimpse of Grim's knuckles, until Aeryn leaned back to give her a better view.

Wynne turned pink. "Sorry. I'm not trying to annoy you. I'm just curious. None of my runes match my family's." She dove her spoon into the cloudy brown liquid. "Quite a way to learn you're adopted."

Now that she mentioned it, it seemed clear to Aeryn. She was the only blonde in the family, shorter than the rest, and had a broad nose unlike either of her adopted parents.

"When did you find out?" Aeryn asked.

"Ten. My birth-mum died when I was a baby, the winter after arriving here." She tore a hunk of bread with her teeth. "They said the rest of my family never made it. But maybe someday a distant relative will show up."

Aeryn pointed in the direction of Grim's knuckles. "Any of his runes match yours?"

"I can't tell, he won't hold still long enough." Wynne took another bite of stew, giving up on the endeavor for now. "So have you seen the Rune Reaper?"

"Yes."

"And you lived? Do you have magic, or something?"

"He let me go," Aeryn said, remembering the day in Bywinter. "So I'd lead him to Grim. Iviss and Wolfe helped us escape."

Wynne's gaze traveled down the table, passing over Wolfe's scarred face, then landing with unmistakable interest on Iviss. "He's cute. So how old are you, anyway?"

"Thirty," Aeryn said, double licking her spoon. "For elves, it's considered very early adulthood."

"Oh. Hold old is Grim?"

"Twenty-three."

Wynne's eyes traveled down the table toward Iviss again. "How old is the cute Shadow?"

"Wolfe is much too old for you," Aeryn said with a straight face.

Wynne choked on her stew, turning several heads. Aeryn suppressed a grin.

Everyone devoured their meal and made quick work of cleanup. The elders arrived shortly after, and immediately launched into hurried plans. Merioake never experienced attacks from marauders during her lifetime. She never realized how much effort went into preparing to defend a village.

There were men to coordinate, general strategy and placement to figure out, and weapons, shields, and armor to account for. No one knew what to expect, only that Ulfur was coming, and he probably wasn't alone.

Everyone had a job. Susi and Wynne were responsible for ushering mother's, children, sick, and elderly to one of three hidden dug-out cellars throughout the village. Ophelia would whip up several nasty poisons to dip arrows. Wolfe would keep vigilant with his dice rolling, and hopefully alert the Enclave forces of which direction Ulfur was coming from before he arrived.

All of the elders, like most villagers who weren't born at the Enclave, experienced the chaos of attacks at some point in their lives.

They, like their people, were eager to strike back at their enemies. But they lacked combat experience and a certain degree of tactical know-how. Iviss, who had undergone Imperial military training, provided some tactical advice, and Grim had many ideas for how to inflict the most damage possible.

"If you have armor and weapons, go get them," Nialls told them as the hurried meeting wrapped up.

"I'll walk with you," Susi said as she ladled the last of the stew into a smaller pot, and loaded the remaining rolls in a basket. "I have to drop this off near your lodgings."

"Once you're armored, come back here," Elric said. "We've a few more matters to discuss."

Daylight waned and the frigid wind whipped Aeryn's hair around as they hurried back to their huts. Susi stopped a few doors down, and they continued the rest of the way without her.

"I plan to work on the poisons here," Ophelia said, as Iviss and Wolfe entered the Keeper's Lodge ahead of her. "Less distracting. I'll meet up with you. Aeryn, be sure to see me with your arrows."

Aeryn nodded. Nerves prickled at the back of her neck in anticipation of the violence to come. Her limbs felt cold even after she and Grim entered their dwelling.

Aeryn lit a lamp and counted her arrows. "I have twenty one left. I hope Ulfur, and anyone he shows up with isn't well-armored. These broadheads aren't very good against metal."

"You don't think they'd puncture?" Grim asked as he began to don his plate armor.

Aeryn shrugged. "Never tried."

"Then aim for the head or neck."

"You say that like it's easy."

"I've seen you with your bow and arrow," he said. "You could do it."

"I appreciate the confidence." She tightened the strap of her quiver across her chest, securing it firmly to her back, and tucked her bow. Her sword was already fastened to her hip. She didn't have armor, but her good leather jacket with the furry lining was better than nothing. "Let me help you with your plate."

When he was fully outfitted, Aeryn stood back. "You look intimidating with your visor down. I mean, more than you normally do."

"Good." He lifted it, and grabbed his axe.

"Have you ever considered naming your axe?" she asked. "Some warriors name their weapon."

He surveyed his weapon briefly. "No. Have you?"

"I named the dagger from Iviss. *Bairb*." Aeryn made sure the weapon was fixed securely in her bracers she wore over her jacket sleeves for extra protection.

Grim turned the axe over. "Retribution. That's its name."

They stepped outside, expecting to find Wolfe and Iviss waiting for them. Instead, they were a few doors down, entering the hut where Susi stopped along the way.

Aeryn and Grim trotted down the lane and slowed as they approached. An infant's cries carried from within. It wasn't a normal, fussy cry. Something was wrong.

The door opened, and the harsh sound grew instantly louder. Iviss poked his head out and waved them inside. In the one-room hut, the noise swamped Aeryn's senses, making it hard to think straight. The exhausted mother stood in the center of the room, bouncing her inconsolable baby in her arms. Her eyes were red. She spoke hastily with Susi over the child's screams. Wolfe listened, casting his dice on the table, asking clarifying questions.

The screams punctuated the atmosphere, setting Aeryn's teeth on edge. A wave of heat rushed over her face.

"Eat something," Susi said to the mother, nudging her gently toward the table where the pot of stew and basket of rolls sat. Susi stepped toward Aeryn, Grim, and Iviss who were clustered at the doorway. She rubbed the worry lines on her forehead, and lowered her voice. "She's frantic. Baby's had a fever for four days. Her husband's gone to fight. She's afraid she's going to lose them both."

"Four days?" Aeryn asked. A cold tingling spread over her chest.

Susi's eyes jumped from Aeryn to Grim. "Iviss mentioned one of you has some skill with healing."

Grim and Iviss turned as one toward Aeryn.

The desperate mother noticed. She abandoned her conversation with Wolfe and the untouched food on the table. She crossed the hut in a single bound, eye begging, and offered her baby to Aeryn. "Please! Can you make the fever leave him? Please..."

Aeryn took the shrieking infant tenderly in her arms. The squirmy baby pumped his tiny rune-marked fists into the air. In discomfort, he rubbed the back of his head into the crook of her elbow. His heat seeped into Aeryn, even through her jacket.

Aeryn stared at the child for a moment. Her ribs constricted. Her ears began to ring and pricks of sweat formed around her hairline. Her whole body felt rigid. She strained to keep her focus on the present, but the memories of Daphne, ill and inconsolable, fluttered around the edges of her mind fighting for dominance. Her heart began to race as the mother relayed the list of symptoms through a thick voice.

"I can't get the fever to break. He's stopped eating," the woman said. She pushed the blonde wisps away from her eyes, then reached out and touched her baby's forehead with the back of her hand.

"Aeryn, did you grab the herb for fever before they led us in?" Iviss asked.

The baby arched his back and shrieked more loudly than before. Aeryn gritted her teeth. Her eyelids fluttered, and she pulled her gaze away from the baby's pinched face. "...What?"

"The herb for fever. Did you get it?"

"I...no." Aeryn shook her head. She felt disoriented. The screaming felt like daggers in her ears. She clamped her eyes shut, as if to prevent the memory of Daphne's last day from slicing through her, but it was too late. It was awake, and it was coming for her. She took a few quick, shallow breaths as a sense of panic coursed through her.

"Can you fetch it?" Susi asked over the noise. "Is it far?"

"No," Aeryn said between breaths. She felt like she

couldn't breathe. "I can't."

She handed the crying baby back to his mother. She pushed her way past Grim and Iviss, she burst from the hut, gulping for air. Her legs slowed as they carried her up the lane toward her and Grim's lodging. Elbows out, she brought both hands to her forehead.

She heard the clunk of metal as Grim jogged to catch up with her. "Aeryn, you can go get the herb. Take Sten. You'll get there and back quickly."

Aeryn's arms tingled. She kept her focus on the packed earth a few feet in front of her. "I can't."

"What do you mean, you can't?"

"I said, I can't," she said, her tone sharp.

"Aeryn, no one else can go right now," Grim said, matching her tone. "You're good at this. Go do it."

Aeryn stopped outside their hut and turned on him. "I'm not responsible for that baby!"

Grim's brows twitched into a frown and he eyed her for a moment before he responded. "No one is going to blame you for this baby's death if you don't make it back in time."

The words caught like hooks and twisted.

"I'm not doing it!" Aeryn said, her voice shrill.

"Everyone else here has a job. Just go do it. You're a part of this team." Grim said, his voice raising.

"Maybe I don't want to be a part of this team!"

A new look passed over his face. Aeryn couldn't tell if it was hurt, shock, or disappointment, but it was gone as quickly as it came. His face hardened and when he spoke, he was curt. "What is your problem?"

"You! You want me to fix this baby. I can't. I can't do this again," she said, the words spilling forth heedless of thought.

"Again? What are you talking about?"

Aeryn pushed the heels of her hands into her temples. Her chest heaved. She felt like she couldn't get enough air. Her vision grew spotty.

"Aeryn, get it together," Grim said, his voice commanding.

"I can't..." she said through gasps. She trailed off as the ground swayed beneath her. She squeezed her eyes shut to keep the world from spinning. Her mind raced. "I thought I could get away... I thought if I left with you..."

"...If you left with me?" Grim said, cocking his head as if to make sure he heard correctly. "Get away from what?"

Down the lane, Susi was leading the mother toward the Keeper's Lodge. "Wolfe said Ophelia makes potions. Perhaps she has the means to whip something up."

Aeryn's eyes settled on the crying infant, her brows pinched in the middle. Grim followed her gaze, then refocused on Aeryn. Aeryn met his eyes, and her throat tightened.

Quick as a breath, ideas aligned in Aeryn's mind.

He could have the truth. Let him hear it. Let him push her away. He'd tell her to leave, surely. Then she'd be free. She could get away from this, and it wouldn't be her fault.

"Grim, I lied to you," she said. "I didn't leave because I wanted to help you. I left so I didn't have to stay in Merioake and work at the tannery."

A brief ripple of surprise passed over him.

To drive home the hurt, she continued. "I used you as an excuse to avoid my obligations. I left for me, not you. Not because I cared about you."

For a moment, he looked as though she'd slapped him. The lower half of his face tightened, and he watched her, dropping into quiet thought. Aeryn couldn't tell what churned behind his furrowed brow, but she read the hurt on his face. Then it passed. Resolved, he refocused his steely blue eyes on her, which seemed to be alive with fire again.

Aeryn braced herself for the stinging rejection. She knew it would feel like being ripped in half, but it was also her release. Her escape from this pain.

"You lied about why you left home," Grim said. "Fine."

He released a breath, and shifted his stance, taking a step closer while maintaining strong eye contact, still frowning deeply. "But you're here now. Has what we've been through meant nothing to you? I thought we were friends. Maybe not when we left Thoen, but now."

She could feel her eyes fill with water and the back of her throat start to ache.

"If we are," he said, watching her closely, "...if what we've endured the last several months has meant anything, then stay. If not..."

He cast an arm flippantly toward the horizon.

Aeryn opened her mouth, but the words lodged in her

throat, unable to even croak out. A new wave of heat rushed over her. This was not how she expected him to react. He was supposed to tell her to leave. Yet here he was, leaving the door open for her.

He studied her face for a long moment. Not seeing what he hoped, Grim pushed out a breath. He shook his head and turned away, leaving Aeryn standing alone in front of their hut.

35

Smoke

Aeryn stormed into the hut, hands on her head. She bent double and released a scream through gritted teeth. Her thoughts spun and hot liquid welled into her eyes.

She had to go.

She needed to clear her head, and figure out what to do next. She couldn't think here.

Aeryn bumped her hip on the edge of the table in her haste. The road was now empty. Sounds of villagers and activity carried from further in town, in the direction of the Thar's house.

She ran.

The roads here didn't make sense, but their hut was close enough to the edge of the settlement that Aeryn only needed to weave through a few dirt lanes to make it to the surrounding pasture. She dodged a few villagers, bustling with preparations. She disregarded the passing noises, lest she hear her name. Though she doubted she would.

She focused on the looming treeline on the western border and shot through the tall grass toward the evergreen forest. That was where she belonged. Arms pumping and hair flying out behind her, the feathers in her hair flipped against each other. Her legs carried her into the woods, startling a herd of pikdeer who grazed along the edge of the field. The shadows of the surrounding forest enveloped her in comforting solitude.

Aeryn's eyes adjusted to the dim light as her boots crunched over pine needles and cones. She was being carelessly noisy for an unfamiliar wood, but she didn't care. She was still far enough away from the Warded Wood not to worry about whatever creepy things may or may not lurk there.

She wasn't sure for how long she ran, but eventually she slowed, catching her breath. The forest was silent apart from the distant hoot of a lonely owl. A line from the lullaby came to her mind. *The owls dance before the moon...*

Breathing heavily, she leaned against a tree, and covered her face with cupped hands, and sank to her knees. The memories of her own sweet baby, who she couldn't save, who she would never hold again, gushed into her mind.

She wasn't prepared for an infant thrust into her arms.

Aeryn began to sob like she hadn't since that day six years ago. She couldn't keep reliving this every time she saw a baby.

Gideon had been upset with her when she came to him, scared, with the news she was carrying his child. He said he didn't want to be a father. He wasn't ready. As if she was.

He warned her not to tell anyone. In Merioake, babies simply weren't born to young, unwed parents. It was outrageous. Most people had the good sense to wait. He said he'd figure something out.

A few days later, he placed his solution, a packet of tiny black flowers, into her palm.

"*Brew it and drink the whole thing,*" he said. "*It will make all this go away. We can forget it ever happened and move on with our lives. Maybe we can try this again when we're older, but not now. You can't be pregnant now."*

Aeryn couldn't bring herself to drink it. This was her baby, her own flesh and blood. Vulnerable, innocent, completely dependent. Though terrified, she made a promise to herself and to her unborn baby, to love and protect her. She'd bite the stigma and grow up fast.

Gideon refused. He pushed Aeryn away and denied he was the father to anyone with ears. She lost him, her friends, and her reputation. All things she could live without. But lastly, she lost the daughter who she promised to love and protect.

She made a promise, and she failed.

She thought she gained distance from the perpetual reminders in Merioake. Disappointing her family and abandoning their livelihood was a small price to pay. But it would never be better. The pain was like a trapped animal, always brooding, always an opportunist. The slightest resemblance to someone she once loved, the mere mention of a song, and the beast would rear its head and maul her. As long as there were other elves, happy families, or children around, she'd be reminded of what was gone forever. She wasn't even safe when she slept.

Aeryn's mind roiled and she got up. Her legs aimlessly began to move.

She could just leave. She couldn't go home. She might travel into Gallendahli and become another person. Just put all this behind her. Try to forget. So what if she made a promise to continue with Grim until he found his family? She was no good at keeping those.

She gritted her teeth, picked up a pinecone at her feet, and hurled it as hard as she could into the shadowy trees. She dropped her gaze and noticed a tuft of fever sorrell growing by her feet.

Aeryn's focus went cloudy. A moment later, she was no longer in the forest, but in her bedroom, at her parents house. Daphne's crib stood in the corner, where it had been. The baby was in the crib. Moving.

Aeryn felt like she was standing outside herself, experiencing a memory which she couldn't place. She was in full control, and it occurred to her that maybe it wasn't a memory. It didn't matter. Her child was there.

Aeryn came to the cribside and gazed down at her daughter. Daphne was wide awake, legs straight in the air as she played with her feet. Upon seeing her mother, Daphne broke into a gummy grin and made a gurgling sound. Her chubby fingers released her foot. She rolled onto her belly, pushed herself into a sitting position, and extended her arms for Aeryn to pick her up.

They'd done this dozens of times. Aeryn's throat tightened, but her daughter's smile was infectious.

"Hi, my little feather," she said. She reached out, feeling the weight of her daughter as she scooped her into her arms. Daphne cooed. Aeryn squeezed her baby into a hug. She sniffed the top of her child's head, which still had that new-baby smell.

It was so vivid that if she didn't know better, Aeryn might've mistaken it for the present. She knew that wasn't possible.

Daphne was gone and she wasn't in Merioake. Whether this was her imagination, or a vision, or something else altogether, she knew it wouldn't last.

She didn't want it to end. Here was her daughter, happy and healthy.

Aeryn relaxed her arms, shifting Daphne so she could cradle her and smile upon her sweet face. "Daphne, I love you. Your Momma loves you."

Daphne blinked her big blue eyes, watching and listening. There was only so much she could understand. More than anything, Aeryn wanted her child to know she loved her and she would've done anything to save her. That she hadn't abandoned her. Aeryn's heart clenched, but she kept it together.

"I'm sorry I couldn't save you. I'm so sorry," she said. "Please know I didn't leave you. I'm sorry I wasn't there when you..." Her throat tightened, cutting off her words.

Daphne watched her for a long moment, then grinned with a garbled happy noise. She squirmed, extending her chubby arms towards her mother's face.

Aeryn felt the little fingers touch her cheeks as if she were really there. Warmth spread from Aeryn's heart. Something released within her as she looked with love upon her daughter, who was delightedly drooling all over her chin. Would it be so bad to remember Daphne this way?

She felt afraid that if she shut her eyes, this moment would end.

But maybe that was okay.

"You will always be my daughter," she said. "I will always carry you with me."

She closed her eyes as she hugged her baby tighter, and when she opened them, she was standing in the dark woods outside the Enclave valley. The forest was quiet and she was alone. Her arms were empty, but her eyes fell to the handful of fever sorrel she clutched in both fists. She hadn't remembered tearing it up.

Aeryn took a moment as her mind rushed over what she'd just experienced, and her thoughts returned to Daphne's bright face, latching onto the image of her daughter, healthy and full of joy. It was good to remember her that way.

She drew a cleansing breath as a peace settled over her.

"I did everything I could," she said out loud to herself. "It isn't my fault."

For the first time, she could accept that as true.

Aeryn's gaze returned to the fever sorrel in her hands.

Her people needed her. Her friends needed her. The sick baby who she still might not be able to save, needed her.

It would've been a lot easier if Grim simply told her to go. Easy, but not good. Instead, he left the door open and gave her the choice, because he was good. Staying would involve major explanations, and as much as she didn't want to endure that, Grim was her friend. They stuck by each other through unending dangers and countless sleepless nights. As much as he pushed her to her limits, he'd always been honest. After all they'd been through, what came out of her mouth? *Maybe I don't want to be a part of this team?*

If she were him, she would probably wonder if any of it mattered too.

She needed to try to make things right. She'd apologize, and hope that he'd accept her. He might not, but she had to try.

Aeryn circled back in the direction of the village. She was still deep enough in the woods that she couldn't see into the valley. She lifted a quick prayer to whatever gods might be listening that she'd make it back in time. With Ulfur on his way, the last thing she wanted was to meet him in the dark.

With the back of her hand, she wiped the water escaping her eyes, then nearly fell over. A herd of pikdeer raced through the nearby picket, so close she could reach out and touch them. They fled deeper into the forest. She didn't have to connect with them to sense the fear rolling off the herd.

As she recovered from the surprise, she slowed her gait to minimize noise. She drew her bow, in case a predator lurked ahead. She moved swiftly through the trees, meeting no creatures. As she neared the forest's edge, she caught the acrid scent of smoke. The smell grew stronger with each step and soon the sounds of conflict carried from the direction of the village. Aeryn breached the treeline and gazed into the valley.

The village was in flames.

Ulfur was here, and had led a group of soldiers to fall upon the Enclave.

She was too late.

Aeryn watched, feeling eerily cold, and momentarily unable to move. Some wicked thought whispered in her ear. *Last chance for Gallendahli.* No one knew she was here.

Screams and the din of battle carried from the valley.

Grim was there.

Settling her mind for action, Aeryn ran toward the Enclave.

36

Battle of the Enclave

The village swarmed with battle violence. Hoards of mercenaries and Cords engaged Enclave fighters in the streets. Numerous huts were engulfed in flame. Burning structures sent hazy whirls of white smoke into the air. Screams and clashes of metal tolled from every direction.

Armed Enclavers fought back, but from Aeryn's vantage point, they were outnumbered. Civilians fled through the streets to escape the raiders, only to be cut down. Dead bodies littered the road, both Cords and Baldomar young and old.

The only light came from the burning structures.

Aeryn had hunted in low light before.

Bow and arrow ready, she fired at the first raider who came into view. She drew arrows in rapid succession, and two more Cords hit the dirt. Never stopping, Aeryn tucked herself in the shadows, like Iviss taught her, and hurried along the lanes. She had to find Grim.

Aeryn had reentered the village from the west. While fighting and chaos were everywhere, the main battle roiled in the southern part of the village. Grim would be there, in the thick of it.

On the road ahead, a pair of raiders cut down an Enclave fighter. They trod over his body toward a hut and kicked in the door.

Aeryn sent two arrows their way and the first raider went down screaming. The second, seeing his comrade fall, shifted his focus to the source of the arrow fire. Aeryn drew another, took aim, and sunk it into his chest. He collapsed onto his comrade, clutching the shaft.

Aeryn raced toward him. Drawing her dagger, she swooped upon him and finished him off without mercy. She cast a glance into the open hut and saw Wynne, hand axes raised. Behind her, a mother clung to her three terrified young children. The brave girl had put herself between the raiders and this family.

Wynne's bulging blue eyes grew even larger. "Aeryn!"

Aeryn shouted above the din. "You're supposed to be at the shelter!"

"I'm trying! Everything happened so suddenly. We couldn't get there. They're everywhere," Wynne said.

"Is it far?"

"No, there's one beneath the Keepers Lodge."

"I'll cover you," Aeryn said. "Quick. Let's go." Nocking another arrow, and checking to see whether the lane was clear, she jogged up the path. Wynne trailed behind, leading the family.

Around the next bend, Aeryn watched three more Cords overwhelm a woman who resembled Tegan. The man she fought alongside was cut down a moment later. Aeryn drew to a stop, and sent several arrows at the raiders. The first sailed overhead, but the next three found their targets.

"Stay to the shadows," Aeryn called over her shoulder. They charged up the lane, making another turn, when the Keepers

Lodge came into view. Aeryn drew to a stop, letting Wynne and the family catch up with her.

"Wynne, here." She dug into her pocket and shoved a handful of fever sorrel into the girl's palm. If the mother with the sick baby made it to a lodge, it was probably this one. "For the woman with the sick baby."

"Tam?"

"I don't know her name. If she's there, you have to give this to her."

Wynne bobbed her head in understanding.

A scream emitted from within the dwelling. An armed raider dragged a woman in a blue skirt outside by her hair.

Ophelia.

It happened so fast. Ophelia slashed at the man's arm with a dagger. He released her. Ophelia reeled back, but the man redoubled his attack and slashed her across the chest. She fell to the ground.

Aeryn sank two arrows into the attacker, and she sprinted for her friend. She dropped to her knees at Ophelia's side.

A guttural yell pulled Aeryn's attention up the lane. Two more enemies charged in their direction.

Aeryn unleashed one arrow after the other until they stopped moving, and Wynne took the opportunity to lead the family into the Keeper's Lodge, and the hidden cellar inside.

"Ophelia!" Aeryn looked over her bloody friend, and her throat felt thick.

Ophelia grasped Aeryn's hand. Her eyes bulged, focused

on Aeryn's, but only for a moment before they grew unfocused. Her grip eased. Her body sagged.

She was gone.

Aeryn fought the shakiness in her limbs, and pulled herself away. *Grieve later.*

Wynne had made it into the hut with the family. She'd have to take it from there. Aeryn needed to find Grim.

✦

Aeryn watched from afar as Grim swung his axe, clipping his opponent on the arm. The weight of the axe sunk into the overturned horse cart nearby, and stuck. Grim yanked, but the unwieldy heavy weapon was lodged.

His opponent took a swipe at Grim's head. He ducked, hunching his shoulders. The sword clattered into the side of his helmet, ripping it off.

Disoriented from the blow, Grim nearly lost his balance. Aeryn's stomach turned to stone as his opponent drew back, preparing to lob off his head. In the maelstrom, she didn't have a clear shot.

Fire ignited in her legs, and she flew at the Cord from behind, drawing her dagger as she ran.

The raider slashed.

Grim launched himself away from the blade, releasing his axe. Another swing forced Grim to make an unsteady dodge backward. This time the edge of the blade glanced off his chestplate.

Grim tripped, and landed with a crash.

The raider raised his sword to bring it down upon him.

Aeryn screamed, pressing into the run to close the distance. She launched herself at the man. Dagger in hand, she jumped onto his back and jabbed him in the neck twice.

The raider crumpled beneath her.

Breathing heavily, she met Grim's stunned face. She clamored over the dead man, and reached a hand to Grim.

He gave her an awed look, almost like he didn't believe she'd be here. But here she was, having saved his life, extending herself to him. Something resolved inside him, and he took her hand.

With Grim on his feet again, Aeryn wasted no time. She snatched his helmet from the dirt. He dislodged his axe.

The sounds of battle were drawing closer.

"Gah!" Grim winced and bent double, dropping his weapon. He held his hands in front of him. "Not now!"

"What's happening?" she asked, though she feared she already knew.

He gritted his teeth. "They've been insistent since the battle started. *And painful.*"

"We need to follow them now," Aeryn said.

Grim cried in agony. His eyes tightened and he staggered to a knee.

Aeryn tugged on his arm, to help him to his feet. "You have to carry your axe or leave it. It's too heavy for me."

"Grim! Aeryn!" Through the smoke, Wolfe rushed toward them, crossbow in hand. He took in the state of the situation. "Runes?"

Grim gritted his teeth and nodded once.

"Follow them. Ya hear me?" Wolfe shouted above the din. "Grim, pay attention. Ulfur is coming. I can hold him off, give ya time. Now get out of here."

"I'm gonna kill him."

"Not like this. Now stop arguing, ya stubborn Northerner," Wolfe said. He helped Aeryn heave Grim to his feet. "Follow the runes to their conclusion. Ya must. The dice don't lie. Now go."

Wolfe looked Aeryn in the eye as much to say, *Make sure he gets there.* She gave a firm nod.

With effort, Grim placed the helmet on his head. Aeryn readied an arrow, and they started to move.

As they passed the first intersection, Grim staggered again, but kept his footing.

The man with the milky eye lumbered across the road ahead. His gaze snapped in their direction. Ulfur stopped short, barring their path. Recognition passed over his face.

"Go!" Wolfe said. He planted himself in the intersection, and took aim at Ulfur. Aeryn didn't wait to watch what happened next.

She tugged on Grim and led him down a turn. His focus drastically improved as they moved away from the Rune Reeper. The pain in his runes lessened.

The battle raged around them. Sticking to the shadows, Aeryn helped clear a path, taking down several more raiders on their way out. At last they made it to the eastern edge of the village. They charged into the open field, headed toward the mountain Grim indicated earlier.

Yells behind them made Aeryn look over her shoulder. Two Cords had noticed them leaving and were attempting to run them down.

Aeryn planted herself, allowing Grim to pass her, and take the lead. She aimed and fired twice. The first arrow met its target and sent him sprawling. The second struck the man in the eye. Then she sprinted after Grim toward the eastern mountain.

37

The Mountain

They ran up the slope for what seemed like an eternity, over uneven ground, dodging roots and trying to avoid rolling their ankles in the dark.

Aeryn urged Grim onward. He was exhausted in his heavy armor, after fighting for his life in the village and jogging uphill for what must've been an hour. But they couldn't afford to stop. Aeryn's breaths came ragged and her body ached, but she'd run like this before. She wasn't going to let someone else die because she ran out of time again.

At one point, Aeryn looked over her shoulder and got her first glimpse of the valley below. The battle raged on, with plumes of smoke obscuring the night sky. She saw the hulking, shadowy shape of four men exit the village for the pasture toward the mountain. They slowed momentarily to note the two Cords Aeryn shot down, and crouched over the bodies. One of them grasped at something around his neck, and released a small animal which shot through the pasture toward the mountain she and Grim were trying to climb.

They were being hunted up the mountain.

"Come on, we can't slow down. He's coming," she said. She urged her screaming leg muscles onward. Just ahead, Grim was sagging with exhaustion. She hooked her arm in his, and tugged, and he pushed on.

✪

Gargantuan rockfaces rose ahead, obscured by the dense-growing aspens.

Panting, Grim leaned into his run and pressed toward the rockface. He touched it with his free hand, allowing his fingers to trail over the surface of the stone. Nearby, there was a sound of thunder, like the crack of split rock.

Aeryn braced herself, searching for an oncoming rockslide, but the stony face of the mountain was still. Grim was completely unphased, but drew her attention to the right. Beneath a rocky overhang, a cave opening which Aeryn hadn't noticed a moment earlier, stood before them.

"This way." Grim staggered toward the cave mouth. Aeryn followed. The stony passage was twenty feet long, high enough for a man to stand, and narrow enough that if Grim extended his arms, he could touch both walls.

"There." Grim indicated a dark opening along the back of the cave.

A pleasant smell Aeryn couldn't place grew stronger as they neared the opening. Passing through, they rounded a curve, and beheld a huge, high-ceilinged cavern, bathed in a bluish glow. They stopped in the doorway, and momentarily forgot how to breathe.

An enormous dragon laid on his belly in the middle of the chamber. Each of his cream-colored scales was rimmed with silver. His many-horned head, the size of a covered wagon, rested on his front legs. Each leg was like a trunk of cedar, ending in curved claws as long as one of Aeryn's arms. His wings were folded against his body.

The dragon took deep, slow breaths. He watched them enter with heavy amber eyes. Then he rumbled low in his belly, and his lip crawled upward, revealing more of his glistening teeth.

Aeryn felt a nudge against her mind. A warm tingling sensation crept over her body.

The dragon spoke in a low voice which filled up the cavern and made Aeryn's insides hum with each syllable. "Welcome, Son and Daughter."

Aeryn stared at the magnificent beast before her. The dragon needed no introduction. They knew who it was the moment he addressed them.

They'd found the lair of Silversaar.

Silversaar shifted his head with effort. "Come nearer so I can see you."

They obeyed, and quietly stepped toward him. Silversaar's eyes focused on Grim.

"I knew someone's runes would lead here one day," the dragon said. He sounded tired, weak.

Then his great eyes shifted to Aeryn, and she felt a nudge wash over her mind again, but this time, she felt it go deeper, flicking through her memories, reading her heart like a book. In an instant, she was known by this dragon. He had seen her mind, and he knew who she was.

"You're the reason he's here, dear daughter," he said. "Pardon my reach, but I'm running out of time to learn about you the old fashioned way. You see, I'm dying."

38

Remember

"Now, son, come here. Closer."

The dragon was not to be refused. Grim took another step toward Silversaar.

"Closer."

Grim drew nearer until he stood only a few feet from Silversaar's snout. Silversaar sniffed him, and shifted his head to touch Grim with his nose. Pulling back to better see him, Silversaar's lips parted. "Do you know what your runes mean?"

Grim cleared his throat. He felt as if he were standing before someone to whom great respect was due, though he also felt uncertain how to properly address him. So Grim answered the question as simply, and honestly as he could. "I know they led me here. I don't know how to read them."

"They were a gift to your people, To protect yourselves. To protect the world," he said. "It was the only way to stop Malachai and his followers. Each person was to use his or her abilities, and together they could do it. No one was meant to stand alone." Silvery tears collected in his eyes. "I waited too long."

"I don't understand," Grim said.

"I waited, because granting magic to mortals was a grave decision. Once given, it cannot be revoked. But I should've done so sooner." The tear spilled over and splashed onto the cave floor.

"Lakhota would still be here. Your people wouldn't have been scattered. The war would've ended differently."

Silversaar blinked his heavy lid.

"My people are in the valley fighting against the Loom now," Grim said.

"I know. The magic protecting this place fades. The Rune Reaper found his way into the valley. I can smell him." There was a hint of a growl in his voice. "He is an abomination, perverting the gift I gave to your people. That's why his presence causes you pain."

A growl rumbled in his belly. Silversaar's lip curled in repulsion. His voice rose, making the stone floor tremble. "He'll be here soon. You must be ready."

"He's already here. Here's tracking up the mountain."

Silversaar's energy waned. "I meant Malachai."

Grim thought for a moment. "Malachai, the King of the West?"

"He's alive, roaming the world. The spell binding him in his form will fade when I die," Silversaar said. "You must stop him. Use the runes as I intended."

"We don't know how," Grim said, a little worried that he'd sound like he was making excuses. "Apart from a few symbols, no one can read them." His mind thumbed over all the things he'd been told. "What about the scroll, or the book the Loom was looking for?"

"There's no scroll. There never was," Silversaar said. "Your people learned directly from me. It connected us. Son, are you willing?"

"Willing?"

"To stop Malachai. To use the runes as I intended. To stand with your people," he said.

Grim didn't know the first thing about how to do this. But standing here before Silversaar, he felt sure that he could. The desire to do so filled him so full it almost hurt.

"Yes," he said.

Silversaar shifted his eye to Aeryn. "And you, Daughter?"

Aeryn swallowed, watching the great dragon with wide eyes. She bobbed her chin and said in a small voice. "Yes."

"Good. You're better together." Silversaar released a tired, heavy breath.

Without warning, a wave rolled into Grim's mind, and he braced himself. It was like the striking of a flint to ignite a bonfire in a darkened room. Runes flashed across his mind. Every curve, every line, every mark, made perfect sense. The entire alphabet of symbols and their meanings.

He felt a warm tingling in his fingers, which drew his attention to the tattoos across his knuckles. In a hurry, he pulled his gauntlets off.

The marks which had been a mystery as long as he remembered were now clear...and they were changed. Instead of crawling down the length of each finger, they circled each one like a ring, and many were different. Though he'd never felt more alive, his breathing stilled. His eyes grew wide as he read the runes scrawled on his hands.

Sense magic. Thunder. Hardiness. Protect. Direction.

Push. Might. Wisdom. Imbue. Healing touch. Crush. Exploit enemy weakness. Dragon. Remember. Silversaar's name and *remember* wrapped around his left thumb.

"I can read them," he said. He'd never read anything before.

"Me too," Aeryn said at his shoulder. She held her hands in front of her, staring at her own knuckles, which now bore their own set of runes, wrapped around each finger like his. Astonished, she met Grim's gaze, and turned her hands to show him. *Lucky. Keen eye. Swift. Speak with nature. Protection. Imbue. Wind. Bolt.*

Most of her's were different from Grim's. She looked perplexed. "Does this mean...?"

"Yes." Silversaar's breathing changed, and his eyes drooped. "Listen. The magic of some runes must be activated. You must know the symbol to use it. Other runes are passive, as part of your being. They remain in effect, whether or not you intend it. But, knowing the mark allows you to implement its magic more effectively.

"Now, Son and Daughter, you know them all. You will read the symbols of your people. You must teach them, and any willing to stand against Malachai, who will not abuse the gift. Do you understand?"

Aeryn's head bobbed and Grim nodded.

"I've seen what happens from here," Silversaar said, addressing Grim. "Son, there are memories which I've placed in your runes. You will not be able to access them until the right time. You've waited for many things in your life. You must be patient again."

The pronouncement of needing to wait settled on Grim

heavier than he was proud to admit. He had the foreboding sense that doing so might involve great difficulty. When he looked upon Silversaar, he had the unsettling feeling that Silversaar knew what he was thinking. Knew, and empathized.

"One more thing. The allur," Silversaar said, shifting his great yellow eye to Grim. "Son, you must remember."

Grim opened his mouth, perplexed. "Remember what?"

"Say the words after me. *Fyrir therr hondum.*"

Grim repeated the phrase.

"The use of magic is more than a recitation, son. Say it again," Silversaar said. "With the deepness of your magic."

Grim didn't know what that meant, but he took a breath, and attempted to quiet his mind. He focused his energy into obeying. "*Fyrir therr hondum.*"

He felt a jolt over his mind, a sense of rushing back in time, to a memory buried deep.

He saw himself crouched behind a rain barrel as an eight-year-old boy. He was afraid. No, terrified. His village was under attack. Night was falling.

It looked so much like the village in the valley, he wondered for a moment if he was seeing the Enclave at present through the eyes of a child. Then he realized. *No, this is me. This was my home.*

Father found him. Ducking behind the barrel, he grabbed him in a hug of crushing relief. Grim's eight-year-old self clung to his father, burying his face and vowing never to let another minute pass without knowing where his family was or how to find them. But it was going to be okay. Father was here.

"Josef. Look at me, son." His father took his face in his rough, rune-marked hands. "Say it after me. *Fyrir therr hondum.* Say it now."

The child, Josef, stared into his father's serious gray eyes and obeyed, repeating the word in a shaky voice.

The sounds of many raiders drew nearer.

"You remember our meeting place?" Father said in a hushed voice.

Josef bobbed his head.

"You must run for the treeline. Do not stop. Do not look back. Find your mother, and go." Josef's father wrapped his arms around his shoulders and pulled him into a tight hug. He kissed the top of his blonde head, prickling Josef with his beard. Father's voice thickened, but he controlled it. "Remember the words. I love you, son. Go. Go!"

Josef obeyed. He shot to his feet and dashed along the row of houses for the woods in the distance. When the row of houses ended, he needed to sprint across a small field to make it to the trees. It wasn't that far.

Josef heard yelling behind him. The raiders had spotted another villager. He heard his father bellowing, and the sounds of violence which followed. Josef felt his whole body tighten.

Do not stop, do not look back.

"One's getting away!" someone called behind him. "It's a kid!"

Josef had been spotted. Panic shot through his legs, causing them to move so fast he thought they might fall off. Dread snapped at his heels. Nothing else mattered but getting to the treeline.

His toe caught on a dip in the ground, and he hit the grass hard, knocking the air from his lungs.

He couldn't breathe. Terror-struck, he gasped for air. He had to keep going and get away. He pushed himself onto his hands and knees.

Strong hands caught him by the arm and yanked him to his feet.

Josef had barely caught his breath but whirled around, screaming, and took a swing at the dirty raider attempting to drag him back toward the village.

His father's word!

"*Fyrir therr -*"

The raider struck him in the mouth. A sharp pain exploded through his head and tears came to his eyes. He felt the warm trickle of blood on his chin. The man jerked him by the arm and handed him off to his comrade. "Load him up."

Josef was dragged through the street, past his father who laid in the road, bleeding, with a raider searching his pockets. He couldn't tell if Father was alive or not, but he wasn't moving.

Invigorated to fight again, Josef tried to break free of his captor's grasp, and received another hard knock to the head. His vision blurred. The next thing he knew, he was thrust into the back of a barred cart with twenty other boys and girls he knew from the village, all older than him, but about his size or bigger.

The memory faded gray.

His arms tingled down to his fingertips. He was on his

knees, fists pressed to the cold stone floor. Silversaar watched him with his great yellow eyes.

Aeryn knelt next to him, studying his face, her eyebrows drawn together in the middle. "Grim, are you alright?"

He took a moment, and sat back on his haunches. He remembered. "My father figured it out."

"Figured what?"

"The allur. I saw him. The day I was taken. He called me by name."

Aeryn waited with bated breath.

"My name is Josef."

Aeryn's eyes softened. "Josef is a nice name."

"The phrase Markus told you will activate the allur. Your symbols will combine. Focus on the effect your runes are capable of producing. You must remember," Silversaar said.

Markus must've been my father's name. But before he could ask, Silversaar spoke again.

"Aeryn, daughter..."

"Yes?"

"Can you pronounce the word?"

Aeryn repeated the phrase perfectly.

"Good," Silversaar said. "Show my people how to use the allur, and anyone else willing to oppose Malachai. You will not have have much time."

He shifted his head to touch Aeryn with his snout. She laid a hand gently on his nose, and Silversaar closed his eyes. His breathing slowed and he grew quieter, as if the conversation had drained him of his remaining strength.

"Do you know why I chose this place to watch over my people?" His voice was a whisper.

"Why?" she asked.

"I wanted to keep my people in their homeland, and it was the closest I could get to Lakhota. I miss her." Another silvery tear formed in the corner of his eye. He took a slow, shallow breath. "I shall see her again soon. I look forward to meeting your daughter."

Then Silversaar breathed his last.

A shift in the atmosphere rolled out from the dragon. It ruffled Aeryn's hair and made the air feel momentarily charged, sending tingles up Josef's arms.

He laid a hand on the dragon's shimmering scales. Beside him, Aeryn's cheeks were wet. She bent forward to touch her head to Silversaar's, and cried quietly.

Her expressions of emotion constantly caught Josef off guard, but he had grown familiar enough with her to recognize pain. He saw it in her when she exploded about the sick baby, during the incident with the lullaby, and in her face when her family argued in elvish in front of him.

She was grieved. Not just for Silversaar. Aeryn had a daughter once, and her child was gone.

Josef reached out and touched her on the shoulder. She lifted her head, and wiped her eyes with her fingertips in an attempt to regain composure.

"What was your daughter's name?" he asked.

Her face bunched with renewed grief. She drew a sharp

intake of breath and let it out steadily. She opened her mouth to answer, but the distant sound of voices outside made her freeze.

"Oh no," she said. "He's here."

39

Reckoning

Aeryn and Josef emerged shoulder to shoulder, and saw Ulfur climbing the mountainside, flanked by three of his hunters. Wolfe's tooth dangled from a new string around his neck.

"The Baldomar belongs to me," Ulfur barked at his hunters. "Subdue the elf, and stand by."

Weapons drawn, they charged.

With a roar, Josef ran at the Rune Reaper.

Aeryn's supply of arrows had dwindled throughout the evening, and she couldn't afford to miss. She readied her bow.

If only she could shoot three at once.

Unsure what might happen or what made her think to do it, Aeryn murmured the spell. Her mind focused. Energy tingled over her knuckles and crept into her fingers. Glowing blue light crawled down the shaft of the arrow to the tip. At the same time, swirling runes spread from her grip on the bow, climbing to the ends.

The enemies advanced. Aiming at the center hunter, she let the arrow fly. Instead of the familiar *thwick* of the rebounding string, a pleasant hum floated past her ears. Halfway to its target, the glowing arrow split into three. The centermost arrow continued straight, while the new ones diverged, angled toward the other two hunters. All three struck their targets in their chests simultaneously.

Something like awe stole over Aeryn, energizing her. But only for a moment.

Ulfur's gaze snapped to his three fallen underlings, then to Aeryn. His eye locked onto her with unmistakable hunger before Josef fell upon him.

Aeryn nocked another arrow and took aim. She noticed the symbols wrapped around her fingers glowing yellow. She hadn't noticed that before. She gaped for a moment, then a clash grabbed her attention. She aimed at Ulfur.

The push and pull of battle made it too difficult to get a good shot. In the desperate throws of the fight, Josef and Ulfur moved around too much. More than once, she nearly released the arrow, only for Josef to move in the flight path at the last second, and she was forced to aim again. She considered the possibility of willing the arrow to find its target with her new magic. But she had never tried it, and with Josef so close, it was too risky.

Aeryn maneuvered for a better position, but there had to be some other way to help.

Using the phrase again, Aeryn utilized a gust of air to pick up loose pine debris, and send it swirling around Ulfur's head. It distracted him enough for Josef to get in several good hits, but the two were evenly matched.

Ulfur pulled out his spear. With its skinny, foot long metal tip, it looked more like a giant bodkin arrow without the fletching. He adjusted his grip, preparing to hurl it and impale Josef.

No, you don't.

Aeryn bared her teeth as she bellowed the allur, using her

power to cast a glowing yellow barrier between the Rune Reaper and Josef.

Then Ulfur swiveled, and shifted his target. He hucked the spear at Aeryn and time slowed.

She could dodge, and maybe survive the impalement. But it was going to strike either way.

She threw herself sideways as the spear connected just inside her hip. She landed on her side in the dirt, the wind knocked from her lungs. A shock of stabbing pain exploded from her lower abdomen. White lights popped in her vision.

Her eyes traveled the length of her body where the spearhead sank into her. She tried not to vomit. It had cut through the leather of her jacket like wet paper. The area surrounding the wound was soaked with blood already, and it dripped up the shaft which protruded from her body, propped against the earth before her. Biting cold clawed from the wound. With a shaky hand, she carefully grabbed the shaft but it sent another wave of pain screaming through her.

She struggled for a breath and a new panic seized her. She knew it was possible to die from the shock of a grievous injury, and she fought to keep herself from losing control.

A deafening crack of stone brought her back to the present.

She looked up to see Ulfur grasping his finger necklace with one hand. With the other, he reached out and made a pulling motion in the air. A moment later, the rockface belched forth a shower of large stones. They rattled down the mountain like a waterfall and buried Josef.

Alive.

"No!" she cried, the slight movement of yelling causing her to shudder in pain. The last pebbles skittered down the mountainside, landing on top of the pile, and then all was quiet. It felt like a boulder landed on her chest.

Ulfur fixed his dead eye on Aeryn. His mouth curled into a grin. He pulled his hunters knife from his belt and stalked toward her.

Her eyes widened in terror.

"I can dig him out and get his later. But first, yours."

Releasing the shaft, Aeryn drew her hands tight against her chest. Ulfur squatted, lifting the spear shaft like a lever, forcing her body to turn. She cried out in agony as mind-rending pain shot through her. She saw spots and her ears began to ring.

The Rune Reaper grabbed her by the wrist and extended her arm, pinning her forearm to the ground with one knee. He spread her fingers.

She reached her free hand across her body to beat her fist into Ulfur's side. Unphased, Ulfur turned a cold eye on her, a smile playing around his lips. He tutted. "I told you I would peel the skin from your bones. But I think I'll add your knuckles to my collection. Never collected runes off an elf before. Your little trick with the arrows ought to come in useful."

He gripped the knife, bending over her hand, his body blocking her line of sight. Aeryn's heart quickened, thrumming in her ears. Hyperventilating, she gritted her teeth and winced in anticipation of the knife meeting her flesh.

A thunderous explosion split the air, accompanied by familiar battlecry.

Ulfur froze, looking up. The color drained from his face.

Rocks burst from the pile which had buried Josef, falling away on either side of him. He stood, holding his axe in front of his body. Golden runes edged the blade.

Chest heaving, he observed Ulfur crouched over Aeryn's hand. He locked eyes with Aeryn, the steel blue burning like blue flames.

"Ulfur!" Josef clapped down his visor. "You're mine."

He charged.

Ulfur dropped the knife. Leaving Aeryn, he leapt to his feet, drew his sword, and ran to meet him.

Their weapons met in a spray of magical sparks.

Ulfur clashed against Josef's brutal advance, matching him strike for strike. Even with the allur, they were evenly matched. If the battle continued this way, its outcome would be determined by whoever made the first mistake.

On her back, Aeryn held the shaft of the spear steady. She took a few shallow breaths. Her body screamed, but as long as she kept the spear still, she could think. She squeezed her eyes shut, trying to quiet her mind as much as possible, but it was getting harder to concentrate. There had to be something she could do.

When she opened them, her gaze landed on the tree nearest Ulfur. She followed the length of the trunk to the ground. She released one hand, and grunted. It was harder to control the spear with only one hand, and the slightest movement sent sickening waves through her.

She dug her fingers into the dirt, and uttered the allur. A tremor traveled through the ground, touching her fingertips.

Josef drove Ulfur back, with a menacing yell.

"*Fyrir therr hondum…*"

The thick, shallow root birthed from the ground in a low arch behind Ulfur's feet.

He noticed, and pushed forward, driving the fight with Josef away from the roots.

No, you are not getting away from me.

Aeryn shouted the words, digging her fingers into the earth until the soil packed beneath her fingernails. Several long, thinner roots snapped from the ground like whips. They snagged Ulfur by the ankles as though they possessed a will of their own. Layer after layer wrapped around his feet, coiling up his legs to the knee. He was anchored to the spot. Horror manifested in his expression as he realized he could not move and had lost control over the situation.

His head snapped in Aeryn's direction as he registered the cause behind his predicament. He knew he had lost.

Josef yelled and swung his axe. Ulfur's head hit the dirt.

The Rune Reaper was dead.

40

The Healing of Harms

Josef knelt beside Aeryn, taking in the state of her wounds. Her fingers felt shaky as she tried to hold the spear steady. Her clothing was soaked with blood.

He dumped his helmet next to him and pulled off his gauntlets. Gripping the shaft with one hand, he anchored his other on her torso. Aeryn drew a sharp breath between gritted teeth and reached for his arm, stopping him before he pulled.

"It has to come out," he said.

It was going to hurt like nothing she'd felt before. But she'd die otherwise, if not from blood loss, than from the unearthly cold clawing its way through her body from the spearhead.

Aeryn's muscles tensed. "Do it."

He yanked it straight out. She groaned and curled inward as the weapon left her body. Blood poured from the wound. Josef covered the area with his hands and pressed. She let out an involuntary whimper.

Her chest rose and fell in rapid, shallow breaths, and she craned her neck to watch the sticky, maroon liquid spread rapidly over her clothing.

It was too much blood.

This wasn't a shoulder wound. This was the sort of wound which punctured organs and made a creature bleed to death. Soon, she'd lose consciousness, and then she'd die. She knew how this worked.

She leaned her head back into the dirt and tried to calm herself. Her heart began to race and ache. Her limbs felt cold. Heavy.

"It's okay," she said, trying to convince herself. The only thing which kept terror from clawing her to the end was the thought of seeing her daughter once more.

Aeryn shut her eyes. She felt as tired as Silversaar sounded. But she needed to get something off her chest before it was too late.

"Grim...I mean Josef. I'm sorry about what happened at the Enclave."

He'd shifted her clothing out of the way for better contact with the wound. "It's fine."

She grunted in pain as he applied pressure to the opening with his bare hands, as if it would stop the bleeding.

"It's not," she said. "I was ready to leave you, and you've been my friend..."

Aeryn's eyes began to leak for reasons unrelated to her wound.

"The truth is, I couldn't take being in Merioake anymore. I had a baby out of wedlock, and everything back home reminded me that she's gone. My baby, Daphne, got sick, and I couldn't save her in time. I went to get medicine, and she died before I got back."

A sob escaped her lips, and when she spoke again her voice croaked.

"When Susi asked me to get the medicine, all those feelings came flooding back. That baby reminded me what I was running away from. And I almost left you. I don't want to leave you." Aeryn covered her eyes with her arm. "I miss her so much."

Josef mumbled something indistinct, his deep voice a comfort. A warm tingling sensation spread from her wound. The throbbing diminished. The slicing pain in her lower abdomen subsided.

Is this what it felt like right before the end? Aeryn had always wondered if it hurt to die. She didn't hurt anymore.

There was one last thing she had to tell him. "I'm sorry I can't help you find your parents."

"Why are you saying that?" he asked.

"Josef...because I'm going to die."

"You're gonna be fine."

Aeryn found she suddenly had the strength to argue with him. She lifted her heavy head and saw the wound had stopped bleeding. She gently prodded it, surprised when she didn't elicit pain.

Josef leaned back on his heels, panting. His hands were covered with her stains, and dark circles gave him a haggard appearance. He was filthy and bruised, and his hair was wet-through with sweat. The glowing runes on his knuckles resumed their natural black.

He watched Aeryn peel back the layers of soaked clothing. Her lips parted in awe.

Her skin was smeared and dirty, but where she'd been pierced, there was a silvery scar in the shape of a four-point star. The wound was completely shut.

Aeryn strained her eyes and gently touched the scar. "Did you do that?"

He bobbed his head yes.

"With your runes?"

He nodded once more. "Hold on."

Josef staggered to his feet. He pulled the necklace of fingers from Ulfur's body, and the separate cord with Wolfe's tooth. He knelt beside Aeryn again, and pressed the small, bumpy tooth into her palm.

"Here," he said, catching his breath. "I didn't have strength to finish...restoring your health...Hold it."

He reached out clumsily and closed her fingers around it, then he collapsed beside her, eyes closed, but still conscious.

Aeryn's breathing and heartbeat steadied. Her chest pain diminished and her head stopped swimming. She felt life energy slowly seep into her body, warming and strengthening her.

"I forgive you," Josef said. "You came back. I don't want to leave you either."

Though still very weak, she eased herself into a sitting position. Aeryn leaned her body close enough to catch him in a hug. She buried her face in his neck. His plate armor shifted as he closed his heavy arm around her shoulder and hugged her back.

She wasn't sure how long they stayed like that. She never felt more tired and relieved in her life.

"We should get back to the village," Josef said. His breathing had steadied, though he still looked ragged. "They need to know what happened here."

His eyes skimmed the carnage around them. Ulfur's spear laid at his side. The exposed roots had frozen in place and still anchored Ulfur's twisted form to the spot up to the knees.

Josef got to his feet and helped Aeryn to stand. Her head spun and her knees buckled instantly. He caught her by the elbow. She tried to take another few steps, but her legs were shaky. She felt weak and sore all over, and her head was spinning again.

She felt herself lifted.

"I'll try not to kill us going down the mountain," he said. Aeryn's mouth flickered into an exhausted smile, and she attempted a snicker, which came out like a drowsy grunt.

Josef carried Aeryn down the mountain. It was still dark but the sky was lighter than it had been, which made Aeryn wonder just how long they'd been up Silversaar's mountain.

In the valley, the bodies of the raiders had been piled outside the village proper, and were being unceremoniously burned. Slain villagers were moved to the tombs cut into the side of the northernmost mountain.

The village itself was a disaster. Some people were crying. Some wandered around in a haze, covered in dust or bleeding. Others kept moving, with graver and more focused expressions, trying to help their neighbors and loved ones. Several plots had been decimated to heaps of charred rubble, and most of the homes bore signs of fire damage, still smoking with gaping holes in the walls and roofs. The smell was awful.

Aeryn insisted on trying to walk as they entered the village.

Her legs felt weak, but cooperated slowly. They made their way to the center, towards the Thar's house, where weapons and shields which had been taken off the bodies of the raiders were piled in the road.

Iviss stood speaking with Elric and Nialls. Jisselle was there, as well as Elric's family and several disheveled villagers.

"Look!" Wynne grabbed her mother by the arm and pointed to Aeryn and Josef as they shambled up the lane.

Iviss broke off his conversation with Elric. He hurried over to Aeryn and Josef. He wore a stained wrap over his head which covered one of his eyes. He looked relieved at first, then saw how drenched with blood Aeryn was.

"Where are you hurt? What happened?" His eyes searched her for a wound.

"I'm fine," she said. "Grim fixed me. I mean Josef."

He didn't look convinced. He offered his shoulder for her to lean on, giving Josef a break. "We thought you two had been taken."

They shuffled toward the group of surviving elders. Josef unhitched the finger-necklace from his belt. He held it out for them to take. "Destroy this."

The elders and nearby villagers dropped silent. Elric, who had been holding Jai with one arm, passed his young son to Susi, who turned the boy away from the ghastly sight.

Nialls stepped forward and took the necklace, his brow set. "This belonged to Ulfur. I know. I've seen. How did you get this?"

Josef gave a nod to Aeryn. "We killed him."

"The Rune Reaper's dead?" Elric said, his voice raising. Several more villagers drew in to listen. "How?"

Josef took a breath to gather his thoughts, his weariness starting to catch up to him. "I cut off his head."

"I meant, how, by the gods, did you face him and live?" Elric said. "Where did this happen? We haven't found his body."

"He followed us up the mountain to Silversaar's lair. We fought him there," Aeryn said.

Several sets of eyes settled on Aeryn.

"Did she say *Silversaar*?" someone from the crowd asked.

Aeryn's head started to pound. "I did."

"That's not possible. How is that possible?" the man said.

Before she could respond, Nialls pointed at her hands. "Your hands. You did not have those before."

The crowd, which had been growing and pressing in, rippled with bewilderment.

"Silversaar gave them to me," Aeryn said.

"She's delirious," said a villager who was missing a front tooth. "She's lost too much blood. Look at her."

"She's telling the truth," Josef said, his voice loud enough to make her wince. "My runes flared up during the battle, and led to Silversaar in the mountain. Ask Wolfe. Wolfe was there. He told me to go."

Josef pointed in the general direction.

Iviss and Elric exchanged a glance, then Iviss spoke. "Wolfe is dead."

There was a quiet moment.

"Silversaar is in the mountain?" Elric repeated slowly.

"Yes."

A stout woman cradling a broken arm remarked, "They're both crazy."

Jisselle thunked her walking stick in the packed dirt. "Pipe down and let him finish."

Josef dipped his chin to her. "Silversaar was dying. Before he died, he showed us how to read the runes and use the allur. He gave those to Aeryn." Josef pointed at Aeryn's runes. "He said we need to use them. With Silversaar's death, Malachai will return to power, and we must prepare to defeat him."

Murmurs of discontent and disbelief rippled throughout the crowd. Mothers hugged their children tighter.

"You say *Malachai* is coming and we're supposed to defeat him?" said one of the scouts Aeryn recognized from their arrival. "We just lost almost half our village. How are we supposed to stop him?"

"We don't know the runes," said a woman in a dented helmet. "Much less how to use them."

"We do," Josef said. "We'll show you, and anyone else willing to learn. And yes. Silversaar says Malachai is coming."

Rakel forced her way to the front of the crowd and pointed a finger at Josef. "We've scouted that mountain. We've never found Silversaar's lair."

Aeryn bristled. Her dislike for the woman made it difficult to talk normally. "It was hidden and protected by magic."

"You're saying I can't do my job?"

Heat rose to Aeryn's face. "I'm saying maybe you weren't meant to find it."

"Or maybe it doesn't exist, Little elf."

It took all of Aeryn's self control not to flick her ear at Rakel. "If you don't believe us, go up the mountain. Go see. The protection hiding the lair has probably faded. See what happened to Ulfur."

"We will," Elric said, raising a hand for them to stop arguing. He gave a sharp glance at Rakel. "But not now. If what you're saying is true..." Elric shook his head. "I hope it is. I want to believe you, Grim, I really do. But I think we need to see this before we settle on any conclusions."

"This is very interesting," Jisselle said. "The way I see it, one of three things is possible. Either they've cruelly concocted this story, or they've lost their minds, or they're telling the truth. I think the evidence leans towards truth."

"I believe them," Wynne said, working her way forward. "How else do you explain her new runes? Those weren't there before."

"It is a good point," Nialls said. He looked toward Aeryn. "If you two can read them, what do they say?"

Aeryn spread her fingers. She pointed to each one as she rattled off its meaning without a hitch. Wynne, Nialls, and some of the other townsfolk drew closer to see. Some grew excited when they noticed a rune they had in common, now knowing what it meant after a lifetime of question.

"What about yours?" Wynne asked Josef. "Wait...yours

look like rings now, too. Those are different."

Villagers pressed in, asking for theirs to be read, when Elric put a stop to it and called for order.

"Give them room." Elric's voice boomed. "This is not the time. We need to finish accounting for the dead. This afternoon, Rakel, if you're able, you may lead a group up the mountain to do a thorough search."

"I'll go as well," Iviss said.

"We don't need your assistance," Rakel said. "Go rest your one good eye."

"Iviss goes with," Elric said, settling the matter.

"It's Josef," Aeryn said, as it occurred to her that the elder had used the wrong name. "Not Grim."

Several puzzled looks met her. Rakel wrinkled her nose. "What is she talking about?"

"My name is Josef," he said.

"What happened to Grim Stonebreaker?" she asked.

"That's what the Loom called me. I didn't remember anything before they took me. Not even my name," Josef said. "Silversaar showed me. My name is Josef."

Aeryn sagged against Iviss. All the time on her feet, especially arguing with Rakel, had drained her.

Wynne pulled a wooden pendant out of her coat. She tapped Susi, urging her mother to look.

After that, Aeryn's vision dimmed. She leaned weakly on Iviss, and was led to bed.

41

Aftermath

Aeryn awoke in a dimly lit room, with her face pressed into Josef's armpit. Her eyes fluttered, and she gasped, pulling away abruptly. This startled him awake. With a yell, he shot upright, groping for Retribution propped beside the bed.

"Josef, it's alright! Calm down," Aeryn said. "I was just surprised."

He scanned for the threat. Realizing they were in a safe, quiet room, he flopped back onto his pillow with a sigh. He rubbed the lines in his forehead. His fuzzy chest rose and fell as he steadied his breathing from the scare. Aeryn's eyes passed over his many black and yellow bruises. She felt suddenly sheepish for having snuggled so close to him. She averted her eyes and took a better look at the room.

This wasn't their hut. There was one bed with a chest at the end. On her side of the room, a wicker table was piled with some of their belongings. Josef's armor had been hung on wall pegs.

She felt hungry and weak, and realized she was gripping something small and hard. She opened her rune-covered fingers on the bumpy object in her palm. Wolfe's tooth. The events of the battle outside Silversaar's lair came back to her. She vaguely remembered coming down the mountain, the argument with the villagers, and not much else.

Josef yawned. He looked filthy and battered, but the dark

circles around his eyes had disappeared.

"You gonna be alright?" she asked. He dipped his chin. A gust of cool air from the small square window made the heavy homespun curtain balloon. Aeryn shivered. Looking down at the bed, she realized that she had invaded his side without realizing it, probaby for warmth.

"Sorry if I hogged the bed."

"Is that what you call it?" he asked wryly.

Aeryn pinked. She rubbed her arm for warmth. "In my defense, you're a furnace."

Josef heaved himself upright, exposing the scars which covered his back. He pinched the bridge of his nose then rubbed the corner of his eyes. "It's fine. Next time try not to scare me awake. I thought we were going to get murdered."

"Do you know where we are?"

"Elric had a spare room. Our hut burned down," he said. "Is there a shirt over there?"

"I haven't checked." Aeryn pushed back layers of blankets and swung her feet delicately over the side of the bed. Gray woolen socks covered her toes and reached her knees. She wore loose coffee-colored pants, and a clean tunic the color of crabapples. She didn't remember where these clothes came from.

She walked carefully to the table. Her body, though weak from lack of food, felt stronger.

On the table, Aeryn recognized the partially charred sketchbook, the leather bracers she had been wearing, her belt, and her father's sword. Bairb rested beside Josef's gauntlets. There was a stack of clean men's clothing. Her bow and empty quiver were propped against the table beside her boots.

"Here." She tossed him a shirt.

There was a gentle knock on the door, followed by a voice which sounded like Wynne. "Everything okay? I heard a yell."

"We're fine," Aeryn called back.

"...Can I come in?"

Aeryn glanced to make sure Josef was decent, then replied. "You can come in."

The door creaked, and Wynne peeked inside, smiling awkwardly. The knot of sandy hair was still affixed to the top of her head. She looked fresh, but tired. "I heard noise. I figured you were finally up. I have these."

She lifted a folded bundle of clothing and blankets. "My Mum and I have been working to make sure scattered belongings make it back to their proper owners. Or, in a lot of cases, passed on. We found a drawing book with some elvish script in the cover. We figured it belonged to you."

She pointed to the wicker table.

"Also, I hope you weren't too attached to your old clothes. They were a mess beyond repair." She grinned at Aeryn. "Lucky we're about the same size."

Aeryn looked down at her new garb, and she had the vague memory of someone, maybe Susi, helping her into these.

"Thank you," Aeryn said. "How long have we been asleep?"

"Almost two days. Don't worry, we checked to make sure

you weren't dead."

Aeryn's stomach growled. No wonder she was so hungry.

"What have we missed?" Josef said.

"There was a ceremony to honor the fallen. Afterward, some folk went up the mountain. They saw everything you talked about." Wynne started to count on her fingers. "...Silversaar's body, his hoard, the remains of the Rune Reaper and his men...." Wynne shivered. "They described it like the trees themselves came alive to fight against Ulfur."

The voices of villagers and the thwack of hammering carried in through the window. Wynne took a few steps across the room and pulled the curtain away from the small square opening. Gray daylight streamed in.

"Everyone has been busy with the clean-up, and repairs," she said. "They're eager for you two to start teaching us about the runes and the allur."

"There was a mother with a sick baby," Aeryn said, remembering. "What happened to them?"

"Tam?" Wynne said. "Their house is a wreck, but their whole family survived. The baby is fine. I gave her the medicine you gave me."

"Okay." Aeryn felt a tightening in her throat even as her shoulders relaxed. She caught Josef watching her, his eyes softer than they had been.

Wynne plopped the fresh linens on the end of the bed and craned her neck out the door, as though checking for anyone within hearing range. She fiddled with her fingers.

"Josef, can I ask you something?" she said in a rush. "You said you had a vision from Silversaar, where you learned your name wasn't Grim. You did say it was Josef. Right?"

He dipped his chin. "Mhmm."

Wynne hesitated.

"I was supposed to wait to talk to you about this." She peeked out the door again. "My parents wanted to be a part of the conversation, but they're busy, and I know it's perhaps a long shot, but...your name is on my necklace, and I thought maybe you were...do you remember your parents at all?"

She pulled a polished wooden pendant out of her beige sweater and unstrung it from her neck. She handed it to him. Josef squinted at the small print carved into it the smooth, dark wood. Aeryn came to his side, and read aloud.

"That says Erlander," Aeryn said.

"It was my family name. I mean, my family before the Thar's adopted me," Wynne said. "My mother made this before she died. She arrived here, pregnant with me. I had a brother and father, but something happened on the way and they never made it."

Josef turned the pendant over and ran his thumb over the carving on the back.

Aeryn noticed more names. "This side says Markus, Inorra, Josef, Wynne."

"Markus." Josef glanced at Aeryn. Something like realization, or confirmation, clicked in his eyes. She remembered Silversaar mentioning the name and she wondered what exactly Silversaar had shown him.

"Wynne, how old are you?" Josef asked.

"Fifteen."

He glanced at Aeryn again, a quiet energy humming about him. He handed the pendant back to Wynne. "I don't remember much. I don't know what happened to my mother. But I saw my father in the memory Silversaar showed me. There was a raid on my village, and I was taken. I was eight. He died trying to protect me. My father called me Josef. Silversaaar called him Markus."

Wynne's blue eyes widened. "So that makes us...wait. You're twenty-three now?"

Josef nodded.

Wynne counted on her fingers, and her blue eyes grew even wider. "Josef, I think you're my brother. I mean, I'm almost completely sure of it."

"Yeah," Josef said. "Me too."

Aeryn's eyes passed between the two of them. Now that she considered it, there was a resemblance. Their hair color and eyes were the same, along with the shape of their nose. The timing, their father's name, and the little they knew about the details made a persuasive argument.

"You do kind of look alike," Aeryn said. "Minus the beard."

Wynne giggled, but she looked like she might shriek with delight, or burst into tears. She dove at Josef and caught him in a hug. She flew to the door. "I need to tell my parents!"

She stopped, eyes smiling at Aeryn. "So that would mean, we're like sisters? Sisters in law? I always wanted a sister."

Aeryn's brow wrinkled. "We're not married."

"Oh…you're not?" Wynne gave Josef a questioning look.

Josef shook his head. "Didn't you hear me introduce her with a different name?"

Wynne assumed a guilty expression and scratched the back of her head. "I was a little distracted…" Her eyes flitted down the hall. "Just so you know, if you're not married, they're not going to want you to room together." Her eyes brightened again. "Aeryn, you can stay with me! Let's go find my Pops."

"Can you give us a minute?" Aeryn asked.

"Sure," she said. "Come right out when you're done. I think my Mum's working on lunch, and Iviss is getting ready to leave."

"Iviss is leaving?" Josef asked.

"I know, it's disappointing," Wynne said. "Maybe you can talk him into staying a few more days."

A door clattered out of sight, and Susi's voice carried from somewhere else in the house. "Wynne?"

Wynne disappeared down the narrow, dim hallway towards the sound of her mother. "Mum, they're awake. Also, don't be mad. I know you told me to wait, but you have to listen to this…"

Alone in the room, Josef met Aeryn's face. "I have a sister."

Aeryn chanced a small smile. "We actually found your family."

"You sound surprised."

"No, no," Aeryn said. "I mean…a little. How do you feel about it?"

Josef thought for a minute. "Glad you talked me into looking for them." His face relaxed into a sincere smile. "Thank you."

Aeryn's gaze softened as she stepped closer. "I'm sorry about what happened to your parents."

He was quiet for a moment, deep in thought. "It's a relief knowing."

"I wonder if the Thar's could tell you any more about your mother."

"I'll ask."

"Josef Erlander," Aeryn said, testing out the name. "I like it."

"Me too."

Aeryn adjusted the lucky tooth in her hand, allowing it to dangle from her fingers. She held it out to him. "Here."

"Why are you giving this to me?"

"You should have it. You were closer to Wolfe."

He looked at the tooth swaying on its string, then back at Aeryn. The wrinkles formed across his forehead. "Why not you?"

"Because you're far more likely to run straight at an enemy. Stop arguing, and just take it. If we're going to deal with Malachai, I'd feel better if you carried it," she said, feeling suddenly vulnerable. "I don't know how long it'll take to defeat him, and I don't want to do it alone."

He closed his hands around the tooth. He met Aeryn's eyes and smiled. "Me neither."

❑

Iviss stood in the road, speaking with Elric and Nialls. He had acquired a backpack full of supplies, and Pippa was saddled and waiting. He had a fresh bandage wrapped around his head to cover his eye.

His face brightened when Aeryn and Josef emerged, and he closed the gap between them to catch them in a double hug.

"I hear you're leaving?" Aeryn said as he released them. "Now?"

"I need to report back to my people," he said. "Silver Shadow needs to know what happened here, and what's coming. And I've spoken with Elric, Jisselle, and Nialls to find out what the Enclave will need. We'll want to send aid, especially with winter coming."

"What about you? Are you coming back?" Aeryn asked.

Iviss' dimples formed. "It's not really up to me. I hope so. If not…" He gave them a genuine smile. "It's been a pleasure, friends."

The business of teaching the runes was a question on everyone's mind. After several long conversations, the elders, Josef, and Aeryn came up with some ideas for training the people, but the implementation of a teaching and training schedule would have to be balanced with the recovery of the village. There was a lot of work to be done.

The conversation about Josef's family couldn't be entertained until after supper. The Thar's confirmed the conclusion which Josef and Wynne arrived at earlier, and Susi teared up at the memory of Inorra and the orphaned baby girl they took in as their own. Aeryn felt her own eyes mist up at the heartbreaking love Inorra bore for her family, which may also have had something to do with the lingering exhaustion and the loss she witnessed throughout the village earlier that day.

For Josef, hearing about his family, where they were from, and the few other details the Thar's shared, provided a settling peace. They hadn't given up on him. They loved him to the end. Now he knew.

The Thar's welcomed Aeryn and Josef to stay with them as long as it took to get on their feet. Elric wanted a private word with Josef, so Aeryn and Wynne worked together to transfer Aeryn's few belongings to the room she'd share with Wynne.

As she gathered up her weapons, Aeryn's eyes landed on a lute propped against the wicker table amongst her things. She crouched to examine the instrument. The wood of its body was stained teal. The fretboard was made of a dark reddish wood. An ornate flower was carved into the soundhole.

She ran a finger over the frets. *Where'd this come from?*

"Wynne, whose is this?" she asked.

"Yours, if you want it," Wynne said as she loaded the sketchbook on top of a folded blanket and a spare pair of trousers.

Aeryn gave her a questioning look.

Wynne paused halfway out the door with her armload. "It doesn't have an owner anymore, and Josef said you played music."

Aeryn must've been occupied during that conversation. Her eyes passed over the lute again. The body had a few dents, and her fingertips brushed the dark wood of the fretboard.

"Do you play lute?" Wynne asked.

"I did." She felt a tugging in her chest. Before she could talk herself out of it, she grabbed the instrument by the neck and brought it with her.

Early the next morning, Aeryn's eyes landed on the instrument which rested a few feet from her toes. Wynne, and most of the household from the sounds of it, were still asleep. She pulled on an oversized sweater. Hesitantly, she took the lute in her hands, then stole away behind the Thar's stable for a smidgeon of privacy.

In the cool gray of early morning, she nestled on a stump, sitting cross-legged and resting the instrument in her lap. She took a deep breath and stared at it for a long moment. Settling her mind, she picked it up, tuned it, and began to play.

The strings pushed against her fingertips as she pressed them into the fretboard. At first, her fingers fumbled slowly over the strings. Their old skill slowly awakened. The thrumming notes stirred her enjoyment of the music once again. She closed her eyes as she finger-picked, allowing the sweet song to wash over her. Her heart swelled in the playing, and a smile eased across her face.

The cool breeze sent her hair flapping.

As she combed the strands away from her eyes and mouth, she breathed deeply of the brisk mountain air, completely at peace.

For the first time in a long time feeling a thrill of hope for her future.

42

Not for Happy Endings

Amber eyes were not a common feature amongst the mortals. The stringy-haired vagabond pulled his hood over his brow to hide them. Wrapped in a ragged cloak, with feet bloody from the cold, he took shelter beneath a bridge just north of the capital city, alongside the other homeless.

He hugged his body for warmth and assessed the filthy men huddled nearby. One scratched himself. Another clung to his bottle of liquor and growled at the other men, like a dog issuing a warning. Two others squabbled in obscenity-laden slurs.

Malachai curled his lip. *Behold, the company of kings...*

Aimless derelicts, addicted to drink and without purpose in the world. If only they knew who he was, they would fall at his feet in worship.

For a long time, Malachai lived as a pariah, skulking around the fringes of civilization, trying to survive in a world which found his very appearance disconcerting. What Silversaar did to him was like issuing a death sentence.

How does a dragon, bound to human form and stripped of magic, survive in a corrupted world? With great difficulty.

To add further insult, his own loyal ones abandoned him. Under the direction of his own chief servant, they even sought his death. One day they'd answer for their apostasy. He would ensure it.

Malachai wasn't totally helpless. He was still a dragon. Magic was knit into the fiber of his being. He still retained access to a teeny whisper of the power he once possessed. It was how he knew the tides of betrayal had swept over the Loom.

It was also how he knew precisely what to say to provoke the Baldomar and his little elvish sidekick to free him from his captors. What a twist of fate, to be saved by one of Silversaar's own.

Malachai withdrew a thick parchment from his pocket, which he snagged from the message board in the last town. He unfolded it. Brushing the stringy hair away from his eyes, he gazed upon the fairly accurate portrayals of his rescuers featured in the poster.

Wanted by the authorities, are we?

When he regained his power, he'd have to change that. *A life for a life.* That was the code. Once all was set to right, he knew exactly how to return the favor.

Malachai sensed the day approaching. He felt the atmospheric shift as soon as Silversaar died. He only needed to bide his time. With his adversary's well of magic empty, the remnants of the spell binding him to this wretched form would soon fade.

Soon, all would be set right.

What he didn't expect was the suddenness of it.

The change happened so abruptly. One moment, he crouched in that shadowy nook beneath a bridge outside Nyassa. The next moment, a rush swept over him. It felt like lightning, pleasantly coursing through his veins, warming and empowering him.

Malachai worked his fingers. Shivers of anticipation made his arms tingle. A deep longing about to be realized surged within him and stirred him into action.

Malachai stood erect. A controlled smile settled into his features.

"Oy, friend. Wha's wrong with ya?" The homeless men had stopped their squabble to oggle him.

"No, mortal. Everything is exactly right," Malachai said. "Follow me."

One of the foul-mouthed men scoffed and strung together a near-unintelligible sentence of curse words. *Was there a question or defiance in there?* Malachai ignored him, and turned his attention to the others, expectant.

The itchy man had stopped scratching long enough to issue a puzzled look, while the growler burst out with a hoarse, "Ha!" then dissolved into manic chittering.

Malachai suppressed a surge of irritation. "Is that a no?"

The man with the foul mouth started up with a second string of obscenities. Malachai set his jaw. He turned his fierce, yellow eyes on the man, and gave a backhanded swish in the air. The cursing ended mid-sentence. The man's mouth moved, but no sound came out. Panic entered his eye as he gripped his throat for a moment, as if to test that his sound-maker still existed. The man continued to jabber, increasingly irate, and mercifully silent.

This got the others' attention.

"You've been existing in a walking death," Malachai said with authority. "I'm extending you an offer of life. Fulfillment. An opportunity to redirect your purposeless existence toward that which is more precious than any treasure. It is time to set things right, and you have a choice to make. Are you with me?"

"Wha are you talkin' about?" one of the men asked, seeming more confused than ever. *Of course he was confused.*

Malachai strode into the open, fifty and then a hundred feet away from the foot of the bridge. The homeless men crept out of the shadows to watch him with curiosity.

There, in the open field beside the river's edge, a magical flash dazzled the onlookers. A gargantuan dragon took the place of the scraggly vagabond. He had an angular face and a pointed snout which widened slightly at the end to accommodate his nasal cavity. Several glossy black horns swept away from his head, like wild eyebrows or a crown blown back by a strong wind. His deep purple scales glittered with flecks of gold. Malachai stretched his serpentine neck, lifting his nose to the sky, and unfurled his leathery wings which were so dark they were almost black. Stretching them for the first time in one hundred years felt like an appropriate first act after his long imprisonment.

He drew a deep breath, relishing the air and the return of his magic. The homeless men, who he'd hoped to recruit, or at the very least offer a chance to change their fate, had lost their minds in fright and retreated under the bridge to hide.

Malachai sighed. Fools. They'd come around.

With a tremendous beat of his wings, he lifted off the ground and bore himself away from his old life.

There was much to set right.

Author's Note

Thank you for your purchase of *The Silversaar Legacy Book 1: When Things Are Set Right.* If you've enjoyed this story, please consider leaving a rating and review.

Be sure to look for *The Silversaar Legacy: On Your Hands,* coming soon.

For more information about upcoming projects, visit HouseofQLLC.com and follow us on Instagram at @HouseofQLLC .

About the Author

Jordan St. James is the pen-name for co-authors Gustavo and Jordan Quintana, a husband and wife duo based in Knoxville, Tennessee. When they aren't writing stories, you can find them spending time with friends and family, playing tabletop role-playing games, and enjoying the wonderful outdoors and the creatures in it.

www.ingramcontent.com/pod-product-compliance
Lightning Source LLC
Chambersburg PA
CBHW021332310726
48971CB00001B/93